About the Author

C.A. Ramsey is an Honorary Research Fellow with the School of Philosophy at the University of Queensland, where she taught Greek Philosophy. She lives the philosophical life, emulating Plato and Socrates by giving free lectures in the public domain and now aims to disseminate philosophical ideas in a way that everyday readers will find exciting and easy to understand. She lives on the Gold Coast, Queensland with her Doberman, Max.

Ladon's Hourdes

C. A. Ramsey

Ladon's Hourdes

Olympia Publishers
London

www.olympiapublishers.com
OLYMPIA PAPERBACK EDITION

Copyright © C. A. Ramsey 2022

The right of C. A. Ramsey to be identified as author of
this work has been asserted in accordance with sections 77 and 78 of the
Copyright, Designs and Patents Act 1988.

All Rights Reserved

No reproduction, copy or transmission of this publication
may be made without written permission.
No paragraph of this publication may be reproduced,
copied or transmitted save with the written permission of the publisher, or in
accordance with the provisions
of the Copyright Act 1956 (as amended).

Any person who commits any unauthorised act in relation to
this publication may be liable to criminal
prosecution and civil claims for damage.

A CIP catalogue record for this title is
available from the British Library.

ISBN: 978-1-80074-462-2

This is a work of fiction.
Names, characters, places and incidents originate from the writer's imagination.
Any resemblance to actual persons, living or dead, is purely coincidental.

First Published in 2022

Olympia Publishers
Tallis House
2 Tallis Street
London
EC4Y 0AB

Printed in Great Britain

Dedication

This book is dedicated to my three beautiful grandchildren, Phoenix, Kenneth and Florence.

Acknowledgements

A big thank you to my 'test' readers, Caroline Blackburne, June Ramsey and Michael Nuske. Your enthusiasm for the book and your meaningful suggestions and comments have helped the writing progress quickly. My promise to you: more is coming soon…

Prologue — Curtain of Time

'Time', its essence abounding — a plenum of dynamic nothingness unfettered by the everyday illusion of space-time, cause and effect. The set of all sets mathematically. The wellspring from which overflows life into all its possible forms, like a spring uncoiling. If God had a name, it would be 'All That Is Possible, Is'. As the ancient Greek philosopher Parmenides put this, "It Is, what is not cannot be thought or spoken about." There would simply be nothing the mind could grasp. Therefore, if we can speak or think about anything, it exists necessarily. You may immediately counter this by telling me, "But I can imagine a myriad of things that do not exist, like a winged horse, for example." My reply: "you can only do this because wings and horses do exist, try to imagine something comprised of non-existence. What could this possibly mean? It is nonsense. We cannot do this!"

Martin Heidegger, some two thousand years later, repeated this thought as 'It gives', and what 'It gives' is be-ing, which to us finite beings, is the space-time consciousness through which we exist. Primordial 'time' is temporal. It consists of our past and future reaching towards and away from each other, so that there is created a 'space' we call now, the present. Heidegger explains this as our 'generation' and in a twofold sense. I am pre-comprised of all those who have gone before me, I carry their genetics and the memory traces, that these entail. Therefore, all my future possibilities are coloured by this past (the way I think and feel about things) which is always already there before my birth. Secondly, there is the contemporary generation into which I have been born. Example: my future possibilities would be very different if I had been born into a poor, African family. So, my time is comprised of the finite temporality of my past, which runs along ahead of me to bring my future possibilities back to me here and now. Past and future made present.

An analogy of my own may make this a little clearer, although I must use imperfect, finite terms to 'speak' of an infinity that transcends my finite understanding.

Clear your mind and picture the inner surface of a soap bubble. This represents the infinite plenum, there is no outside of this. Picture the myriad colours that appear and disappear caused by the surface tension of the bubble and light (life force energy). This is the world of space-time, cause and effect. As some colours appear, others disappear. This is the infinite becoming and dissolution of finitude, the world as we understand and conceive of it. There is no end to this streaming in and out of existence of the colours, and there is always an infinity of colours yet to appear, so long as the bubble is. The soap bubble is not itself the colours, neither are the colours the soap bubble, but as long as the surface tension of the bubble holds, there will be colours. No colours, no soap bubble, no soap bubble, no colours, yet each maintains its integrity without being subsumed one into the other. This is analogous to the overflowing of an infinite, dynamic life force which finitely we conceive of as that present 'space' we name 'time'. The end of 'time' is not the end of temporality as such (all colours), but simply the end of *my* 'time'. Innately I know this, but how? Death means I am no longer a being in the world, a colour. What comes after death, I cannot conceive. I come up against that which I *am not,* that which is wholly other (bubblehood). What would happen do you think, if we could 'discover' how to navigate through the infinite plenum, the wholly other without which we could not arise before the end of our own most 'time'? I use italics around the word *discover* to signal what this word is saying, which most of us do not notice. To *discover* means to uncover something that is there but covered over from our immediate consciousness, as with a veil or curtain. To *discover* does not mean to bring something new into existence, rather it relies on the existence already there, of what is brought to light!

If this brief exposition and the question it relates to appeals to you, read on!

Athens

Late afternoon settles over the Aegean Sea like a light cloak. Colours so vibrant during the middle of the day begin to fade gently into deeper, shadowed hues, and the heat of the sun lessens as a zephyr breeze brings the first hint of coolness and the coming night. The shoreline glistens as the heat of the day that brought a white haze to the golden sands, gives way to a softer glow that allows the colours to show through. Jagged cliffs of age-old stone crazed with myriad hues of sedimentary rock kiss the shoreline that gleams wet from the wavelets of clear, blue water.

It is late June 2020 and summer in Athens, the height of the tourist season. The streets should be bustling with visitors, setting out to eat in alfresco bistros and listen to live music. Streetlights should be activating soon as the sweltering heat of the day begins to subside, and twilight sets in. The beach should be littered with small, wooden fishing boats, pulled onto the sands at the close of the day, amid the last sunbathers, beachcombers and children frolicking in the shallows. Nothing of the kind is apparent here. Instead of the multi-coloured, semi-modern buildings and meandering, bustling streets, a stark, jagged landscape of ruins greets the eye. There is no evidence of any living being; a silence born of desolation shrouds the scene, giving an eerie feel to the landscape, as if the very earth is holding its breath. Higher up, the ruined Acropolis seems to watch out over Athens like a crouching beast ready to strike.

Aletheia

Back in the wooded hills above Athens, a stone house built into a cavern of rock, nestles among other rocky outcrops. It is surrounded on two sides by trees such that it is camouflaged from all but the sharpest eyes. A young woman of nineteen years, slim, lithe and beautiful, Aletheia, sits in the semi-dark; a darkness that shields her from the worst of her pain. Weeks of turmoil have brought a weariness that she finds difficult to endure and even harder to overcome. Tiredness clings to her, and her movements drag at her like a weighted chain. Taking this brief respite to just sit, she gives herself over to pondering for a moment; her brothers will return soon and Antheia, her sister, has gone. One last trial for the family and their tasks will be completed here — then they can leave this place behind them. So much has happened over the last several years and there is so much more yet to come. She knows that time is necessary for her to re-gather her strength, but will there be enough time? She knows she can only wait and see.

Her sister, Antheia, left before dawn. If she returns, she will be forever changed. Antheia's life stands in the balance — either she will survive, or she will not. The outcome lies in her own strength and goodness. If she survives her encounter with Ladon, then Ladon will lead them all through the next phase of their destiny. One does not confront the dragon without injury, not only the physical injury afforded those who survive the encounter but the psychological shock of suddenly opening into the spirit realm. Well does Aletheia remember her own awakening and the weeks of confused dreaming that precluded her understanding of what she 'saw' there? —Then, there was the loneliness of never speaking of it to another living soul, for only those who survived as she has done would 'hear' when she spoke. The archaic language of the spirit realm, recovered automatically by those who survive the encounter, cannot be countenanced merely by human ears. A mind-to-mind communication is the only way. The images stand in stark relief below the surface of human ego consciousness, have always been there, surfacing nightly in dreams when rational consciousness is lowered sufficiently, but oblivion reigns and like a veil shielding the face of a Muslim woman, the dragon stands guardian. The spiritual awakening brings with it the ecstasy that this forgotten knowledge has always been known and the question: Why could I not see this before? Answer: one has first to survive the dragon, demigod guardian of the spirits and their archaic, image language.

Crystals afford a little light and a greenish tint bathes Aletheia's alabaster skin in warmth and serenity. Her physical wounds are healing, the worst of the pain dissipating. Tomorrow she must decide whether to consult with the Delphic Oracle again — the thought of another wounding does not concern her rather, the worry of leaving her brothers for a day, and what she might learn there makes her head throb in tempo with the beating of her heart. As always in times of stress, she summons into her mind an image of her mother, Florence. She misses her mother terribly, yet the memory of her always brings back the last words spoken between them:

"Fear not, my child, I must leave you now, but I am not gone from you forever. When the time is right, search for me. Ladon will guide you."

Four years later, in a dream, Florence laid out instructions for Aletheia. The directions and directives necessary for both daughters to find the dragon's lair and brave the encounter that will lead them back to her. Alone with this knowledge, Aletheia followed her mother's directives, and now, when sufficiently recovered from her wounds, she has prepared her sister to do the same. Before leaving, Florence spoke to Aletheia at length about Ladon, about her fire-born brothers and the challenges they all faced ahead.

From the day Florence left until now, Aletheia has mothered the three younger children with a care and attention well beyond her tender years. Set the example by experiencing her mother's kindness and firmness, she has weathered many extremes, both good and bad with the fortitude born of her kind — the fire-born. The ways of the fire-born are singular and as different from normal human being as the animal kingdom is from rational intelligence. Philosophers well into the future of Aletheia's 'time' mention this growth in human spirit, not the least Freidrich Nietzsche, who termed this 'new' form of man — the Overman — a rational and moral human leap that encompasses spirit and intuition as well as intellect, and that takes mankind to a higher level of understanding in which moral codes are no longer essential. Such a man or woman does what is right simply because it is the most rational way.

What puzzles Aletheia again as she ponders her mother's words, is the fact that Florence made no mention in the dream of her father, Canath. As oldest child, she should remember him clearly; how can she not, when her brothers are only twelve and eight years old respectively? Is the Curtain of Time somehow responsible? How can he have fathered her sister and brothers if, as her mother related, he was killed some twenty years ago? At that time, she had not yet been born, but shadowy images of him that she cannot bring to full consciousness defy the facts as she knows them. As always, these unanswerable questions are unhelpful to the present situation, so Aletheia rises to light the rush torches and to busy herself with tasks that must be done before the sun sets tomorrow.

Antheia

Antheia moves on silent feet as she draws closer to the dragon. A fetid, warm breeze assures her that he sleeps. Discovery of his lair has been accomplished by carefully following her sister's instructions. How her sister made this discovery puzzles her — she realizes just how difficult this task is and knows beyond a shadow of a doubt that alone she would never have succeeded. She remembers well, the wounded state of her sister when she returned from this place. Trepidation makes her heart beat faster, and she purposely banishes thoughts of what will ensue from this awesome encounter.

The passageway begins to widen, and blackened stone shows in the semi-darkness. The faint rumble of breathing can now be heard, or more truthfully, felt through the cavern floor and with this, Antheia's heartbeat ratchets up again. Slowly and carefully, she moves towards the faint rumbling.

Aletheia described the dragon and his lair in great detail, in order that Antheia be prepared for the enormity of what she is about to experience, but even so, any precognition is wildly inadequate to the reality she faces as she draws nearer. The cavern grows suddenly into an immense space; the rooftop so far above her head that she can scarcely make it out in the gloom. The rumbling through the floor makes her unsteady on her feet and the noise grows in intensity in direct attunement with the vibration through the floor. Still there is no visible sign of the dragon, just the effects of his sleeping state.

Following the carefully described pathway of blackened granite, Antheia comes at last to the sigil that marks the final turning; she takes a few moments to steady her breathing and prepare herself for the last time. Her mind shrieks for her to turn and run as the fight or flight instinct takes hold, but she resists, and before she has the chance to think, she resolutely steps forward and rounds the final turn.

Phoenix and Kenneth

Phoenix listens carefully. Visibility is poor and he knows he is nearing the settlement of the enemy camp. The silence does not for a moment lure him into a feeling of safety. He has much more knowledge of his enemy's abilities, than to suppose there is nobody near. He signals Kenneth to remain in the gully and slowly, carefully, he moves to the top of the outcrop. Down below he can discern nothing, so he reaches out with his telepathic power. Very softly he searches for other minds and is not surprised when thoughts in the language of the Ketters enter his mind. There is incessant chattering, and he listens carefully to what is being thought and said. The force is about a score strong and the leader's thoughts and voice he recognizes. Slowly he returns to the gully and with a crook of his finger, signals Kenneth to follow him back along the track.

The two brothers move swiftly, their reconnaissance vital to the survival of their sisters and their eventual return to their mother. The brothers implicitly understand that Antheia must be protected for some time if, or when she returns from her encounter with Ladon, and Aletheia is still recovering from her wounds.

    The fact that both brothers are naturally fire-born affords them innate kinship with Ladon, the dragon-God. Their sisters were born before their mother, Florence's own encounter with Ladon, and her survival from this encounter means that her subsequent children do not need to make the visit to the cavern. Both brothers are endowed with the dragon's mark gifts of telepathy, empathy and telekinesis. For the last four years, the boys have grown fit and strong under the mothering of Aletheia, and now at the ages of twelve and eight years, they are on the brink of becoming manhood. Phoenix has already flexed his fire-born powers and learned to control them, and with his help, Kenneth is learning to do the same. Both boys know Ladon with the intimacy born of blood. The archaic image language is second nature to them both; and

Ladon warned them from birth, not to reveal their powers to another living being. This implicit, ethical demand, no fire-born human being can overcome or forget — the dragon's mind is simply there, always.

The ruins of the Acropolis come into view and the brothers scramble up the slope and into the shadowed portico of the Parthenon. Flitting amongst the columns, they skirt the main floor and exit the ruins via the underground vault. The sun is already sinking into the Aegean Sea. Below them, the ruins of Athens are briefly coloured in rosy hues, then darkness falls swiftly, closing the view into velvety, black night. The clear night sky shimmers with starry brilliance and the ruins take on the jagged shapes of crude, unmoving creatures. The shoreline silvers with the rising moon and the waves ceaselessly slide over the sand and retreat with a susurration that soothes the soul.

Sir Henry Bonnington and the Ketters

Sir Henry Bonnington listens carefully for any unusual resonance or sound. He, Brandon and his eighteen strong party have remained under the cloak of invisibility for the best part of two days. It is now time to move and begin the search for the dragon's lair. The journey from Kettering has afforded Bonnington the time to make sure his plan is as fool proof as is possible, given the fact that he has not walked this shore for more than twenty years.

The scientific advances he has made at the university during those subsequent twenty years are the means by which he now begins his quest. He understands well enough, that further advances in the realm of transpersonal psychology require a way to access the deeper realms of the human spirit and that which underlies the human spirit as its form. Jung's work on the collective unconscious enabled his research to move in the direction of an underlying plenum, and the letters between Jung and physicist, Wolfgang Pauli, over a twenty years' period sufficed to corroborate Jung's findings. The second human language — the images born before the rise of human consciousness and largely forgotten since, remain at the forefront of his advances, yet he has been unable to find an access point. There is most obviously a 'guardian' of some kind, and he has discovered a tiny clue when delving into the works of the Alchemists of old, thanks to Jung's lead.

The university situated in Northampton proper is renowned for its STEM programs and Kettering itself has become a vibrant town of budding academic researchers. Henry Bonnington was first drawn to the university, not by its scientific excellence, but because of its extensive Religious Studies program. Having excelled in his undergraduate studies, he stayed to complete his doctorate based on his growing fascination with the works of both Jung and Martin Heidegger. Knowing full well that in the nineteen twenties, the Japanese Zen Buddhists from Kyoto

University were enamored with Heidegger's Being and Time, he followed where Heidegger's works led, and was not disappointed with what he found. He understands now that the modern scientific mindset has blinded Western man to his own essential constitution and hence, to following through the quest that Henry has set as his task. Objectivity has foresworn subjectivity, and this move could easily mean the end of humankind. Is it not obvious to the scientists that there would be no objects to pursue without a human subject through whose intuition and cognition the objects of the 'world' take on form and meaning?

Henry signals with his hand and the cloak of invisibility fragments and then completely dissolves. The men look about them; all of them seeing the vista before them for the first time. The cloak was erected before the landing from the submersible, and not only did the cloak affect them with invisibility, but it also worked the counter way as well. They were guided to their position by satellite imaging alone. For two full days they have been blind to their surroundings, so that even the silvery star and moonlight seems bright to their eyes. Brandon Fellings detaches the noise suppressor from his satellite connection and signals that the men can speak quietly.

Astonishment and confusion can be read on the faces of the men — how is this possible? Some have visited modern Athens and know the streets and buildings that should greet their gaze — what stands in stark relief is something else entirely. Where streetlights and outdoor alfresco restaurants should be commonplace, there now stands the darkened ruins of an alien and what appears to be, lifeless Athens. Realisation comes over them slowly. No wonder Henry was such a stickler for them memorizing every detail of the map before they embarked on this journey! These men, however, know better than to ask the myriad questions that accompany the vista before them.

Henry leads the group into a crevice in the cliff face and briefs them on what is to happen. "We are going to search the shoreline for the following," he says and produces an image of a sigil on his iPad. "I want you to split into your designated pairs and follow the instructions we drilled at Kettering. Are there any questions?"

"How long do you want us to look, and at what time do we meet at the designated spot?" Brandon asks.

"We reconvene at 0.400 hours. If you find the sigil, remember to signal on the open channel. Now good luck and good hunting!"

The pairs of men move off into the night, guided only by the map they have all memorized in Kettering. Henry and Brandon move away, out of earshot of any of the pairs, to discuss what they alone know — that it is unlikely any of the men with them will survive to return home.

Twenty years ago, when Henry first landed on the Aegean shore, he stumbled upon evidence of an archaic Greek culture, not of old, but extant. The answer to the hypothetical question of many years' research resulting in this discovery made Henry ecstatic. Here was proof positive that time as we understand it is indeed a human construction! It is not merely the measure of movement as Aristotle and Kant argued. Here he was, in full view of a vista temporally remote from his own time.

Hubristically, his first thought was to make contact with this archaic group and illustrate the leaps and bounds in technology and civilization that he was sure would astound them. He had somehow expected them to welcome him and his men as God-like strangers, even though he was familiar with the lives and times of the historically recorded ancient Greeks. To his consternation, instead of extending him and his men an awed welcome, the men were surrounded by a group of these archaic people and asked firmly and not too politely, to leave.

The fact that these people were able to speak the Ketter language puzzled Henry, and when he asked them how, their leader produced a device that looked to all intents and purposes, like a crude translator. Unlike a translator, however, when held to the ear, it enabled the holder to assume a full understanding of the language of whomever he was confronted with. So much for Henry's expectations of wonder and awe from these strange people! A scuffle broke out when it became clear that Henry and his men were not simply prepared to leave. Henry's legendary anger resulted in the leader of the group, Canath, being accidently killed, and the intruders escaped largely by the skin of their teeth in a perilous evacuation to the submersible. Wounded but alive, Henry was already plotting his return.

This initial landing corroborated Henry's scientific calculations. Blending the psychological and philosophical tennets of Jung and Heidegger, together with the physics of Pauli and Heisenberg, he surmised this exact possibility — that time travel as expounded by the mediocre, scientific mainstream was fictitious, while entry to the plenum was not just a possibility but easier to accomplish than the time travel that relied on time being somehow a spatial dimension. Even Aristotle had gained a rational notion of an 'unmoved mover' towards the end of his Metaphysics, although his short treatise on time smuggled in space, to define time as the measure of movement.

From the work of Jung and Pauli, Henry slowly came to understand that underlying our everyday consciousness of time-space, cause and effect, there is a substratum in which everything that is, was and ever could be, already lies. Gaining entry to this plenum was a huge, calculated risk, but his patience and research had been well worth the effort and time. Herein lay the seeds of a quest for the knowledge that lay beneath the everyday level of human thinking. This is what Heidegger had called the 'home-coming', the return to what human being always already was, and yet with the rise of Western scientific culture, had been forgotten, then receded into oblivion. Simply put, the forgetting itself had been forgotten! It came as no surprise, then, that the Athens of his initial landing was temporally remote from his present-day world in Kettering. It was just as he had hypothesized.

Antheia

Nothing could have prepared Antheia for what now hits her. Blinding light and almost unbearable pain instantly envelop her and, she falls to the cavern floor, unaware of anything but trying to breathe. She feels blood gushing out of her from between her legs, and her head feels as if it has been split asunder. A resonance so loud, it makes her ears bleed, fills her head and archaic images dance before her inner eyes. How can she survive such an assault on her being? There is a sense of burning over her entire skin, such that her skin begins to smoke and with blessed relief, she loses consciousness.

The bleeding slows, then stops, cauterized by Ladon's breath. Ladon's claw marks Antheia's skin like a brand, and with the patience born of living infinitely, he waits for her to awaken or not. If she survives the visions, she will survive her wounds, if not, she was not meant to be fire-born, and Ladon knows as he has for time immemorial, that her spirit must envelop the fire-born way for her to have any chance of survival. Her future and his own depend on it!

In the twilight of fleeting but gradually returning consciousness, Antheia listens to the deepest voice that can be discerned within her hearing range. She immediately recognizes the voice and the creature it belongs to, as if she has always known him. A fierce joy enters her whole being; a knowing that had not been possible before, takes hold now, and she is swept up into a lightness of being she had never before thought possible.

"You are now my fire-born daughter as will be any progeny of yours. Welcome, daughter, and know you that I will protect you forever. I am always here, and you must now return to your fire-born, human family."

As Antheia becomes fully conscious again, she feels the terrible pain of her burnt and assaulted body, yet she fully understands for the first time, the meaning of her life and the gifts she has been granted. Slowly, agonizingly she drags herself upright and staggers back along the passage, now silent and cool. Ladon no longer inhabits this physical space — Ladon now goes with her, in and as her.

Phoenix and Kenneth

Phoenix and Kenneth enter the portal of their home, breathless and sweating profusely. Aletheia looks up from her work, a smile breaking out to lighten her countenance.

"Well met, my brothers. Have you any news?"

"We have confirmed the arrival of Sir Henry Bonnington and his men," Phoenix answers. "Now we must decide what is to be done! Any news of Antheia?"

"Not yet," Aletheia replies, "but I would not expect to know for a little time yet.

"We can't decide what to do about the intruders until Antheia is either back safe here with us or ingested by Ladon. We must wait another day to learn the outcome. Eat and then go to your beds, boys, you still need the sleep of growth, and who knows how long we can stay here with the arrival of our nemesis. Tomorrow we must make plans and preparations for Antheia's recovery and our own safety, should we need to go from here quickly."

The boys, as always, do their sister's bidding. As they silently eat their spartan meal, each boy thinks about what the future may hold. If only they could be sure of Antheia's safe return! If only they were sufficiently grown to help Aletheia more. Their love for their sisters has grown to an all-encompassing concern. After their meal, the boys clean their dishes and prepare for bed. Safe within the confines of the only home they have ever known, they go to bed, and both fall into a deep, dreamless sleep.

Sir Henry Bonnington

Bonnington's men fan out around the coastline watching carefully for any sudden movement or noise. Each pair searches the rocks and caves for any sign of the sigil shown them for the first time after the removal of the invisibility cloak. Questions and confusion assail Greg Jackson and Tim Freeman — they are finding it difficult to concentrate on the task assigned to them.

"What do you make of all this?" whispers Tim.

"I don't really want to think about it," replies Greg. He just wants to be done and get the hell out of this nightmare. Why had Bonnington not told them what to expect? The only reason he can think of is that he didn't want them to refuse to go, which is exactly what Greg's response would have been! He dares not think about what else could be out there — the time-lapse is terrifying enough!

Tim stops so suddenly, that Greg almost falls over the top of him.

"What the hell?" Greg hisses. Tim holds up his hand and points to the ground.

"Look at this!" he exclaims as Greg's eyes follow to where Tim is pointing. The marks of huge and alien footprints litter the sand at the entrance of yet another grotto. The men are unable to tell whether the feet were entering or leaving the grotto, so alien are the footprints.

"What in God's name made those?" Greg exclaims, his heart beating so hard he thinks it might jump right out of his chest.

"More to the point, where the hell is it?" breathes Tim. The men search the gloom with fear and trepidation — just what kind of creature is out there? Anything with feet that big is not something either man wants to encounter.

"Let's get out of sight," whispers Greg, "we need to collect our thoughts and decide what to do." Both men look askance at the entrance to the grotto, but there is simply no other shelter in sight. As quietly as they can, and skirting the alien prints, they tiptoe past the entrance into what they sense is a narrow passageway. At least nothing can surprise them from either side, the passageway is too narrow for that.

"How far in should we go?" whispers Greg. "We can't see for any distance ahead and I for one, don't want to get lost in here!"

"Let's just sit here for a minute and think," Tim suggests. Both men crouch carefully down until they are sitting on the rock floor.

Aletheia

Aletheia awakens with a start. Has she heard a faint rustling, or was that part of her dream? She focuses her senses and slides carefully out of bed, donning a woolen cloak. Swiftly she moves to the window and staying out of direct line of sight, glances at the moonlit pathway and the wooded grove beyond. An owl calls mournfully, and a small creature skitters amongst the shadows and into the tall grass at the side of the path. The rustling sound comes again, more pronounced this time, and she freezes in position, hoping the beating of her heart cannot be heard beyond the window. She feels in the pocket of her cloak for her knife, but it is not there; she remembers she put it under her pillow before retiring for the night. With the return of Bonnington and his men, she can take no risks, but now, she *is* at risk as are her brothers!

On silent feet Aletheia creeps slowly around the perimeter of the room until her hand touches her strung bow and quiver. She carefully nocks an arrow and waits in the shadows for whomever, or whatever is making the rustling sound. Reaching out with her mind, she gently wakes her brothers and instructs them to arm themselves and stay low within their rooms. She will summon them when she knows who or what is coming.

A fluttering of branches accompanies a louder rustling, and Aletheia searches the moonlit path with her eyes. Whatever is coming may know of her presence if she uses her mind. Then out of the gloom looms what looks to be a giant wolf, snaggle-toothed and shaggy grey with moth-eaten fur. It trots quickly on almost silent paws and is soon out of sight, moving away along the path. Aletheia lets out a breath she is not aware she has been holding and puzzles about what she has just seen. The creature should not be here, in this place. It is not native to this region and certainly, it is not known in these parts. The physical damage to the beast suggests it is slowly disintegrating, as if it is out of its own time.

What on earth could this bode; nothing good as far as she can discern.

With this strange visitation, her return to the Oracle is assured, and as she moves to speak to her brothers, she wonders if the Curtain of Time might not be fragmenting.

Without knowing how or why this thought brings with it more than trepidation. Suddenly, she knows they must move on.

"Antheia must return today, or you must leave without her!" This imperative comes to her unbidden, and although she immediately tries to resist, the mind of Ladon cannot be denied. All she can hope is that the Oracle will give her the advice she needs — will help her to make the decisions she knows will affect them all, and from which, once made, she cannot deviate. After speaking with the boys and alerting them to her need to make the journey to Delphi, they all return to their beds. None of them sleep further that night and as dawn approaches, Aletheia rises and begins the rituals and cleansing that must preclude her visit to the Oracle at Delphi. Alone, the boys prepare a spartan breakfast and eat silently, knowing that one sister must soon leave, and hoping against hope, that both sisters will return this day.

The Oracle of Delphi

The distance between Athens and Delphi is about a hundred miles. Aletheia knows she will need to pass through the Curtain to arrive there and return again within the period of time before they must take their leave. As always, she is beset with trepidation lest her journey take her astray, either to some place other than Delphi, or the return to her home. There is simply no guarantee that the time lapses will coincide. With a prayer to Ladon, and assuring the boys that she will return swiftly, she trots downstairs to the underground grotto. As she comes to the grotto's back wall, and the sigil announcing an access point to the Curtain, she shuts her eyes, summons up an image of the temple of Apollo in Delphi and lets her mind relax.

When she opens her eyes again, she stands on the threshold of the temple. The sun is just beginning to lighten Mount Parnassus and the valley below. With a bow and on silent, bare feet, Aletheia enters the portico and makes her way to the Oracle. The Oracle is seated as before on the raised dais in the sacred centre of the temple. As previously the blinded girl child lifts her head as Aletheia approaches and kneels before her. An image of light passes into Aletheia's mind, the old scar on her forehead opens and begins to bleed anew, and she knows she is both recognized and welcomed.

"You don't have much time, Aletheia," the Oracle's thought speaks directly to Aletheia's mind. "What is your question?"

"I know we must leave, Holy One, but I don't know where we are going, can you aid my decision? The lives of my family depend on my choice, so can you tell me where we are going and what we will face next?" The child stares blindly beyond Aletheia's kneeling form and speaks directly to Aletheia's mind.

"You must be blinded as I am, Aletheia. To choose the right path is to see through your inner eyes. The centre through which you must pass is within you. You are the beginning of your journey and the end of all that must pass. May Apollo go with you."

With this, the Oracle rises and walks back through the forbidden door leaving Aletheia alone. As she rises to her feet and turns slowly to leave the temple, Aletheia tries to make sense of the answer she had been given. She trusts, as she must, that the answer will become clearer so long as she lets her mind gently contemplate the words of the Oracle. For now, she must return to her family and direct her attention to making the preparations necessary to leave Athens.

Antheia

At long last Antheia arrives at the top of the slope and the ruins of the Acropolis. She leans heavily on the outermost column to try to catch her breath. She has lost consciousness several times since leaving the grotto and the pain is enormous now, encompassing her entire being. She knows she must reach home before she passes out again. Her breathing is ragged, and her head swims with archaic images, making her dizzy. With the last remnants of her remaining strength, she crosses the main floor and passes down the stone staircase into the underground vault, and with faltering steps sets out along the path towards home. Only her mental strength and determination keep her on her feet. She knows she must get to the house soon, or she will die.

Phoenix and Kenneth

Phoenix watches as Kenneth undertakes the exercise in telekinesis that he has set him. Slowly and with concentration so great that beads of sweat break out across his face, Kenneth manages to lift the boulder an inch above the ground.

"Don't struggle so much," Phoenix advises, "relax your physical muscles, this is not a physical contest."

"Easy for you to say," Kenneth drops the huge rock back with a thump. "I still can't do it like you can without trying. Will I ever be able to?"

"Of course, you will, Kenny, it just takes time and practice. Rest now and you can try again in a minute or two."

Suddenly, Phoenix raises his head, closes his eyes and listens. "Quickly, Kenny, come with me!"

The boys jump up, race up the stairs, out the door and along the path. They reach the top of the first rise and looking down, see the prone form of their sister, Antheia. They hurry down to her and using all their inborn gentleness, lift her between them and as quickly and quietly as they can, carry her up the path to the house.

"First we must get her to her bed, and then, I want you to fetch me water and mint," says Phoenix. Both Antheia and Aletheia have schooled him in what he must do, and how to do it.

"I hope that Aletheia returns soon. I don't want us to hurt Antheia any more than she is already hurt," Kenneth worries as he goes to follow his brother's instructions. He watches Phoenix anxiously as he begins to bathe the burns on Antheia's face and skin with the mint infused water.

"Kenny, get me the potion Aletheia left ready for us, I will try to get Antheia to swallow a little. Without it she may die. Hurry!"

Kenneth races back to the kitchen and reaches up to the shelf where Aletheia keeps the medicines. He pulls down the bottle of potion and fetches a small piece of clean cloth as well, knowing that trying to get

Antheia to swallow may be a challenge while she is unconscious.

"Good thinking, Ken," says Phoenix, "now wet the cloth with the potion and put it in Antheia's mouth, then gently squeeze it. If you lift her head back a little, it will help to keep the potion from oozing out again. Just make sure she doesn't choke."

With shaking hands, Kenneth does as Phoenix instructs, and within a few seconds, Antheia gives a cough and begins to regain consciousness.

"Where am I?" Antheia looks around fearfully until her fevered eyes fall on Phoenix and then Kenneth. She drops back with a sigh of relief and loses consciousness again. "Is she going to be all right?" Kenneth asks, his voice tremulous.

"Yes, Kenny, she will be fine, we just have to watch her carefully and feed her the potion for the next several hours."

Phoenix has already helped care for Aletheia under Antheia's instructions, when she returned from her encounter with Ladon. He knows the signs are good, though he hopes Aletheia will return soon just in case! The boys continue with their ministrations, tenderly watching over their older sister. Although her wounded state terrifies them both, they also understand that she is now fire-born. Ladon's dragon mark is red and raw but gives them the assurance that at long last, the entire family will soon be ready to move into the next phase of their destiny.

Aletheia

As soon as Aletheia opens her eyes in the underground grotto, she knows Antheia has returned. Quickly she enters the house and makes her way to her sister's room. The scene before her strengthens her resolve, and she places a hand on each boy's shoulder in thanks for their care and concern for their sister. Both boys look up at Aletheia, relief writ large on their faces. With gentle hands, Aletheia examines Antheia's body, and with her mind, she gently soothes her sister's fear.

"Well done, my brothers, you have saved our sister's life," says Aletheia, "go and prepare a meal, and I will take over here. Then we must all rest because tomorrow we must leave here, and there will be much to do to prepare."

"Did the Oracle give you any answers?" asks Phoenix.

"I will talk with you about the answers tomorrow, Phoenie. Go now and remember, we are all now under the protection of Ladon, whatever befalls us. We are now a fire-born family, and our task here is done. Our true destiny awaits."

In a flash of understanding, the Oracle's initial words become clear to Aletheia. She pauses for just a moment to collect her thoughts and then says, "It may not be for us to know, we may be blind to what is coming, so instead of searching for answers, we must put our trust in the powers that protect and go with us."

Phoenix and Kenneth, relieved and thankful for the safe return of both sisters, move towards the kitchen to prepare their last evening meal here. Wherever their journey takes them tomorrow, any leftover food will remain here, so they do not need to use anything sparingly. Phoenix decides that this last meal will be a feast to celebrate their sisters' return.

Greg and Tim

No sooner have Greg and Tim seated themselves on the cavern floor than there comes from deep within the floor a rumbling and vibration sufficient to make them believe that an earth tremor is in progress. Suddenly the rumbling decreases, and the floor stills beneath them.

"What are we going to do?" asks Greg. By now he is ready to flee regardless of the fact that he has no idea what he is fleeing from or to.

"Let's get out of here and try to find somewhere safe, whatever that could mean in this nightmare!" Tim responds. The men care little now whether their orders are carried through; their main concern is to get out of this nightmare as soon as they can find some way out.

The bizarre circumstances they find themselves in override any loyalty they initially felt to the man who is paying their outrageous wages. What matters money anyway if you do not survive to spend it! Both men have university degrees, Tim in science and Greg in ICT, as do all those Bonnington approached, so they hope they can use their combined knowledge to figure out what is occurring and how to make their way back to their own time and Kettering. If not, they know their only other option is to use their own wits to survive in this alien place and time. With only these two unappealing options, Greg and Tim begin to devise a plan.

Antheia

Suddenly, soaked in sweat and receding dreams, Antheia jolts awake. It is still dark, but she can see clearly. The terrible pain assaults her anew, but unlike yesterday, she manages to put it 'behind' her mind somehow. Slowly and carefully, she stretches her body and then flexes her mind and finds a suppleness and complexity alien to her everyday consciousness, yet it is at the same time, comfortingly hers and amazingly agile. Images that assaulted her yesterday now make perfect and startling sense, and she is beset with a freedom of soaring intelligence that sharpens to crystal clarity and resolve — she is he, and she sees through his eyes and thinks his thoughts. There is cleared vision lit by brilliant fire, the unadulterated, dynamic fire of pure existence. Antheia knows that she and Ladon are now one! She is at one with his vital force, and she welcomes him with an expansion of mind, opened fully for the first time in human history. The Overman awakes!

Silently, Antheia rises and examines her face in the mirror. What she sees shocks her, and yet she is at the same time, filled with jubilation. The eyes that look back at her have an alien cast, they have the dark exterior and crescent shaped yellow pupils similar to those of a cat, but with the vertical, black line through the centre of the pupil that she now knows, only dragons' eyes portray. Her skin is luminous and clear of yesterday's burning, although the pain reminds her that the wounds still abound. As she gazes on her countenance, she begins to accustom herself to this alien presence and with deft mental acuity, Ladon begins to imprint the necessary understandings directly onto Antheia's conscious mind. Only because of her innate strength and goodness is this possible. Ladon has waited millennia for just this mind, this spirit; his future and hers are now assured, and he is ready to lead his hourde into the next phase of their destiny; that which was written before the dawning of finitude — of 'time'.

Aletheia, Phoenix and Kenneth

Although it is still dark, a silent summons awakens Aletheia, Phoenix and Kenneth. All three become aware of an alien yet familiar presence close by, and all three arise in answer to the summons. The boys leave their room and meet Aletheia in the hall as she is coming from hers.

"What is happening Lethi?" asks a sleepy Kenneth.

"I am not quite sure, but let us go and see." She leads the way down to the kitchen, and all three are startled to see the shadowed form of Antheia seated at the table.

The boys are filled with joy at seeing their sister up and well, but Aletheia is wary and not a little concerned with this unforeseeable and rapid recovery. How is this possible when her own recovery sufficient to be able to rise and walk around took many days? Carefully she lays her hands on the boys' shoulders to stop them approaching any closer to Antheia. Something is not right here!

"Antheia, are you all right?" she asks. At the same time, she reaches out with her mind and gently probes Antheia's. The changes she encounters make her gasp aloud and the boys turn their faces to her with concern.

"What's wrong?" both boys ask. They look from one sister to the other with trepidation.

"What is going on?" asks Phoenix fearfully, aware that Aletheia has begun to tremble.

With great effort and determination, Aletheia closes her mind to the contact and calms herself. When she knows she can speak normally, she asks both boys to complete a task that will leave her and Antheia alone for a few minutes.

"Can you boys please fetch some water from the well?" she asks, her voice now steady, not betraying her inner turmoil. "We all need some mint tea and then we can think about breakfast. Today we leave and there are things that we must complete beforehand."

Phoenix and Kenneth, worried and unsure what is happening, but relieved that Antheia seems to be recovered, reluctantly obey Aletheia as they have been schooled always to do.

As soon as the boys have gone, Antheia stands and crosses the room to her sister, taking her in her arms in a gentle embrace.

"I am now who I have always been," she whispers, "don't be afraid of me, Aletheia. We are now safe, and as we go forward through the Curtain today, remember we move towards our reunion with Mother and Father. I have such a lot to tell you, but I must sort it all out in my own mind first. I can tell you now though, that Ladon has gifted me with eternal life and unsurpassable intelligence, and I also carry his child, the dragon child of our future. We must protect him at all costs, including with our own lives if necessary. Immortal Ladon is soon to become mortal through me."

Aletheia is silent for a few moments, so taken aback that she is hardly able to breathe, her mind in turmoil tumbles as if she has vertigo. Perspiration breaks out on her brow although the room is cool, and a faint nausea threatens to break through. She stumbles to a chair and sits down until the dizziness recedes. The implications of these bizarre facts are startling. Her steadiness returns gradually as Antheia's revelations begin to take hold. Slowly her mind calms enough for her reason and resolve to return, and she smiles weakly at her sister.

"I'm sorry if I seemed afraid, Antheia, the changes in your mind gave me an awful shock," Aletheia gazes intently at her sister, looking for any signs of physical changes, but she is the same even in the shadows, beautiful with the gentle countenance that Aletheia is accustomed to.

"I didn't lay eyes on Ladon, so I have no idea what he looks like," says Aletheia.

"Neither did I," Antheia replies, "but I know him now when I look in the mirror, for I have his eyes."

Aletheia crosses to her sister and takes hold of Antheia's shoulders. She turns her sister towards the window where the lightening sky glints on those alien eyes. She puts a hand to her mouth, again in shock, as

Ladon's eyes look into her own.

"This will take some getting used to," she breathes, "you must explain what happened to you in detail — to me and the boys before we decide how to undertake the next phase of our journey. Do you know where we are going next, Antheia, or should I call you Ladon?"

Antheia walks to the window and looks out on the coming dawn. She ponders her reply for a few moments, then turns back to Aletheia.

"This is all so new to me, Lethi, I hardly know what to tell you, but I am and always will be your loving sister. Please give me a little time to collect myself. Just know that I love you and our brothers, and in that respect nothing has changed. I hardly know myself what or who I am yet, but I will, I promise, and when I do, you will be the first to know."

Just at that moment Phoenix and Kenneth enter the kitchen with a bucket of water and with practiced skill, fill the iron kettle and place it on the embers of last night's kitchen fire. Phoenix adds more wood and with the crudely fashioned bellows, gets the fire burning brightly. Kenneth spoons crushed mint into the pot, ready for the water when it boils.

"Would you ladies like some scrambled eggs?" asks Phoenix, delight written on his face. He has his whole family back in the one place again, and he is mightily pleased and mightily hungry.

Bonnington

Henry and Brandon have made a command room in one of the shallow cave recesses, setting up the apparatus and technology that connects directly to the satellite. Brandon powers up the computers and enters the passwords that allow them to watch from the satellite view. Most of the pairs of men are going about their task, following the orders given and several are discussing their situation animatedly. One pair, Greg and Tim, are sitting in a grotto, talking.

"How are we going to maintain discipline if the going gets tough?" asks Brandon.

"We will simply apply a psychological fix by explaining this as an elaborate exercise in psychology," Henry replies, "at 0.400, when we all reconvene here, I suggest we pre-empt any problems before they have a chance to become real. Before leaving, I prepared a power-point for precisely this situation, so I am expecting relief from the initial shock of the time-lapse when the men are shown this information. Of course, we may still have a few who can't take the pressure, but the vetting process and psychological testing done in Kettering indicated that all the men are strong enough mentally to endure the alienness of this quest."

Thinking through what Henry has said, Brandon asks, "Have you allowed for any protests or refusals? We could have a full-scale rebellion on our hands if there are any dissenters."

"Yes, of course," Henry assures him, "I have been most careful to bring the means to deal with just such a problem."

Brandon does not miss the subtle threat contained in Henry's words.

"Do you really think the men will find the sigil?" Brandon asks skeptically, "or do you already know the answer to that?"

"Don't worry yourself with second guessing me, Brandon, you know what I expect, and you know why. Why don't you get some rest while we wait for the men to return? We have two more hours and if you want to sleep, I will wake you when I see them coming back."

Brandon stressed and weary, yawns and without further urging, settles himself down on the sleeping bags brought from the submersible. In a few minutes, his breathing becomes rhythmic.

Henry checks to make sure Brandon is asleep, then moves to the computer, looking back over his shoulder one more time before typing a complicated sequence of numbers and letters in an algebraic code. The screen goes dark and then a screen view appears of his office at home in Kettering. Henry checks his apartment, going from room to room to make sure no intruder has managed to break in. The cameras show everything as he left it, so he again types in a complicated sequence and the darkened screen lights up in his office at the university. Again, Henry checks with each camera to ensure nothing has been changed or moved and nobody is in evidence.

He types a sequence again, this time connecting to his computer at home, and what appears on the monitor is something so alien to the senses that had he not been prepared for it, Henry himself would have been floored.

Henry ponders as he peruses the alienness on the screen. The next step is crucial; without it, the whole project will be doomed, and this knowledge belongs to Henry alone.

He resolves, as he has many times already, to sacrifice the lives of all those with him, if necessary, to complete this quest. There will be no second chance, the alignment with the Curtain cannot be maintained indefinitely and the infinitesimal calculations and computations necessary to find the sigils again would require three of Henry's lifespans or more. He simply cannot fail now; failure is not an option regardless of the human toll. With his resolve hardened, Henry disconnects the computer, stands and stretches. He makes his way to the makeshift kitchen and pours himself a large mug of coffee from the battery powered coffeemaker. Resuming his seat, he sips the strong, hot brew and waits for 0.400 hours, going over his well-laid plans once more.

The Curtain of Time

Atop a rocky outcrop and within sight of the stone house, the snaggle-toothed wolf lays, weary, panting and watching with rheumy eyes. He knows he will need to act as soon as the family begin their descent to the underground grotto. He knows that he will know when this happens, without any thought whatsoever. This knowledge is innately imprinted so that he does not and cannot be otherwise. His whole life has led him to this point unconsciously, there is, and never was any conscious choice, just an instinctual urge. In satisfying the urge, his future will begin. The physical deterioration he silently suffers continues, his strength ebbing with the fragmentation due to passing through the Curtain. He has no rational thought, just the feelings available to him through pure instinct. His life-force fights the disintegration, but his consciousness is unaware that he does so. He has no fear of death, neither does he consider it in any way, he simply obeys the laws of his nature. He has not eaten since passing through the Curtain, but his hunger is assuaged he knows not how. Tufts of his fur fall out amongst the rocks, but he keeps his vigil unmoved by whatever else is happening to him.

Atop the Acropolis, an owl prepares for flight. She knows of the wolf, and she knows she must join him as he waits. With a leap she spreads her snowy wings and soars high above Athens, riding the thermals as the lightening sky prepares to greet the dawn with the kiss of a rising sun. She dips and rises with the breeze and soon sees the wolf lying, panting on the outcrop of rock. He is weakening fast, so she begins to hunt and soon she spies a young leveret feeding in the long grass. She flies directly overhead and gliding on her wings silently, drops out of the heights and down, snagging the screaming creature with her sharp, long talons and rising up again to the heights with the creature grasped tightly. Down below, the wolf looks up; with a shake sufficient to break the baby hare's neck, the owl drops the body so that it is within the reach of the wolf. He grabs it thankfully and with several sharp bites, devours the creature. His eyes brighten with the sustenance in silent thanks. Athena-Minerva, the owl, alights in the branches of a nearby tree, shielding her eyes from the brightening light. She will wait now with the wolf, she too knows what must be done, she too is obeying the very laws of her nature, written before the dawning of time.

Antheia and Ladon

"Phoenix, Kenny, please come and sit down as soon as the tea is ready. Antheia has much to tell us, and we don't have much time." Aletheia considers how to begin, but she already knows how, by showing the boys Antheia's eyes. How are they going to cope with this revelation? she wonders.

"Brothers, come to me," says Antheia, "I want to show you what happened to me in Ladon's cave."

Unsuspecting the boys cross to Antheia, but she keeps her face downcast and grasps each boy's wrist. "Now when I raise my head, don't be frightened," she says and with that she lifts her head and gazes directly into the two expectant faces. Phoenix smiles widely and hugs his sister to him; next Kenneth does the same. Aletheia is shocked at her brothers' responses, but Antheia seems to have been expecting just this reaction.

"Hello, Ladon," the boys say brightly.

"Hello, Antheia, when will our brother arrive?" Kenneth asks breathlessly. His smile is beautiful to behold.

"How could you possibly know what is happening?" asks Aletheia, startled now more by her brothers' reactions, than the changes in Antheia.

"Ladon told us this morning while we were fetching the water," says Phoenix, "why do you think I am so happy?"

With no further ado, the boys pour the tea and settle to making breakfast for them all. Aletheia sits quietly thinking about these strange events and hoping that they can all settle down now. Antheia will give them all an account of what has happened when they finish with breakfast, and she is relieved that the boys are taking everything in their stride. It will make the revelations easier to deal with.

Thinking through what has happened this morning, the Oracle's words return to her, and again Aletheia is stunned to discover that this is what the Oracle was telling her. "The centre through which you must pass is within you", refers of course, to the dragon child now carried inside Antheia's womb, and "You are the beginning and the end of all that must pass", refers of course, to Ladon's physical presence to come. Aletheia says a silent prayer of thanks to the Oracle for her truth and wisdom.

Phoenix passes out plates piled high with scrambled eggs, and Kenneth passes around thick slices of homemade bread and butter. With relish, the family sets about eating their hearty breakfast.

Greg and Tim

Opening his laptop, Greg tries to connect to the satellite so that he can begin the research to confirm what he deep down suspects. Brandon has given each of the pairs, the means to be able to transmit on the open channel, so Greg assumes the connection will hold for the intranet as well. After deciding to leave the grotto, the two men climbed up to a rocky platform about halfway up the cliff above the beachhead. They had discovered a crude pathway, steep and crumbling, but at least leading away from the grotto. No longer trusting that they are safe because Brandon and Henry have been truthful about the quest, they now intend to set about trying to discover where they are, and when. The time to reconvene at the designated place is looming. The false dawn is already beginning to lighten the darkness and the two men know that unless they return with the others, they must be far enough away from here to have a head start on Henry and Brandon. Both know beyond a shadow of a doubt that Henry will not let them escape into the surrounding area. They have seen enough of his reactive anger to know that this quest is his highest priority. Neither man doubts that he will kill them rather than simply let them go.

At last Greg has an internet connection, and with deft hands, searches for the university home page and Henry's profile. There are few personal facts, but there is an email address for Henry's office at home. Greg knows that he must now show his hand should Henry have set any traps within his computer systems to stop hackers from breaking in, but the situation calls for speed, so Greg does not have the time to disable any back-door traps. The two men have discussed this issue but agreed that this is the only chance they may have to find out what they need to know to escape this place, and within the short time left to them.

"I am ready, Tim, are you sure you want me to do this?" Greg asks, "there will be no turning back once I am in, and we may have to move quickly."

"I don't see that we have any other choice," Tim replies, "just do it Greg and let's get away from here as soon as we can. I don't want to be anywhere near here when Henry finds out we are missing. Our lives are now in danger, but I have a strong feeling they already were as soon as we signed up for this quest. What else have we got to lose?"

Without further delay, Greg begins the break-through into Henry's home computer. In a few seconds, he types in a trojan horse code, and the screen becomes filled with scrolling lines of computer coding. It takes several minutes, and the men hold their breaths as the trojan horse goes to work, finally opening the screen into Henry's personal files. Racing through the file icons, Greg clicks on the one with the sigil shown them tonight. The screen darkens, and when it lights up again, both men jolt with the alienness of what appears.

"I think we have just discovered what made those footprints near the grotto," breathes Tim, "now we have to find out what this means. I think we should get moving while a download of Henry's files completes." Tim hands Greg a flash drive, and hoping the connection with the satellite holds, Greg plugs it in and types the command. That done he closes the laptop and carefully stows it in the backpack. Both men begin to scramble for the clifftop, keeping to the shadows and feeling their way with their hands. They cannot afford to slip or dislodge any stones and the path they discovered earlier is rough and steep. The laptop now sits in the backpack on Greg's shoulders, and he knows he must protect it at all costs. The going is slow and arduous, but both men persevere with the knowledge that if they want to live to see past tomorrow, they must endure whatever hardships confront them, and move along as quickly as is possible.

Antheia

The kitchen chores done; the family sits down to hear what Antheia needs to tell them. She begins with the sigil signaling the last turning in the cave and relates what she remembers from the ordeal. Aletheia listens carefully, sorting what was the same in her case and what was clearly different for Antheia. At last, she speaks to them all.

"This is the beginning of our true quest and was foretold by the Oracle when I visited her," says Aletheia. "I think we must prepare to leave as quickly as possible; time may be of the essence. Antheia, are you recovered sufficiently to make this journey right now?"

Antheia looks up, "Yes, my dear sister, I am fully recovered, although I feel there are more changes to come for me over the next several hours. Ladon is giving me the strength necessary for all of us to travel to our next destination. Please trust in Ladon to get us to the right place and in the right time."

Aletheia gathers herself and directs the others to pack only what is essential and to meet her in the underground grotto as soon as possible. With one last look around at what has been her home for as long as she can remember, she sets about the tasks necessary to leave here. Silently, she thinks to her mother, "We are coming, Mother, please wait for us, we need you."

The family gather near the steps leading down into the grotto and together they descend towards their destiny. As soon as they are all close to the back wall and the sigil, Aletheia asks each of them to empty their minds and relax.

"The way this would normally work," she says, "would be for us to picture the place we want to go and then close our eyes and relax our minds. This time we need to let Ladon take us, so I do not want you to think of anything, just empty your minds and relax. Are we all ready?" The others nod and holding hands, they all close their eyes, empty their minds and relax.

Bonnington

It is nearing 0.400 hours and Henry rises to wake Brandon and prepare for the men's arrival. He has made a fresh pot of coffee in preparation, and he and Brandon help themselves to a cup and make ready for the power point presentation.

"Did you sleep, Brandon?" Henry asks.

"Yes, and thanks, Henry, I must admit, I was more than a bit frazzled and very weary."

"Good," Henry replies, not looking at Brandon and keeping his voice light as if he is really just being polite. He moves to the laptop to prepare for the presentation and just then, what sounds like a bell tolling erupts from the screen. A red flashing light announces a breach of Henry's personal files. Someone has broken into his private, home computer.

With astonishing speed, Henry types in a complicated series of algebraic notations and waits for the command to process. With steely eyes, he reads what comes up onto the screen and with one almighty bellow, he sweeps everything from the table, the laptop included.

"We have a real problem, Brandon, and I must deal with it NOW!"

Although younger and fitter than Henry, Brandon steps back from the raging countenance of Henry Bonnington. There is no way that Brandon wants to be within Henry's reach; he has learnt from past experience how possessed with inhuman strength Henry can be when he becomes truly angry!

The actions that had first cemented their uneasy partnership resulted from the death of a young man who had deigned to question Henrys' competence. Before Brandon could intercede, Henry, enraged, had broken the man's neck and pounded his face into the floor. The threat written in Henry's eyes at that moment warned Brandon that he was now a partner to the murder and that Henry would not let him survive to tell anyone. Acting quickly and quietly, Brandon had sworn his allegiance to Henry. He had helped Henry dispose of the body and make sure there was no evidence to point to what had happened. Brandon had typed a letter of resignation from the university in the young man's name, explaining that he had been offered an internship on a dig in remote African territory and so would be incommunicado for several months, thus giving Henry the time to complete the preparations for this quest. With these actions, their partnership was forged. Henry had kept Brandon on a leash from that day on but sweetened the deal with more money than Brandon could have earned in two lifetimes. Brandon had made a deal with the devil, and the devil had demanded his soul.

The first of the pairs of men begin to arrive and Henry directs them to help themselves to coffee and then go and sit on the cavern floor in front of the table. The laptop is again set on the table, albeit with a large dent in the casing and scratches from the stone floor on the lid. Henry has calmed down enough that the men do not suspect his rage, but the forbidding darkness of his shining eyes warns the men against making any complaints.

Soon all the pairs of men, bar one, are assembled and Henry, unwilling to wait any longer, begins to explain to them that what they have so far endured is a form of psychological experiment. With deft reasoning and the presentation, the men begin to show signs of relief, and some are smiling and nodding their heads as if they knew this to be the case all along. When Henry has finished, the men begin to discuss the experiment animatedly, the relief written in their smiles. Soon Henry directs the men to prepare a meal and opens several bottles of whisky, pouring liberal amounts for each man.

"A toast to the success of this venture, men," Henry proposes, and the men all raise their mugs and drink. With no further ado, Henry slips out of the cavern and stands looking out over the Aegean Sea as the sun begins its ascent. His eyes betray his anger once more, and he silently plans what he must now do. The fact that two of the men are still missing speaks volumes, and Henry vows to deal with them both before they have a chance to discover the truth.

Wolf and Owl

As soon as the family is assembled, the wolf leaps up and sets off at a run, and the owl takes flight. They are only a few hundred yards from the stone house and the grotto, and they cover the distance quickly. Just as the human forms begin to disintegrate as they pass through the Curtain, the wolf and owl race into the grotto. As soon as the humans' forms are but a shimmer of light, both wolf and owl enter into the shimmering, and both begin to shimmer too. Ladon welcomes them both, for he knows them from time immemorial.

"Brother and sister, thank you both for your presence. We go forward together; our family grows."

Aletheia, Antheia, Phoenix and Kenneth open their eyes and look around them in wonderment. The vista before them is so vastly different from Athens that it takes a few moments for them to take it all in. Tall, age-old oak and ash trees filter the weak sunlight, and the forest glade glows dimly with a faint, green light. Antheia is first to notice the wolf and the owl, and she smiles. She recognizes them and knows that they will make the family stronger in ways that their own human forms cannot.

The wolf is fully restored once more, and beautiful to behold. His fur is sleek and his muscles bulge. Eyes lit with fire and intelligence meet Antheia's own.

"Do you know me, Antheia?" he asks silently.

"Oh yes," she whispers, "I have always known you and Athena-Minerva, too. I thank the gods you are coming with us." Antheia stretches out her arm and Athena-Minerva alights on her wrist. Antheia kisses the head of the small owl and turns to the others.

"My sister and brothers, let me introduce you to our very own familiars — wolf and owl," she pronounces. The others turn to her with astonishment written on their faces as they take in the sight of Antheia and the animals redolent of their own spiritual realm.

Aletheia is the first to speak. Her brothers are smiling widely and move to touch both creatures with wonder shining in their eyes.

"Who are you," she asks, "and how do you know our sister?"

"We have known you all since you came into this world," the wolf announces without speaking, "and we have been your protectors here, in Athens and beyond." Aletheia is astounded with this revelation, but as so often happens, she somehow recognizes the truth of what the wolf has said. Athena-Minerva, spreads her wings and says silently to Aletheia, "Stretch out your arm for me, dear girl."

Aletheia does as she is bidden, and Athena-Minerva alights on her wrist and looks deeply into her eyes. "Do you not know me girl?" she asks.

With a sudden gasp, Aletheia breathes, "Athena-Minerva, can it be you?"

"It is me, Aletheia, and your second familiar stands beside you, look into his eyes and see."

Lykaios, the wolf, looks up into Aletheia's eyes and tears of joy gather in the corners.

"Oh Apollo-Lykaios," she says, "thank the gods, I love you both more than you can know. I am so glad to have you here with us. Please tell me you will both stay with us?"

"Your future is now a constant but dangerous quest for truth and wisdom, Aletheia," speaks Lykaios silently, "and we will stay with you, but not always in our physical forms. You have been true to yourself and your family. Our way of showing you this is to appear for you, to become present, but this very presencing belongs to another. You know him as Chronos, but remember, names are only ways of making present. Names are finite, we are not, neither are the other named gods. We will always remain in touch with you through the Oracle, our duty-bound daughter. Today we go with you, but there will come a day soon when we are no longer present to you. Take heed of my words, for Athena-Minerva and I are merely archaic images of your own unconscious, the light of your imagination — it is there to which we must eventually return, for we are not of this world."

With renewed strength and vigor, and wonder in her eyes, Aletheia surveys the scene around her and vows to remain true to her quest, whatever that may entail. She understands now why the visit to Ladon's lair was essential, and she thanks the gods with all her heart and all her being.

Tim and Greg

The two men at last climb onto a rocky outcrop at the top of the cliff and pause briefly to catch their breath and look down towards the sea. Searching the dimly lit surrounding scenery, Tim notices the Acropolis higher up and further towards the inland side of their present position.

"I suggest we try to make our way up there," Tim points to the ruins, "we should be able to hide within the shadows." Greg takes a moment to think.

If they are to keep ahead of Henry, they need to make sure he cannot track their progress.

"We have to take the time now to check the download," says Greg, "if we are to get a head start, I have to turn off the laptop. If I don't, Henry will be able to track our movements. The laptop will act as a beacon! We can't go any further until that's done, and we are running out of time!"

The men sit and Greg removes the backpack from his shoulders. Taking out the laptop, and with practiced fingers, Greg opens to the screen, saves what has downloaded, removes the USB and blanks the screen. He has no idea how much of Henry's data they have, but he knows that whatever they have will have to be enough. There is simply no more time. With the laptop switched off and stowed again, both men turn towards the Acropolis and begin the trek they hope will save their lives.

Dawn begins to break as the sun's rays reach the edge of the horizon. The two men pick up their pace — they cannot afford to be seen from the beach below. Searching amongst the boulders, they look for some kind of depression that will cover their progress. Speed is impossible in this rocky terrain.

Bonnington

The men have all eaten and settled down to sleep the day away. Henry fetches his backpack and packs his laptop and enough meagre supplies to last the day. He signals Brandon and steps outside the cavern.

"I am leaving you in charge today, Brandon. Make sure the men stay here and do not allow them any satellite connection. I am sure you can conjure up some mundane tasks to keep them busy until I return."

"I assume you are going to take care of the problem you foresaw earlier?" Brandon asks the rhetorical question. "What do you want me to do if you do not return?"

This question is not rhetorical and Henry stares at Brandon with disdain.

"If I don't return, you may do as you wish for it will not matter in the least to me. But beware of making any autonomous decisions until you are quite sure that I am dead. A mistake could cost you dearly!"

Brandon knows exactly what Henry means, and he asks nothing more. He watches until Henry is out of sight and returning to the cavern, stretches out on his makeshift bed to think. His situation is becoming untenable as his nervousness about Henry's intentions towards him take form. He knows he must use the time of Henry's absence carefully to formulate a plan if he is to survive this quest.

Henry follows the beacon signaling the direction and distance from Greg and Tim. He has already decided his course of action and steadfastly begins the ascent of the cliff face taken earlier by the two men. As soon as he has taken care of them, he knows he must reckon with Brandon, another problem to be eliminated. Brandon has never been able to hide his true feelings, and Henry has read the fear and mistrust in his eyes. He hoped to be able to use Brandon more substantially before getting rid of him, but the chance to do so has now vanished. His return to the cavern must be camouflaged so that he can catch Brandon unawares. As the sun rises above the horizon, Henry tries to quicken his pace, but the sheer, jagged cliff face slows his progress. The path, a mere indentation of the rocks, allows only slow and careful movement, so he grits his teeth and moves slowly upwards.

Ladon's Hourdes

The forest glows more brightly as the sun rises, although to call this light bright would almost be an oxymoron. The family survey the old growth trees and low brush and briars that hide their presence from the world into which they have passed. A dawn chorus of birdcalls reminds them all that this place and time are unfamiliar to them. Aletheia and Antheia know that they must think about and form a course of action. Without scouting out the immediate area, they will have no idea what or who lives in the vicinity, and if by chance they have passed into an inhabited area close to a village or town, their appearance and oddness of garb may make them conspicuous. Antheia seems preoccupied and sits quietly — the others do not understand the enormous changes that are happening to her mind and body, but somehow, they sense that she needs to be left alone.

"The chill suggests we have passed into a colder climate, and the bird calls are nothing I have heard before," Aletheia peers around the forest glade trying to gain some semblance of understanding.

Lykaios stands still, sniffing the air and twitching his ears. Silently he relays a message to them all.

"I will scout the area and bring you the information necessary for you to plan." With a flick of his tail, and on silent paws, he moves off swiftly. Aletheia moves with the family to find a hide large enough for all of them to be out of sight. Phoenix lets his telepathy range carefully so as not to alert another telepathic adept to his presence, should there be one nearby. There are hardly any signs of other minds or voices, but he widens his range to the limits of his ability.

Kenneth sits with Athena-Minerva, stroking her soft feathers and trying to adjust himself to what is happening. He has not learned yet to fully encompass the sudden and what seem to him to be, forbidding changes.

His short life seems to be filled with nothing but continual and abrupt change, and sometimes he wishes he could just be a little boy with a mum and dad. Athena-Minerva snuggles up to him to give him a semblance of comfort and support. She understands that his wish will come true and perhaps sooner than he can imagine! Weary and sad, Kenneth snuggles up to the small owl and falls asleep, his head resting at her feet. She enters his unconscious and summons the dream images that will soothe his soul and give him rest.

Tim and Greg

At last Tim and Greg reach the portico of the Acropolis. Both stagger into the shadowed ruins of the Parthenon and collapse on the floor. The climb has taken the last reserves of both men, and they know they need to sleep. Water is becoming a problem and the heat of the summer day is becoming more evident. With just their backpacks for pillows, both men fall into a sleep of exhaustion. It will be several hours before they wake and as they sleep, Henry moves closer.

The cry of a hawk wakes Greg suddenly and it takes him a few moments to remember where he is. He has slept, but his sleep has been beset with lurid dreams. Stark images of gigantic proportions have chased him through shadowed passageways, but he has been unable to see clearly what these images are. His heart is still beating overtime as the dream fades with his return to consciousness. Drenched in sweat, he stands and stretches his aching limbs — the hard granite floor has done nothing to ease the painful stiffness caused by the climb. Before waking Tim, he removes the laptop from his backpack and powers it up to see if he has managed to download Henry's files. After a quick appraisal, he turns it off again, just in case Henry has been alerted to the download. His worst nightmare is to be confronted by an angry Henry. He knows that if a confrontation ensues, he will have to fight for his life, because Henry will not let them live. With that thought, he wakes Tim and both men eat a frugal meal and drink the last of their water. It is nearing midday and time to move on, hopefully to find water and some place safe where they can stay long enough to get their bearings. Food and water will be the critical issue today, so they set out to search the ruins, looking for any clue of a way forward. What remains of the Parthenon seems to be the lesser ruined of the ancient buildings, and Tim notices one rear corner that is darker than the rest. While Greg walks the inside perimeter, he moves in that direction.

"Greg, quick, come here!" the excitement in Tim's voice brings Greg on the run. In the shadows, the men notice an ancient and narrow stairway at the back wall.

"Shall we try it?" asks Tim. There is at least the chance that this may lead them to an underground area not so easily found as the rest of the complex of ruins.

"At least it will be cooler than up here, and who knows we might find another way out," Greg sounds more positive than he feels, but they have little or nothing to lose. Tentatively at first, they test the crumbling, stone steps to make sure they will take their weight, then with little further ado, they carefully descend down many feet into a dark passageway. It is definitely cooler here, but they can also feel a current of air. The passage must lead to the outside, so they hurry as much as is possible through the winding darkness.

At last, the darkness begins to lighten and the air warms. With renewed hope, the men quicken their pace and before long, they can see quite clearly. The passage begins to wind upwards getting steeper as they ascend and within a minute, they break out into a wooded grove with a well-defined pathway. Scanning the woods and pathway to make sure there is nobody near, they begin to follow the path upwards through the grove. The higher they climb, the less the trees obscure the way. Soon they come in sight of what appears to be a stone house, although it is obscured by a cliff face into which it seems to recede. The sun is directly overhead, and so shines down through the surrounding trees to glint off the rock facade of the house. Another hour sooner or later, and the house would not have been visible from the path.

Moving with great care now, and as quietly as they can, the men approach the house, ready at any moment to fade into the trees should anyone appear. The windows are open to the outside, without even shutters to hold back the weather, and they eventually find the doorway hidden by bushes growing down from the cliff face. By now the men recognize that the house is deserted; they would most certainly have been detected if anyone was inside or in close proximity.

The door is unlocked, but still with great care, the men push against the stout beams and slowly and silently, the door moves inwards until they can slip into the darkened interior space. Standing quite still, they listen intently for any evidence of habitation. At last, satisfied that they are alone, they make their way into the house proper and begin to explore the rooms. The entrance leads onto a passage paved with flagstones and leading in both directions. Unlit rush torches rest in sconces at regular intervals along the walls. Going right, they encounter four bedrooms, starkly furnished, but with sturdy beds.

There are various items of strange clothing folded in wooden boxes in each room, some befitting boys and others most obviously female attire. A short bow and a quiver of strange-looking arrows are propped against the wall in the last bedroom; the clothes define it as obviously the room of a woman. Tim lifts out one of the strange arrows and examines its structure. The fletching looks to be that of a small owl. He recognizes the feathering having seen these same birds in Kettering. The barbed point of the arrow is engineered to cause maximum damage to flesh and bone — this is a serious weapon for anyone to use let alone a woman! Hopefully, they will not have to encounter the owner! This rudimentary weapon will certainly be a welcome addition to their meagre supplies.

Leaving this last room, they return to the central point through which they entered and carry on along the left side. They pass a doorway with steps leading down into darkness, but for now they pass this by. Towards the end of this wing, they enter a large kitchen space with a fireplace and various iron pots and pans. Recessed into the stone, there is a store containing a meagre supply of food — what appears to be some kind of flat bread and dried fruit together with small pots of dried herbs. Lifting one of these, Greg sniffs and declares the contents to be dried mint. The contents of others contain familiar smells although the men can put names to only a few. On a higher shelf, they notice various stoppered bottles labelled in what appears to be ancient Greek script. Neither can read Greek, so they examine the contents using smell alone. There is nothing familiar, but the stringency to their noses suggests that these bottles contain a variety of strong, herbal potions probably used as medicines.

Beset with relief, exhaustion claims them once again, and after drinking from a wooden bucket of water found on the kitchen table, they return to the furthest bedroom and both lie down on the bed, with the bow and arrows within close reach. Separation is not an option at this time just in case they are discovered by the owner of the house, or worse, by Henry Bonnington. In minutes they are both unconscious, sleeping the sleep of the dead.

Henry

Henry takes the final steps onto the clifftop, and with great relief, collapses onto the rocky ground and reaches for his water bottle. His tortured breathing begins to subside towards normal, and he looks around him searching the vista for any sign of movement. While he rests, he muses. How have his well-laid plans come to this? He felt sure with all the painstaking planning at the university and months of testing and drilling, that the men would follow his instructions to the letter, yet already three have been found wanting.

The beacon has ceased to function, so he knows Tim and Greg have had enough foresight to turn off their laptop. Certain proof that they are making a dash for freedom! Knowing this only serves to harden Henry's resolve, and after a short respite, he begins the further ascent towards the ruins atop Athens. His painstaking, geographic surveys of the area prior to leaving Kettering give him the surety that this is the only way forwards for anyone wanting to leave the immediate vicinity. He has not, however, walked these tracks himself, nor been able to procure any map as ancient as the time he figures he now inhabits, although he cannot be sure. The time may be more or less than he has calculated; there is simply no surefire way to know, so he must be careful to remember that the map as he memorized it, may not be the same as the reality that now presents itself. Steadfastly and taking care to watch his steps, he slowly rises towards the Acropolis.

Brandon

At last Brandon fell into an exhausted sleep, but as the sun begins its afternoon descent towards the Aegean Sea, he jolts awake. He spent most of the morning planning what to do next; carefully thinking and weighing the consequences of the plan as it formed and firmed in his mind. The only decision left to him now is whether or not to take the other sleeping men with him. Leaving without them means they will be doomed to live out their lives here or worse, become the targets for Henry's wrath. The decision he makes gives him the best chance of survival, assuming that what is necessary to accomplish this is possible at all.

When they first arrived here, Henry made sure he was the last person to alight from the submersible. Henry and Brandon are the only ones with the transponder codes and satellite coordinates. There will be only one chance, and this may already have been taken care of by Henry! Brandon knows that Henry can foil his escape at any time. The only way he will know if Henry has taken the actions to prevent escape, is when he tries to activate both the invisibility cloak and summon the submersible. The remote system requires no human contact, but human contact to the system will most definitely alert Henry and may provide him enough time to shut down the underwater portal — access to the Curtain. Any possible alternative is a non-starter, there simply is no other way. Brandon resolves to activate his plan now, before Henry returns.

With haste in mind, he starts to pack up his meagre belongings, careful to make no noise to wake the others. He must be gone from here as soon as is possible, or he may not get away at all. Shouldering his pack, he steps outside and carefully scrutinizes the surrounding area, searching for any movement or sign that Henry is in the vicinity. With shaking hands, he sets the coordinates to connect to the satellite, then sends out the signal to bring the submersible to life again. At first, everything seems to be working as it should; the invisibility cloak settles about him shielding him from human eyes. Watching only his enveloped feet, he moves swiftly along the track towards the beachhead. The cloak provides a lighted pathway towards the submersible, so tracking back is no problem. Just as he reaches the access point, the lighting along the pathway blinks out and the invisibility cloak disintegrates leaving him clearly and starkly visible to anyone looking in his direction. With renewed haste, Brandon scrambles down the rocks and leaps aboard the submersible. As soon as he gains a foothold, he sprints to the control centre set into the aft quarter deck. As quickly as his shaking hands can manage, he sets the coordinates for the Curtain portal and sinks down into the seat, strapping himself in. The watertight dome lowers, and the seals activate and seconds later, as the submersible slips silently below the water, his form inside the submersible begins to shimmer and shake. The control panel of the submersible glows with heat and condensation begins to form around the controls. A few seconds later, both Brandon and the submersible have disappeared. The silence on the surface is broken only by the cry of a sea eagle that drifts away as it takes flight out over the sea. Only the gentle lapping of the waves onto the shore disturbs the afternoon's peace. The men in the grotto sleep on.

Lykaios

Testing the air with all his senses, Lykaios moves swiftly and silently through the forest, checking for any scent of human habitation. The forest stretches for miles, and although the forest floor seems to be mostly flat, he recognizes that with each mile, he is climbing steadily higher. Oak and brambles give way to ash and pine trees. All of a sudden, he senses a change in the air and carefully cuts his trot down to a walking pace. Up ahead, the light changes, becoming brighter, and signaling the emerging edge of the forest. Five hundred yards further on he emerges at the edge of the tree line. He must go no further, until he senses it is safe to do so.

Lykaios notices a rocky outcrop a few yards from the forest edge and testing the air in all directions for any sign of danger, he moves carefully towards it until his form is hidden within the shadows of the rocks. Slowly he lifts his head to survey the scene below. Spread out in all directions are swathes of emerald, green, split only by hedgerows into discreet fields. Different greens in harrowed rows signal different crops and sheep dot the grassy verges. Evidence of human interaction with the natural landscape! This is obviously a farming area, and the colour of the grassy fields says much more to Lykaios. This is the green he remembers of Ireland, named the Emerald Isle for this very reason, and well into the future of when and where he now stands. He is high enough to be able to overlook the fields and notices darker areas in the nether landscape that he recognizes as peat bogs, more granite outcrops and beyond, the movement of water. Narrowing his eyes, he also sees the top of what appears to be a tower built of stone, and beyond the water. The tower beckons.

Taking the time to take in every small detail, he warily returns to the forest and sets off at a fast trot to rejoin the family. The smallest nuances in the scene he has surveyed, enable him to estimate the 'time' they have passed into and with this knowledge, he can help Aletheia formulate a plan of action. The fact that this is Ireland is no coincidental passing through; the spiritual saturation of this land is the necessary catalyst for the fire-born humans to refine and enhance their own spiritual powers. Above all he understands perfectly well that spiritual and intellectual growths must happen together if one is to become whole. The underdevelopment of either will stunt the other and lead to a lack of understanding. Without this experience, he knows without thinking about it, that they cannot survive their quest. His own physical appearance and that of Athena-Minerva are embedded within the Zeitgeist of Ireland. It is here that all the members of the family must gain the fullness of their fire-born powers and innate humanness because it is here that the sigils abound. Using the Curtain of Time must become second nature to them all before they can leave here, so that when the sigils disappear, as they surely must, the Curtain will always remain open to them. A bridge between consciousness and the collective unconscious must be securely constructed by each member of the family. Ladon has led them all here for just this purpose. A family reunion is to happen, and soon.

Antheia

Sitting alone in the far side of the hide, Antheia is no longer conscious of the outside world. As her body and mind metamorphize, she wanders through internal realms filled with archaic images that 'speak' silently to her with messages from the gods. Ladon grows inside her. As her understanding grows, she begins to feel a lightness of spirit, ineffable in worldly terms. She is free to fly here, no longer hampered by bodily form and all communications come from the deep, eternal silence of existence. There is a simplicity here, so beautiful that it cannot compare to anything finite, and she is filled with the pure light and fullness of the power of existence.

The joy is so acute that there is simply nothing negative. Pure existence is ecstatic. Here is the abounding fullness of nirvana, the pure, dynamic nothingness from which overflows life into all its forms, described by the poets, philosophers and prophets. Every nuance of this unquiet silence makes perfect sense. A deeper unconsciousness descends upon her, and she lets herself go down, down into the nether 'world' of her spiritual core. There is at once every living thing in all its abundance, in every singular possibility, growing and waning before her inner eyes. She 'dreams' in every possible colour far surpassing those of the mere worldly spectrum. Each colour has its own unique sound, like a million strings of unknown instruments all in perfect harmony. Memories of reading about the music of the spheres as written down by Pythagoras fleeting before her mind; now she understands! A faint vibration begins from beyond this heavenly realm and down deeper she goes, towards it. Suddenly there is light so wonderful that she can scarcely believe it. She wavers as she nears the pulsing source of universal vibration, terrified that she may not be admitted, but with wonder she is immediately enveloped and held in the warm light of the living God. Welcome Antheia. She is home at last!

Florence

The family has arrived! Florence sits in the tower room on the island of Inis Cealtra set in Lough Derg, only three hundred metres off the later to be named, Mountshannon shore. Studying under the guidance of abbot Marcom, she has reached the pinnacle of her spiritual powers. The history of this place will later tell of Christian pilgrimages and churches manned by renowned Irish saints, but this is only the apparent practice of what happens here. Brian Boru and his brother, Marcom, are much more than mere Christian clerics.

The island is small and set out on a plain with few trees, but a calmness lies over the island, most unusual in this part of County Clare. The round tower in which Florence sits acts as a beacon for the mainland. Built of stone, tall, cylindrical and with a narrow, spiral stone stairway, its highest rooms abound with ancient charts and scrolls. There is hardly space to step or sit, but this has been Florence's home for the last several years, and she loves every inch of it. From the window, she can survey the granite flats, peat bogs and green fields of the mainland. This area is windswept on the Western side by howling storms rolling straight off the Atlantic Ocean. On this Eastern shore, they are protected by the inlet of the lake.

Her own spartan room has only a narrow straw palliasse as a bed and a narrow arrow slit window open to all weathers. Sheep on the island provide both food and a thick fleece used to spin the light, but warm cloth made into clothing and blankets used by all here.

What later history will describe as the church is more akin to a college and here a stone fireplace warms them in the worst winter months, although the winters in this region are milder than the rest of the country. Peat is plentiful, cut from the bogs of the mainland and carried across by coracle. There is a large store of peat blocks for burning. At the back of the 'church' building is a large kitchen area with a huge fireplace for cooking and a huge oak table with benches along the sides for sitting and eating. Barrels of mead are stored here, and a new kind of spirit made from fermenting grain, much later to be named whiskey. In winter, a warming brew is made by mixing these together and heating the mixture by plunging a red-hot iron poker into the brew. This hearty brew sustains them and seems to keep illnesses at bay.

The effects of drinking the brew also aid in lowering the rational thinking threshold, so that exercises to bridge consciousness with the unconscious core of human being can begin. It is this strengthening and widening of consciousness that allows the human to become truly what he or she already is. Without the exercises performed here, oblivion of the deeper regions of the human spirit would remain. In the everyday world of space-time, cause and effect, these hidden depths remain hidden. Inis Cealtra is a sacred and spiritual centre, not merely Christian by origin but adopted as a sacred place of ritual by the Druids long before this time. It is to this place that Ladon has led the family knowing full well that only this place can provide access to the work necessary for the spiritual learning to be accomplished. A family reunion is coming and soon!

Tim and Greg

Awakened by birdsong and hunger, Tim and Greg leave the room they have slept in and head for the kitchen at the other end of the house. From the window, the dawn light brings with it the smells of summer. Both men are very hungry, and Tim notices the sounds of chickens coming from somewhere close by. From the vantage point of the kitchen window, the men survey what is visible, and although there seems to be nothing or no one near, still they ponder whether they are safe. Do they go outside and look around or stay put? The specter of Henry Bonnington imbues their every action!

"Greg, stay here and watch. I will go outside and see what I can find." Tim gets up and picking up the bow and two arrows, he heads back towards the door. Greg concentrates all his attention to alert to any movement or sound coming from the trees and path. Can they be lucky enough to have found an abandoned house? Skeptically, he doubts it! Half an hour goes by, and Greg begins to feel nervous about the length of time Tim has been gone. He resolves to wait for ten minutes more and then go in search of him. There is a rustling of leaves, and with heart beginning to pound, Greg notices Tim's form returning. "Thank goodness for that!" he thinks.

Moments later, Tim arrives back in the kitchen and puts a makeshift bundle wrapped in his shirt on the table.

"Breakfast, Greg," he smiles, opening the bundle to reveal six large, brown hen's eggs. "The chicken run is hidden from view in the middle of that grove of trees off to the left of the path."

With great relish, the men find an iron skillet and risking the smoke, set and light a fire in the kitchen hearth. They fill an old iron kettle with water from the bucket and search for something to make tea, if there is any such thing here. No tea, but they decide to slake some dried mint in boiling water and see if it will do as a hot drink. Soon both men are tucking into scrambled eggs and flat bread and drinking a soothing mint tea.

Henry Bonnington

Henry wakes from his sleep in his makeshift bed within the ruins of the Parthenon. Late yesterday afternoon he managed to climb to the ruins before fatigue claimed him, and he managed to provide himself with a rudimentary sleeping pad softened by his thick jacket and pack. Unable to go on and not having slept for nearly thirty-six hours, he succumbed almost immediately he laid his head down. His senses tell him that he has slept the clock around — the sun is again dropping towards the Aegean Sea. He scrabbles in his pack for the meagre rations left from yesterday and drinks deeply from his water bottle. He must find more food and water if he is to continue his hunt for Tim and Greg.

Restlessly, his mind returns to Brandon, and he has the uneasy feeling that leaving him in charge any longer may produce problems. He is in a quandary; does he go on with his search for the two missing men or go back to the grotto and try to resume his search for the sigils? Perhaps it was foolish to leave Brandon in charge of everything just for the chance of revenge. The two men cannot leave this place so what is more important, to catch the men and deal with them or accomplish what he set out to do in the first place? Of course, there is really no question. He should not have given in to his angry impulses. In doing so, he may have put his whole quest in peril.

Hunger and thirst slaked for now, Henry quickly returns his pack to his shoulders and without looking back, sets off to descend once more to the grotto. The unease he felt earlier is more pronounced now. With trepidation, he realizes that the tiredness of yesterday clouded his judgment and that leaving Brandon in charge was foolish at best! The 'leash' he had used to bind him only worked in close proximity. What if Brandon escaped his clutches? This did not bear thinking about. Slipping and sliding with the haste of his descent, Henry tries not to imagine the worst.

Lykaios

Loping along the forest path, Lykaios formulates a plan to put to Aletheia. Afternoon is coming and the sun has reached its zenith and begun its descent towards the horizon again. Lykaios knows this by the subtle changes in the light through the forest growth. Even in summer, the days here are not very long, and he knows they must find shelter before the coming darkness. At the same time, he is filled with hope and joy, because he knows they are quite close to their destination. If he can gather the others and start out soon, they will reach their destination before another morning dawns. This is the most important task and the least risk to all! Finding shelter will have to wait, the best shelter is to reach their destination without delay. Yes, this is what they must do! As he runs, he sends a message to Athena-Minerva.

The family have been napping, but now the coolness in the air has made their hide uncomfortable. Aletheia worries that Lykaios has not yet returned and although Antheia seems to be merely sleeping, Aletheia is not sure that is in fact the case. Summoning her resolve, she wakes the others and reaches out to touch Antheia. Her sister shakes her head, and her alien eyes adjust to their surroundings once more.

"We must find food and water soon, or we will not be able to last the night here."

Antheia smiles at Aletheia and moves to 'speak' to Athena-Minerva. Kenneth and Phoenix look rested and quietly listen to the silent conversation. The family are wearing the clothes they left Athens in. The boys are beginning to shiver, and everyone is now very hungry.

"What can we do to find warmth and sustenance?" asks Antheia.

"Do not worry," the small owl answers, "Lykaios is near, and he has news to warm your hearts if not your bodies. Prepare yourselves to move on as soon as he arrives. We will need to move quickly, and we have a way to go, so you will soon be warm. Hunger must wait, but there is a brook along the way to slake everyone's thirst."

Just then Lykaios emerges from the undergrowth and sits panting before Aletheia.

"There is no time for me to explain where we are and why we are here, so you must trust me. We must travel through the night to reach our destination," he says, "I know you are all hungry, but I promise you, the journey you are about to make will be worth your continued discomfort. Do not stray from my sight because the forest stretches for miles, and it is easy to become lost. Are you all ready?"

The family gathers together and with Lykaios loping ahead, they move quickly through the forest. Athena-Minerva flies from tree to tree, watching to make sure all are together, and she waits until everyone has passed her position before moving on again.

As the sun moves closer to the horizon, the family moves closer to Lough Derg, winding their way through the forest to the rocky outcrop already visited by Lykaios. Turning left, they descend to follow the line of fields towards the granite plains fronting the lake. As night falls, the moon is almost full, so out in the open the darkness is not as forbidding as within the forest. Lykaios listens for the babbling of water over stones and skirting the peat bogs, he at last leads the family through a thicket to the edge of a fast-flowing brook. Sinking onto the spongy edge, each family member drinks his and her fill before Lykaios does likewise.

"We are about halfway now," he silently communicates, "rest for a few minutes before we set off again. Tomorrow you will sleep in the shelter and comfort of the place that has been waiting for you since before you were born."

The boys are tired, but the excitement of travelling at night keeps them going. Everyone is wondering where they are and towards what destination they are moving. Lykaios sets off again and the others follow closely behind him. Ahead, someone prepares for their arrival.

Brandon

Passing through the portal of the Curtain, Brandon has lost consciousness. The submersible has been damaged but before breaking down altogether, it has re-emerged into a fast-flowing current of an in-going tide. Brandon remains unconscious as the submersible bobs and plunges with the waves, moving slowly towards the tidal estuary of an inland bay. Night shields the disabled craft from view.

Unseen by Brandon, dark shadows move along the estuary bank. They have not caught sight of the craft. They are travelling at night to meet with men from neighbouring tribes. It is a meeting of secret men's business. Each shadow carries a woomera and spear, and each body displays the ochre markings defining their spirit animal. Soon they are lost to sight, moving swiftly through the bushland. Brandon remains unconscious. The craft has arrived in Kettering, but this is a Kettering across the world from Brandon's Kettering in Northamptonshire, England. This Kettering, as it will be known well into the future, is at the bottom of the Great Southern Land known as Terra Australis, this is the Kettering of Van Diemen's Land, much later to be named, Tasmania.

Tim and Greg

The two men have now eaten their fill and after disposing of the cleaning up, using the water left in the wooden bucket, they decide to search the house more thoroughly. As they move away from the kitchen, Greg remembers the stairway that they passed by yesterday and again this morning. The men are still wary, worried that they may yet find someone else here. Carefully and with as little noise as possible, they descend the stairs and find themselves in an underground grotto. It appears to have been cut directly into the rock face that hides the house from view outside. Strangely there are several items that do not naturally belong here: a large boulder lies in the centre of the rock floor, and there is a wooden ramp constructed from oak beams. Ropes woven from some sort of strong fiber lie curled in neat piles and a hooded robe hangs on a piece of rock that has been hewn from the grotto wall for just this purpose.

The men move past these items towards the back of the grotto. An unlit rush torch sits in a sconce carved into the wall, and reaching into his pocket for a box of matches, Tim lights the torch so they can see the dim rear of the grotto more clearly. There does not seem to be anyone or anything else here; with the light, the men can clearly see the back wall. They move towards it to check for any sign of another ingress from the outside. As Tim shines the torch around the wall, suddenly a sigil becomes visible carved into the wall to the left. The men move closer to examine this carving.

"This is what Henry showed us when we arrived!" exclaims Greg, "this is what we were looking for when we searched the shoreline! What on earth is it doing here and what can this mean?"

Both men try to make sense of what they are seeing, but there does not seem to be anything meaningful to either of them. Extinguishing the torch and replacing it in the sconce, carefully, they return to the stone stairs and ascend back into the house proper. Greg goes to the room they slept in the night before and picks up his backpack. With this in hand, he leads Tim back into the kitchen where the light is now brighter.

"We must try to work out what all this means," he says to Tim. "It's time to look through Henry's files. We need to know what is going on, to decide what to do next!"

"What about Henry?" Tim asks, "can we risk him finding us here? Surely it is too risky, it might let him know where we are. He could be close behind us for all we know, or even watching the house right now from outside!"

"I think we should go outside and scout the area before I open the files," agrees Greg, "if it is all clear, then we must risk it. We can't make any move without knowing more about what the sigil in the grotto means. It must be important, or Henry would not be so keen for it to be found. But why, that is the question! And without a reasonable answer, we will be acting blindly."

Looking around the kitchen, Greg picks up a crude knife from the hearth, and Tim shoulders the bow and takes an arrow. Both men move towards the door and quietly pull on the beams to open it enough to slip silently though into the grove of trees. Using a hand signal, Tim leads Greg to the left where the chicken run is. The men creep silently past the run and continue for about a mile, until the trees begin to thin out. They can see an area beyond the glade where the land slopes down again towards the beach. There is no evidence of anyone here. Returning back the way they came, they move off to the right of the path, making sure not to step on anything that will snap and being careful not to move the foliage of the lower branches enough to cause any rustling. A few yards past the house, they discover what looks like a well, set with a handle above the stonework. They have at least, found the house's source of water. The wooden bucket in the kitchen must have been filled from here!

Again, they move on until they can see the end of the tree line on this side. There is nobody here either. The land again slopes down steeply. Gaining the lie of the land, the men realise that the house stands on a naturally fortified hilltop ledge, so anyone approaching from below should be able to be seen before they can see the house. As quietly as they can, they return to the house and move back into the kitchen.

"If we have to stay here, we can set some alarms on either side, and on the path we used to get here, that should alert us to anyone coming towards the house," says Tim, "so now let's look and see what we can determine from Henry's files. At least that way we can make up our minds as to what to do next."

Florence

In the kitchen of the college, Florence and her maid bustle about preparing enough food it seems, for an army. There is a full lamb roasting on a spit in the great fireplace, and every now and then, the maid bastes the meat with herbed oils and turns the handle to turn the meat. On a large, floured board, Florence is kneading down for the last time, the seeded dough that will be baked on a shelf above the fire but behind the lamb, to produce a variety of tasty, crusty loaves. Vegetables have been peeled and cut into pieces to be boiled or roasted. It is just after midnight and the two women prepare for the arrival of the family.

Rooms have been readied with straw palliasses and soft, warm blankets of wool. New beeswax candles have been set on their holders and placed on small tables in each room. The small firepits in each room have been lit to provide warmth and cheer. All is ready. Florence has been advised by Athena-Minerva how each of her children fares, and what they have most recently been through, although she will elicit all the details from them herself over the next few days. She can scarcely believe Antheia is now an immortal, and that she carries Ladon inside her. This outcome could never have been foreseen by anyone, but knowing now what she does, it makes perfect sense to Florence.

Others in the small community of eight prepare the table with bowls, knives, spoons and wooden mugs. Brian releases the bung on a new barrel of mead, tasting the first sip to make sure it is aged sufficiently. The sweet honey wine is just right! Alongside this barrel he places an earthenware jug of the fermented spirit, ready to mix the two together to make the warming brew.

Marcom uses this time to meditate in preparation to read the minds of each new comer. There is an unspoken law here that all who enter must be sufficiently powerful to withstand the mental testing to come. Knowing the strength of Florence, he assumes this will be merely a formality to fulfil the rules by which they all abide here. The brothers know that the task set before them with this family will be their last, after which they can retire and live quietly, free at last to research their chosen areas of study. There is nothing more to do now but await the arrival of those who are slowly but surely coming closer.

Henry Bonnington

By the time Henry reaches the beach again, he is beset with a feeling of dread so deep that his breathing has become rapid and shallow. Carefully, so as not to alert the men in the cavern to his presence, he creeps along the cliff face in the shadows cast by the sinking sun and the coming night. He can hear men in discussion, but he cannot hear what is being said. The men have powered up lights sufficient to cast their long shadows towards the spot where Henry stands. He knows there is no sense in trying to surprise Brandon now that the men are all awake. He will have to take care of that problem later.

Taking a moment to steady himself, Henry at last steps into the cavern to the surprise of the talking men. With his entry into the cavern, the men cease their talking, and a hush falls over the scene. Henry looks around him but cannot see Brandon. The men watch Henry with concern written on their faces, and several avert their eyes from his gaze.

"Where is Brandon, men?" Henry inquires.

The men shuffle their feet, looking at each other; each hoping another will answer Henry's question.

"We awoke around three this afternoon," replies Peter, "but Brandon was not here then, and he left us no clue as to where he has gone, or how long he will be. We were just talking about what to do when you arrived back. We have prepared plenty of food though because we have not eaten since yesterday evening. Would you like some, Henry?"

"Thanks, Pete," Henry replies, careful not to let the men see his consternation. "I have been to the ruins above the beach here to check out the landscape. I was so bushed after the climb, I slept up there, so yes, I am very hungry too. Let's eat."

The men share relieved glances, and nobody dares mention Brandon's disappearance again.

Henry eats with the men, listening to, and chatting about their ideas regarding the experiment. He deflects any mention of their return to Kettering before the question becomes overt, instead, reminding them that they need to find the sigils before they can contemplate the end of the test or their return home. When everyone has finished eating, Henry sets them some housekeeping tasks to do before they move out for the night search. Although they have all slept well, they are at last becoming attuned to the day-night difference between Athens and Kettering, so Henry decides to shorten the night search and let the men sleep again at midnight.

As the men go about their tasks, in preparation for heading out again, Henry sets his laptop on the makeshift table ready to connect to the satellite when the men have left. He issues some final instructions and informs the men that they need to return at midnight. He wishes them all good luck, and the men set out in their designated pairs to resume their search.

As soon as he is sure that the men are well away from the cavern, Henry connects to the satellite. Firstly, he checks his offices at home and the university. As he suspected earlier, his backup system alerts him to the Trojan Horse attack. Typing a few lines of algebraic script, he is able to see which of his files have been downloaded. Careful to keep his face guarded, and his temper under control, he tries to think about how he can complete the quest as quickly as possible now that Brandon has gone. But where has Brandon gone? This question is most worrying! He scarcely wants to contemplate the possibilities of where Brandon is, or what he may have done, but he knows he must.

Taking a deep breath, he types in the transponder codes to summon the submersible. He waits for the transponder to send back the automated message to his laptop. When there is no response, he cancels the summons and sits stock still. Could Brandon have done such an abominable thing? The question is merely rhetorical as the memory of the fear and mistrust written on Brandon's face the morning before, provides the answer. With shaking hands, Henry tries a second time with no result.

Greg and Tim

Greg takes out the laptop and opening the lid, he uses his satellite connection to power up sufficiently to open Henry's files. The familiar sigil icon stands out, and having clicked on it previously, he knows what it opens onto. Greg moves on to another that looks like a stylised curtain. With deft hands, he opens the file, and an index page of sorts appears on the screen. Reading carefully, he selects the first item titled 'Time-Lapses'.

This page opens to a paper written recently by a renowned scientist known to the two men. Sitting side by side they begin to read carefully. After about an hour, they are both finished reading the paper and each sits silently, thinking. After a few minutes, Greg rouses himself and returns to the index screen.

For the next several hours, the men methodically and carefully read through the full contents of the file. A fledgling understanding begins to dawn as they wend their way through the papers, articles and plans; the meaning of what they are reading begins to weigh heavily on them both. The enormity of the situation that Henry has led them all into is mind-boggling. If they can believe what is in this file, then they know beyond a shadow of a doubt that Henry never had any intention of returning to Kettering with any of the men. The Curtain of Time and the sigils that signal an entry point require the sustenance of living bodies to remain open. They were all to become human sacrifices to the dragon, thanks to Henry's insane, all-encompassing ambition.

At last, the men have read everything there is, and both understand their predicament. They thank their lucky stars they did not touch or get close to the sigil in the grotto! The day has quickly turned to twilight, their research has taken their full attention, but now hunger, thirst and weariness rear their heads, not to be denied. There is still a little food in the store, and Tim rises to get it as Greg turns off the laptop. The bucket needs to be replenished too, and both men set out together to the well. They simply cannot take the chance of being separated.

"I figure we need to plan in case Henry comes," Tim says, "I think I have an idea that might work in an emergency."

"Let's get back safely inside before we talk more," Greg advises, "I don't want to get caught out here if there is anyone around."

The kitchen is darkening quickly, but the men are worried about any light being visible from the path outside, so they light one of the rush torches back from the kitchen in the passageway. This provides enough light for them to see what they are doing without broadcasting their position in the house. They do not light the kitchen fire for the same reason, so their makeshift meal consists of dried fruit and water from the refilled bucket. They eat silently, each pondering on what has been discovered and how they can best go forward, given their present predicament.

"Do you really think Henry will waste time on us?" Greg muses. "Surely, he will try to complete the quest as quickly as possible. The sigils will disappear without the sustenance of living flesh, so I think he won't risk everything just to find and kill us."

"Perhaps you're right, maybe we are safe enough here, it's not as if we can just up and leave, is it?" Tim is beginning to see Greg's point. More concerning though is the fact that they are now stuck here with no possibility of returning to their life in Kettering. This thought weighs heavily on both men and neither speaks for some time. There really is nothing to say and everything to think about!

Brandon

In the distance, Brandon can hear chanting. As consciousness slowly returns the chanting gets closer. There is something grating about the sounds as if someone is trying to sing but is tone-deaf. The nearer the sound gets, the more Brandon's head hurts. A blinding headache and nausea threaten to overwhelm him. He experimentally tries to open one eye a crack, but the pain makes him shudder and he closes it again quickly. Where is he? He can't remember what has happened. Is he sick, is he in fact dreaming? The pain is too real for this to be a dream, he must be sick. With this last thought, he drifts back into unconsciousness again.

The droning chant continues and firelight dances on a dark figure stamping the ground near the place where Brandon lies. This figure is the source of the chanting and other men sit on their haunches silently watching. The stamping figure shakes what appears to be a bunch of smoking leaves, and with each shake, the droning chant continues. The Clever Man is singing Brandon back to life, he is aided by the spirits of his ancestors, springing up in the puffs of dust raised by his stamping feet.

At last, the figure is still and speaking in the alien tones of a strange language, squats next to Brandon and checks his breathing. He moves to join the men squatting around the large fire. He reaches into the flames with a long stick and removes what appears to be a blackened body of some long, strange animal from the heart of the fire. The men wait patiently as the older man breaks off the hardened black, clay shell and with just his hands, dismembers the goanna, sharing the pieces out amongst the waiting men. They all eat their share silently watching while Brandon sleeps on.

The Family

As the false dawn begins to change the quality of the darkness and the brightness of the moon begins to fade, the exhausted family look out from the Mountshannon shore, over towards an island not far removed by water from their present position. They have travelled the night through, and hunger is all that stops them from succumbing to their exhaustion. Lykaios waits with the family as Athena-Minerva flies over the water to the lighted tower visible from the shoreline. There is only one more short trek and that will be made by coracle for all of them. As the small owl flies toward the tower, a tall figure holds out an arm for her to alight on, and a sudden recognition tries to break through the tired minds of the four children of Florence. They are all too weary to notice that their power of telepathy is blocked. Lykaios has blocked all the fire-born powers they possess, but they do not notice. There will be time for reflection later.

Jaded by exhaustion and their strange circumstances, they do not immediately see who awaits them; just that there is something very familiar about the tall figure that they cannot quite seem to grasp. Everything of late has been so strange that none of them has the energy to give too much heed to their thoughts and feelings.

Yawning hugely, Kenneth sits down on the ground, but Lykaios moves to him and nudges him with his nose.

"Stand up, Kenneth, you must not go to sleep yet, there is someone in the tower who is waiting for you. Stand, boy, the wait will soon be over now."

With an effort Kenneth stands again, resting his hand on Lykaios's broad, furry back.

On the island, there is movement, and several figures can be seen running from the tower entrance, down to the shore with what seem to be huge baskets on their backs. As the family watches, these figures drop the baskets into the water, and each has a second basket secured to the one being carried. With deft movements, each figure climbs into one basket and begins to paddle towards the family. Each manned basket is towing another empty one behind and soon the features of the figures can be seen quite clearly. In minutes, the first basket arrives, and the person paddling guides the small boat into the shore, making sure to secure it before jumping out onto the grassy edge.

"Welcome, children of Florence," the beaming man announces making a sweeping bow from the waist.

"How do you know who we are?" Aletheia asks sternly. She is tired and worried about what awaits them on the island.

"We have always known you, Aletheia," the man says warmly, "we have been waiting for you since time began."

Lykaios steps forwards and the shocked man pales and quickly prostrates himself on the ground.

"Stand up, man," Lykaios orders and the man stands eyes glowing with wonder at the sight of the wolf. "Please take the children across as quickly as you can, they are exhausted."

By this time, the other boats have arrived, and the leading man issues the instructions to get the whole family across to the island post haste.

Phoenix and Kenneth are the first to climb into the coracles and the men quickly jump into the leading basket-boats and take up their paddles once more. Looking back, Phoenix sees that all the family and Lykaios are crossing over now too. The boys are fighting to keep their eyes open with the lull of sitting in the bobbing boats, but they watch tiredly as the island grows in size before their eyes. In minutes they will be there. Who is it that is waiting for them? Neither has the slightest idea who it could be.

Henry

Sitting in stupefied silence, Henry now knows beyond a shadow of a doubt that Brandon has taken the submersible, passed back through the Curtain and left them all stranded here. The fact that the transponder does not show the slightest sign of life means also that the submersible is damaged or possibly destroyed. Could this be the case? Henry knows he must try to find a way to move back through the Curtain before the sigils disappear or his worst fears will be realized — he will spend the rest of his life in this desolate place! But how to calculate how much time there is left?

Before utter hopelessness can descend on him, he rises, pours himself a liberal amount of whisky and taking a large gulp, returns to his laptop on the table. He knows his savage temper has led him to this impasse, and the only way to salvage his own life might be to sacrifice to the dragon, if he can find its lair. But how can he do so, when he has not yet found any of the sigils that can grant him access? With fresh determination, he opens his files and begins to read. The answer will possibly be here if only he can skim through quickly enough to find it! As he skims, he opens a paper that discusses the meaning of fire-born in relation to human beings. He has not bothered with this at length previously because he could see no relation to his present quest and time was of the essence. Perhaps it is the right time to read it more closely now, since he is looking for something that as yet, he is not cognizant of. As he turns to the second page, his eyes narrow and he gives his full attention to what he is reading.

Along the shoreline, the pairs of men are searching each rock and crevice. As they move further away from the grotto in the search pattern devised by Henry before they left Kettering, many of them are beginning to think about what they have been told and whether this is really what is going on. If this is purely a psychological experiment, as related in Henry's presentation yesterday, then why is discovery of the sigil so important?

There does not seem to be any rhyme or reason to continue the search unless they have not been told the full truth about this quest. Since they have already been told that the point of the quest is the experiment — if, of course, what they were told is true — then why the search? Why not return to Kettering and go through the normal debriefing procedures that such experiments entail? Why is Henry so set on finding the sigils? They all understand that a psychological experiment is no longer useful once the participants know they are under observation in a certain way. There must be more to the quest than they have been told. There simply is no other explanation for their continuing with this search. An uneasy silence prevails between the pairs as their own private thoughts and misgivings on the matter take hold. Another hour on, and Peter connects to the open channel to talk to the other pairs of men.

"Have any of you found the sigil yet?" he asks, "only, we have been thinking, and it seems to us that there is something not cogent about what is happening."

"We agree," comes back an answer from another pair, "I think we should all meet up and try to work out what is really going on here. Where are you, Peter?"

"There is a headland just about five hundred yards ahead of us, can you see it from your position?"

"I think I see what you are talking about," answers John, "you try and direct the others on your side, and I will do the same from this side. Let's all meet at the headland as soon as we can get there."

"Roger that," says Peter, and he sets in the map coordinates to guide the pairs he knows are along his side of the search pattern. The nine pairs of men all move towards the beacon of the headland, visible only as a darker shape rising above the height of the shoreline. There are still two hours before midnight and their return to the cavern.

Brandon

Suddenly, with a great gasp, Brandon jolts awake. His heart is racing, and he gulps in great breaths of cold night air. He shudders and sits up with no memory of having laid down.

There is a fire burning brightly and as his eyes clear, he notices a group of painted men squatting around the edge of the fire. What on earth is happening? Where on earth is he? These questions rise unbidden, and with uncomprehending fear written on his face, he tries desperately to remember what happened to him. He watches the group fearfully; they are like no people he has ever laid eyes on before. Their painted bodies make them look like the reverse images of a photographic negative. He swoons as his splitting headache makes itself known and a nauseous dizziness envelops him. With a groan he lays back down, closing his eyes in the hope that when he opens them again everything will feel and look normal.

A seizure suddenly grips him; shaking uncontrollably and foaming at the mouth, he loses consciousness again. He does not see the figure that rises and grasps his head, pushing a flat piece of bark into his mouth to hold down his tongue. Without this intervention, he would have surely swallowed it and death would have been certain. When the shaking begins to ease the figure removes the bark and speaking in alien, guttural tones to the others seated at the fire, he moves off quickly, loping through the bush. The other men remain, watching Brandon from the edge of the fire. Still now, Brandon sleeps on.

The Clever Man lopes with long seemingly effortless strides, covering the ground quickly and moving through the forested bushland with the obvious knowledge of where he is going. To an uneducated eye this landscape seems totally unrecognizable as anything through which one might have any sign of direction. At last, he enters an area less scrubby although the crude bark dwellings erected here are hard to notice amongst the trees and bushland. The only clearly visible aspect of this camp is the thin spiral of smoke from a large firepit set into the ground and in which the coals of burnt logs flicker with redness and occasional sparks.

He quickly enters through the hide flap of one of the bark humpies, and just as quickly he re-appears again, his hands firmly grasping what appears to be a bundle wrapped in bark and tied with a fibrous string. He lopes back the way he came with the bark bundle firmly under one arm.

The Family

Lykaios, last to arrive on the island, jumps from the coracle onto the grassy shore and bars the way towards the tower. He searches the faces of the family and the men and women who have brought them here from the mainland. Athena-Minerva arrives at the same time, having left the arm of the person high up in the tower.

"Hold out your arm," she orders Aletheia, "I have news that you all must hear before you enter this sacred place."

Aletheia does as she has been bidden, and the small owl alights on her wrist.

"You have been destined to this place since before you were born," the small owl looks directly into the faces of each family member, as well as each of the faces of the tower people. She scrutinizes each one carefully; the scrutiny leaves each one with the sure knowledge of the seriousness of what she is about to impart.

"When you leave here again, you will be changed, a necessary change, for you have been chosen to decide the fate of all our futures. All our lives will rest in your hands. None of you has chosen this odyssey to come, but the gods have chosen you, so before you enter here, you have one chance only to decline.

"Once you enter, your life will be forfeit should you try to leave. Harken to my words, for the duty that lies before you is not for the faint-hearted. Please take a few minutes to decide if you will stay. If any of you wishes to leave, you will be taken back across the water and all memory of what has passed in your life thus far will be erased. Your memories and your life will be supplanted into families who live here in the farming community. You will happily continue that life, having no other memory and with no chance of recollection of what is occurring here, now."

There is complete silence as the enormity of the choices put before them sinks in. Some have been holding their breath, and now begin to breathe normally again. The first to speak is Antheia.

"I welcome this duty Athena-Minerva with all my heart and soul," she swears, one hand over her heart and the other over her belly, "please lead me towards my future here."

As soon as she has so sworn, the rest of the family swears also, the boys watching their sisters with pride. The tower people go down on their knees and swear their allegiance to Athena-Minerva, Lykaios and the family, hands on fast-beating hearts. At last, Lykaios turns to lead them all to the entrance to the tower, where a tall, thin figure waits to bid them enter. Marcom will now read their minds so to ensure none enter here without the mental stamina for what is to come.

Greg and Tim

There is no chance of sleep for the two men. Their situation is too bizarre for rest. The problems that beset them are overwhelming and it is difficult to sort them out into any order of priority. Food is now a serious problem, but at least they have water. What of this house? Will the owner return, or will they be able to stay here? If they stay, how are they going to live? Will it be possible to return to the beach so that at least they can return to Kettering with the others, or will Henry kill them on sight? Are the others still there, or have they left already? The problems flash though each man's mind until both become disoriented and terrified. Is there anything that they can do to alleviate the unbearable stress?

Tossing and turning on the bed, Greg eventually decides to get up; he can't keep going over everything like this. Surely, he must act, or he will go insane! Tim is lying still, but his eyes are like saucers, and he rises with Greg.

"What the hell are we going to do now?" asks Tim, eyeing Greg with fear written in his features. "Can you think of anything? I have no idea what to do, do you?"

"The only thing I can think of," answers Greg, "is to go back down to the grotto and try to work out how we might be able to use the sigil. We know at least, that it is a pass way through the Curtain, but how it works is anybody's guess. Let's go down and see what we can come up with. Anything is better than lying here worrying."

The two men move quickly along the passageway to the stairs leading down to the grotto. Tim has already picked up a rush torch, and he lights it with his dwindling supply of matches. At the bottom of the stairs, Tim shines the torch towards the back wall where they found the carved sigil earlier. There seems to be a change! As they approach the back wall both men see that the relief carving is less apparent than earlier. It almost looks like it is fading into the wall. Surely there must be some explanation for this.

"What if the sigils are beginning to disappear?" Tim whispers, remembering what they read earlier. The paper about time lapses had proposed the notion that without sustenance, the sigils would slowly disintegrate, and the Curtain would close. Although only a proposal, this seems a likely explanation for the fading sigil.

"We might just have a chance to move through before the Curtain closes," muses Greg, "but that may mean we are ingested by the dragon if the dragon image on Henry's file is in fact a reality. What do you think, Tim?"

"I don't see how a mythical creature like a dragon can have anything whatever to do with the time lapses," says Tim, "that was probably a story put about to stop anyone using the sigils and the Curtain. How can a dragon reach out from a carving on the wall? I think that it's all rubbish! Let's see if we can get out of here, shall we?"

"We need to get our stuff from upstairs," says Greg, "then yes, let's get out of here if we can."

The men retrieve their belongings including the bow and arrows found in the house and head back downstairs, then to the back wall of the grotto.

"I don't know how precisely this works," says Greg, "but I suggest we hold onto each other just in case we do go through. We don't want to get separated and end up in different times and locations. At least together we have a chance to survive, I reckon."

The men grasp hands and try to imagine Kettering, when and where they want to go. Nothing happens! "I think we will have to touch the sigil for this to work maybe," says Greg, "I don't know if it will work but let's try it."

"But we can't reach it from here," says Tim, "how are we to remain standing here and at the same time, touch the sigil?"

"Look what you brought with you," says Greg pointing to the bow, "if you stand here, you should be able to make contact with the sigil by stretching out the bow, yes?"

"Sorry, yes of course," Tim replies and unshouldering the bow, he reaches towards the sigil. Just as the end of the bow shaft makes contact with the sigil, an enormous flame bursts from the middle, engulfing the end of the bow entirely. At this very moment, and before Tim's hand feels the heat of the flame, the forms of Greg and Tim begin to shimmer, and then disappear altogether. The remains of the burning bow turn quickly to ashes on the grotto floor. Where once the sigil was carved into the wall, a smooth, blank surface now meets the eye.

Henry Bonnington

At last Henry stands to refill his whisky glass. The paper on the meaning of fire-born has tickled something at the back of his mind. What is it that he cannot remember? He steps outside the cavern to let the darkness wash over him and sips from his glass. Something he once read, and a long time ago, but what was it?

Henry knows from experience that often he needs to let go when he cannot bring something to mind and allow his mind to work on it alone. Many times, he has woken in the night with the solution to a problem that he could not solve during the day or from days previously. He must do this now and trust that his subconscious will bring it to mind. It is 20.00 hours, and he has the time before the searching men return. Henry lays down on this makeshift bed, setting an alarm for two hours on his iWatch. Closing his eyes, he tries to empty his mind altogether. He begins to doze.

There is a room at the bottom of a round tower, bones lie half buried in the floor. Ancient stone flags bedeck the floor and walls, and Henry thinks to himself, "This is the tower that Jung described in his dreams, what the hell am I doing here?"

As he searches with his eyes, an understanding creeps in and he shuts off his questing, rational thinking. He is aware that he sleeps and that the images are trying to tell him something. Calmly he lets the dream go to work. He hears a buzzing far away and slowly, reluctantly, he rises towards the sound. Henry wakes up to the alarm set two hours ago. What seemed like a few minutes has in fact, been two hours! Lying still, he thinks about the startling dream and suddenly the sense of it comes flooding into his mind. It is to Jung's work that he needs to go, the inkling from his reading, he now knows, is something read in one of Jung's works and most obviously, the dreamwork! The question this raises is how on earth is he going to be able to retrieve this text? Without access to the submersible, there is no way to get to the book, unless he can retrieve it from the university library in online format. He vows that as soon as the men have returned, eaten and bedded down for the night, he will find the text, hoping fervently that he will be able to get access to read it online. The answer he is searching for, he is sure, will be within the pages of Jung's work.

Brandon

Removing the string from the bark parcel, the Clever Man unwraps what looks like a set of long, animal bones. From these, he selects the shortest one and advancing to the fire, sets his whole hand into the flames. Silently he keeps his hand amid the fire and begins to chant anew. Rather than flinching from the pain of the flames, he closes his eyes and repeats a three word phrase several times. Out of the fire, he pulls the blackened bone, still within his hand that retains no signs of damage wrought by the flames. How is this possible?

Moving to the sleeping form of Brandon, the Clever Man lays the smoking bone against the bare chest of Brandon. With a guttural roar, Brandon leaps up from the place he has lain for several hours. His chest shows a reddened burn mark deep into the flesh, and with eyes wide with fear, he stumbles forwards. The Clever Man reaches out and places his hand on Brandon's head. The chanted three-word phrase brings Brandon to a standstill and his eyes although open wide, have the glazed look of a man in a trance. The Clever Man holds Brandon and leads him to the place where the fire is brightest. Without removing his hand and with no discernible words, he beckons Brandon to sit. Brandon sits.

The Clever Man spits on his hands and wipes this over Brandon's face, chanting all the while. Soon, Brandon awakens, and a startled look accompanies his return to full consciousness. Looking around him, Brandon recognizes the men; they are Australian Aborigines. For several moments he tries to recollect what has happened to him. Memory of his escape from Henry floods back, and he silently wonders to himself how on earth he has arrived here. With a sinking feeling he knows that something untoward must have happened when he passed through the Curtain. The burning question: "Where is the submersible?"

Greg and Tim

As if waking from a dream, the two men open their eyes and look around. They appear to be in a town; a cobbled laneway lays beneath their feet and strange overarching buildings block out sight of the sky. Darkness tells them that it is night and a cold breeze, whips by as they try to get their bearings. The crooked, wooden buildings seem to lean out towards each other, as if cantilevered regimentally, and held up by God knows what. They all appear to be on the point of collapse! The men make their way carefully down the alley, trying to make no sound and aware of the creaking coming from the boards of the buildings above their heads. The sound of hoof beats on the cobblestones has the men scurrying for the shadows of an ancient doorway. Just as they press themselves back against a stout wooden door, a horse plunges past, ridden flat out and foaming at the mouth. The rider wears a hooded cloak so the men can't tell whether it's a man or a woman. Suddenly both men fall backwards into the building for which the door is the entry point. A startled man gasps as he, too, is knocked off his feet by the falling men.

"Who are you?" asks the man querulously, dusting himself off and staggering upright again. He seems as taken aback as Tim and Greg. "What do you want here, and where did you come from?"

"We're really sorry," Tim holds up his hands in response as if to hold back the man's words. "We have no idea where we are?"

"What do you mean?" asks the man. His face takes on a serious countenance. He feels no obvious threat from these two strangers, and they certainly do look perplexed. Taking in their appearance as they regain their feet, he notices that their clothes are very odd indeed. In fact, he has never seen anything like what they are wearing. They must have travelled from some land across the ocean!

"What do you mean, you don't know where you are?" he asks more forcefully, "surely you set out for some destination in this city, or how could you be here in the first place?"

"We are time-travelers," Greg interposes, "we have travelled through time to get here, but where this 'here' is, we do not know."

The man's face creases up with laughter at this ridiculous reply, tears appear in his eyes, and he slaps his thighs in mirth. Eventually he brings himself under control. Frowning now and taking a more threatening pose, he remonstrates with them.

"I suppose you think that's funny, do you?" He folds his arms across his chest and watches Tim and Greg carefully. "Please state your business here or leave!"

"Please, sir," Tim begs, "we really are lost. Can you please let us in so we can talk with you? I promise you we are not dangerous."

"A likely story," the man replies, "and how do I know you won't rob me blind and then kill me? You look so strange that I scarcely recognize you as men!"

"Let us in and we will show you magic to make your head spin. Arm yourself if you wish, we are no threat to you," Greg stands his ground and keeps his eyes level with those of the man. Making a decision, the man steps aside and Greg and Tim enter a dark hallway, at the end of which, a light shows in a room of large proportions.

The room is furnished with low tables and thick rugs. Floor length damask curtains cover extensive windows on one side; the opposite side to the passage they entered from the alley. There is an enormous fireplace with a stone mantel and several items adorn the mantel that are not known to the men. Their host watches their reactions closely, indicating for the men to sit at one of the low tables. Tim and Greg do so. The man crosses to the mantel and tugs on a bell pull hanging next to the curtains. Deep within the recesses of the house, a faint ringing sounds. Within seconds a woman dressed in an old-fashioned maid's uniform enters and bows to the man.

"How can I be of service, master?" she says.

"Bring refreshments please and ask Petyr to fetch more wood for the fire."

The maid bows and leaves to do as she is bidden. The man paces around the room hands behind his back watching the men and with a thoughtful expression on his face. At last, he sits down opposite Greg and Tim and speaks.

"You have come to the house of Gavinar the Great," he speaks quietly but firmly, "before we embark on the subject of how you got here and why, I offer you refreshment in the name of hospitality, the common law of this land."

"We thank you, sir," Tim replies, "for it is many days since we ate a full meal, and we are certainly both thirsty and hungry. When you are ready to hear, we will tell you honestly what has happened to us, but please listen carefully because our story is bizarre."

Gavinar the Great bows his head in acquiescence, and they talk no more before the maid reappears with another young girl struggling with a tray laden with fruit, bread and cold meats. The maid carries a large foreign looking coffee urn from which the rich scent of real coffee steams. The men's mouths flood with saliva with the rich scents of food and drink, and the maid and her girl retreat leaving the three men alone again.

"Please help yourselves," Gavinar hands each man a large plate and an eating knife and pours hot coffee into three large earthenware pots. There is neither sugar nor milk, but the men do not care, and both begin to eat with obvious relish. Gavinar watches them, with a thoughtful expression on his face. He lifts his cup, sipping his coffee to hide his perusal of the men as much as is possible.

The Family

Lykaios reaches the door to the tower first and with a barely perceptible nod, Marcom acknowledges the wolf. Antheia smiles at Marcom, and sudden recognition lights his eyes. He seems to start involuntarily for the briefest of moments and then Antheia has passed through. Aletheia and the boys enter next and Marcom nods to each, his eyes not leaving their faces. Lastly Athena-Minerva flies through the door, and Marcom bows low to her. The tower people pass by Marcom slowly, and he tests each. At last satisfied with all who enter, he shuts the stout oak doors, and with a boom, a sonic lock renders the doorway impassable. These mighty doors will remain closed now until the family are ready to leave this place.

A dimly lit passage leads quickly to a warm, lighted and spacious area used obviously as a kitchen and dining room. The family look around, and suddenly, a tall woman steps out of the shadows of the pantry and turns to face them. A small shriek erupts from Aletheia's throat before she throws herself into the arms of the woman, tears of joy streaming down her face.

"Oh, Mother," she cries, and suddenly, all four children surround the woman pressing into her arms and the folds of her clothes. The boys are shy, they barely remember her, but once snuggled against her, the familiar smell of her has them reaching for her. Florence hugs her children to her with all her strength, and then, just as suddenly, pushes them back so she can look at them all in turn.

"Aletheia, my beautiful child, how you have grown. Thank you from the bottom of my heart for caring for your sister and brothers so well. We have much to talk about when you recover from your ordeal.

"Antheia, immortal vessel for Ladon, how wonderful you look and how well. We will care for you here and help you reach the zenith of your spiritual power.

"Phoenix, my beautiful big boy, what a man you are becoming and a what a wonderful, kind and strong man you will be soon.

"Kenneth, oh my baby boy, how I have missed watching you grow. We have time to make up, and I promise you both, I will not disappear from you again."

As the children watch their mother with unadulterated joy, none are aware of the disappearance of Lykaios and Athena-Minerva, except Marcom who bids them silently farewell. In another time and place, they may become apparent once more, but for now, they are no longer needed. The family is complete — well, almost!

Amid the celebratory mood and kitchen preparations, a loud booming resonates, and the room becomes hazy, slightly tilted and out of focus for anyone looking on. There follows a flash of brilliant light, and with long strides and fierce countenance, a tall, broad man appears as if from out of the air. His long, blonde hair streams out behind him as he strides towards those gathered here. A flowing beard hides his lower facial features, and he carries a broadsword in his right hand. At his approach, Marcom kneels and touches his forehead to the ground. The children look on with shock! Florence calmly walks to the front, shielding the children from this ostentatious stranger.

"How are you, my darling?" Florence asks, and open mouthed, the children realise they are looking at their father.

Canath reaches for his wife and hugs her to him. His eyes alight on the four children and his face registers recognition.

"Come to me, my little ones," his voice resonates deeply. He holds out one arm and keeps Florence at his side with the other.

"Are you, our father?" asks Phoenix, protectively stepping in front of his sisters and little brother, "only, I do not remember you."

"Come, Phoenix," Canath replies, "for I certainly remember you and Aletheia, Antheia and Kenneth. Your mother and I have much to explain to you, but I have kept watch on all of you since you came into this world. Here we meet again, and here we stay until you all reach the powers that are latent within you. Ladon has cast the stones and he will soon be delivered to us in the form of your very own spirit brother. Antheia, immortality is now yours and with the birth of Ladon, you will join the ranks of the gods, there to watch over us, always. Until that time, I, Canath, your father and Florence, your mother, will be your mentors and protectors."

Aletheia is stunned! Her father was killed twenty years ago, as related to her by Florence. What is happening here, and from where has Canath appeared? Of all four children, only Antheia smiles, for she is now aware of the details surrounding Canath and his death and reappearance. She alone understands the circle of existence, thanks to Ladon's gift. She is the first to move towards her father. Warily and with misgivings written on their faces, the children approach, but as soon as Canath places his hand on each of his children's heads in turn, memories of this man flood into their minds. He is indeed their father. Tears spring to their eyes, and they embrace him with all their strength. They are a family again at last!

Henry

The eight remaining pairs of men stand together at the base of the headland, and a heated discussion ensues. Peter raises the question of what is really going on in this place, and why they have been brought here: is it to ensure the success of Henry's quest, or something altogether more sinister? They do not actually understand what Henry's quest is because they have not been given any straightforward answers to their questions in this regard. The fact of Brandon's disappearance is one more reason to suspect that Henry has not been truthful about any of this. The real 'elephant in the room', so to speak, is the continued search for the sigils. Why have these not yet been found and why are they so important? This question is taxing the men, for they know they must have used something like this to pass through the Curtain from Kettering. This entire quest cannot be a mere psychological experiment as outlined by Henry, or why the Curtain and the time lapses? These are real enough and no mere psychological framing. What on earth is really the point of this quest anyway? The men realise that nobody here assembled has the slightest idea of the purpose of the quest, and there seems to be no rhyme or reason to this puzzle. They simply do not have enough information, and this in itself, is telling. Thinking about it now, all their questions about the quest have been skillfully deflected by Henry and Brandon from the start. Peter calms the men, and signaling for silence, begins to speak.

"I have thought at length about what has ensued so far, and although we are being extremely well paid, I don't believe we will ever get a chance to spend what we have earned."

As the men listen, a kind of uneasiness begins to take hold. They have all been holding similar thoughts at bay, but now that Peter has voiced their own fears, it somehow seems to become reality for the first time.

"What do you mean?" John asks skeptically, "surely you don't believe we are in danger, do you?"

"I certainly do," Peter announces, "why has Brandon disappeared, and where are Greg and Tim?" The men remain silent as they ponder Peter's question.

"Do you think they just walked away from here? I think the three of them discovered something so dire that they felt the need to escape from here. Do you think that Henry just happened to climb to the ruins yesterday for his own amusement? I think he set out after Greg and Tim, because he knew what it was they found out. What do you think happened when he caught up to them? Why did they not return with Henry? I think Henry killed them to stop them from escaping with knowledge he did not want to get out. I think Brandon left in the submersible while we slept because he feared Henry would kill him too. What does that bode for the rest of us? If any of you have a better explanation of the events so far, please tell all of us now."

None of the men say a word as the implications of what Peter has voiced begin to sink in. If what Peter says is true, that means they may all be marooned in this desolate place. How will they survive? They have not the slightest idea if anyone lives here if there is food to be foraged or anywhere for shelter bar the caves and grottos along the shore. They have seen no animals or any signs of people. The ruins are age-old and show human habitation at some time in the past, but there are no habitable houses evident, except those whose ruins jut along the old pathways. Their grim thoughts and growing fears turn to anger and to a man, they vote to return early to the grotto and confront Henry. They are afraid of his temper, but with sixteen of them to one of him, they surely can subdue him and find out some answers, regardless of how terrifying those answers may be. It is 23.00 when they all set out together to confront Henry.

When the men have left, Henry connects to the satellite and opened his university web page. With shaking hands, he turns to the home page and clicks on the university library's website icon. Entering his username and password, he holds his breath until the library site opens. With relief, he exhales loudly and types Jung's name and the text he needs into the search frame. He sits back and waits.

A few seconds later the text appears in the results section, and Henry clicks on the text icon and again waits. The text is indeed available in hard copy or online read only formats. Henry thanks his lucky stars! Excited now, he opens the online version of the text. Checking through the index page, he opens the chapter he needs to read. He focuses in on the text and reads.

Completely focused on what he is reading, Henry does not hear the returning men enter the grotto. He jumps when Peter clamps a hand on his shoulder.

Brandon

Looking around him, Brandon checks the immediate surroundings to see if there is any sign of the submersible. It is too dark for him to make out more than mere shadows from where he sits in the light of the fire. Although there must be a waterway close by, Brandon cannot see or hear it. The Clever Man watches Brandon carefully and signs to one of the seated men to fetch some food. The painted man brings some of the white goanna flesh and places it next to Brandon. The sight of this food reminds Brandon that he cannot remember when he ate last, but he is unsure what the meat is, so he lifts a tiny piece to his mouth to taste it before eating it. There is a fishy like flavour to it, and it is not unpleasant, so with little more ado, he reaches for the strip of bark and eats the meat. The seated men nod their approval.

The burning question Brandon faces as he eats is how he is going to make himself understood by these people. Unless the time he has now passed into is similar to his own contemporaneous time, these painted men may not yet have come into contact with white men. If this is the case, he will have to devise a way to make signs to communicate with them. Another more troubling thought takes hold: if the submersible is damaged or destroyed, he will have no choice but to remain in this place and time. He knows without a doubt that the only way he can survive here is with the help of these people, so it is crucial for him to befriend them. He rises from his seat by the fire and crosses to where the others are sitting. Holding his hands in a prayer-like attitude, he kneels and bows low touching his forehead to the ground. Hopefully, there is a kind of universality to be read in his actions. He sits back on his haunches and waits. The men look at him askance, curiosity written on their features.

The Clever Man rises from his seat and stands directly in front of Brandon. Again, he puts his hand on Brandon's forehead. For several minutes and with blank eyes, he seems to silently 'listen' to Brandon, then, as if coming back from a trance, he speaks to the others assembled, and it appears that some resolution has been reached. He turns on his heel and the others follow. Brandon rises and follows too. The bushland is difficult terrain to move through, and Brandon finds himself scratched by low hanging branches and his feet encounter roots and stones. He wonders where his shoes have gotten to and suddenly realizes he is no longer dressed in the clothes he left Athens in. How could he have not noticed this before? Scrabbling to keep up with the others, he does not have the strength to ponder these facts.

As the false dawn begins to lighten the solid darkness, the men approach an inlet of water. From the faint sounds of waves breaking on a shore, Brandon realizes that this is where he must have passed through the Curtain from Athens. If he is correct, then the submersible and his belongings must be around here somewhere! The Clever Man leads them down through the bush to the sand near the edge of the inlet. There, propped against a tree stump lies the submersible. Almost out of the water, its size belies the fact that twenty men crammed inside it for the ride of a lifetime. Brandon looks to the Clever Man, as if asking permission to approach the strange craft. There is an inaudible consent given, and Brandon runs down the sandy track to the beach to see if he can find out what has happened to the craft.

The Aboriginal people stand well back and watch Brandon as he clambers aboard. Soon he is lost to sight as he moves down into the bow of the craft. The men squat on their haunches and wait patiently. At first Brandon can see no obvious damage, so he goes through all the usual checks and balances made before embarkation of the craft. This, of course, he did not have time to do before leaving Athens! He discovers the problem when he reaches the console on the fore deck. There has been some extreme heat here, plastic has melted and blackened around the command module. He dares not try to further adjust or test it until he has time to think, but crucial to any kind of test is his satellite transponder, and so, he searches the craft for his pack. He finds his shoes jammed under the console and dons them thankfully.

Back on the shore, the men begin to talk quietly amongst themselves. The words they use to describe Brandon loosely mean 'ghost' or 'spirit'. They have never seen a 'white' man like this before! The Clever Man calms them and indicates they must wait for the 'ghost' to reappear. The backpack has fallen into the hold, and as Brandon tries to pull it free, the transponder inside the front pocket snags against the bulkhead. There is a whirring sound and the beacon light on the submersible lights up. Brandon quickly removes the transponder and switches it off. The light dies again, but Brandon's heart soars with the knowledge that all may not be lost. With his pack in hand, he once more climbs back to the deck, jumps onto the sandy bank and walks towards the squatting men.

Greg and Tim

Having eaten their fill, Greg and Tim know it is now time to speak. Gavinar remained silent and watchful as the two men ate, now he rises and beckons for the men to follow him back through the house. He guides them into what appears to be some kind of office or study and gestures for them to sit down before another fireplace bright with warmth and cheer.

"Well, now you have partaken of my hospitality, perhaps you might explain yourselves to me." Gavinar sits opposite the men and waits.

"As I told you at the door," starts Greg, "we have travelled through time to this place, but we have no idea where we are or what time this is. I know it sounds bizarre, but it is the truth."

Gavinar scrutinizes Greg's face for any sign of dissention but finding none signals for him to continue.

"We were taken through what we know as the Curtain of Time, in a strange craft to Athens, only the Athens we arrived in was temporally remote from our own time." Greg explains. "We were tricked by the man heading the quest, and we managed to escape into the hills above Athens."

As Gavinar listens intently, Greg and Tim try to explain where they have come from, and what has happened since they left Kettering. They try to make it as clear as possible, although they do not fully understand themselves what has happened to them. Succinctly, they describe each hour in Athens as well as the sigil through which they managed to escape. They both know that further help will only be forthcoming if they can convince Gavinar to believe that what they are telling him is true. At last, they fall silent and Gavinar sits thinking.

"What year do you come from?" he finally asks, "and where do you come from?"

"The year as we know it is 2020, and as we mentioned, we come from the university city of Kettering in Northamptonshire, England," replies Tim. "Can you please tell us where we are and what year it is here?" he asks.

Gavinar sits back but does not reply immediately. He again scrutinizes both men before deciding to speak. "I want to see some proof of what you have just told me," he demands, "or you can leave now and be on your way."

"That is fair, sir," Greg says and asks Gavinar if he can get his backpack from the room in which they ate. Gavinar rings for the housekeeper and asks her to fetch the men's belongings from the dining room. Handing the backpacks to Greg and Tim, Gavinar warns them to be careful. The men look up to see that Gavinar now holds the hilt of a wicked looking curved sword, the end of the long blade is resting on the floor.

Slowly and carefully, Greg removes his laptop from the backpack and opens the lid. With a silent prayer, he tries to connect to the satellite, not knowing if there is the slightest chance that this will work here.

"What is that thing?" Gavinar asks sternly.

"This is a machine that allows us to connect to our university back home," Greg answers the question as best he can, given that Gavinar has never seen computer technology before. "I can show you what my office looks like in my own time."

"That I would surely like to see!" Gavinar's countenance loses some of the distrust and in its place curiosity becomes evident.

As the laptop becomes active, Greg breathes a sigh of relief and offers a silent thanks to the powers that be. With shaking fingers, he opens the screen into Henry's office.

"Would you care to come over here and see what I have opened?" Greg asks politely.

Gavinar rises, leaving the sword next to his chair and stands behind Greg to look on. Greg moves the cursor so that a panorama of the office and the objects and furnishings within appear to follow his fingers. Gavinar's eyebrows rise in surprise and fascination, his eyes follow the screen as it moves around the office. He reaches out to touch the screen with his own fingers and pulls them back as if burnt when his touch causes another page to open into Henry's office at home. He is immediately taken aback! Greg manipulates the screen so that Gavinar can see the layout of the room and what appear to him, to be very strange objects within. With a shift of the cursor, Greg opens to a vista of Kettering showing the town and its surroundings as well as an inset map of the area. Gavinar is spellbound at the sight of modern cars and houses. He looks on for some time, then as if waking from a dream, he walks back to his chair and sits down. He sits silently pondering for some time.

"I see that what you have told me is true. I have never before seen such a machine. What is its name?" Gavinar asks.

"This is what we call a laptop computer," answers Greg, "it was developed in a much larger form in the early twentieth century. In our time it is commonplace for almost everyone to have one. It can be used to search for information and to send messages to others."

"Can you use this to travel back to your own time again?" Gavinar asks with a guarded look in his eyes. From the look on his face, the two men read that he desires to travel with them if it is at all possible.

"We have no way to return," says Tim, "we hardly understand how we got here."

"Will you now tell us where we are?" Greg asks the question again, "and what year this is? If we are to try to work out how to return, we need that information."

"I will do my best to help you," Gavinar states. He has made a decision to trust the two men, but he wants to keep them and their magical machine close. "You will both stay with me, and we will work on the problem together, no?"

"Thank you, sir," Tim says with relief. "We don't have anywhere else to go right now, and if you help us and we find a way back, we will take you with us if that is what you wish."

The three men seal the deal by shaking hands and Gavinar rings for the housekeeper. "Please ask Petyr to find a suite of rooms for these men," he orders, "and make sure they have everything they need for the night. I wish you both good night and we will meet again for breakfast."

Gavinar has successfully evaded their questions several times, so the men do not push him further for answers. Both men are aware that Gavinar is not to be fully trusted; there is something of a sly fox to his demeanor that neither has missed. They will have to proceed carefully and find a way to plan an escape, should the time come that they need to.

The men follow as the housekeeper leads them towards a set of stairs at the rear of the house where Petyr appears to light their way upstairs, with two tapers set in a candelabra. On the floor above, the doors to several rooms reveal a substantial house, and Petyr opens a door that leads into two or more rooms, all adjacent to each other. He shows the men in and lights several candles set in lamp-like holders to reveal the space.

"There is a lock on the door, sirs," he says, and with no further ado, he leaves and closes the door behind him. Tim and Greg look around at the comfortable, large room, obviously a sitting room with divans, tables and carpets. Two doors lead to two bedrooms directly off this room. The bedrooms are furnished with four poster beds and thick rugs on the floor.

"What do you think?" asks Tim, "are we safe here?"

"We don't have much choice at the moment," Greg replies, "but I don't trust Gavinar as far I can throw him. I am going to hide our backpacks, so they don't go missing while we sleep. We can lock that door, but I have the feeling that it won't make any difference, should Gavinar decides to visit this room while we sleep. Make sure you keep the knife from Athens and your laptop with you. I shall sleep with my laptop and the arrow under my pillow."

"Good thinking, Greg, and I agree with you," Tim replies. The men search the bedrooms, and as soon as they have found a reasonable hiding place each for their backpacks, they retire to their beds to sleep. There is nothing more to be done until morning.

"Are they sleeping in the rooms with the false ceilings?" asks Gavinar.

"Yes, master, and they believe that they can lock their main door," Petyr replies, "and the spyholes are ready for your use."

"Thank you, Petyr," Gavinar dismisses the manservant, "you may go now. I will not be needing you further tonight. Please make preparations for the morning before you retire." Petyr bows low and leaves Gavinar alone. He sits quietly to ponder all that has happened tonight and to think how he will maintain control of the men in his keeping. It seems the gods have dropped them right into his lap. How opportune!

The Family

Florence shepherds the children towards the table, now set with platters of food. The maids and tower people have taken their meal on trays and left the family alone. Hunger overcomes the children's tiredness and all tuck into the feast as if they have not eaten for a month. As soon as the boys have eaten their fill, their eyelids begin to droop, so Florence leads them up the spiral staircase to a room warmed and ready for them. Both boys are only just able to remove their outer garments before falling upon the beds into deep sleep. Florence leans over each boy and kisses his forehead. "Sleep well, my darlings," she whispers, and descends again to the dining room to begin what will be days of explanation, interrogation, speaking and discussion with her two older girls. Canath fills a jug with brew, and after wishing his wife and daughters goodnight, leaves the room to the women, retiring to the workroom at the top of the tower, there to peruse the charts left out for him by Florence.

"I don't understand any of this, Mother," Aletheia is the first to speak. "There is so much here at odds with what I know."

Florence places her hands on Aletheia's shoulders and kisses the top of her head.

"I know, my darling one," she sympathizes, "I must begin at the beginning because things are not at all as you know them to be." Florence walks to the barrels set behind the table and from the jug, fills three earthen goblets with the warmed mead and whisky brew.

"I want you both to listen carefully, for the tale of your lives is stranger that you can possibly believe. I will start now but only for as long as it takes for this drink to take hold of you both. Then you must sleep, and we will begin anew tomorrow." She places a goblet in front of each girl. Antheia smiles at her mother with knowledge besetting the alien eyes of Ladon.

"Mother," she begins, "I think it best for Aletheia and I to go directly to our sleeping places. We have had such an exhausting day, and we both need time to just rest safely before you begin to explain what must be explained."

Florence looks deeply into her daughter's alien eyes and recognizes that she already knows much of what is to come. She returns Antheia's smile.

"Then just drink and then rest, my dears, I will show you to your rooms. They will be your own domains for as long as you remain here, so please set them up as you wish."

The girls rise and with goblets in hand, Florence leads them up the spiral staircase to two adjacent bedrooms, warmed, lit and readied for her daughters. The girls hug and kiss their mother, and with the relief bred of being children once more, sink onto the soft woolen blankets covering their beds. Aletheia is too tired to drink the brew, so setting her goblet on the small table next to her bed, she falls almost instantly asleep. Antheia drains her goblet with the knowledge that the drink will infuse her unconscious with the power to work on as she sleeps.

Florence returns to the kitchen room to ensure the cleaning up is done to her satisfaction. While she works, she wonders how the children will cope with what they must all now be told and how they will fare in the ordeals to come. Her thoughts move to Canath and the journey he must make as soon as the children are strong enough to manipulate the Curtain without using the sigils. The child, Ladon, when he is born, must be protected from interlopers, whether they be accidental arrivals, or the result of Henry Bonnington's machinations. When grown to adulthood, he will be sorely needed to strengthen and maintain the bridge with unconscious forces if the task crucial to saving the world as they know it, is to be successfully completed. As Canath has spoken, the stones have been cast and at last the family has arrived safely at the beginning of their odyssey. For this, Florence sends her silent prayer of thanks to the gods. She knows that Lykaios and Athena-Minerva await.

Henry Bonnington

"So, Henry," Peter begins, "now is the only chance you get to tell us all what the hell is going on!" Peter does not remove his hand from Henry's collar, and Henry feels the anger and resolve in that hold. He knows he cannot withstand sixteen pairs of hands, so with resignation written on his face, he agrees to speak to them. Peter allows him to stand and make his way to the other side of the room; six men stand to block the entrance to the shallow grotto, the menace on their faces plain to read. Henry sinks down on his makeshift bed and asks the other men to do the same. He signals for Peter to fetch his laptop.

"Before I start," Henry says, "there is something you should know. Brandon has left in the submersible and travelled back through the Curtain. There is no response from my transponder, which means the submersible is either broken down or destroyed, so we are stuck here unless you help me find the sigils. They are our only hope of leaving this place!"

"Then you need to explain just what the sigils are and how they relate to this so-called quest of yours," Peter demands. "And while you are at it, where are Greg and Tim? Have you killed them, Henry? Did they discover your real purpose here?" Henry looks at the men's faces and realizes that they have figured out more than he has told them. How is he going to maintain control of the situation?

"You are right to some degree," Henry answers carefully, "Greg and Tim decided to break into my private office and home computers to find out what they could. I had alarms set on both. They stole my personal files, so I set out to find them and bring them back here. However, after reaching the ruins and sleeping, I decided that I could not trust Brandon either, so I returned here. I did not find Greg and Tim, and I have absolutely no idea where they are. I was right about Brandon though, for as you see, he has left us all stranded here!"

"OK Henry," Peter does not bother to question this answer yet, he wants to know more about the purpose of this quest before interrogating Henry further.

"Tell us about the sigils, what they are, what they do and why you brought us here to find them. Be careful not to prevaricate, we have all had enough of your lies. Whether or not you survive depends on you supplying us with the information we need to decide what we do next."

Henry stays silent for a few seconds then begins.

"Some years ago, I discovered that time as we understand it is false. After researching the works of several philosophers and psychologists, I accidentally came across a text that defines the Universe differently to what scientists today believe. I followed where this text lead and after many years of painstaking study, I found a clue to a way to enter what this philosopher terms as 'the plenum'. Do you want me to spend the next several weeks going through the basic ideas and connections that got us here, or do you want me to explain by answering the questions you have put to me?" Henry is relying on the fact that the men want quick, definitive answers to their questions. In this way, he can give them answers that are not definitive and that they will not fully understand. If they go with this calculated response, he need not allow them to see what is in his files. He prays he is right to read anxiety displayed as anger and that perhaps this subterfuge may save his life, he can only hope.

"I can't see the point in going step by step through the ways and connections to what Henry found, can you?" Peter asks the men to judge which way to answer Henry. He does not and cannot know why Henry has given them the decision in this way. The men just want to find a way home.

"Let's skip the history lesson, Henry," John says, looking to the others for their agreement. "We are not giving you the time to prevaricate again. What do you say men?"

The other men nod their agreement, and Peter again asks Henry to just answer the questions. They do not see the relief written on Henry's face as he shuts his laptop; he disguises it well. He sighs as if they have gotten the better of him and slumps his shoulders as if resigned to doing as they have demanded.

"The sigils are entry points to the plenum," Henry starts again, "at these points you can move through time because time is not objectively real as we understand it. What we understand by time is really only Aristotle's notion of the measurement of movements in space, as our analogue clocks illustrate."

The men do not fully comprehend what Henry is saying, but none of them want to ask a question to show their ignorance or to prolong Henry's explanation. Henry moves on.

"This Athens we are standing in, I visited once before but more by accident than design. I returned to Kettering and resumed my studies sufficient to build the new submersible in which we arrived here. I knew that the sigils must be here simply by deduction — I have already moved through the Curtain three times using the sigil underneath the sea. The reality of time-lapses gave me the clues to figure it all out. The thing is, more importantly, I also discovered that the sigils disappear after a certain period of time, so you see, we need to find one or more before they disappear altogether. I have calculated as far as is possible, the length of time, I can be sure they remain active, and we are nearing that known limit. If we pass that limit and they disappear again, we will never be able to leave this place or this time. The calculations necessary to find them again in the plenum would take more than three of my lifetimes!"

The men stand rock still, each trying to think through the implications of Henry's exposition and what that means in terms of action. If Henry is telling the truth, and there seems to be no reason now for him not to be, then the search is paramount. None of them want to be stranded here for the rest of their life. Peter is the first to speak again.

"Henry, we have no alternative but to believe what you have told us, but you will be watched constantly by the six men at the entrance. The rest of us will try to find the sigils. When this is all over, you will be held accountable for your selfish actions in bringing us here. If we have to stay here, you will not live long enough to feel remorse, we will execute you. If you try to leave here before we get back, mark my words, you will be killed."

Peter turns away from Henry to speak with the six men left to guard him, then the ten remaining men set out with purpose to find the only means of their route back to home. Henry plays at being downcast and resigned, but secretly he revels in how easily he has been able to hoodwink this group. They did not even ask about how he could possibly know that the sigils would disappear after a certain length of time. They had been too anxious to take note of what he had said, thank goodness! Henry decides to sleep now, for he will need to be at his sharpest when the others get weary. The six guards set about preparing a meal, all the while keeping watch on Henry. After surreptitiously sliding his laptop under the head of his sleeping bag bed, Henry lays down to sleep.

Brandon

The squatting men rise as Brandon approaches them from the beach. The Clever Man steps forward and puts out his hand. Brandon recognizes that he wants the backpack, so he hands it over and stands still. The Clever Man closes his eyes as if to read through his hands, what the backpack contains. The other men look on, watchful of Brandon as well as his backpack. They have never seen anything the like of it before. The Clever Man opens his eyes and hands the pack back to Brandon. He again turns on his heels and sets off at a jog back through the bush. The others follow, and Brandon has to scramble to keep up with them. He does not even have time to properly secure his pack to his back, so it drags along beside him as he tries to keep up. As the dawn breaks, Brandon is able to see where he is going even though he has absolutely no idea of direction. He just hopes he can keep the others in sight.

Near the end of his strength, Brandon gradually falls behind the others, and eventually, he sinks to the ground. He cannot go on and his raging thirst and dry throat make it impossible for him to shout out to the receding men. Hopelessness overwhelms him and weakens any remaining resolve. He drops his head into his hands and weeps. Perhaps facing Henry would have been easier! Resting for what seems like minutes, Brandon remembers the pack beside him and with anxious hands, he delves into it hoping against hope that he brought water with him. Too much has happened, and he is simply too exhausted to remember. His hand grasps a plastic water bottle, and with huge relief, he draws it out. It is barely half full, but it is liquid gold to the parched man. After drinking sparingly, Brandon decides to try to find his way back to the beach. There are occasional footprints from the passing men, so he follows slowly, not wanting to miss the signs that are far and few between. As the sun rises higher, the heat of the Australian summer begins to take a toll on the weakened man, and the continual buzzing of insects in the gum trees, irritates his ears. Morosely Brandon plods on.

Taking a rest in the shade of a grove of gum trees, Brandon searches his pack to see what else he has brought with him. There is a change of clothes at the bottom. Gratefully, he dons socks with the shoes, and his fingers alight on a packet skewed against the bottom seam. The sight of the muesli bar brought from Kettering brings tears to Brandon's eyes, and as he slowly chews, to savor each mouthful, he ponders what he must do if he can find his way back to the beach.

First and foremost, he must painstakingly check and test all the operating systems in the submersible, only then can he start the machine using the transponder. He reminds himself to check the heat damage as a priority. The big problem will be to find the sigil through which he gained entry to this place and time. Hopefully, his satellite connector will be able to pinpoint the spot! With these plans in mind and a little food in his stomach, Brandon starts to feel better, so he sets off again, much more comfortable with shoes and socks on and his pack secured to his back.

Greg and Tim

Gavinar smokes a long, curved pipe and thinks carefully as he waits for time to pass. It is nearing two a.m. — the time he knows, when most people are at their lowest conscious ebb and deepest sleep — when he rises and moves silently to the foot of the stairs leading to the upper floor. Quietly he climbs and turning right at the top, passes the door to Greg and Tim's suite of rooms. He moves to the far end of the passage and ascends another set of narrow stairs. These stairs lead to a long, narrow space directly under the eaves, and Gavinar expertly moves along it until he estimates he is above one of the rooms in which the two strangers sleep. Lifting a loosened board, he gains access to the wattle and daub ceiling of the room below and drilled into this is a spyhole, big enough for him to see through by lying flat on the floor and putting his eye to the hole, yet small enough so as to be almost unnoticeable to anyone sleeping below.

Greg is fast asleep and unaware that he is being watched from above. Gavinar searches the room with his eye, but he cannot see the backpack or the magic machine. "So," he thinks, "the men have hidden their possessions! They do not trust me as much as I thought, unfortunate, because it makes my plans harder to accomplish." There is no point in remaining longer, so Gavinar replaces the board as silently as he can and returns downstairs to the sitting-dining room. From a decanter on the sideboard, he pours himself a goblet of port wine and resumes his seat. He has little time before the men wake, so he must remain here to make the plans essential for him to maintain control over what happens next.

Sunlight and street noises from the window wake Greg, and for a few moments, he does not know where he is. He sits up quickly and looks around him. Memories come flooding back of the previous night, and he rises and dresses quickly in the clothes he wore yesterday. He opens the heavy drapes partially covering the window and looks down onto the street below. He recognizes the buildings and streets from pictures he has seen of Medieval Europe, but this gives him no clue as to where in Europe he might be. The cobbled streets are busy with horses and carts and poorly dressed peasants going about the day's business. Nowhere in sight is there a person dressed in finery, so this part of whatever city he has landed in must be the poorer quarter.

The house in which he stands does not reflect this however, so perhaps the time is still too early for gentlemen and women to be afoot. He leaves the window and crosses the outer room to Tim's bedroom. Tim is in the process of dressing, so both men talk about what to do next. They know they cannot leave here without at least knowing where in Europe they are, and what year they have passed into, so they decide to pack their things and carry them downstairs. It is imperative to keep their possessions with them at all times. As they descend the stairs, they hear Gavinar talking to Petyr, so they creep further down to try to pick up what is being said. The voices are quite clear, but the men are talking in a language that is foreign to both Greg and Tim, so there is little point in eavesdropping. If they can pinpoint the language, however, they will know where in Europe they are. The men continue down the stairs and listening carefully, follow the voices back to the dining room.

"Aha, our guests have arrived at last," Gavinar, reverts quickly to English and, smiles broadly at Greg and Tim, bidding them join him at the table for breakfast. Petyr bows and leaves the three men alone.

"I trust you slept well?" Gavinar asks and before the men can answer him, he summons the housekeeper to bring in the breakfast.

"Let us eat, and then get down to business," Gavinar is all smiles and civility, but the smiles do not quite reach his eyes. Greg and Tim seat themselves on the floor in front of the low dining table.

"Would you like coffee?" asks Gavinar, "I buy the best from the East, and I declare there is no better coffee anywhere."

"Thank you, that would be wonderful," Tim replies and Gavinar rises to serve the men himself from the sideboard. There is a pot of honey on the table, but both men decline. The coffee is hot and very good, so the men do not speak further while enjoying the fragrant brew.

"There is someone I would like you to meet," Gavinar tries to sound casual, "this person may be able to help you, and as he is a good friend of mine, he can be trusted."

Greg and Tim smile politely, but do not answer Gavinar directly. They are saved from further discussion by the arrival of breakfast, consisting of thick bacon, eggs, and a platter of flat bread. As soon as the housekeeper has left, Gavinar bids the men tuck in, so there is no further talk until they have all eaten. After dabbing his hands and mouth on a linen cloth, Gavinar asks Greg and Tim to follow him.

The three men climb the stairs, but instead of entering the rooms set out for them, Gavinar leads them towards a room at the opposite end of the passage. Inside there is a hanging rack and on the rack are two sets of clothes similar to those worn by Gavinar.

"I suggest you both change into these," Gavinar advises, "you cannot go outside in what you are currently wearing without drawing undue attention to yourselves, and I am sure you would appreciate your travel clothes being cleaned, yes?"

"That is extremely thoughtful and kind," Tim smiles at Gavinar.

"I will leave you both to change, and you can leave the clothes you are wearing in a pile on the floor. I will ask the housekeeper to attend to them immediately. When you are ready, please join me downstairs again." Gavinar turns on his heels and leaves the men alone again. Back in the dining room Gavinar's brows draw together in thought. This is not going to be easy! He paces the room while waiting for the strangers to reappear.

"We must find out where we are today," Greg speaks in a whisper. "At least then we can form some sort of plan. I don't want to stay here any longer than necessary. The more I see of Gavinar, the more I get the feeling he is as slippery as an eel."

"I know what you mean," Tim agrees. "If we can't get the answers we need from Gavinar, we must try to speak to someone else in the house or out on the street. Gavinar wants to take us to meet someone, so keep your eyes open for any signs of the year or the place. There have to be street names or some kind of telling signs."

The two men change into the clothes provided by Gavinar: breeches, shirt, waistcoat and long hose as well as leather shoes with buckles, all of which are well worn, but fit reasonably well. There is not much that can be done with their hair however! Greg puts the satellite connector into a voluminous pocket in his breeches to make sure it does not get taken or lost. With a cursory glance around the room, the men return downstairs.

The Family

Florence brews a pot of 'coffee', a form they drink here made from berries collected and dried from the hedgerows. It is time to rejoin Canath at the top of the tower to discuss how they are to proceed. Bryan and Marcom are already seated at the chart table with Canath, and all three men rise as Florence sets the coffee pot on the table.

"Well, the children are all sleeping, although Antheia will be working hard while she sleeps," Florence informs the men. "We will all be learning as we go as far as her metamorphosis with Ladon is concerned."

"That is indeed the case," Canath agrees, "Marcom has been researching, but there seems to be nothing like this recorded anywhere or at any time, past, present or future." Canath frowns as he pours the coffee, and the four adults sit down ready for a long night of discussion.

"That in itself is an enigma," Canath growls, "for if the plenum is infinite reality, how can there not be anything? Of course, I must constantly remind myself that in some senses our finitude conceals what is beyond our human understanding."

"We must firstly decide how much to tell the children tomorrow," Florence says, "time is short for the amount of work that needs to be done, and we must ensure everyone is ready."

"I say we should go as far as we can, beginning with a brief family history, so they understand the gravity of the odyssey to come," Canath's deep voice reverberates through the room.

"They are all still very young, but I sense the strength that lies beneath the surface of their minds," Marcom reports his findings. "It would be better if we could proceed with caution, if only we had the time to do so, but we must trust that Ladon would not choose to become mortal at a time of great risk to any of the family."

"Well, the seals have been set, so the sooner we get started, the sooner our task can be undertaken. Are we all in agreement?" Canath searches their faces for any misgivings. Nobody speaks further. "Good, let's get to work, we begin at sunrise."

Antheia has fallen into a dream-like state which is on the threshold of sleep but with still a slight consciousness of what is occurring within her body. The child, Ladon, is growing rapidly and his thoughts 'speak' to his new mother as he becomes. He is implanting knowledge of millennia past as fast as she can manage to take it in. He understands that this task must be completed before his coming to birth, for at that time, he will lose the memory of it for the formative years of his human growth. During that time, he will need Antheia's strength to maintain the bridge with the unconscious from which human consciousness has only just arisen. This task has never been entrusted to a mortal before, and although Antheia is becoming immortal, still there is much yet to be done to ensure this metamorphosis is completed successfully. Ladon continues implanting until he senses Antheia is becoming exhausted. Shutting off the direct communication between them, he soothes Antheia's mind and spirit. Finally, she falls into a deep, dreamless sleep.

In the tower room, the four adults work together deep into the night, reformulating, testing and reinforcing the steps to be taken, until they have as fool proof a blueprint as is possible, given that they cannot prepare for every unknown contingency. At last, Canath speaks.
"Let us all sleep while we can before we must start the rituals that herald the dawn. Once this is begun, there will be no possibility of going back. The future is already written in the plenum, so the only way forward is to patch the damage created by our nemesis."
With no further ado, the four stand and bow their heads in supplication as Brian intones the benediction for the odyssey to come.
"May the gods give us the wisdom and strength to go where no human has ever been before!"
Bone tired and needing sleep, they leave to retire, Florence and Canath to their room and Bryan and Marcom to theirs. The time for planning is now over and tomorrow they will set in motion the final steps. They are all very well aware that once they leave the sanctuary of this place, they will be marching into the teeth of every danger that the forces against them can muster. If they do not succeed, the Universe as we know it will be totally and utterly destroyed. Nothing will prevail.

Henry

"We need a plan to find the sigils as quickly as possible." The men have moved away from earshot of the cavern and Peter states the facts they are all well aware of. "Since we began, we have just blindly followed Henry's instructions and that has gotten us nowhere, so I suggest we broaden the search now, including the inner caves and the ruins above the beachhead."

"The fact that Greg and Tim possibly found something that led them to Henry's files means something," John enjoins the discussion. "If that's the case, and I know we only have Henry's word for it, then we need to begin in the area they were sent to search. We may stumble upon what they found."

"That's good thinking, John," Peter replies, "You and I will go there and see what we can find. We may have more luck if we change Henry's search parameters.

"Why don't the rest of you split into two groups and one climb to the ruins above, and the other look for caves that lead underground. If you can find a safe way up to the ruins, climb carefully and watch where you put your feet. If it is too difficult in the dark, leave it until after daylight and search the surrounding area."

"What do we do if we discover something, Peter?" asks Rob, "We don't know if the sigils are dangerous, or how they work, so I suggest we signal you and the other group and we all meet together to decide what's to be done next."

"That sounds sensible," Peter considers the options and can think of nothing better. "We need to rendezvous after a certain time anyway, so send out two beeps if you find a sigil, and if there is no headway by four a.m., then let's meet back at the headland again. I don't want Henry to know anything about what we find or decide to do."

The three groups set out towards their allotted destinations to search.

Peter and John connect to the satellite to recall the search coordinates used by Greg and Tim, and with Peter leading, they make their way along the Western side of the cliffs until they come to a path sloping gently upwards. About twenty yards ahead they spot a darker patch in the cliff face, so they make for it carefully. As they near, the darker shadows form the entrance to a cave. Peter shines his torch towards the shadows; in the light the entrance becomes visible, and they see that it is narrow but high enough for them to stand upright. Just as they are about to go in, John looks down to check for any underfoot obstruction and gasps aloud.

"Good God!" he exclaims, "what on earth are those?" He has found the alien footprints first seen by Tim. Peter looks on in amazement; he has never seen anything like them in size or shape.

"I think we just found a clue to Greg and Tim's disappearance," Peter breathes, "but what it means is still not clear. I think we had better go in and see where this passage leads, don't you?"

"Yes," John agrees, "this could well mean the presence inside of a sigil, or at least some clue as to what made those footprints and why Greg and Tim did not come back to the grotto. I don't think we have the luxury of choice, so let's move inside."

Unlike Greg and Tim, the two men seem to discount the possible presence of whatever made the prints as they make their way into the cave. The inside is cool and silent with walls of roughened stone, although the stone floor is smooth as if the passage has been used regularly over a long period of time. There is a slightly familiar smell that Peter suddenly recognizes as the whiff of burning as if someone long ago had a fire in here. The passage winds slowly upwards and it is several minutes before the cave opens into a large, cathedral like space. The roof is high above their heads, so high that the light from the torch scarcely reaches, and in the torchlight, the men can see that the walls have become smooth and black, as if great heat has melted the rock to form a glass-like surface. They continue through this heightened passage until they come to a tight, ninety-degree turning. It is so tight that they cannot see around the bend, but just as they shine the torch against the angled walls, a sigil can be seen engraved in the blackened stone. At first, the two men stare in disbelief. So, here is the proof of what they were sent to find.

They had all half believed that the sigils were a fabrication to hide Henry's true intentions, yet here it is in plain sight at last! Peter reaches out to touch the raised design, but John quickly hits his arm downwards to stop him touching it.

"Don't touch it, Pete," John warns, "we don't know anything about it, and it could be dangerous. Let's just signal the others and wait for them to get here."

Peter sends out the two-beep signal as well as the coordinates of where they are. The two men then retrace their steps to the cave entrance to await the arrival of the others. They are both buoyed by the discovery and a new hopefulness lightens their spirits. They might just have found the way home!

Brandon

Brandon's return to the beach is slow and arduous. He stands upright, stretching his back to relieve the bent posture of the last two hours. It seems to be taking forever! Each time he moves, he has to try to find a footprint pointing away from the direction in which he is moving. If he loses the prints, he knows he will never find his way back from the way they came through here, in what seems like days ago. They were only jogging for about an hour before he could no longer go on, but the way back is torturously slow. There is no option, he must carry on. Once he is back at the beach of the inlet, he can at least try to get out of his predicament. If nothing else, the submersible can act as a boat even if it is not working. He is sure he can rig a couple of oars or long poles out of tree branches. The thought of regaining at least some control over his situation spurs him on.

He is so intent on looking for footprints that Brandon does not immediately recognize what he is hearing. At last his brain registers the sounds of waves breaking and he looks up, surprised when he notices not too far ahead, the beachhead where the submersible lies. With high spirits he races towards the sand leading down to the spot where the submersible lays half out of the water. He sinks to the sand weak with relief and takes a few moments to collect his thoughts, then with no further ado, he once more boards the submersible. It is sitting higher in the water with the incoming tide.

Brandon begins the checks that must be done to safely restart the submersible. The blackened, melted plastic surrounding the console is his first priority, and he collects the toolbox from the hold. As he unscrews the bracket holding the cover, he looks for any signs of broken wiring or damaged parts. Slowly and carefully, he removes the bracket completely and lifts the cover to reveal the inner working parts. Although there is a slight skewing of the mountings here and there, there does not appear to be anything other than surface heat damage. He does not want to completely dismantle the console, given the conditions here, so he carefully inspects every visible element before carefully replacing the cover and bracket. Next the skin and inside surfaces must be examined to make sure there are no microscopic splits, for as with a rocket ship, this is the main way fatal damage can occur. Reaching into the hold, Brandon opens the door that secures the sonic tool necessary to complete the examination in a short time. The sonic waves will produce colour on the screen, should there be any split, no matter how microscopic. Holding his breath, Brandon turns on the tool and waits. The computerized machine makes its own examination over the complete inner and outer surfaces using a special kind of sonar. The task usually takes a few minutes and on time the machine beeps three times. Brandon lets out a long-held breath. The worst that can happen to cripple the submersible, has not happened, the beeps signal the all clear in this regard. He continues the learned routine for checking the craft.

Brandon has been working with such focus that only now that he has successfully completed all the checks, does he realize the sun is beginning to sink and the heat of the day has faded leaving a slight chill in the air. He jumps down to the sand and drinks the last from the water bottle. Now is the time of revelation; he must try to start the submersible again as well as trying to connect to the satellite. So crucial are both these actions, that Brandon must screw up enough courage to try. Right now, there is the faint hope of returning home, but if either of these tasks does not work, then he knows he will be here for the rest of his life. His hands are shaking, and he tries to calm himself in preparation for either the best or worst results. He must act now, there is no time to waste, he does not want to find himself surrounded by Aborigines again.

Brushing the sand from his clothes and shoes, and steeling himself, he boards the submersible once more and with trepidation tries to connect to the satellite with his transponder. If it worked earlier, he hopes with all his heart, it will work again now. The red light on the console begins to flash on and off, but then remains on in solid red, and with the whirring sound familiar to Brandon, the submersible's powering up sequence begins. Seating himself at the console, Brandon lowers the dome that seals the submersible, and with heart beating overtime, sets in the coordinates for Kettering. The whirring winds down and lights on the console blink on in sequence. The sigil icon lights up, meaning the submersible has found the sigil through which Brandon must have passed, and slowly he pushes the joystick to fully forward position. The craft moves out from the bank and stays on the surface until the water depth is sufficient, then sinks down, so that Brandon loses sight of the surface altogether. He checks the lights once more to ensure there is nothing untoward happening, and lastly, closes his eyes to await the disorientation that occurs when passing through the Curtain. There is no awareness of time passing, just a hint of nausea and the dizziness associated with time lapses.

The Family

Phoenix wakes with a jolt, and sitting up, recognizes the tower room from the night before. Relief makes him feel weak, and he lays back down again, allowing a feeling of security to take him over for the first time in as long as he can remember. It is so good being in the same place as his parents. He looks over at his brother sleeping on his side and wonders at all that has happened to them in the last two days and nights. Slowly, he reaches out with his telepathy and his mother bids him good morning from the kitchen room below. He smiles and relaxes against the warmth of the soft blankets.

As Florence works to prepare the children's breakfast, she considers how to begin the truncated training her sons will need. They must accept the burden placed upon them with all their hearts and this is what worries her. Without an adult's life-experience, they are both still too young to fully embrace the odyssey that awaits. Canath has gone to the tower to prepare the family history lesson, and she hopes that he can provide the impetus necessary for both boys. Her thoughts move next to her two daughters. Antheia is now assured her safety and the security that she cannot be killed, although this will become a burden as she sees her friends and family age and die. Florence hopes with all her heart that she is filled with the will to live to such an extent that she can overcome her depression as the ones she loves leave her. At least Ladon will be her constant companion in one form or another. Aletheia is more of a mystery to Florence, although she knows her well enough to have trusted the lives of the others to Aletheia's care. This first child is quiet and undemanding, and Florence believes that they have not seen the depths of her yet, perhaps they never will, or perhaps the odyssey will change that. Breakfast is ready and Florence mentally summons all of the children to come down and eat.

Canath stares at the screen and thinks through the lesson to be given soon. How much to tell them and how much to keep unrevealed! The gravity of the situation cannot be discounted, so perhaps it will be better to give them the full picture and then leave them for a time to digest the facts and think about what they mean. Florence is leaving this first part of the program for him to decide and decide he does. With his plan in mind his fingers fly over the keys and the research from eons past is transferred at an amazing speed from the scrolls to the laptop. As he completes the last page, Florence summons him to breakfast. All is now in readiness to begin!

Antheia has been awake for several hours; she does not seem to need much sleep now. Ladon has, as is now usual, been imprinting knowledge and the familiarity of the process leaves her to ponder as he goes to work. This morning she will discover who her family really are and how they have come to this point. The fact that she is blocked from this knowledge is an enigma; perhaps her father has done this to protect her until now. As she rests, she allows herself to relax until Florence summons them to the kitchen below.

Aletheia wakes in a sweat with heart beating ten to the dozen. Where is she and how did she get here? As realization kicks in, she sighs deeply and allows the vivid dreams to recede. She is so used to being responsible for the others that she hardly knows how to let go of the anxiety necessary to ensure everyone's safety. Resting her head on the soft pillow, she luxuriates in the sense that she no longer needs to be in charge. What a wonderful way to rest! Today is a new beginning and the security of having her parents close by raises her spirits and helps to chase the deep weariness from her body. Soon enough, she 'hears' Florence's silent summons, and with a lighter spirit, Aletheia rises to dress and make her way down to the kitchen.

As the children arrive, Florence examines their faces for signs of stress. She is much relieved to see that all four of her children appear to be rested and well. The table is set with platters of meat, eggs and fresh bread with a basket of fruit in the centre. Before each place setting is a cup filled with the brew of mead and whiskey, mulled by a red-hot poker from the fireplace. The children sip carefully unsure of how this will taste, but as soon as their lips meet the hot, bitter-sweetness, they all declare it delicious. Kenneth is first to enquire where Canath is, and before Florence can answer her youngest son, his father arrives from the room at the top of the tower.

"Good morning to you, Kenneth, Phoenix and my beauties," Canath beams with the pleasure of seeing his family all seated before him. "Today you will learn who you are and why we had to leave you for a time."

Kenneth's smile lights up his face, and with no further ado, the family set upon the food as if they have not eaten for a week!

As they eat, Florence and Canath speak silently one to the other, and Canath blocks the children from this conversation.

"I think they are ready," Florence says carefully, "but I guess we can only wait and see."

"I have taken this into account, my dear, and I have decided to tell it all and then allow them sufficient time for the facts to sink in. If we allow them this one chance to understand who we are, then there cannot be any questions later. Let them ask their questions now before the real work begins."

"Thank you, Canath," Florence replies, "I myself would have made the same decision. Have you consulted with Brian and Marcom?"

"Yes, I have let them know our decision, and they are readying the lessons to begin tomorrow or the day after, depending on how the children take the news we have for them. Florence, how do you want to do this?"

"After we have eaten, I suggest we take the children to the tower room for the lesson and show them what we have been doing over the last several years. That way they can understand the seriousness of the situation."

Florence and Canath are as ready as they can be. The next few hours will be telling, but with Ladon so close now, they hope they cannot fail.

Greg and Tim

Gavinar sits as the men enter the room, and he inspects both of them to see how they look in the clothes he has provided. Satisfied, he speaks,

"As I told you, there is someone I want to introduce you to; someone who may be able to help you return to your own place and time. This person owes me a great many favours, so I don't need to ask him before I take you to him."

"Why are you doing this?" asks Greg, "You hardly know us and yet you seem anxious to help us get out of here as soon as possible, and I don't see how you can. What's in it for you?"

Gavinar searches the men's faces for any hint of outright refusal; he may have to use force if it is necessary. He has given Petyr the instructions to prepare for any eventuality.

"I merely wish to help and as you promised, if there is a way, you will take me with you, no?"

"Gavinar, you don't understand, we may end up somewhere other than where we want to be. That is exactly what happened to us last night," Greg begins to argue logically in the hope of dissuading Gavinar from joining them, but as he soon discovers Gavinar is not to be put off, he wishes he had not made the promise last night!

"Come, both of you, we are arguing about something that may not even be possible. What harm for you to meet with my friend? Let's go, I arranged the meeting at nine a.m. in a coffee house not far from here. At least you can enjoy another cup of good coffee."

The men cannot see any way out of this, so they allow Gavinar to lead them to the door and out onto the cobbled street. Both men have donned their backpacks, taking everything except the clothes left to be washed. The men look about them with curiosity, trying to find any sign of where they might be and in what time. As they pass by, local tradespeople who are just opening the shutters on their shopfronts wave and speak greetings to Gavinar. He returns their greetings, smiling and waving as he does so. Greg and Tim do not notice the fearful looks of the townspeople when they notice the strange bags carried on their backs.

Tim notices that the overhanging buildings continue, and the shops are part of the street level of the houses. He tries to remember his history lessons, to estimate what year they may be walking through. Ahead, the narrow street opens out into a broader thoroughfare of sorts, where horses and carts and horses with riders pass slowly by, going about their business. The three men cross over and enter another narrow laneway where up ahead, a board hanging from the eaves of a house announces refreshments. Greg and Tim cannot read the language, but the painted images leave them in no doubt. They enter a wide doorway that opens out along the pathway with rough wooden tables and stools set up for customers. At one such table sits a tall, thin, bearded man dressed oddly in a cloak of dark red velvet. On his head sits a wide black hat adorned with an enormous plume. If they were in Kettering and their own time, the men would consider him to be from a travelling show or circus, but this is indeed, not Kettering!

As the man's eyes alight on Gavinar, they exchange a hardly visible nod, and as they make their way to his table, the stranger scrutinizes Greg and Tim almost to the point of rudeness. Again, there is a hardly perceptible nod exchanged. Gavinar reaches his friend and bows.
    "Please be seated," the man speaks in strongly accented English.
    Gavinar, Greg and Tim pull out stools and sit while the stranger signals to the serving girl to bring coffee.
    "Please let me introduce you to my good friend, Felix," Gavinar makes the introduction, "and Felix these are the men I told you about, Greg and Tim." Both men wonder when last night Gavinar could have met with this man; they spent the night talking, then slept. Perhaps Gavinar met with him while they slept, but why would he do that so late at night?
    Felix makes a half bow from his seat, and Greg and Tim nod to him. A strange sense of light-headedness overtakes them both as they meet Felix's gaze. There is something not quite right about the scene, but the

two men cannot put words to it. They glance at each other for a second and miss the slight movement of Felix's hand. The serving girl brings the tray of coffee pots to the table as well as a dish of tiny, honeyed cakes. Gavinar pours from the pots into mugs handing one to each and the men take a sip of the rich brew.

"I believe the two of you are time travelers," Felix concentrates on his coffee, giving Greg a chance to decide how to answer this.

"We are unwilling time travelers, Felix," Greg replies, "we came here by accident, and Gavinar tells us that you might be able to help us to get back to our own place and time, although I can't see how that would work. Can you please tell us where we are and in what year? We certainly need that information before we can make any attempt to return."

Felix looks at Gavinar and the two men sip their coffee as if playing for time. At last Felix answers.

"Why you are in Gothenburg, Sweden, young man, and this is the year of our lord, 1762. Now, tell me where and when you are from."

"Felix, we come from Kettering, Northamptonshire in England, and the year as we know it, is 2020."

"Well, well, well," Felix exclaims as he plays for time to respond to Greg's reply. If he can believe the men, then they truly have been dropped into their laps as Gavinar excitedly reported. Felix quickly dampens his excitement so that the men do not notice his reaction. He knows he must not show any signs that he recognizes the name of Kettering. All their predictions and calculations depend on the men remaining stum.

"I suppose you are both wondering why my friend Gavinar brought you to meet me?" Felix speaks carefully and with as much nonchalance as he can muster.

"First let me tell you who I am. I belong to an order of Alchemists, a group of scientific researchers and scholars. We also study the works of the great philosophers. Have you heard of this order in your own time?"

The two men understand far more about the Alchemists than either wants to admit; Henry's work was centered on the Alchemical treatise for some considerable time back in Kettering, although what he discovered or learned, neither man knows fully. The fact that Felix is associated with these people, however, is a clear warning to them both. How are they going to extricate themselves from this situation of deepening danger? It is some seconds before any one of the four seated men speaks.

"I would have expected the weather here to be colder," Tim tries to deflect the conversation. "I don't know much about your country, but Gothenburg seems to be a commercial centre. Is that the case?"

"Gothenburg is the centre of commerce for the whole country," Felix advises, "the Dutch came here about a hundred years ago and established this city for trade purposes. The port here is sheltered and many vessels from all over Europe visit bringing most of what we need, like the coffee you are drinking, but let us not forget why we are here together. Are we agreed that you will accept my help? I do not want to waste your time unless you wish to continue your journey."

Felix does not want to seem to rush the men, but he knows that the time to act will be limited within strict parameters and he and Gavinar have come too far to miss this golden opportunity.

Henry

The men guarding Henry have eaten and Henry is fast asleep — or so they believe. As the night advances, they begin to tire and slowly their concentration begins to ebb. As midnight approaches, most of the six men are dozing and some are fully asleep. Henry opens one eye a fraction and gauges the likelihood of making his escape. Slowly and silently, he withdraws the laptop from under his head and having laid down still fully clothed, he edges his way to the back of the shallow cave and sidles along the shadowed back wall. His backpack — he placed there earlier, before he laid down and he lifts it carefully and heads to the corner of the entrance furthest away from the sleepy men. With one last, ironic smile, he slips out into the night.

"Is everyone here?" Peter has been counting the faces as the other pairs arrive. "OK, let's go inside, and John and I can show you what we found. Before you do, look down."

There are a few gasps as the giant, alien footprints shine up at them from the light of John's torch. Nobody says anything, and each man tries to bypass the prints to enter the narrow cave mouth, as if whatever made them might feel their tread. Peter leads the way, and the men stare in surprise at the point at which the cave opens to the cavernous, blackened space. Some distance ahead, at the ninety-degree turning point, Peter stops and shines his torch onto the wall. The sigil shows clearly, and they all draw closer.

"This is what we were searching for, and my guess is Greg and Tim found it, but what happened to them at that point?" searching their faces, Peter asks the question on everybody's lips.

"We don't know how the sigils work; except we needed one to pass through the Curtain to get here. Do any of you think that Greg and Tim might have used this to get away from here, and if so, how?"

The gathered men remain silent, thinking. There must be an

explanation for the disappearance unless Henry killed them after climbing to the ruins above the beach.

"We saw no evidence of foul play when we climbed the cliff," Jason replies, "although we didn't reach the ruins before you summoned us back here."

None of the others can offer anything else, so Peter takes up the reins once more.

"OK, well now, we have to decide what to do," Peter thinks aloud.

"What do you suggest?" John defers to Peter as all the men seem to do. They are all seeking a leader to follow, and Peter seems to be their choice.

"The facts are these," Peter starts using his fingers to count off the points he wants to make. "One: we have found the sigil that was the exercise we were brought here to carry out. Two: by using the coordinates to where Greg and Tim were sent, we find alien footprints as well as a sigil. Three: Greg and Tim have disappeared, but before they did — if Henry was telling the truth — they accessed Henry's files back home. Why? Four: there is no evidence that they were killed here at least. Five: they found something in Henry's files that made them run, if that is what happened. Six: Brandon escaped too, and he was part of the planning process from the start, so what is it that we are missing? I think it's time to put the pressure on Henry; I don't think he has told us the half of it, and we must know how the sigils work if we are going to leave here, especially if there is a time limit on their use."

Nobody dissents from the points Peter has laid out or his final statement. The only thing in the back of his mind is the matter of time; do they actually have the time to get the information out of Henry, or will the sigil disappear before they can make it back here? He decides to put this question to the vote.

"If we take the time to go back and confront Henry, will the sigil disappear before we return? That is the question, and I want to see a show of hands for which way we should go. All those in favour of questioning Henry, raise your hands." Peter counts the response. "All those who think we should stay here and try to use the sigil?" The response is clear; the majority of the men want to try to use the sigil before it disappears.

"Has anyone brought their laptop with them?" Peter asks. One man raises his hand.

"Jason, could you try to connect to the satellite, please; we can see if Henry's files are still accessible, although I would imagine he has safeguarded them more thoroughly after Greg and Tim's access."

Jason manages to connect to the satellite, but there is no possibility of breaking through the security behind which Henry's systems lie; none of the men gathered have the expertise.

"OK, so let's vote again; should we try touching the sigil or not? Who is for it?" Peter waits for all the men to make up their minds. It seems they are stuck between a rock and a hard place. If they don't try, they may lose the chance. If they do try, they may end up somewhere they don't want to be or worse, they may be killed or badly injured by contact with the sigil. From their responses, the men believe there is no real choice. If they don't try, they are stuck here for the rest of their lives. The question now is: who will be the first to try? Peter asks for a volunteer.

A man steps up to Peter, a man nobody really knows very well. He was chosen for the expedition because of his expertise in ancient philosophy. Steven has always been somewhat of an enigma to the others because his skill set does not seem to fit with the rest. The other men have practical, scientific skills quite obviously necessary for the purpose of the quest, yet for some reason Henry chose Steven as well. The men wait for him to speak.

"I know you don't understand why Henry chose me for this task," Steven looks at each man in turn, "but this kind of situation is precisely where my skills can come to the fore. I have studied deeply the treatises from all the major ancient writers and religions, and I think I may be able to guide us all through this impasse."

Peter and the others remain silent, and Peter asks Steven to continue.

"One of the major works of ancient literature is the arcana of the Alchemical Treatise written by several authors around the time of the Middle Ages. Although it is usually interpreted as the scientific quest to turn base metals into gold, there is another more psychological interpretation, largely thanks to the work of Carl Jung. This interpretation looks to the woodcuts that accompany one of the treatises and which are discarded as mystical mumbo jumbo by the mainstream scientific community. When these are married to the hidden inner work of ancients such as Pythagoras and taken seriously, there is a clue to the fact that mathematical knowledge contains all the principles of the infinite. These are principally a form of images so ancient as to be impossible to translate into discursive logic, but they contain all the memory traces of the human race from the beginning of 'time' as we know it. This image language we know from dreams that accompany our night sleep when ego consciousness is lowered sufficiently. This is our second human language, a collective unconscious from which ego consciousness has risen and provides access to a deeper knowledge that scientific logic skates over the top of. Jung named them archetypes. I can't go into further detail, but if you grant what I am saying is possible, then we can use the sigil, simply by interpreting the image through which it is represented here."

The other men are taken aback by what Steven has just related, and it is obvious that some of them find his statements ludicrous. Peter, however, remembers how Henry shut himself away for several weeks at the university to study the works that Steven has just mentioned. Perhaps this man can provide what the scientists cannot, a way home!

"I think we must defer to Steven, what do the rest of you think? This may be our only chance to get back to Kettering."

The men look at Peter and again at Steven, and John brings up the elephant in the room.

"What about the six men we left back at the cavern and Henry, of course? You are not suggesting we just leave them there and try to go without them, are you?"

"This is the problem; do we have enough time to go back and collect them, or will we lose the chance to leave here, and all have to remain for the duration?" Peter puts this to the men. Nobody wants to think about the impasse they face.

"Peter, let's try to interpret the sigil before you decide — it may be safe to return, but first I need to brainstorm with all of you here to think of as many meanings of the image as we can."

"OK," Peter is relieved not to have to make the terrible choice. Perhaps Steven can really do this, at least they have to give it a shot!

Brandon

As the feeling of disorientation begins to fade, Brandon opens his eyes and looks around him. The sun is rising, so he knows it is early daytime, and as he depressurizes and slides back the dome, a warm, summer breeze wafts down on him. The sea is calm and small wavelets wash softly against the hull of the submersible. He is in some kind of enclosed bay, sheltered from the open ocean, but he cannot make out where he is. The rising sun is reflected back at him from the land, so it is impossible for him to see clearly. This surely can't be Kettering though; the warm ambience is far too humid, the water too clear and aqua blue and the sun too bright. Brandon's hopes begin to plummet again. As the wavelets wash him slowly towards the shore, Brandon readies himself to disembark and shut down the craft into dormant mode. He must go ashore; that is the only way to try to discover where he is. As soon as he hears the rush of water over shingle, he jumps down into the shallows. Using his transponder, he connects to the satellite and readies the submersible to slide back under the waves within ready recall distance. Wading ashore in his sneakers, Brandon sinks down onto the narrow strip of sand and looks around. At least there is nobody within discernible distance this early in the day. He listens carefully for any sounds of habitation, but all that is visible is high cliff faces. He searches as far as he can see and soon spots a man-made path meandering upwards towards the cliff top. The cliffs are too high for him to see what lies at the top; they are also a strange dark colour. After allowing his shoes to dry out somewhat, he begins the trek towards the pathway.

The beach is littered with sharp, black shards of rock that jog his memory. Yes, it has the look and feel of lava that has flowed down from the cliff to meet the sea. As he carefully picks his way towards the path, he notices rock pools filled with the moving shapes of tiny, darting fish. Again, his memory is jogged. This time his mind moves back to childhood and watching documentaries about volcanic beaches, just like this. The pathway looms now and using the handrails on both sides, he quickly makes his way upwards towards the crest of the cliff. The meander of the path means it takes longer to climb, but he recognizes that this is the only way a pathway could be built to scale the cliff from below. At last, he crests the cliff and steps out onto the land.

His spirits soar as he sees the view in front of him! A beach-comber style, small resort lies spread out before his eyes and lit signs in the windows of shop fronts invite customers to try their Hawaiian cuisine from pineapple ice cream to coconut fish salads. Brandon has never seen anything more beautiful in all his life. He is on the Hawaiian island of Maui, and he is back in approximately his own time regardless of the fact that he is half-way across the world from home. He thanks his lucky stars and taking some deep breaths, he crosses from the cliff-top landing to the resort building and civilization at last! If he can find someone willing to allow him to borrow their cell phone, he can make contact with his family and arrange the funds for the journey home. He is so overcome with relief that exhaustion grips him, and he has to make a supreme effort to keep his shaky legs moving.

Inside the cool lobby, he searches the lounge area for a discarded newspaper, the better to find out the date. Popular magazines lie artfully placed on several low rattan tables and before long he spots a folded newspaper, obviously left by a guest, finished with reading it. His hands shake as he picks it up, turning the folded pages back to the front page. There before his eyes, the date! He can scarcely believe what he sees: 17th June 2020, just seven days after he left Kettering and yet a lifetime after he left in terms of what he has seen, experienced and been through. He sits down heavily, his whole body shaking. He feels as though he has just been born again, and it takes several minutes for the shaking to subside enough for him to risk standing up.

The Family

As breakfast comes to an end, Canath stands and addresses those seated at the table.

"Well, my children, it is time to initiate what you were summoned here to do. Please follow your mother and me to a room at the very top of this tower. There we will begin by showing you what we have been doing and why. Then I will explain our family history and you can ask any questions before the real work begins."

"Father, will we be staying together now of do you have to leave us again?" Phoenix is worried about this.

"Phoenix and Kenny, please just let me get through what I need to show and tell you before we start to look at the dynamics. I am sure you will understand more clearly once you have the information. That is why we are doing it this way."

The whole family climbs to the tower room. Brian and Marcom are already seated at a larger table; room has been made by returning the scrolls and books to their shelves and eight stools have been squeezed around the long table. Canath and Florence take their places at either end, and the children sit two to each side, alongside Brian and Marcom. As Canath reaches for his laptop, the children exchange puzzled glances. None of them has ever seen such a thing before. A SmartScreen drops from the wooden beams above Canath's head and illuminates as he sets the laptop to project. This time the children sit open-mouthed. There is nothing in this room that speaks of their life thus far.

"It is time for your mother and me to explain what you see here. The year we live in is 2020, but your lives have been lived in an ancient Greece, although the time there is also 2020. None of you have seen anything but Greece in a time of ruin, but this ruin is man-made in the sense that there has been tampering within the plenum, by men with no sense of what they are doing. This tampering with time itself cannot stand or everything that has existed, does exist, and will exist will cease to exist. The power of existence itself will cease. There will be nothing at all." Canath looks at each child in turn to make sure they are able to take in what he is telling them.

"The damage is like a tear in the fabric of the Universe, and unless we can repair the damage, all will be lost universally. Please ask me questions now about this before I proceed to the next stage."

For several seconds nobody speaks, then Antheia raises the first question.

"Father, does Ladon have a role to play in this?" she asks plaintively.

"Yes, child, he has much to accomplish, which is why he is becoming mortal through you."

"Then, Father, who are we and why are we the ones chosen to do this?" Phoenix's mind flickers with images that he can't quite make out. They seem to be speaking to him, but the sounds are just below his hearing range.

"All in good time, Phoenix, do you have any questions about what I have just explained?" Canath scrutinizes his oldest son's face. This is not going to be easy for any of them to understand, but for the younger boys, it could prove too much. He must be careful now.

"No, Father," Phoenix replies, "it all seems somehow like a dream that I can't wake up from."

"Father, why were we born and raised in the ruined Athens that we know as home?" Aletheia has been thinking while the others asked questions. "There certainly was nothing but scarce food and few people, most of whom we only saw signs of; why did you and mother leave us there for so long?"

"This is symptomatic of the problem I have just explained briefly to you. I will explain all this shortly," Canath is worried that the gravity of their quest has not sunk in. "Do you all understand how crucial our part is in saving all living forms?"

The children quietly think about what is written on the screen. This is so much to absorb in such a short time. Dizziness begins to overcome Antheia, and her face pales to such an extent that Florence rises from her seat and moves to her daughter.

"Are you feeling all right?" Florence asks, but Antheia swoons in her seat and Florence catches her before she falls to the floor.

"Canath, I must attend to Antheia," Florence gazes at her husband.

"Take her back down to her room and make sure she is comfortable, Florence," Canath looks on gravely as his second daughter returns to consciousness once more. "Perhaps we leave this for the moment and allow the children some time to think about what they have been told so far."

Florence looks gratefully at Canath, and he stands to make way for Florence and Antheia to pass. He addresses the others.

"Children, go back to your rooms and think about what I have shown you. If you have questions, you will find me in the kitchen with Brian and Marcom. We will begin again after lunch, so make the most of your time. Try to understand."

"I am so sorry, Mother," Antheia lies on her soft bed. The colour has returned to her face, but she is still feeling weak as a kitten.

"Antheia do not concern yourself; this is part and parcel of being pregnant," Florence soothes her daughter and brushes her hand through Antheia's long, golden hair. "I will leave you, but only for a minute to go down to the kitchen and bring you something to make you feel better. Are you hungry, child?"

"No, Mother, I am still full from breakfast," Antheia is starting to feel better and smiles wanly at Florence to reassure her.

"I will only be a minute," Florence rises and leaves the room. In the kitchen the three men look up expectantly. "She is all right," Florence assures them, "just tired and a bit nonplussed by all that she is learning. I will take her a warm brew so she can sleep, and Ladon can then soothe her."

Henry

"Right," Steven walks the men over to the site of the sigil, making sure everybody has it in view. "What is this the image of, can you all try to give your interpretation and, Jason, can I use your laptop, please?"

Jason quickly hands his laptop to Steven, who opens it to a blank word document ready to type in the responses.

"It kind of looks like a stylized dog or some creature, but with more pronounced nose and teeth," John suggests.

"If it is an image of collective dreams, wouldn't it be something from fables or fairy tales?" another of the group suggests.

"That is a vital point," Steven types this response, "what are the creatures that we all remember from fairy tales?"

"Well, wolves and dragons are the ones I remember," Peter replies, "do either of these seem likely, Steven?"

Steven looks thoughtful, "Well, in the ancient Greek pantheon, a wolf called Lykaios was the familiar of Apollo. That would seem to fit. Dragons were considered to be the most ancient of creatures with wisdom born of their infinite age. Of course, we all know that they were said to be fire-breathers, and in some ancient civilizations, they were considered to be the guardians of the spirit realm. In this way a dragon stood between the finite knowledge that we have access to and the deeper archaic knowledge that the archetypes represent. Dragons were also considered to be immortal in many Asian cultures, especially China and Japan. In fact, the dragon image is by far the most prolific throughout all times and all geographic regions, so we might be on to something."

"What does it mean then if the sigil is a dragon?" Peter wants to get to the bottom of this as soon as possible.

"Well, it could represent a guardian of the Curtain, and if so, it could also be a warning."

"In what way, I can't see it." Peter wants to hurry this process.

"What does the Curtain represent as far as you understand?" Steven needs to explicate this crucial point so that he can make them understand how the sigil works.

None of the men feel sufficiently knowledgeable to provide a theory. Steven continues.

"The Curtain acts like a gateway from one kind of reality — the finite realm of time-space, cause and effect — and ultimate reality or infinity. For a finite being to transgress the universal laws that govern all of reality means that a filter of sorts, much like a catalyst, is essential. An approximate example is the speed of light. This represents the fastest possibility of universal movement, yes? Light is nothing but pure universal energy. What do you think would happen if a human body approached the speed of light? I won't go into the particular facts of changes that occur during that approach, just to keep it as simple as possible."

The men are absolutely stunned that Steven, a supposed philosopher, should be speaking understandingly about the metaphysics of what are principally highly complex scientific ideas.

"All matter at the speed of light just becomes light," Steven's point begins to sink in. "So, what do you think would happen if there was no filter between consciousness and the unconscious or finite reality and infinity?"

"Chaos," Peter responds.

"Actually, Peter, reality as it is, is its only possibility. Think about it. Infinity means everything that can exist does exist and cannot be otherwise, or infinity would be nonsensical. So, without the filter, infinity, finitude and anything whatsoever could not exist. There would be no possibility of existence at all. But the fact that existence quite obviously *is,* then the filter also *is,* so the sigil 'tells' us in image language form, its purpose and use. Dragons represent wisdom, guardianship and fire breathing, so if we examine each of these properties, what does that tell us?"

The men are intrigued; they have never even thought of the concepts that Steven has cleverly introduced and explained. His explanation makes sense, and there is certainly no other explanation that does, so they are willing to follow where he is leading them.

"Let's take wisdom first, what does it mean in the context of the sigil? To me — and I have been interpreting these images for a long time, — wisdom speaks of ultimate reality, age-old if you like. The dragon image itself tells us that the sigil is a gateway into the plenum of ultimate reality, where everything that ever did, does or will exist, already exists. Since the dragon is the guardian of the gateway, he acts as the filter that allows movement through primordial 'time', or movement within the plenum which contains all possible realms of finitude and infinity, much like the infinite set, in set mathematics.

"The dragon breathes fire, so I expect that if contact is made with the sigil, fire will erupt from it as with a dragon. Look around you, the blackened glass walls of this cavern speak of rock melted at super high temperature. My explanation is just what the sigil tells us in its image language form."

Henry moves quickly and quietly towards the men in the cavern. He has surreptitiously connected to their coordinates and immediately recognized their position as that to which he sent Greg and Tim on the first night. This is an aha moment for Henry. He had not thought to check where the men who accessed his files had been. It makes perfect sense now to Henry. They must have found something that made them leave in the first instance. All he has to do now is stay incognito by avoiding the others. As he nears the pathway leading up to the cavern mouth, he slows his pace and keeps to the shadowy cliff face. It is still very dark, but he does not yet know if there are any men here guarding against his appearance. Could the men ahead realise he has escaped the six men guarding him? He must take every possible precaution. Slowly and carefully, he follows the pathway until he spots a darker patch on the cliff face. As he nears the darker spot, he stops to listen. There is no discernible sound, so he continues until he reaches the entrance to the cavern. Although he cannot see more than a few feet ahead, he does not want to turn his torch on in case he alerts the others who must be inside. He is about to enter when his feet begin to react to a burning sensation. He looks down at his feet but finds he cannot move them. The burning pain is now very acute, so without thinking too much, Henry switches on his torch and searches the ground on which he stands. To his dismay, he recognizes the footprints on which he stands. In a panic now, he calls out hoping the men inside the cavern can hear him. He screams as the burning passes through his shoes to the skin of his feet. He claws at the cliff face in an almighty effort to move his feet away from the glowing prints, but with growing understanding, he knows he is doomed. All of a sudden, Henry is engulfed in flames so hot that it takes only seconds for his form to disintegrate into ashes.

The path on which Henry stood is now slick and black. The prints have disappeared along with Henry.

Inside the cavern, the sigil begins to glow and the awestruck men back away from the wall where the sigil stands, now in deep relief.

"What the hell is happening?" Peter is alarmed, and Steven looks puzzled.

"Something has triggered the mechanism of the sigil, but how," he wonders.

The outline looks sharper and more in focus. The sigil now appears as the dragon, there is absolutely no doubt, but the eye of the creature appears to glow and look out from the wall. All the men look on in stunned silence. Slowly, the glowing dims until the sigil is once more, no more than a two-dimensional figure cut in relief, into the rock wall.

Greg and Tim

Felix looks at Gavinar, and the two men seem to come to a silent agreement. Felix is the first to speak.

"Gavinar and I have something to tell you, but we cannot do so here. There are too many ears in close proximity. Would you both be willing to come back to my house? I have servants who ensure my confidentiality."

Greg and Tim look at each other, and they also make a silent agreement. They will go, but they will get away from these two strange men as soon as they can do so. As they stand to leave, Gavinar remarks that he has left an important document at home; he will return home to retrieve it, then meet them at Felix's house. Felix leads Greg and Tim towards the main thoroughfare and turns right. Nobody says anything, but Greg and Tim take note of the available landmarks, especially a road leading downhill towards the wharf. There the men can just see the highest spars of the masts of several sailing barques, either unloading their cargo or taking it aboard. This may be the fastest way to escape the clutches of Gavinar and Felix!

"Petyr, I want you to come with me and bring Damon with you. Felix is taking the two strangers to his house, and I may need your help to detain them there."

"Yes, master," Petyr replies, bowing low, "Damon and I will make sure they do not leave. Are these men dangerous, sir, or do they hold the key to your experiments?"

Gavinar does not reply immediately, gauging how much to tell his faithful servant. If everything goes to plan, he and Felix will simply disappear.

"Whatever happens, Petyr, I want you to take control of my finances until I return, should anything happen to me. Do you understand?"

"Yes, master, you can rely on me." Petyr does not show it, but he is puzzled as to what Gavinar can possibly mean by this statement. Surely with the four of them, these two strangers cannot pose any real danger.

Felix leads Greg and Tim for about a kilometer before turning up another cobbled lane. They have left the bustle of the city behind and the houses here are larger and appear to be better appointed. Felix stops before the wooden door of a house about halfway along the lane. Using an old-fashioned, large key, he unlocks the door and ushers the two men inside. Immediately inside the door stands a grandfather clock, the like of which neither Greg nor Tim have seen before. The ornately carved wood of the oversized case seems somehow sinister, and both men get the feeling that something is not right here. It is the same light-headed feeling they had, when looking into Felix's eyes at the coffee house. Felix leads the men down the narrow passage and into a large sitting room. Here large bay windows let in light and the furnishings are in a style similar to that in Gavinar's house.

"Please take a seat, I will be back in a moment," Felix leaves Greg and Tim alone.

"We need to get out of here ASAP," Tim whispers urgently, "did you feel the clock inside the door?"

"I sure did," Greg replies, "it felt as if the clock was watching us. Did you get the same light-headed feeling as at the coffee house?"

"Yes, something is not right here," Tim looks around the room nervously.

"Well, now we must wait for Gavinar to return," Felix saunters back into the room, carrying a large, wooden box. "I have asked my servants to leave while we talk."

"What is it precisely that you want to talk about?" Greg asks.

"Please bear with me until Gavinar arrives. I am sure you will want to hear what we have to tell you because it affects you both personally." Felix tries to smile, but it does not reach his mesmerizing eyes. Both men look away from his gaze.

"I still don't see how that can be the case," Greg stands his ground, "we don't even know you or this place."

"Oh, but you do," Felix replies silkily, "please, let's just wait on

Gavinar."

Just then, there is a rapping on the door, and Felix hurries to answer it. Gavinar stands at the door with Petyr and Damon. Felix signals for the two servants to enter the yard from the rear of the building.

"Wait in the kitchen until we need you," Felix orders, "there is tea and food set out, but do not eat the bread, or you will sleep for a week!"

Gavinar steps into the hallway and follows Felix to the sitting room.

"Ah, my good friends," Gavinar greets Greg and Tim, "at last we can divulge a great secret. Then you will understand why I wanted you to visit here with Felix."

The men note that Gavinar does not carry a document with him, so the forgotten paper was merely an excuse to leave them with Felix. The hair rises on both men's necks. Something is definitely amiss here!

"Gavinar, I think Tim and I must leave now," Greg has had enough of this game.

"I think not," Felix fixes Greg with his eyes again, and Greg begins to feel faint. He struggles to stay conscious, and Tim looks at him with terror written on his face.

"What the hell is going on?" Tim demands, but he is also stricken when Felix turns to face him. The men cannot move; they seem to be held in place by Felix's gaze.

"You have nothing to fear, but you must listen to what Gavinar, and I have to tell you. Our fate depends on it, not only yours. I am going to release both of you now, but do not try to get up, or I will have you bound." Felix's voice brooks no dissent, and neither man wants to be transfixed again, so they sit as instructed. Gavinar and Felix remain standing, and Felix waves his hand over the wooden box, then lifts the lid. Greg and Tim cannot see what is inside from their seated positions, but Gavinar's eyes take on a manic kind of light. Whatever is in the box has taken possession of him. Greg wonders if these two people are crazy. He does not have time to consider this thought, for just then, an orb rises from the box of its own accord. It is silver and about the size of a large grapefruit with a strange, crazed pattern in black. It slowly spins as it rises, and Gavinar seems transfixed by it.

With another wave of his hand, the slowly spinning orb moves towards Greg and Tim and stops directly in front of them. Felix moves behind the men's seated positions, and the orb begins to glow. Within the surface scenes become visible, and without any spoken directive, a living scene of Kettering appears. The scene is a moving picture of cars and streets, buildings and people walking to and fro, going about their daily business. Greg and Tim can scarcely believe their eyes as the scene of life they are both so familiar with plays out. At last, with a click of Felix's fingers, the orb returns to its normal state and moves slowly back towards the box. As soon as it is above the box, it slowly drops back into its boxed position, and Felix closes the lid. There is utter silence in the room, and the men can scarcely draw breath.

Brandon

His legs feeling like they are made of jelly, Brandon carefully stands and walks to the front reception desk, where a casually dressed concierge is busy with setting up the counter for the day's guests. He looks up at Brandon with distaste written on his face. Brandon is immediately aware of what he must look like. He is, at the least, disheveled and dirty, and the unkempt state of his clothes must make him appear as if he lives on the streets. He takes a calming breath and speaks.

"Apologies for my disheveled state," he starts, "but I have been in an accident, and I desperately need to call home to arrange funds. Would it be possible to use a telephone please? I can let you speak to my family if you wish, but without your help, I am afraid I am stuck here."

The concierge pauses from what he is doing and looks Brandon over.

'You don't look injured to me," he says suspiciously, "you look like a bum off the street!"

Brandon opens his shirt and the red, swollen burn made by the Clever Man's bone is stark against his otherwise, pale skin.

"You see?" Brandon replies, "I need help and my family will ensure I get it. Please, I just need to make one call and I am happy for you to speak to whoever answers the phone. Tell them you have Brandon Fellings with you."

With a sigh and doubt still writ large on his face, the concierge acquiesces and asks Brandon for the phone number. He writes it down and presses the numbers, watching Brandon as he does so. The phone is answered reasonably quickly, and the concierge relays the message given to him by Brandon. He listens for a few seconds, then passes the phone to Brandon.

"Here, and make sure your mother sends you money, or you will have to leave immediately you finish the call."

Brandon takes the phone with shaking hands.

"Hello, Mother?" Brandon asks querulously.

"My god, Brandon, where are you? We have been so worried! You seemed to just drop off the face of the earth."

"Mother, please listen, I need you to transfer money for me, and I don't have my cards or wallet with me. Can you do that please? I will immediately organize to fly home, and I will tell you all about what has happened to me when I get there. I am on the island of Maui, Hawaii, and I need to get home as soon as I can. I am going to hand the phone back to the concierge here, and he will give you an account number to transfer the funds into. Please transfer five thousand pounds, and I will give it back to you as soon as I get back there."

Brandon listens for a few moments and hands the phone back to the concierge, who is standing by with a pen and paper. He is weak with relief, but the concierge watches him still. He finishes writing, then puts down the phone and says to Brandon,

"Your money transfer should be in the account within the hour, would you like a room to clean up and some food?"

Brandon can scarcely stand, and holding on to the desktop, he nods weakly.

"That would be so kind of you," he says, "I won't forget your kindness."

The concierge takes a keycard from behind the desk and directs Brandon to the room.

"I will have a meal sent to your room shortly," he replies, and Brandon slowly makes his way to the allotted room. The stress of the last few days is beginning to take its toll, and Brandon just makes it into his room before he collapses on the floor. He realizes he has been living on adrenalin and not much else for several days.

The Family

Canath, Marcom and Brian watch as Florence warms a jug of brew with the poker from the fire. When she leaves with a pot for Antheia, the men begin the serious thinking that must ensure the family are ready for what awaits them ahead. Canath frowns deeply as they consider the plight before them and how they can turn the children's resolve in such a short time.

"I cannot see how we can burden them with all the knowledge born of centuries past and then expect them to acquiesce immediately," Marcom states the obvious facts. "Just how do you plan to do that, Canath?"

"I am afraid I can't plan too far ahead because they have to understand that this is their birthright," Canath muses, "however difficult this task is, it is essential and nothing can soften what they need to know about themselves, about Florence and me, and about what will be expected of them. I have to trust in Ladon's understanding of them, and in the directives of the Oracle of Delphi. None other than these two beings have the ability to read the spiritual realm of the plenum and foresee the future, as we call it. Only in the plenum is there the answers to every question that can ever be asked."

"Then we will leave you to continue," Brian replies, "but be aware that we are both here if you need us for anything whatsoever."

"Thank you both," Canath bows to the men, "and may the gods come to our aid also."

Brian and Marcom stand to leave as Florence re-enters the room. They bow to her, and she bobs her head in return. Florence sits next to Canath and takes his hand in hers.

"Do not worry so, my love," Florence tries to soothe Canath's mind, "they will come through. They are fire-born and the offspring of immortals, trust in Ladon and the Oracle, for they cannot speak untruths. Our children have been born to this task, and without them, there would be no hope for existence. Just follow where your intuition takes you, and everything will happen as it is meant to."

"Thank you, dear one," Canath holds Florence's hand to his lips and kisses it reverently, "without you I could not go on."

Phoenix and Kenny are both lying on their beds, hands behind their heads and thinking deeply about what Canath has shown them so far. They both feel disconnected from reality as if they have been thrown into another world, and not of their own choosing. They are too bemused to be frightened, and yet they also feel the comfort of being in their parents' close proximity. At least they are no longer four children alone.

"How come Father is here at all?" Kenny tries to fathom how a father who was killed before they were born is here, and very much alive.

"I think Father must be immortal," Phoenix replies, "perhaps he was to all intents and purposes, killed, but then somehow his body reanimated itself. Remember he just appeared in the kitchen from nowhere. He must have passed through the Curtain to get to us, so perhaps immortals can travel when and where they like without the sigils."

"Do you think mother is immortal too?" Kenny asks, his eyes wide with wonder.

"I think we will find out soon, Kenny," Phoenix is also wondering if this could be true.

Aletheia is sitting in her room, combing her long hair and musing about what her father has shown them. She understands now that he and their mother must be immortal, and perhaps this is why she recollects fragments of her father after his so-called death. Now she is beginning to understand how this could be so. The question she put to Canath still remains unanswered, and she hopes he will tell them more soon. If as he related to them, the current year is 2020, how is it possible for the Athens of her home to be in ruins? Has this to do with the damage to the plenum? Questions keep coming to her, and Aletheia keeps brushing.

Antheia lies with her eyes closed but is far from sleep. She is aware of Ladon going about the imprinting as is now her normal, but as she thinks about him, there is a fluttering under her skin. She opens her eyes in surprise and reaches with her hand to lay it flat over her swelling belly. Again, the fluttering comes, and she is able to feel movement under her hand and under her skin. These are the first movements of the baby, Ladon. The fact of carrying a tiny being within her own body becomes real to her for the first time. This is really happening!

She closes her eyes once more and thinks about this tiny being who is a part of her own body. Her hands lay over him as if to protect him, and she is filled with an immense love for this tiny child.

It is time to eat their midday meal, so Florence reaches out with her mind and summons the four children back to the kitchen. Each smile in response and slowly they make their way down the spiraling stairs, to the flagstone passage leading to the kitchen room. The children are all silent, still lost in their own thoughts, but they take their places along the bench seat as their parents seat themselves at each end of the table. There is a platter of cold chicken with fresh bread rolls and butter; each partakes, but they do not seem to notice what they are eating, so absorbed are they. At last, Florence addresses her brood.

"Children, we must get on with your lessons soon and to help you to understand, I want each of you to drink a cup of the brew we use here, when we need to work efficiently. It is strong, but it will enable your conscious mind to relax sufficiently for the unconscious imagery to go to work. You are all aware of your fire-born powers even though you, Kenneth, are still learning control. These powers must be flexed and exercised before you leave this place. Each day, you will drink the brew, and each day, your powers will become stronger. This is essential and what you were all born to. Antheia, go to your room and rest, I will join you shortly. Now let the rest of us take our cups and get back to work in the room at the top of the tower."

Henry

As the sigil cools and returns to how it was before, the men begin to whisper to each other, and Steven and Peter look at each other. Peter raises his eyebrows to signal Steven to continue.

"I think we have just witnessed the sigil at work," Steven starts, "but how and why I cannot tell you. I can't see how it could have been triggered though because none of us touched it."

"Could there be some other way to get it working?" John asks, "maybe an animal or bird?"

"Surely we would have seen it if that was the case," Steven thinks aloud. "There is no evidence of that, and if my reading of the sigil is correct, then we would have noticed flames emanating from it. Let me think for a minute."

Steven squats down and puts his hands over his face. He can't imagine what caused the sigil to operate, but it is quite obvious it happened, they all witnessed it! "I suggest we all move ahead as far as we can to see what lies beyond the turning, and if there is nothing explanatory there, then let's go back towards the entrance and look more closely at the walls and floor there. I don't want to touch the sigil until we can find the answer to this conundrum. Do any of you have a better idea?"

Peter and John nod, and the other men can think of nothing, so they set off again, torches lit, being careful not to touch the walls, and watching the floor for any signs that could explain what they have just witnessed. As they round the turning, they gasp aloud and many of the men crouch down as if expecting something to launch an attack on them.

"What on earth is that?" Peter's eyes are like saucers, and the crouching men sheepishly rise to standing position again. There, at the end of the cavern, lies what looks like a gigantic, petrified nest, now turned to glassy rock. Although there is no sign of anything living here, there are signs that something indeed lives or lived here recently.

Scattered around the nest are partial skeletons of large animals, and some of the bones look disturbingly human. All have the appearance of being burnt around the edges, and there are still fragments of dried flesh attached to some. There is no smell of putrefying flesh however, so whatever feasted on these unfortunate creatures must have caused their bodies to be thoroughly cooked. The gigantic proportions of the nest, originally built from large tree branches and now reduced to glassy rock, suggests the creature to be of gigantic proportions too. But if this is so, as the evidence attests, how on earth did it get in and out of the cavern? It is only at this end of the cavern that the roof is high enough for whatever creature lived here to be able to move around. What is it that they are evidencing here? That is the question on everyone's minds!

Steven walks forward and carefully lays a finger on the rock of the nest. It is cool to touch, and he cannot intuit anything from it, but his mind is working overtime, and suddenly, he spins around to face the others.

"I think what we have here, is a dragon's lair. There is nothing else that makes sense. The sigil warns of the dragon's presence and the evidence of what happened to anything or anyone who braved to enter here is spread all around us. Look at that dark patch on the floor. I would lay odds on that it is blood and quite a lot of it at that! The only question is, does the dragon still inhabit this cavern, or has it gone?"

This last question has the men searching around them nervously. None of them wants to meet the owner of this nest.

"Let's get out of here while we can!" Liam is terrified more by this than by the idea of living here for the rest of his life. The other men are looking askance too. Peter, John and Steven are too absorbed in this mystery to feel the danger that is troubling the others, but it might be as well for them to carefully check the way back to the entrance. Then if they find nothing else, they can take a vote on what to do next.

Henry cannot feel anything, Henry does not inhabit a body now. Yet there is awareness as if his spirit is flying through nothing at all. Space there is not. Time there is not. There is the awareness of light, and suddenly, the answer to the Universe is clear and rapturous. How simple, how magnificent, how so unlike anything carnate. A deep peace descends, and

Henry, who is no longer Henry, knows that only here is there nothing negative. Only here is everything wonderful and exactly as it has always been. Disembodied, Henry floats on.

The men arrive back at the entrance to the cavern; they have seen nothing else to indicate why what they witnessed inside occurred. As they shine torches around the entrance, Liam notices the colour of the path just outside.

"Will you look at that!" he exclaims, "this was not here before. And what happened to the giant footprints?"

Steven moves up to examine what Liam is looking at, and suddenly, he understands what has occurred.

"I know what this is," he says breathlessly, "and I think I know who triggered the sigil. The prints have disappeared and in their place is the same smooth, black, glassy surface as the walls inside. There has been an immolation here and that is how the sigil was triggered. Thank God none of us stood on the prints because they act in the same way as the sigil. Whoever stood here was immolated by superheated fire; the glassy surface indicates just that."

"But who could have been outside while we were in there?" Liam asks, "Were we followed by someone?"

"I think that our nemesis followed us here and unwittingly stood on the prints. If Henry waited until the men guarding him were at a low ebb, then made his escape, he would have come here as we did, to find out what Greg and Tim found, yes?"

The others consider Steven's idea, and it seems the most plausible.

"I think we must return to the cavern," Peter suggests, "let's find out if Steven is right, and if so, we need to get the others and return here as soon as possible. If we can get back quickly, I think we can work out a way to connect with the sigil and perhaps get home."

Greg and Tim

Gavinar is the first to recover his senses and speak.

"So, my friends, do you understand now why I wanted you to meet with Felix?"

"I don't understand," Greg states, "how can you possibly have recognized us? Were you responsible for us landing here, in this place and time?"

"Absolutely not," Gavinar replies, "believe it or not, that was pure chance."

"Utter rubbish!" Tim is beyond frightened and turns his fear to anger. "You want us to believe that in all the Universe, the fact that we landed here was a random occurrence? That is too far-fetched even for you, Gavinar, who we wouldn't trust as far as we could throw you!"

Gavinar does not react to this slur; he understands that Tim is fearful, and the startling facts do indeed appear to be contrived, even though he and Felix have no conception how that could be the case. The orb is also a random discovery; Felix happened on the box, its contents and how it operates by pure chance and still does not fully understand how it works or why. It has been the subject of his experiments since he found it some two years ago.

There are too many coincidental facts that when merged together speak of contrivance and with a great deal of skill and planning. All four men think about the intricacies necessary for the facts to emerge at all. This can be no mere human contrivance, because so few humans are cognizant of the plenum at all, let alone how to traverse it. As far as Tim and Greg understand, their quest with Henry is the first experiment of its type ever undertaken, so none of what they have now just witnessed makes any sense at all in everyday scientific terms.

"We need to get to the bottom of this right now, Gavinar, or you can try to stop Tim and me from leaving, but in that case, someone is going to die, I swear to God!" Greg jumps to his feet, furious and unable to take any more, obviously this is the last straw. Greg, like Tim is now fed up with the subterfuge and ready to fight or flee. Both men are at their wits end with everything that has happened over the last seven days, and they are no longer willing to be patient with anyone, let alone the two crazies standing before them at the moment.

"Please calm down, both of you," Gavinar raises his hands in a placating gesture. "There must be a way we can all work together to discover what has happened and why. We solve nothing by fighting, and there is much to solve. Felix and I really don't know how you came here; we barely know what the orb actually is, let alone how it works, or why your city should be the scene played out on it. I don't think anywhere else is displayed in the orb, so your problems are our problems, or so it seems to me."

Greg's face is set, and his hands are balled into fists; he stares angrily at Gavinar and Felix in turn. "If you want any cooperation from Tim and me, Gavinar," he turns his face to their host, "then you had better call off your watch-dog there; if he tries to hold me down with his gaze again, I will smash his face into a thousand pieces. I have had enough of your games, so you had better tell us immediately what this is all about. One chance only, Gavinar!"

Gavinar stands completely still, trying to think how to defuse the situation. It is apparent to him that unless he and Felix can elicit the cooperation of these men, then their hopes of finding out what the orb is, will be compromised. After a few seconds, he tries once more to placate Greg.

"I think, Felix," he says, "you need not try to hold these men again; their future and ours is tied so inextricably, that without both sides working together, they will not get back to their own time, and we will be left with what we have so far, an unsolvable conundrum."

Felix understands what Gavinar is implying and immediately sets about apologizing for his aggressive tactics.

"I am truly sorry, Greg, please accept my apologies, and please let's try to work this out together. As a gesture of goodwill, if you and Tim wish to leave right now, I will not try to stop you. But I would much rather we all tried to figure out what has happened in our two completely different times and places. As you say, it all smacks of contrivance, but by whom and why? That is the question we must start with, yes?"

"Then it is time for you and Gavinar to tell us what has happened here. After that Tim and I will decide whether or not we will cooperate. That is our only offer, and you can both decide right now."

"We accept," Gavinar replies, and with little further ado, he summons Petyr from the kitchen and asks for coffee to be prepared. Felix does not look askance at Gavinar taking charge of his house this way. He realizes how close they have come to losing their one and only chance to solve the puzzle of the orb.

"So," Tim speaks now, "you and Felix were going to have us tethered by your servants, were you? I see big Damon is here, too."

"I am sorry for making such a disastrous mistake," Gavinar looks suitably abashed. "It is just that we so desperately need your help, and we couldn't countenance losing you. Please forgive us, and let's start again. I promise you we will not make the same mistake again."

"I want to speak to my partner alone, Gavinar, so you and Felix can leave us. We will call you when we have conferred." Greg sits down next to Tim and stares at the two men. Quickly and quietly, they leave the room. Greg breathes a sigh of relief. He knows full well that if push came to shove, he and Tim would be unlikely to be able to overpower all four of the men. His bluster has served to communicate their unwillingness to be part of any game playing, however, so now he and Tim must decide whether or not to trust Gavinar and Felix.

"What do you think?" Greg asks Tim.

"I think after what we just witnessed with the orb," Tim replies, "we must trust that both of them want to solve this as much as we do, and that will keep us safe. Perhaps the orb is some kind of portable sigil, or perhaps we can work out a way to use it. Once we are back in Kettering, regardless of whether Felix and Gavinar come with us, we are back on home turf, so I don't see how they can be a danger after that."

"You are right," Greg thinks the same, "we can lose them anytime we want if we can get back to our own time, so we cooperate?"

"Yes, Greg, I think that is our best chance of getting home."

Greg calls for Gavinar and Felix to come back, and they enter with a tray of coffee and cakes. Both sides are still wary of each other, but both sides are hoping that this unlikely truce will lead to a win, win situation for them all.

Brandon

Several minutes pass and gradually Brandon's lethargy begins to subside. So much has happened in so short a time that he can hardly believe it is all real. He feels as if he is just now awakening from a nightmare. Slowly, testing his legs carefully, he stands and makes his way over to the bed. He sits again and runs his hands over his face. Taking several deep breaths, he starts to feel better and looks around him for the first time. The room is well appointed but simple, and there is a full-length mirror on the wardrobe door. He makes his way over and glances at his reflection. He scarcely recognizes the man looking back to him. No wonder the concierge looked askance at him!

His clothes are grubby and stained and wrinkled beyond normal. His face is grey, and his eyes have a haunted look similar to those of a battle-scarred soldier. He lifts his bloody shirt and the angry red scar on his chest looks swollen, so perhaps it is infected. Brandon walks into the bathroom and turns the shower on to hot. Quickly he shrugs out of his disgusting apparel and sits down under the cascade of hot water. He does not know how long he just sits there, but eventually he rises and using the bar of soap provided, washes first his hair and then his whole body, grimacing with pain as he scrubs the burn mark. At last, he turns off the water and dries himself with the soft, white towel. He ties the towel around his waist and returns again to the bedroom and lays down on the bed. In seconds he is sleeping, so he does not hear the gentle knocking on the door.

It is dusk when Brandon once more opens his eyes, and for a second, he can't remember where he is. As soon as his memory fills in the gaps, he sits up and swings his legs down off the bed. On the chair beside a small table at the opposite side of the room, sits a man with long grey hair tied back in a ponytail. He is watching Brandon, and as soon as he sees the look on Brandon's face, he rises and crosses the room.

"How are you feeling, son?" the man inquires.

Brandon stands, and moving to the other man, he grasps him in an embrace.

"Dad, how did you get there so quickly?" Brandon can scarce believe his eyes.

"I was already in San Francisco at a conference," his father replies, "so when your mother called to tell me you had turned up in Hawaii, I jumped on the first flight I could get. The concierge let me in when he realized I was your father."

"I have never in all my life been so glad to see you," there are tears in Brandon's eyes, and he grips his father hard. So much has happened to me, and I hardly know how to explain to you what I have been through."

"Before you do that, you need to eat, and I will go downstairs to the shopping mall and find some clothes for you. I gave what you were wearing to the cleaning staff to wash. I ordered a meal for you, so it should be here soon. They left a sandwich on a tray at the door, but I sent it back to the kitchen when I found you asleep in here."

"I don't know how to thank you, Dad, I was nearly at the end of my tether."

"Just rest and eat as soon as your meal gets here; I will be back as soon as I have what you need. You are quite safe now, and I will check you over myself after you have eaten." His father quietly moves to the door and leaves. Brandon sighs deeply and at last begins to relax. He tries desperately not to think about Athens and the men he has forsaken there. He will tell it all to his father, and maybe they can work something out to rescue the others. For now, there is simply nothing further he can do.

Dr Fellings takes out his phone as he descends the stairs. The call he makes sets in motion what will soon become an international incident. If he had known what was going to ensue from this call, he would have thrown his phone into the ocean. He has no idea what his son has been involved in, and so, he cannot choose to do other than he has just done. In years to come, he will remember how he did not think about this move for a second. Outside, the sun is setting as only it does in Hawaii, and the colour show is extraordinarily beautiful.

As Brandon picks at the best meal he has seen in over a week, he looks towards the door, hoping his father will return soon. There cannot be too much to choose from in the way of clothes, and Brandon does not care what he wears. His main concern is getting back to Kettering as fast as is possible. There is the matter of his passport too; how is he going to be able to depart Hawaii without it? Worries begin to beset him again, and he tries desperately to keep his anxiety at bay. Hyperventilation makes him light-headed, and he rushes to the bathroom to throw up. What on earth is he going to do? He slumps onto the bathroom floor, a headache beginning to pound.

The Family

Florence sits down next to Antheia while she sleeps. There is much to plan for the coming birth, not the least of which is how it will be accomplished when she has no idea what the baby will be like. Will it resemble Ladon, or will it be a normal human baby? This question worries Florence most of all; she does not want to lose her daughter to an impossible, alien birth! She worries about how this birth is possible at all. In all the literature written about dragons, they are hatched from eggs, so what does this live birth mean? Florence pulls her thoughts together; she admonishes herself to remember that all dragon stories are just that — stories born from the imagery of the unconscious archetypes. In fact, nobody alive today believes that dragons are in any way real, they are the stuff of fairytales and urban myth. Nobody in this age of science has stopped long enough to think about the fact that the dragon image is extant in all places and all times. This is the most apparent clue to whether or not a form of reality stands behind the legends.

Although it is mere weeks since Antheia visited Ladon's lair, Florence knows that the baby is growing at an exponential rate and that the birth is not far off. She and Canath have recalled the children to the tower room to go on with their personal history lesson, but Florence leaves Antheia to sleep. She must rest while she can and reserve her strength for the ordeal to come.

As Canath speaks, the children listen attentively; the story of their birth is now to be told. First, Canath reverts to the time of his and Florence's meeting and the reason for their bond. He sets a page filled with their family tree on the laptop for the children to follow. There is so much to relate that he knows this will merely be the first step.

"I was born the son of Achilles, himself the son of Poseidon and Thetis, a Greek Nereid." Canath begins, "Thetis's husband was Peleus, and he was reportedly Achilles' father, but the seed of an immortal cannot be displaced by that of a mortal. Poseidon had captured and raped her before her marriage to Peleus, and she swore she would only give birth to an immortal. Each time she became pregnant with Peleus's child, she dropped the child at birth into a bucket of sea water to drown. At last, angry with each child's so-called still birth, Peleus swept into the birth tent and saved Achilles from drowning in the bucket like the rest by grabbing him by the heel. This child, Achilles, the son of a goddess and an immortal father would later save the Greeks at the battle of Troy. During that battle, Achilles' wife was given to him as a prize by the Trojan priest of Apollo, Chryses. Her name was Briseis, and she fell pregnant with me during the battle. I have been named many names in many different times, but for now I am Canath, and I am an immortal through my grandfather, Poseidon." Canath watches as the children absorb this lineage and follow it back through the family tree displayed. As soon as he has their attention again, he begins once more.

"Your mother, Florence, has a different lineage. Her name was originally Flora, a Roman nymph living in the Elysian fields. She became Chloris when our lives came together. Chloris is the Greek Goddess of flowers like Flora and of new birth and fecundity. We were destined to be together from the beginning of mortal 'time'. Your coming into being, was destined then. Your sister, Antheia, carries the immortality of your mother, Florence as you know her, and this is why she was destined to become the mother of Ladon, the immortal, who is to take mortal form. Only another immortal can undertake this gravely, onerous task.

"Aletheia, your name means 'truth' or 'unconcealing', and you are the true spirit of truth; the rock against which all must be tested because only you can judge whether or not another is telling the truth. You are to be the glue that holds the Universe into its configurations; you, the uncovering of reality into all its forms, unsullied by untruth, falsity or dissembling. Your part to play in this quest is to remain true so that none can pass through the sigils without your assent. You must take Ladon's place as guardian of the unconscious plenum until he grows into his immortal powers once again." Canath watches Aletheia absorb this, her fated role, and she does so with aplomb. Canath then addresses his sons.

"Phoenix, my son, you are the way of being that rises from the ashes of your own death; your death can only be your rebirth, so son, there are hard times ahead for you, but you are up to this Herculean task. You are the meaning and the way of eternity. Being fire-born, you will die by immolation from time to time, and from the ashes of that immolation, you will rise anew. You are the eternal cycling of finite reality. Without your recycling motion, infinite finitude could not exist, and if that were the case, then there could be no existence."

Phoenix assents to this, his destiny with a barely perceptible nod to his father.

"Kenneth, your name is a derivative of my own, Canath. Together, you and I must protect the others from harm and watch over the Universe. Your destiny is entwined with mine, son, so soon I will need your strength, wisdom and calm to advance what needs must be done. Together, we must heal the rifts created by men who do not understand what they have done. We may well perish from the effort, even though we are immortal, for the Universe holds sway in every way, and we are but the tools of infinity."

"Father, I am ready," Kenneth pledges his life to Canath and the quest ahead.

"That is enough for now, my beauties," Canath stops speaking to allow the children time to contemplate their history and their future. Soon enough it will come to pass, and they must be given time to absorb all the implications of what they have just been told and form any questions that come to mind.

"It is time to break for the day, so you can all think about what you have been told and what your futures will be," Canath and Florence both rise and let the children descend the stairs before they do. All children return to their rooms. The boys begin to talk quietly, and Aletheia remains silent and thoughtful.

"Well, my dear," Florence addresses Canath, "you have done your best, and we must now await the results. I must begin the preparations for the birth, and I pray to the gods that Antheia will bear up under the ordeal to come. This is the most dangerous time for us all, for without the live birth of Ladon, everything will cease to exist."

"You speak the truth, Florence, but I have the feeling that Ladon would not have put himself or Antheia at risk. Yes, the birth will be an ordeal, but he has chosen Antheia, so I am sure she will come through. Let's get ourselves a drink and some food and retire to our room for a time. We have to conserve our strength as well."

Henry

"Are you sure we have the time to go back and collect the others?" John asks, "this may be our only chance to get home."

"How can I be sure of anything?" Peter replies, "you know as much as I do, but I am not prepared to give up and leave the others stranded here with no hope of returning home. Does anyone want to challenge that?"

The men talked quietly amongst themselves, but silence soon asserted itself again without any further dissent.

"Good, well let's get going so we can be back as soon as possible." Peter turns and begins the descent of the path. The others follow quickly — the false dawn is almost upon them, so the darkness is no longer absolute. As he descends, Peter tries to lay out plans for every contingency even though he really has no idea what to expect next. His supposition that it was Henry who followed them and who ultimately was immolated is his greatest worry, for if it was not Henry but someone else, then he will need to deal with Henry first and foremost. Wracking his brains for quick solutions is not helping, so he concentrates on getting back to the cavern quickly; the rest will have to happen as it will!

"Peter and the others are coming back," Derek calls from his lookout near the entrance. Since the moment the men realized Henry had escaped, they had kept a watch in case he returned. Now, with the return of those who had trusted them to guard Henry, they have a different set of worries, not the least of which is how angry the returning men will be. Geoff wakes the four sleeping men, and they all gather together to receive Peter and his band.

"Peter, thank goodness, you are back," Geoff begins, but Peter lifts his hand to silence the man.

"It's all right, Geoff, we know Henry escaped your clutches, so stop worrying. I assume you haven't found him?"

"I'm so sorry, Pete, we must have nodded off for a few seconds, and when we woke, he was gone." Geoff looks suitably contrite but at least he does not try to shift the blame.

"Well, we have news for you about Henry," Peter looks at the men, "he is no longer a danger to any of us. He must have followed us to the cave where Greg and Tim were sent to search, because not only did we find the sigil there, but Henry accidentally stood on some huge, alien footprints at the entrance of the cave, and they acted like a sigil. We now know, with Steven's help, that if the sigil is touched, flames of enormous heat immolate the toucher. So, Henry got his come-uppance, I should say."

Relief and puzzlement in equal measures flood the faces of the men, but Peter does not give them time to consider his news.

"We must get back to the cave immediately," Peter cuts through any other thoughts, "the sigil is still active, but we don't know for how long. It may be our last chance to get home, so pack a few necessities and let's get going."

As the others prepare, Peter searches through the equipment for something he can use to make contact with the sigil. A rod or long stick will do, so long as they can maintain themselves out of the reach of the flames for long enough for the sigil to do its job. At last, he spies the satellite antenna connection for the submersible and quickly he takes a screwdriver from his pack and disassembles the main rod. It is only about sixty centimeters long when fully extended, but beggars can't be choosers. This should do nicely! Dawn is beginning to break when the band of men leaves the cavern to return to the cave.

As they near the entrance, which is now almost visible because of the coming dawn, the men try not to imagine what occurred here to turn the rocky path into a black, shiny glass-like surface. Thankfully, there is nothing left of Henry's body at the scene. Careful not to touch the clearest patch, they sidle past and into the cave. Quickly now, and with torches ablaze, the men hurry to the main cavernous space. There, as before, and cut into the rock face stands the sigil. It is not as clear as before, but it is still there, nevertheless.

"Steven, I think I should allow you to work out what to do now," Peter defers his leadership role and steps back with the others. Steven approaches the sigil and careful not to touch the actual carving, he runs his hands over the rock face around the image. Several seconds pass before he stops, his hands still against the wall and closes his eyes. The other men watch silently. After what seems like an age, he gasps a huge breath, and a shudder passes through his whole body. He opens his eyes, which are now overly bright, and his whole visage appears to be shining. The men show their consternation but say nothing.

"OK, now comes the most dangerous part of all," Steven looks at each of them in turn. "From what I can glean, we must retain contact with each other, or we might find ourselves scattered throughout space and time."

"Do we know where we will end up anyway?" asks John.

"I can't tell you any more than you know already, but I think that our minds are the key." Steven is thinking out loud now. "If we all concentrate our minds on a scene from Kettering, perhaps that is the way to direct where and when we will go. Can anyone suggest a scene we all know?"

"How about the university green?" Peter knows that they have all been there.

"I think that's a great idea," Steven replies, "is there anyone here who does not know the green? OK, now I suggest we all link hands and do not let go whatever happens. Peter, do you want to hold the rod?"

"I guess someone has to," Peter does not want to do this, but he can't ask anyone else to do something he is not prepared to do himself.

"OK let's get ready for this," Steven takes control again. "Is everyone ready? Now empty your minds and picture the university green. Peter, now is the time to reach out to the sigil."

As soon as the rod makes contact with the sigil, there is a blinding flash, and Peter drops the white-hot rod. Before it hits the ground, their bodies begin to shimmer and then break up into what looks like dust mites. When the dust mites have disappeared, the surface of the wall is smooth again with no evidence left of the sigil.

Greg and Tim

"Tim and I have decided to trust you for now, but don't try to play games with us again, or we will leave regardless of your servants." Greg makes no show of fear, and his simmering anger is still written on his face. "In return, Gavinar, you and Felix will now tell us everything you know about the orb and how you found it. Do we have a working arrangement?"

"Yes, yes, Greg, and you won't regret it," Gavinar replies immediately. He and Felix breathe a sigh of relief. They really do not stand a chance of discovering anything further without the help of these two strangers. To seal the bargain, Felix signals for Petyr to fetch a bottle of his best wine. The four men begin to relax, but each pair regards the other still with some suspicion and trepidation. When they have all toasted their agreement, Gavinar stands to face the others.

"So, now I will tell you everything that happened and what we know. Two years ago, Felix and I were taking a walk through the fields near the coastline of Kungsbacka, about twenty-four kilometers from here. We took the journey because Felix needed to examine the mineral rocks along the cliffs around Kungsbacka. His work with the Alchemists had struck a problem, and he volunteered to undertake this task. We rode out in the change of seasons, spring was just turning to summer, so we did not have to contend with snow and ice. Our horses were well shod and fed, and both mounts were strong enough to make the journey. We arrived at our destination just after sunset on the second day and made for a shelter known to the Alchemists. It was a crude but strongly built hut with a fireplace and a larder stocked with dry goods. There was a lean-to barn for the horses, and after we had settled and fed them, we lit the fire, prepared a spartan meal, and then got ready for bed. We banked the fire so it would last the night.

"Around midnight, we were woken by the terrible noise of a storm coming in from the ocean. In that part of the country, and at the change of seasons such storms are common, but this one was ferocious. We did not dare to open the door to check the horses, so we boiled some water over the fire and made some coffee. We sat and talked until well after daybreak when the storm started to abate, and it was safe to go outside. The lean-to was mostly gone, trees were down, and the horses were very spooked, wet and bedraggled, so we did our best to calm and dry them and make sure their tethers were secure. Eventually during the morning, the sun came out and the storm was gone. It seemed the right time for us to walk down to the sea front and check out the cliffs. The sooner we finished the task, the sooner we could leave and ride back to Gothenburg.

"To get to the coast, we had to cross fields used for cattle and sheep. The stormwater runnels had carved long channels through some of these fields, and it was difficult to traverse. There were no livestock present; the farmers had not yet put them to this pasture, so at least we did not have to contend with storm infected animals. It was essential to watch where we stepped; we did not want to turn an ankle or step into a hole and break a leg, so we were looking intently where we were going. Felix was the first to spot what at first appeared to be a tree trunk sticking out of the ground. We had to walk in that direction, so we took care not to trip on any submerged roots, or so we thought at the time. As we got closer, the 'log' as we thought it, took on a different aspect, it was suspiciously proportioned with clean, geometrical lines. This was no log but obviously something man-made! Up close, we could see that it was a large wooden chest, bound with copper, and when we dug down and pulled it out, there was a large brass lock holding it secure. Someone had buried this box in the field at some time. We thought that it might contain gold or silver, so we quickly carried it back to the hut and gathered the horses and our belongings, all thought of the original task forgotten. We rode back to Gothenburg as quickly as we could, and again, arrived just after sunset the following day. Felix's house was closest, so we went there directly, and after they tended the horses, we sent the servants away. The chest was filthy, as were we, so we bathed and cleaned the chest as best we could, before setting about opening the big, brass lock. You can imagine our surprise when we saw the clear orb nestled in its velvet lining. What could this possibly be?

"At first, we could make no sense of it, but Felix has gained a semblance of power over inanimate objects by studying the ancients, and he intuited the orb was somehow 'alive', in the same way as Heraclitus described the lode stone to be. As he raised his hand to scratch his chin, the orb began to rise from the box. We were both transfixed, and even more so, when the scene from your Kettering played out through the orb's surface. We had never seen anything like it; the people moving about, their strange clothes, the even stranger buildings and the machines that people climbed inside to move about. You see, when you showed me the similar scene on your machine, I just knew it could not be coincidental. But what it signified, I had absolutely no idea. Paramount, however, was to keep the two of you here by any means necessary and take you to Felix so we could try to discover what was going on. The point is, we had to try to gain your favour. When you related to me your ability to move through time, then the possible purpose of the orb became clearer, or so I reasoned. That is the tale of our strange encounter with both the orb and with both of you. Do you think it could possibly be sheer coincidence, or are there other hands or minds at play here?"

Gavinar sits down again and looks intently at Greg and Tim. Both men remain silent for some time, gob smacked by what they have just heard. How could this alignment within the infinity of time and space occur if not by well and intricately laid planning? There seems no possibility of coincidence and yet, how could this happen otherwise? Greg decides they must research any and all written philosophies relating to the reality of space and time, and he knows this is going to take time. How to broach this with Gavinar and Felix?

"Felix and Gavinar, we have no idea what all this means either, but it surely cannot be coincidence. Tim and I are scholars at the university in Kettering, and by using my machine, we can start to try to gain some understanding of what is going on here. This may take time, because we will need to read through texts written over several hundred years by philosophers, past and present. There has been much argument over the years about the reality of space and time, what they are and how they are, and it is to this literature that I think we must go to try to find an explanation for what has occurred or at least an understanding of how it has happened. That is all I can suggest. We have access to the university library and the libraries of all universities in England and Europe, so we should be able to get any text that is relevant. My machine works by connection to what is called a satellite, a massive man-made object that has been launched onto space above the earth and held into orbit by the earth's gravity. It is connection with this that will also renew the charge necessary for my machine to keep working. I cannot explain beyond that now; so, what I have said will have to be enough for you, there is simply not the time to teach you both the science of how this works sufficient for you to fully understand, but this is where you will both have to trust us. Can you do that?"

"I don't think we have a choice," Felix intercedes in the discussion. "It seems to me that we have gone as far as we can in this, but if you can access your modern scientific principles, then may we at least join you in reading and trying to decipher them?"

"Of course," Tim replies, "we will need all our brains if we are going to find a solution to where we find ourselves right now."

Brandon

Dr Fellings let himself back into the room, suspecting that Brandon would be asleep again. He glanced at the small table and the hardly touched meal still sitting there; perhaps his son was more traumatized and anxious than he seemed earlier. No matter, the plan he forged earlier while waiting for Brandon to wake has been set in motion, and soon he will be able to get his son on a plane for home. How fortuitous it was that he was in San Francisco!

Unbeknownst to Brandon, his father is part of an intelligence cadre, formed ten years ago, largely at the behest of MI6. For some time, those in the know have been watching Henry Bonnington as he set in motion his plan to return to a time and place that he broke into purely by accident. Most scholars at the university found Henry's fantastic story to be merely speculation and aggrandizement, something Henry was well known for. This intelligence cadre had already become aware of the plenum as written about especially by Jung and physicist, Wolfgang Pauli, and Dr Fellings was a major contributor to that knowledge, having studied Pauli and Heisenberg's physics closely. Only those working on the classified project recognized what Henry had stumbled upon.

More to the point, they are seeking him regarding the disappearance of a highly classified piece of equipment being developed by the aeronautical and space engineers at the University of Northampton. After the twenty men and the submersible disappeared, the cadre was deeply worried. Without the knowledge of the reality underpinning time and space as we know them, those who had disappeared could create universal havoc and endanger all life.

Fellings needs to get his son home, where he can gently debrief him and find out whether his disappearance has anything to do with Henry's disappearance and the disappearance of the new submersible. He knows that Brandon is known to Henry and to the others who have also disappeared. Dr Fellings has alerted the head of the task force in MI6 and organized a plane to get Brandon back to the U.K as soon as possible. He will let Brandon sleep now until it is time to drive to the airport. Hopefully, he can give him a full physical and psychological check up in the privacy of the plane.

Brandon's backpack is still on the floor where he dumped it when he first entered the room, and his father now opens the top to see what is inside. Perhaps there is something that will indicate where Brandon has been. There is his laptop, of course, an empty water bottle, crumpled shirt and underpants, a packet that once contained a muesli bar, and at the bottom, what looks like, the transponder for the submersible! Fellings looks stunned, then realization begins to dawn. Could his son have used this to get here? An awful thought suddenly hits him. How involved in all this is Brandon? What if his son was a willing participant in the theft of the submersible and the disappearance? Fellings immediately regrets not checking the backpack when he first arrived, and Brandon slept. What he has done by alerting the authorities before checking with Brandon is tantamount to turning his son over to the full force of the law if, as it now seems, he is up to his neck in all this. Dismay hits him like a mack truck; this could be the end of Brandon's as well as his own career and even his freedom! He sits down to think.

Brandon opens his eyes once more, still groggy with exhaustion and anxiety. His eyes alight on the figure of his father, and the look on his face tells Brandon he has discovered the transponder. But how does his father know what it is? Fellings senior crosses quickly to the bed, and he sits on the end.

"Brandon, you must tell me quickly what this means." He holds out the transponder.

"Father, how do you know about this?" Brandon answers with his own question.

"I can't go into that right now, but suffice to say, I am part of the development team at the university. It is imperative that you tell me how you came by this."

"Father, Henry Bonnington recruited me along with eighteen others to make a journey through time." Brandon searches his father's face to see if he is believed. There is no sign of incredulity, so Brandon continues.

"I really had no choice, Father, I witnessed Henry kill another academic, and he made it very clear that I would not survive to tell the tale should I choose to do so."

"Go on," his father encourages.

"I told Henry I would not reveal anything, and from then on, he schooled me in the use of the new submersible, then made me second in command of his trip. We arrived in Athens, but there we found ourselves in a time warp. Instead of Athens as we know it, there was a ruined landscape and no signs of habitation. Henry sent the others out in pairs to find his sigil, but I don't think anyone did find it. I have an image on my laptop.

"Two men broke away from the main party and this angered Henry to the extent that he set off after them. While he was gone, he left me in charge. I think he was going to kill them if he found them, and he warned me not to do anything until he returned. I think he noticed my fear and distrust, and I thought he would take care of me in the same way when he got back. The only thing I could think to do was to escape before that happened."

Brandon began to sob; he buried his face in his hands. Fellings senior encouraged him to go on, telling Brandon they did not have much time.

"Father, I took the submersible and left all the others behind. I feel like such a coward. I left the other men to their fate. How are they ever going to get home again?"

Dr Fellings tries to calm his son enough for Brandon to tell him the rest; he must know what else occurred before he can decide what to do.

"Brandon, you must tell me the rest now; together we can try to work out how to rescue the others."

"I must have passed out when the submersible passed through the portal because when I awoke, it was night, and I was surrounded by Aborigines. I have no idea what time I crossed into, but they seemed not to recognize a white man. Their chief or witchdoctor helped me, and I fully awoke when he burnt my chest with a hot bone. See?"

Brandon moves the towel so his father can see the swollen burn. It is still red and angry looking, but Dr Fellings is more concerned with the information from his son.

"Tell me what happened next."

"I knew we were near the beach because I could hear the breakers, and I tried to communicate with these people to help me find the submersible. They must have understood to some degree because they took me down to the beach, and I found it wedged on a sandbank. I went on board and checked it. There was a burn mark over the console, so I was worried that it may no longer work. I took out the transponder, and when I switched it on, the console lit up too, so I quickly turned it off in case it was not fully operational. I took my pack and rejoined the Aborigines because if I was stuck there, I would need their help to survive. They took off running through the bush, and I kept up for about an hour, but by then, I could go no further. I couldn't even shout out to them because my throat was too dry. I was lost, hungry and thirsty and with no idea where they were going. I sat for a few minutes and then decided to try to backtrack to the beach. It was very hard going; I had to find footprints to be able to get back. I had on my runners but no socks, so my feet were getting blistered. I remembered I had my pack, so I looked inside and luckily, I found half a bottle of water and a muesli bar as well as socks.

"It took about four hours to find my way back, but when I did, the transponder was working. Like I said, I had tried it before and the light lit up, so I was hopeful it would work. I checked all the main components before trying again, and when I connected it, the console light showed that there was a portal there, so I left immediately. When the submersible surfaced again, I was here, at the base of the cliffs, which I climbed and found myself in this place. Father, what is this all about?"

"Brandon, where is the submersible now?" Fellings ignores Brandon's question.

"I sent it into standby mode near the shore at the bottom of the cliffs, Father, what's going on and how are you connected to all this?" Brandon senses his father knows much more than he has admitted so far, and he searches his father's face for any clues.

Dr Fellings sits thinking deeply. He must decide what to do and quickly if he is to save his son from the authorities. If only he had not called it in so soon! He banishes any recriminatory thoughts; they are not helping. He has to decide whether to tell Brandon everything, including his call, or manage the situation alone. Two heads are obviously better than one, but if he goes along this path, there will be no turning back. He, along with Brandon will be hunted. It comes down to his loyalty to the government, or his love for Brandon, and he has only one choice. He prays he might see his wife and daughter again, but for now, Brandon must be his first concern.

The Family

"Canath, how do you propose to help Kenneth achieve his necessary potential before we have to move on?" Florence is worried about their youngest son; at merely eight years, he of all the children will have the most gruelling path to forge him into his allotted role.

"Don't fret, my love, I will take him under my wing. He will be fine; our paths are one and the same, so he will remain with me for the foreseeable future."

"Do you think all the children will be able to undertake their roles? I cannot help worrying for each of them; I suppose it is a mother's burden."

"Florence, they have all been tested over the last several years, and none of them has been found wanting. If anything, they have surpassed what we expected, especially Aletheia and Phoenix. They have the hardest tasks, but they also have the finest of natures, and don't forget, if Antheia's pregnancy is anything to go by, Ladon will mature much faster than a mere human child could possibly do. He will then lead us all through those tasks necessary to hold infinity into its shining."

From sleep to wakefulness in a flash, Antheia feels the first signs that indicate that the birth of Ladon is imminent. Ladon calms her and reassures her that they both will be fine. Savage pains begin to beset her, but she grits her teeth and silently calls out to her mother. Florence jolts awake and immediately knows that the birth is coming now. Quickly she rises and wakes the others as well as Brian and Marcom. Marcom has a role to play in this birth and has been waiting all his adult life for what is soon to materialize. Florence bids them all to dress and make their way to Antheia's room, and she and Canath dress and leave their room to head there too.

Marcom rises and slowly, carefully dons the robe made for him over a span of several centuries. The spinners, a family in which the craft has been passed down from father to son for as long as anyone can remember, have painstakingly fashioned it from the finest gossamer silk, spun by millions of spiders for this singular occasion. He feels the weightlessness of it and begins the chanting that will open his mind into the plenum to enjoin with the light of existence; his whole life to this point will now be tested. He empties his mind of everything, down to the last vestige of conscious thinking, until pure nothingness begins to shimmer. As the shining begins to encompass him, he lets himself drift into it. He is ready and should he die in the process, he is totally at peace.

Brian dresses quickly before going to check that Marcom is ready. His brother is barely visible, except for the light shining through him, and the small vial he carries in his hand. All is in readiness. He takes his brother's hand and leads him down the stairs to Antheia's room. The girl is in great pain, her hair already drenched with sweat, and she is barely able to keep still. Marcom kneels across the room from her bed and waits in trance.

"We are all here, Antheia, you are about to bring the Healer of Rifts into the world, and the gods will sing your praises forever." Brian raises his hand and makes the sign of the benediction over the writhing girl. Florence, Canath, Aletheia, Phoenix and Kenneth enter, the boys and Aletheia are unnerved by the sight of their sister in such great pain. Phoenix puts his arm around Kenneth's shoulders to give him moral support.

Florence moves to Antheia's side and takes her hands in her own.

"It won't be long now, child," she soothes her daughter, "the midwife is ready, and we will all remain to bear witness to this monumental event."

Canath approaches the bedside and puts a strong piece of leather into Antheia's hand.

"For you to bite down on, child, should the pain become unbearable." He steps back and allows Florence to take over. Silently, Florence summons the midwife. She is a strong-looking, older woman, who bows low to Florence and Antheia as she approaches the bedside. Firstly, she checks Antheia's pulse, then her heartbeat using a trumpet-like device. She then places the device on Antheia's huge bulging stomach and listens carefully. She nods to Florence, and the two women converse silently. Florence has blocked the communications from the others here present.

The midwife lifts the soft blankets to check Antheia's cervix for dilation and tells Florence that she is ready. All the normal timespans of regular birth are thrown to the winds in this case. It is happening at such a swift rate that Florence is slightly alarmed, but the midwife stays calm and watchful; she has years of experience and knows that each birth is singular. There simply is no accurate guide of times and events where birth is concerned. Within minutes the contractions come closer together and the midwife encourages Antheia to start to push. The poor girl is pale and stricken, but with every ounce of her strength, she pushes when the midwife asks her to. In between she gathers herself for the next contraction, and she silently speaks her love to her infant. At last, the child's head is crowning and with one last almighty effort, Antheia sets her baby free.

There is no cry from him, and Marcom stands and crosses to the bedside. With infinite care, he takes the newborn baby into his arms and sings softly in an archaic language that nobody else present has ever heard. The silver-haired child watches him intently with colorless eyes, and as he sings, Marcom removes the stopper from the vial of spider venom and gently tips the contents into the baby's mouth. At once there is a thunderous roar that shakes the very foundations of the tower. The rest of the family look disconcerted, but no more than that. The baby opens eyes that are now bright green and closes his fingers around Marcom's finger. The two converse silently in the archaic language of the song. At last Marcom returns Ladon to Antheia's arms, and she holds him tightly against her body, crooning to him with absolute love. Unnoticed, Marcom slips from the room.

The midwife shoos the rest of the family and Brian from the room as she prepares Antheia for one last effort to shed the afterbirth. Florence remains with her, and as she begins to bathe her daughter, she praises her for her bravery and strength in delivering this immortal child. She also notices that Antheia's eyes are her own again. Ladon nestles against his mother but peeks at Florence and the midwife with his large, green eyes.

"What was that terrible noise?" Kenneth whispers to Phoenix as soon as they are clear of the birthing room. He is still clinging to his brother; he really does not understand what has just happened.

"That was the Universe announcing the birth of Ladon, Kenny," Phoenix answers his brother, "Marcom anointed Ladon with the most potent spider venom."

"What?" Kenny's eyes widen at this revelation. "How do you know that and how come it didn't kill him?"

"I don't know how I know, but I also know that Marcom's robe was made from spider silk, the lightest and strongest natural fiber in the Universe. I don't know how long it took to make, but you can be sure, hundreds of generations of a family of spinners have worked on it."

"What does all this mean, Phoenix?" Kenneth is awed by the revelations and not just a little scared.

"It marks the beginning of our odyssey, Kenny; the start of what we were born to do as father told us yesterday. Our whole lives have been marked with these tasks since before we were born, and not by our own choosing."

"Does that mean Mother and Father don't really love us?"

"No, Kenny, it means just the opposite; we are the product of our mother and father, and they love us more than anything else in the whole Universe. If they did not, we could not do what must be done."

As soon as the midwife allows, the family file back into Antheia's room to greet the new family member. Canath and Florence both take turns to hold the child and whisper their greetings and love to him. Aletheia is next and she holds the child close. Phoenix and Kenny step up to take their turn, and Ladon looks each brother in the eyes. He smiles at both boys and melts their hearts. As Kenny takes his brother in his arms, he feels the greatest love he has ever known and Ladon whispers to him silently,

"I am your loving brother, Kenny, and I will never let anyone, or anything hurt you. Our future has begun!"

Kenny kisses his new brother and hands him back to Antheia.

Henry

There is a twinkling of dust motes and as they become more solid, the echo of a massive sonic boom reverberates. The forms of the men from the cave begin to shimmer and then solidify into human form. The faces of the men are white and each stand on shaky legs as they try to clear their minds. There is darkness, total and absolute. It is impossible for them to see their hands in front of them. Hearts start to pound with fear. Where on earth *are* they, and are they on earth at all? As the booming echo begins to fade, there is a return to the night sky of a plethora of bright stars. From absolute darkness to silver star light in moments, the men look on in awe. The heavenly show continues with the electric green, red and purple swirling colours of the northern lights, Aurora Borealis. Suddenly, as if coming out of a stupor, the men feel the icy air and the snow under their feet. None is dressed for this cold, but at least they are wearing their climbing boots!

"Where do you suppose we are?" John turns to Peter, shivering.

"Is everyone OK?" Peter asks, more concerned about whether or not there are any injuries from passing through the Curtain. His left hand is throbbing with the burn sustained from holding the rod, and he squats to take a handful of snow. The relief is immediate.

"Well, we certainly left Athens behind, but for what and where?" As usual, most of the men are under the impression that Peter knows what they do not. Derek peers around him sulkily.

"Why would you think I have the answers to your questions?" Peter is tired of having to think for them. "I am as clueless as you; we are all in this together, so quit asking me stupid questions that I can't answer!"

"Obviously, we have come into somewhere in the far north. I suggest we look around for any signs of human habitation before we become meals for polar bears or arctic wolves," Steven takes the lead, "We may be able to find signs that tell us where we are."

"Thank you, Steven," Peter replies, "at least one of us is able to think."

"I don't think we are too close to the Arctic Circle, the air is frigid but not freezing, so it is either spring season coming into Arctic summer, or we are somewhere in Scandinavia or Russia; perhaps even Canada or Iceland. Until daybreak gives us more light, if there is daylight here, we just have to be patient and try to find some sort of shelter. At least we haven't landed in a blizzard!" Steven has the men calming down again, and Peter is very grateful.

"Did you all hear the massive sonic boom echo when we materialized?" Steven is not going to give in to fear, he knows that to do so is the quickest way to become paralyzed and unable to act. Rather, he is considering and reflecting on the process they have all just experienced, and he wishes he had a notebook to record his thoughts.

"Was that a condition of passing through the Curtain, do you think Steven?" John is also trying to remain calm and think.

"No, I think it was something else, but what I don't know."

"Right then, let's get moving men, before we all freeze to death." Peter takes control again, and the men are more than happy to do his bidding. At least that way, they don't have to make any decisions for themselves.

There is light enough for the men to see where they are putting their feet, and the ground seems to be relatively flat as far as they can see. As their eyes accustomed to the faint light, they can make out the darker form of a range of mountains or perhaps icebergs off to their right, so they begin to trek in that direction.

"Take it slowly," Peter advises, "and watch where you are putting your feet. We have no idea if there are any patches of thin ice below the snow; we could be walking on top of an ocean!"

This idea ensures that the men are indeed careful to test the ground beneath their feet before putting their full weight down. Slowly and carefully, the men move towards the higher landmark. The walking may be slow, but at least their movements slacken the icy grip of the cold, and soon the men begin to regain feeling in their feet and hands. They set their minds on the trek and try not to think about anything else. All ears are vigilant, however, for any sounds of movements other than their own. Steven's suggestion of polar bears has been taken seriously.

As the darkness gradually begins to lighten, the men can see that the snow beneath their feet is becoming thinner, and within minutes, breaks in the snow announce solid ground beneath their feet. Relief begins to set in, and the men become less frightened and less morose. The ambient air temperature seems to be less cold as the dark begins to lighten slightly.

"I think it is safe to say we are on solid ground," Peter stops and takes in the surrounding vista. "We seem to be leaving the snowfield behind, so I am hoping that there will be a settlement of some kind where we are headed."

There is no reply from the men, so with Peter in the lead, they keep moving, quickening their pace now, heading towards what now appears to be a barren mountain range. There is no clue to the time of day or the time they have landed in, but at least they are on solid ground, and the gradually increasing light suggests dawn is on the way.

Another hour passes and now faint light can be distinguished behind the mountains. They are indeed barren, but there seems to be some low growth in dark green patches, and there is the hint of smoke, merely a haze rising from near the bottom edge of the rising land. The men head towards the rising haze, hoping against hope that it signals a house or cabin. They are all very thirsty and ravenous as well as cold.

As a faint sun, really only a glow, begins to lighten the barren mountains, the men can make out a row of low houses, their rooves overhanging the walls almost to ground level. There is so sign of movement, but the haze has definitely materialized into smoke rising from several chimneys, built into the middle of the roof of each.

"We need to approach this settlement with caution," Peter suggests, "we don't know if they will welcome strangers here."

"Pete, the houses are obviously contemporary with our own time," John is much happier now, "don't you think they will offer us hospitality. At least we can find out where and when we are."

There is the faint sound of dogs barking at several houses, and as they get closer, one door opens, and a large dog comes running towards them. The men stop, hoping they don't have to contend with a savage guard dog. The last thing they want to do is to harm anyone's pet; that will not endear them to the inhabitants of this settlement!

The dog stops about twenty yards from the men and stopping barking, it tests the air with raised nose to get their scent, but it does not growl. Steven steps forward and whistles through his teeth, then squats and puts out his hand. The rest of the men step back as the dog approaches. Warily, the dog approaches Steven, the hackles along its back raised. It reaches out to sniff Steven's hand, and he reaches out with the other hand to lay it gently on the dog's head. It snuffles Steven and its tail begins to wag. Introductions are accepted and the dog turns tail and heads back to the house. The men begin to breathe again.

"That was very brave, Steven," Peter says, "I thought we were dog meat."

"I have two large dogs of my own, so I know reasonably well whether or not they are going to attack. That fellow was just checking us out, and we can now approach his house safely so long as we don't show any sign of aggression."

As the men approach the house, a bearded, middle-aged man steps out onto a low porch fronting the house. He carries a shotgun under his arm, and the dog stands next to him, both watching the approaching men. The man tells the dog in English to sit. He drops to the floor and puts his head on his massive, shaggy paws.

"Good morning, sir," Peter addresses the man politely, "could you tell us where we are, please?"

"Why, you have just arrived in Savissivik. Lucky for you it's almost summer, or you would have frozen to death out there." He points in the direction the men have come from. "From where have you come?"

"That is one long story," Peter replies, "I know there are many of us, but could we prevail on you for some water? It is more than twenty-four hours since we ate or drank, and thank goodness it is cold here, or I think we might have perished from thirst."

The man looks sharply at the group standing around his front porch; he is not quite sure what to make of these men. He has never seen one man arrive from out of the snowfields, let alone sixteen. They may be dangerous.

"Please, sir," Steven speaks, "we have a bizarre tale to tell, but we are very cold, hungry and thirsty, so could you find it in your heart to let us into your house? We are not armed, and my friend here has a bad burn on his hand. We are all scholars from the university in Kettering, Northamptonshire, England. I have a laptop in my backpack, and I can verify who we are from the university website, if you are willing to help us and can spare us some food and water."

Still the man assesses those in front of him for a few moments more, but then makes a decision and steps aside so they can enter. The dog follows them into an open area containing a large wood burner in the centre, with a kitchen, table and four chairs at one end, and a large sofa and a desk at the other. The contents of the room confirm that this is contemporary with their own time; and the men begin to relax. At least they are back in their own time!

The house is obviously the home of a single person with two rooms leading from the open space. There is only room for seven men to sit on the furniture, so the others sit on the floor, which is blessedly warm and cosy. The dog climbs into its large basket, and after turning several times, flops down, all the time keeping the men in sight.

"Now then," the owner of the house speaks, "I can offer you water or black tea, what would you prefer? I am afraid you will have to take turns; I only have a dozen cups and glasses all told."

"Water first, please," Peter immediately replies, "and then if it is not too much trouble, the tea would be very welcome."

"You are lucky you came to my door," the man says, "not everyone here speaks English. In fact, I am English."

"This may sound like a really bizarre question, but in what country are we precisely?" Peter is now happy to engage this man; if he is

English, then they can prove to him that they are also.

"This is Greenland," the man replies, a surprised look on his face, "how can you be here, and not know that?"

"Well, first let me prove to you that we are who we say we are, then I will tell you the most bizarre tale you have ever heard, even more so because it is true."

"That sounds fair," the man is intrigued now; he prepares the tea and fetches a loaf of bread and a pot of butter from a small pantry and puts them on the kitchen counter. Peter removes his laptop from his backpack and connects to the satellite. Soon he opens to the university webpage and clicks on the staff inventory. The man is watching him as he prepares the spartan meal.

Peter summons the man to come near and begins by opening the staff pages applicable to each of the men present. Their photographs are displayed along with their academic credentials and lists of their published work. The man carefully reads each and checks the faces in front of him to ensure they are the scholars from the staff list. At last satisfied, he sits with them and proffers cups, mugs and glasses along with slices of buttered bread. The men thankfully tuck in.

"Can I ask why you are here?" Peter regards the man with interest.

"I assume you don't live here permanently."

"I am part of a research team from Leeds University; we take it in turns to volunteer to stay here for a year to monitor the earth's magnetic field. About three thousand kilometres beneath your feet lies the liquid iron core, the earth's magnetic core. This can cause interference with the magnetic north pole. There are changes occurring that we don't fully understand yet. I work in conjunction with Professor Chris Davies. Please call me Charlie."

"I hope you are willing to hear what I have to tell you now," Peter tries to explain, "as you have seen we are also researchers in different fields, mostly science and IT, but Steven here, is a philosopher, and without his knowledge, we could not have gotten here."

"I am happy to hear what you have to say, so why don't we clear the decks now, and then you can tell your tale. I have two nice bottles of scotch to share while you speak." Charlie stands, and the men help clear the table and quickly wash the cups, plates and glasses. Soon they are all back near the fire, and Charlie signals for Peter to begin.

"We set out from Kettering on the 10th of December on a highly secret mission to test out an innovation developed by the aeronautical and space engineers at the university. Our team leader, a man called Henry Bonnington recruited us, and we went into intensive training for four months. To cut a long story short, using the new submersible, we passed through what is known as the Curtain of Time, some kind of rift that allows movement through primordial time unfettered by space-time, cause and effect as we understand them."

"Hang on," Charlie stops Peter for a moment, "are you aware that there was an all-points bulletin issued last week and an arrest warrant for Henry Bonnington? Apparently, he is wanted for espionage." Charlie stops, maybe he should have kept that information to himself!

Peter looks at the other men, and he seems to make a decision. If Henry is wanted, then possibly they are too. "Was there any mention of anyone else?" Peter asks casually.

"Sorry, I don't know," Charlie replies, why couldn't he keep his mouth shut! He has now put himself in real danger. "Do you want me to find out?" Charlie offers.

"That would be good," Peter watches Charlie closely. "I assume you are able to contact your university people?"

"Do you want me to do that before you go on?" Charlie asks. Perhaps he can alert the authorities through the university security staff. One of his friends works in that department, but he will have to be very careful.

"I think you should wait until I have told you the rest," Peter is now playing for time; he needs to talk Charlie out of alerting the university in case they are all named in the bulletin.

Greg and Tim

As Gavinar and Felix look on, Greg removes his laptop from his backpack and connects to the satellite, explaining his actions as he goes. The two men are amazed at the technology and watch every movement with avid attention. Greg connects to the university web page, and using his ID and password, moves through to the library page. Again, he uses his ID and password to access the collection and begins to search using the terms 'space', 'plenum' and 'time'. Within seconds he has three hundred forty-seven hits, and he then begins to scroll through the titles looking for texts by Bergson, Heidegger, Kant and Jung in particular. He adds in Heisenberg and Pauli, knowing that Jung collaborated with Pauli over a twenty-five years period. The science, he knows, must include the psychological aspects of the experimenter who sets the frame for the research. As he searches, Gavinar and Felix become enthralled; they cannot believe how many texts are accessible, and some they too recognize.

The first text Greg summons for reading is Heidegger's 'Being and Time'. He remembers Henry having a well read, dog-eared copy with him most times at the university. Recalling the papers read from Henry's files, Greg ponders whether or not this is actually a scientific problem. Perhaps this is the reason Steven was included in the team; the philosopher was conversant with texts such as this one. As he opens to the first page, all four men gather around the laptop and begin to read. The first thing Greg notices is that the style of writing is different to anything he has encountered before. Thankfully, the two-part introduction explains a new method used here by Heidegger. Phenomenology and Ontology are clearly and painstakingly explained with the reasoning necessary for the men to grasp where Heidegger is going to lead them. This is indeed going to take time.

"I can't for the life of me understand why this text was a constant for Henry," Greg muses, "I am starting to think that what we are seeking is more akin to philosophy than science. If that is the case, we are going to be here researching for the foreseeable future. Are you all prepared to do that?"

"I think we must, and I think you may be right," Gavinar replies, "there doesn't seem to be any other way, and certainly Felix and I have tried everything we can to get to the bottom of the puzzle. There are certain philosophical notions used by the Alchemists that seemed like they might lead somewhere, but we have not been able to decipher them."

"Right, then let's prepare for a long stay and work out how long we read and how long we separate to think." Greg suggests a work roster to allow them to take in what they are reading and then think it through before going on to the next stage of the reading.

"I suggest when we separate to think, that we all write down questions or ideas that the reading raises," Tim knows how research can be lost when not recorded in the first light of the details read.

The men brainstorm until they have a rudimentary work plan, and by that time, it is lunchtime. They break for food and wine and each sits silently contemplating the enormous task ahead. Thankfully, they are safe and in comfortable surroundings with servants who will see to the everyday tasks so that they can concentrate on their work, so conditions for progress are optimal. While the servants clear away the lunch dishes, the four unlikely partners resume their reading.

Brandon

Having made the only decision possible, Dr Fellings tells Brandon to dress quickly. Both men are agitated, and Brandon again notices the extreme change in his father's demeanor.

"Dad, what's wrong? You seem very stressed," Brandon asks.

"Brandon, just do as I ask and pack what you need to leave here," Fellings does not want to tell Brandon more until they are safely away from this place. "We need to get moving, and we may need to go out and buy enough supplies for some time. Once we are out of here, I will explain, but time is of the essence now."

"The concierge has money that mum sent; we should collect that on the way out." Brandon settles into following his father's instructions, and they quickly remove all traces of their presence from the room. Fellings does a quick look around to make sure there is nothing left for others to follow, and they step out and lock the door. Downstairs, they approach the desk and clear their bill. The concierge counts out in cash, the amount left from Brandon's mother's deposit; Brandon has already organized for them to be paid in cash, following his father's instructions. They thank the concierge and leave the building.

"Can we get something to eat," Brandon is starving from not eating yesterday.

"I was going to suggest exactly that," his father replies, "how about we make our way into town and find a diner."

It was only a short walk to the town centre, and they soon found a café with seating outside. A young waitress took their orders and the men sat at the edge of the seating area; Fellings wanted to be able to talk and at the same time, to see if anyone approached. How to explain to Brandon what he had set in motion!

"I have made a huge mistake, Brandon; once we have finished here, we need to get back to mainland America as soon as we can get a flight."

"What about the fact that I don't have my passport, Dad?" This has been worrying Brandon since he arrived.

"I need to think about that, but first, let me tell you what you don't know about me and the work I have been doing for the British government."

"OK Dad, let's talk while we eat."

The waitress comes with their meals, so they stop talking while she serves them and pours coffee for them both. Fellings begins:

"For the last ten years I have been part of a secret research team assigned to MI6. We have been trying to gain an understanding of how and why the Curtain of Time, as you call it, works. We have also been watching Henry because we realized through his spouting off at the university of Northamptonshire, that he had discovered the Curtain by sheer accident."

"Hang on, Dad, do you mean to tell me that Henry was not part of the research team?" Understanding begins to dawn on Brandon.

"No, he was not! In fact, Henry stole the submersible from the university research team and set you all up for charges of treason."

"Oh my God!" Brandon now sees why his father is so worried, "please, Dad, tell me you did not report my return to MI6?"

"I am sorry, Brandon, but I wanted to get you back to the U.K as quickly as possible, so while you were sleeping, I rang in and ordered a plane to get you back home for debriefing. It wasn't until I looked in your backpack and found the transponder, that I realised how mixed up in all this you are."

"What the hell are we going to do, Dad?" Brandon starts to panic; he knows what will happen if MI6 get their hands on him.

"I have decided to get us the hell out of here before the authorities arrive. It means we will be hunted, and if caught, we will be lucky to be thrown into prison for the duration." Fellings does not hold back; he needs Brandon to fully understand the implications of either going with the authorities, or more so, trying to outrun them. "As soon as we finish here, we must stock up and recall the submersible," Fellings has just made this decision; he knows they cannot take a commercial flight now because one, Brandon does not have his passport, and two, they will be too easy to track down.

"We will call your mother first and let her know that we are going to be uncontactable for the foreseeable future, and to let her know to help the authorities to the best of her abilities and without reserve. We can't involve her and your sister in this; they have to live in England, and I don't want them to come under suspicion of helping us." Fellings already knows that they are unlikely to get through this unscathed, but he must do all he can to lessen the impact on them.

"Are you sure you want to do this, Dad?" Brandon asks, perhaps it would be better for them all if he throws himself onto the mercy of MI6.

"Believe me, Brandon, it is not what I want, but there is simply no other viable option. MI6 do not care about the welfare of individuals, and they will make mincemeat of you, especially if they can't get their hands on Henry."

"I assume you want to stock the submersible with enough supplies to last us for some time," Brandon starts to think now, forming plans along with Fellings.

"Dad, the trouble is, there is a problem with coordinating the thing; it seems to travel to who knows where and who knows when. Twice I have found myself totally off course from where or when I intended to be. What if we become lost in time, like I did initially? We really have no way of directing the machine that I can see."

"I understand, Brandon, but what other choice do we have?"

Fellings looks deeply into Brandon's worried eyes, and Brandon realises his father is as worried as he is himself. Gathering his resolve, he nods and determines to help rather than hinder the older man.

"Okay Dad, lets finish our food and get going. As soon as we have the supplies, I will summon the submersible, but I would rather do that when we are at the bottom of the cliffs, close enough to get aboard quickly and disappear from here. We don't want anyone to see what we are doing. Did you report that the submersible was here with me?"

"No, at the time I rang in, I didn't know that fact, so at least we have that on our side."

The Family

Canath and Florence return to their room to sleep; with the safe arrival of Ladon, exhaustion hits Florence like a sledge-hammer. She did not realise just how stressed about the birth she had been. The midwife will stay with Antheia for the next few nights, so Florence can at last, relax. Canath is tired too, but he knows that he now has limited time to set his inherited plans into motion, so he waits until Florence's breathing becomes regular, and he knows she is asleep, then rises, kisses her gently, and moves quietly to the tower room.

"I have been expecting you," Marcom is sitting quietly by the fire, unnoticed until he spoke. He is still wearing the spider silk robe.
"There is much to do and not much time."
"I know we must work quickly now, Marcom, before your real journey begins."
"I want you to fetch me the real Doomsday Book; it is at the top of the farthest shelf, covered by a blanket. Quickly now, we must proceed with all haste!"
Canath does what Marcom bids him, removing the dusty, gigantic tome from its hiding place. He does not look at it because he knows that only the foresworn, Marcom, can survive opening the pages and reading.

Closing his eyes and sitting in yoga pose on the floor, Canath empties his mind of all rational thinking. Slowly, he becomes aware of the lilting, archaic language spoken by Marcom to the baby, Ladon. The room begins to swirl as Marcom's chanting becomes louder, and Canath opens his eyes. There is a mist swirling towards the ceiling, filling the tower room and thickening with each syllable that Marcom utters. Lightning flashes through the mist as it begins to solidify, and soon Canath can make out a strange shape. The shapeshifter takes the form of a large spider, its head human-like, and he gasps as the 'thing' begins to move.

Marcom stops his chanting and waits patiently. Canath holds his breath; never has he seen the like of what stands before him on eight gigantic and hairy legs.

"Greetings friend Marcom," the spider speaks in a deep and dissonant scratching voice, much like fingernails running down a blackboard.

Canath shudders deeply. He can barely avoid screwing up his face as the spider gathers itself.

"I bow to you, oh Rift Spinner," Marcom indeed bows deeply as he politely addresses the spider. "We welcome you in the name of the immortal Ladon. He is now mortal through Antheia. The time is come for you and me to travel into the plenum together and begin the necessary preparations for the healing process to begin, so that as soon as he is grown, Ladon can take over."

"I am ready, Marcom, and I bid you adieu, Canath. Without your presence here tonight, I could not have been summoned. May the gods provide you with everything you need. Marcom and I will surely watch over you as the danger increases."

As the last excoriating syllable is pronounced, Marcom and the Spider simply disappear along with the Doomsday Book, the real one. Canath releases a long-held breath and continues to sit in pose, making a stellar effort to calm his shaking form.

As soon as he can stand, he makes his way to Antheia's room to check on his daughter and new grandson. The room is lit only by the glowing embers of the firepit, and he notices Antheia is sleeping peacefully. He crosses quietly to her bedside so as not to awaken the midwife sleeping nearby and leans low to kiss Antheia gently on the forehead. As he rises again, he hears the soft voice of the baby, singing in the archaic tongue of his forebears. Tiptoeing, he crosses to the crib and looks down into two enormous green eyes. The child's hair has grown long over the last three hours since his birth, the silver locks shining with their own power. Ladon fixes Canath with his gaze, and Canath cannot move.

"I am getting stronger, Grandfather," Ladon silently conveys this message to Canath, "it will not be long before I can do what must be done."

"May the gods bless and keep you, darling boy," Canath replies, also silently. The child resumes his crooning and allows Canath to leave the room. As he climbs to his and Florence's own room, he wonders not for the first time, what is to become of his family. Theirs is not an easy or simple path to live; he hopes with all his heart that they might have a brief respite together before the burdens become real. As he drifts off to sleep, the faint, lilting voice of Ladon soothes his troubled soul.

Henry

Peter stares at Charlie, who cannot meet his gaze. It is clear that he has just now realized how much danger he is in.

"Charlie, it's OK," Peter tries to reassure the man that they are no threat to him. He must reason with the man, or they are all in danger, and not just from the authorities. "Please tell us all you can about the search for Henry, because we have to decide what to do, and I don't want you worried that you will come to any harm from us."

Charlie looks at Peter and at each man in the room; his fear is palpable. Can he trust them and what they say?

"It looks like I don't have much choice," Charlie utters his concerns, well aware that the other men all understand he is now afraid of them. As his demeanor changes, the dog looks up from his resting place and a low growl emanates from his throat.

"Charlie, you must listen to me," Peter realizes that if he does not diffuse this situation immediately, someone will be attacked by the dog. They do not have the means to deal with it safely, and if there is a melee, then it is likely someone from a neighbouring house will intervene and maybe with a gun. There could be a police presence here too, given that the research station is here.

"I think you should all leave now," Charlie has hedged his bets and knows that if push comes to shove, someone will call the police.

"Please, Charlie, don't send us away; we have nothing and no means of support. Contact the authorities if you are really concerned, but we have come here not of our own choice, and we have no means of getting back home without your help."

Charlie thinks about this and suddenly has an idea.

"If you are genuine, then you will not have a problem with me contacting the police and handing you on to them. They may be able to help you, but I am afraid there is nothing further I can do for you," Charlie speaks forcefully, not allowing his fear to show.

"OK Charlie, we will leave, but please don't call the authorities. We have done nothing other than follow the orders of a man we thought was a genuine scientist," Peter pleads, "I will try to contact my family and see what they can do to help us. Thank you for your hospitality." With that, Peter stands, gathers up his laptop and backpack, and signals for the other men to follow him. They must get away from here quickly before Charlie has a chance to call the police. It will be touch and go whether or not they can succeed, but they must try.

As soon as they are away from Charlie's house, Derek starts his moaning again.

"What do we do now?" Derek is expecting Peter to think for him.

"Shut up, Derek, or we will leave you to find your own way home!" Peter explodes. He looks at Steven and asks, "Do you think we could get back to the entry point? There must be a sigil there, and maybe we can move through to somewhere safer now that we know about the arrest warrant for Henry."

"Let me think for a minute," Steven stops and ponders. "I think you could be onto something, Peter, and it will be faster than trying to outrun the police. I agree with you that Charlie will already be on the blower."

"Let's see if our footprints are visible. If we can make our way back to the snowfield, we may be able to follow them to pinpoint our entry."

Peter is more hopeful about this course of action. "OK, let's give it a shot; I think I can remember our direction reasonably well."

There is light enough to see now but definitely not daylight as they are used to in England, even in winter; the men follow where Peter is leading, and each man carefully searches the ground for any signs of a footprint, even though they are on solid ground. Every so often, Peter turns to view the scene behind them; trying as best he can to line up with the view they had when moving in the opposite direction. It takes about an hour and a half before the first signs of snow appear, and another hour before Savissivik is but a dark shadow in the distance. Peter breathes a sigh of relief. Now perhaps they can move faster if their earlier footprints can be found. The sky is clear, and there doesn't appear to have been any recent snowfall, so as soon as the snow becomes thicker underfoot, Peter asks the men to spread out and look for signs of their earlier footprints. Although it is only hours since they passed through this area, there doesn't seem to be anything here to find. The men keep walking forwards but spread out in a widening line, being sure to keep each other in sight. Peter begins to think that they have made an error in their mental calculations and is just at the point of summoning the men to group together, when Steven shouts and waves his hand. The others converge on Steven's position, and with great relief, they can see the gradually degrading outline of someone's boot print.

"OK, now let's be really careful we don't step in any further prints," Peter cautions, "the last thing we need now is to mess up the track."

"Should we walk in a line, do you think, Peter?" Steven asks, "that way we can step in each other's tracks without risking messing up the ones coming towards us."

"I think that is the best idea," Peter can't think of anything better, "that way we stay together too."

Reversing the direction that the boot print is pointing towards, and with Peter in the lead again, the men begin to follow their earlier tracks. They are making good time now, and Peter begins to think they might yet get home, when he and the others hear a faint, but unmistakable sound, As the sound gets louder, Peter's spirits sink; a helicopter is approaching fast, and is coming from the direction they have left behind. There is nowhere they can take cover or try to hide, so the line of men stands still, awaiting the inevitable.

Tim and Greg

The four men have been reading for nearly a week now, and with each section of Heidegger's text, a transformation is gradually taking place. The hardest time was the initial reading, but as they, through necessity, gradually and painstakingly became accustomed to the phenomenological method, understanding began to creep in. Each has had to do as Heidegger teaches; he has had to use his own being to check the veracity of Heidegger's notions of Dasein or 'being-there', as Heidegger suggests. Gradually the idea that human being is an object amongst other objects has given way to the understanding that human-being is verbal and cannot be otherwise. As understanding grows, each man has had a revelation, described by Heidegger as the Augenblick or lightning strike. All of a sudden, they are able to reach beyond the everyday world that they were socialized into from birth. They have broken into a deeper human understanding that has always been there, but with the dominance of scientific logic, has been 'skated' over and hence remained unseen. Suddenly, they are able to 'see' below the surface of everyday thinking, to a deeper level not accessible in the everyday mode. Things begin to take on a vibrancy and the reading at last, makes perfect sense.

Felix now senses what the Alchemists were really doing. It was not gold from base metals they were trying to accomplish but gold in terms of understanding from the base metal that each and every one of us is until we begin this introspective journey. "How could he not have seen this before?" is the question he asks himself.

Gavinar is now reaching the understanding that everything he thought was important in his life, is but chaff. But is he demolished by this thought? No, not at all, suddenly he realizes that what he has been searching for, wealth and possessions, are really hampering his spiritual and intellectual growth. He is ecstatic with this new understanding because what he has been searching for is now becoming clearer and no amount of 'things' can any longer keep his real purpose obscured, or usurp his joy in this fact. There is no feeling of loss with the need to gather more and more gone; in fact, it is the opposite. He just now understands his life has real meaning and purpose, and he needs to be still and listen rather than grab as much of everything as he can lay his hands on. How startling is this new revelation! How refreshing!

Greg and Tim are no less affected by the text reading. They have both struggled to become recognized as academics. But to what end? To write papers to present at conferences? Now, with the journey Heidegger is taking them on, they both see that this is nothing but the total abrogation of responsibility. Now they understand that they must contribute to the world of others, not build a walled, ivory tower around their learning in which to sit and pretend to be learned; pretend to be doing something useful. How could they not see this before? How could they be swayed by the boastful Henry into joining an expedition to ruin? Did money mean so much? Well not any more; they sold their souls to the devil, but now they both know beyond a shadow of a doubt, that they must wrest their souls back! The reading continues and understandings grow. The hermeneutic circle is working its magic!

Brandon

Beset by worry now, the two men quickly and quietly go about the preparations necessary to leave Maui. As soon as the stores open, they gather together everything they consider to be a necessity for their journey. At last, and with the morning closing in on midday, they begin the descent from the cliffs near the resort, winding down the pathway to the beach. Brandon leads the way across the volcanic scree and into the sheltered cove, where he made landfall. They both carry large packs on their backs to hide the supplies from view. The transponder is at hand, and with trembling hands, Brandon connects to the satellite and presses the send button to recall the submersible. Fellings senior is sweating with regret; he has made the call home and is beyond worried about his wife and daughter. His wife is terribly upset and cannot fully grasp the implications of Brandon's return, however, she has listened and agreed to do as her husband has asked. Luckily, there are no financial problems; Fellings has inherited a fortune from his father, and they can live comfortably for the rest of their lives, even if he and Brandon do not return. At least that thought gives Dr Fellings some small comfort.

The light on the transponder goes green, and it is with a sigh of relief that Brandon tells his father the submersible is on its way. They just have to get on board now and leave before anyone sees them. Please God they can make it!

Within minutes, the transponder beeps, and Brandon searches the shoreline for sight of their vehicle. There, just beyond the breakers, Brandon spots the dome. Bidding his father to wait and hold the transponder, he removes his pack and rushes into the water, and as soon as it is deep enough to swim, he makes strong strokes towards the dome. When he reaches the side of the submersible, he grabs hold of the ridge just below the dome and begins to swim the submersible closer to the beach. He gives his father a hand signal, and Fellings senior, loaded down with both packs, wades slowly into the water, making his way closer to Brandon. As soon as he is within reach of his son, Brandon takes the transponder and releases the dome. He clambers aboard, wet and shaking, then carefully takes each pack from his father and reaches down to take his hand and help him aboard. He shows his father how to strap himself in and as soon as he is also strapped in, he closes the dome, applies the hydraulic seals and looks to the console for the sigil to light up. As soon as it does so, he directs the submersible below the surface and instructs his father on how to hold his body ready for the Curtain. There is a shimmering, starting with the outer shell of the submersible, then the inner surface, and lastly, the two men begin to shimmer. The submersible disappears leaving not even a ripple on the surface.

About three miles away, at the airport, a private jet touches down and makes its way to the side of the public terminal. The engines shut down, their whine steadily decreasing, and the door lifts upwards, allowing four men in suits, one with a briefcase, to disembark. They are met by a man dressed in police uniform, and he salutes the four men. They all make their way quickly into the terminal building, bypassing the customs desk, and exiting out into the sunshine. A dark, four-wheel drive vehicle waits at the kerb, and the four men climb in. The police officer watches as the vehicle drives off in the direction of the resort. He then climbs into an unmarked police vehicle and makes his way back to the police building. Once inside, he walks swiftly to his office, shuts the door and picks up his private telephone. He dials a number committed to memory and not written anywhere.

"I assume you have news for me?" a voice known only to the police officer asks as soon as the receiver is lifted.

"The men from England have arrived. I left them to make their own way to the resort. What do you want me to do now?" the police officer asks.

"Keep them under surveillance, but do not approach them again directly." The phone goes dead. The police chief sits for a moment; he wonders, not for the first time, just what he has gotten himself into. At least he can now get back to work and forget about the four men for the time being. He contacts the patrol car and instructs the two officers to keep the resort under surveillance and discretely follow if or when the men leave. The island is small, so the presence of the police car will not seem conspicuous.

The four-wheel drive pulls up in the forecourt of the resort and the men step out and hurry inside. The concierge looks up from his work and addresses the four men.

"Good day, sirs, would you like to book rooms?" he asks politely.

"Thank you, no," the man with the briefcase replies, "we are here to meet with Dr Fellings; he is expecting us."

"I am sorry, sir," the concierge looks puzzled, "but Dr Fellings and his son left here early this morning. Are you sure they were expecting you?"

"Yes, we have just arrived from the U.K at the invitation of Dr Fellings. Are you sure they are not coming back?"

"Well, they settled their account and took everything with them." The concierge is becoming suspicious. "May I ask who you are?"

"We would like to see the room they stayed in please," the man replies, ignoring the question.

"Well, that could be a problem unless you can show me good cause." The concierge is more than a little suspicious now, and while he maintains a polite demeanor, he hardens his resolve at such an unusual request. He does not like these strangers at all.

"Please call the police chief; he knows who we are, and I am sure he will authorize our request."

The concierge picks up the phone and does what the man has asked. He listens for a few moments and replaces the receiver.

"If you wouldn't mind stepping this way," he leads the men to the first-floor room and opens the door. The men enter and close the door behind them, making it evident they do not want him to accompany them inside. He returns, miffed and mystified to his desk.

The men begin a painstaking search of the room, concentrating on the bathroom and the bed. They have donned disposable gloves, and they check every inch of the two rooms for anything at all that may lead them to the whereabouts of Brandon and Fellings senior. Soon enough they realise that the room has been 'sanitized' of any clues, and this means that the Fellings have indeed absconded. The four men know there will be hell to pay if they cannot find them. The man who carried the briefcase removes his mobile and dials a number. When the call is answered, a woman with an English accent asks him to hang up and wait. The man watches the others complete the search. After about forty seconds, his phone rings, and he presses the call button.

"We are now encrypted," a male voice says, "what is your progress with the problem?"

"They have left the building and sanitized their room," the briefcase man reports. "What do you want me to do now?"

There is silence for a few seconds indicating the man on the other end is angry and trying to control his temper.

"Return as soon as you finish up there." The phone goes dead.

The briefcase man dials another number and speaks to the head of his plane crew.

"Make sure the refueling is done immediately and prepare to takeoff as soon as we return."

"Certainly, sir," the man at the other end replies, "what is our flight plan?"

"We return to England soonest," the briefcase man orders, "so make sure everything is ready by the time we return to the airport."

With no further ado, the four men leave the resort, ignoring the concierge as they walk past his desk on the way out. As soon as their vehicle is back on the road, a police cruiser leaves its parking spot about fifty metres behind them and carefully follows. The policeman in the passenger seat watches the four-wheel drive turn off towards the airport. As soon as he is sure of their destination, he advises his partner to return to the station house.

The Family

"Canath, did you and Marcom manage to contact the Rift Spinner?" Florence has just woken, feeling much better and rested.

"Yes, they have left to begin," Canath replies, "now our burdensome tasks begin also. I cannot leave the issue of Aletheia any longer, so I must steel myself to do what must be done — today. Ladon is no longer guarding the entrance to the Plenum, so she must replace him immediately. We can't leave the Universe unguarded, but it breaks my heart that I have to cause my daughter so much pain."

"Oh, Canath," Florence winces with his statement, she knows what her daughter must endure this day, and she can hardly bear to think of it.

"We must wake the children then, and the boys must start their training with Brian today too. At least let us all eat together before we begin." Florence is aware of the lack of time, but she wishes, not for the first time, that they could be a normal family with normal aspirations instead of having the heavy burden of saving all life on their shoulders.

"Shall we go down and check on Antheia and our gorgeous grandson?" Florence cannot wait to see the boy and hold him again.

"I checked on them after Marcom left," Canath says quietly, "he is such a beautiful child, and you won't believe how much he has grown overnight."

"Oh, my darling boy!" Antheia greets her baby son; she cannot believe how much he has grown during the night and how beautiful he is. Two huge, luminous, green eyes look into her own, and he smiles at his mother beatifically. She lifts him carefully from his crib and places him next to her in the bed. He reaches with his tiny hand and touches her face. There is a frission of power in his touch that takes her breath away. She is reminded that this is Ladon, the dragon, guardian of the Universe. The child begins to sing in the archaic language of his forebears, and Antheia watches his face with rapt attention. He holds her for a few seconds and then reaches with his mouth for her heavy breast. She settles him to feed, all the while watching him with love evident in her eyes. She has never felt the like of this love for her infant. As she watches him, her father and mother enter the room. They cross to her bedside and look down on the feeding child.

"Oh my gosh!" Florence notices Ladon's silver locks, "how he has grown during the night."

"Mother, he is Ladon after all, you should not be so surprised," Antheia laughs.

"I know, my dear, but still, to me he is my first-born grandson, so I suppose I expect him to grow as all of you children did."

"We will leave you to finish up with feeding him, Antheia; we are all going down to the kitchen to eat together. Do you feel strong enough to join us?" Canath needs to speak to all his children before the burden he has to deliver to Aletheia begins.

"Yes, Father, try to stop me," Antheia smiles. "The midwife has checked me already this morning, and I am so ravenous, I could eat two horses!"

"We will await you then, precious girl," Canath smiles in reply, and he and Florence leave the mother and child alone.

"Good morning, Mother, Father," Phoenix is already sitting at the table with his brother when Canath and Florence enter the kitchen, "What's on the agenda today, Father?"

"I want to speak to all of you before we begin today's tasks, Phoenix, but you and Kenneth will begin your training with Brian after breakfast."

"What will we learn today, Father?" Kenneth looks pleased and hopeful. "Will we learn to use a bow and a sword?" The expectant look on his younger son's face, nearly breaks Canath's heart.

"Today, my boys, you will begin to learn how to use your mind, in ways that you never thought possible."

"Oh, Father," Kenneth's face falls, "I am no good at that, ask Phoenix. I couldn't even lift a big rock."

"Today you will learn about more than lifting rocks, my boy," Cananth replies, "today you will learn how to repel without rocks, and soon you will be strong enough to help me save the Universe, both of you. Ladon will be well pleased with you both."

As the boys take in this news, Aletheia, beautiful and stately as ever, enters and sits down next to her mother.

"Good morning, all," she says, "how are Antheia and Ladon this morning?"

"Oh, you should see that boy!" Florence looks dreamy, "his hair alone has grown long overnight and those bright green eyes!"

"Can we visit him after breakfast?" Kenneth can't wait to see his brother; at last, there is a sibling who is younger than he is.

"You certainly can, all of you," Canath beams with pleasure at the way his children have taken to this new arrival. He could expect no more. There is not even a question about his brotherhood; he had expected the others to ask why he is their brother and not their nephew. Yet each of them recognizes him as a sibling, no questions asked.

At last, Antheia enters the room. She is looking radiant and glows with the love for her son.

"Hello, my lovelies," she beams at each of them in turn. "Can we eat now, I for one, am starving!"

Laughter tinkles around the room, and for the moment, the mood is lightened, and the family share their breakfast with smiles and chit chat. There will be plenty of time for seriousness soon enough.

Henry

As the men watch on, the helicopter circles overhead, and then hovers nearby and descends, its skids touching down gently onto the snowy field. Before the rotors have stopped spinning, a group of soldiers in the uniform of the green berets rushes from the craft and surrounds the men, rifles held pointing towards the ground. The officer approaches, and Peter steps forward, indicating that he is leading the others.

"What can we do for you?" Peter tries to brazen it out.

"You can come with us quietly, if you value your lives." The officer's face tells Peter that resistance would be futile.

"What is this about, and who sent you?" Peter does not give in to his fear; he knows that to do so will immediately give the officer the upper hand.

"I think you know well enough who sent us and why." The officer needs these men to cooperate, so he tries a conciliatory approach. "There is another helicopter coming to transport you all initially to Canada, then probably back to England. Which one of you is Henry Bonnington?"

"I am afraid Henry is no longer with us; he is out of the reach of anyone," Peter continues.

"What do you mean?" the officer asks, listening carefully.

"If you know who we are, you will also know that we left England on the 10th June. Henry recruited us for an unusual expedition, but it soon became apparent that he had lied to all of us, and we tried to escape his clutches. In his effort to stop us, Henry was immolated by the dragon sigil, so he is no longer a concern for anyone. We are just trying to get home, and we certainly did not know that the expedition was not authorized."

"I think it would be unwise to say any more," the officer knows that what Peter is relating is classified top secret, and he should not question them further. "If you wouldn't mind sitting, we will wait for the other black hawk and then we can transport you all back to Nunavut, where you will be checked by the military doctor, and you can rest and eat. Later tonight, you will be put on a British aircraft and flown to Quebec, where MI6 will take over. Do you have any further questions?"

"Sounds like a plan." Peter begins visibly to relax. At least they will be going home, and he fervently hopes that the authorities will listen to what has happened to them all. At least they will sleep in a bed tonight and be warm. There are worse things that Peter can imagine happening, and he knows this is for the best.

Soon, there is the unmistakable sound of the other helicopter coming closer, and with no show of resistance and some measure of relief, Peter and the others stand up to await their fate.

Tim and Greg

There is an animated discussion in progress; the end of 'Being' and 'Time' has created a great many conundrums for all four unlikely partners. What to make of their newfound understandings, and where to next?

"Personally, I think we should look into the psychology of being-human. It is obvious to me now after this reading that science cannot get close to answering the question of 'time'. As Heidegger shows quite clearly, space is essential to any notion of time as we know it. We are really just measuring movement in space in the same sense that Aristotle reckoned in his metaphysics — locomotion or movement in a circle. All our clocks have been the proof of just that for centuries!" Tim is mystified by the fact that this has been before his eyes since he was born, and yet it is just now that he is seeing it clearly.

"Well, Jung was contemporary with Heidegger, so who thinks we should take a look at his work?" Greg asks for a consensus.

"Can we search his works through your library?" Felix asks.

"Sure, we can," Greg answers, "is that what we all agree to do next?"

The four men agree, and so Greg sets a library search using Jung's name as the search criterion. He is moving through the titles and ready to select 'Modern Man in Search of His Soul' when Felix suddenly shouts "Stop!"

"Can you move back to the last page, please, Greg?" he asks breathlessly.

Greg does so and Felix gasps.

"This is the one we must read!" Felix's hand shakes, as he points to a text called 'Mysterium Coniuctionis'. "This is a translation of an Alchemical text, Greg," his excitement making the others pause. "I am sure we must read it; I remember some from the Latin but not all of it, and if Jung is a psychologist and is using this text, it must grant us access to the psychology of Alchemical thinking. What do you say? Can we read this, please?"

Greg looks at each man in turn, and since there is no dissent, he selects the text and opens the first page. The first thing he notices is that there are listed a series of pictures taken from original woodcuts. There is something uncanny and arcane about the first, which shows what looks like a fountain bowl with four pipes flowing water into it. There are other symbols in each corner.

"What do you suppose this means?" Greg asks the others.

"I think we need to start at the beginning and carefully read each page and refer to the pictures when Jung refers to them," Tim suggests. The men all nod their agreement, and they begin to read.

There is so much more to the notion of 'mind' than any of the men could ever have countenanced. Jung, step by step, shows them how the Alchemical Treatise is actually one of the first descriptions of what he terms 'individuation'. This has nothing to do with individual egoism and should not be conflated with it. Rather it means the breaking down of the 'hard shell' of the human ego to bring to light the deeper Self. This core of the human being is the 'soul' so called; but is much more than has been uncovered scientifically. Here is what the Christian bible refers to as 'being made in the image of God', or what Plato referred to as 'the stamp of the maker'. The men are transfixed as they read. Thank goodness they read Being and Time first; they would not have been able to understand what they are now reading without doing so!

Jung recounts how the human being has always and everywhere been drawn to what he calls the quaternity or square in a circle. This signifies the balanced human mind. These graphic depictions he names mandalas, and they appear in every religion, both extant and extinct. The square defines the four functions of the human mind; Jung had discovered these earlier and could not break them down further. The functions are thinking, feeling, intuiting and sensing. His text 'Psychological Types' was the text in which he outlined his conclusions, stating that every single human being has a singular psychological makeup including all four functions. Each function plays a role, but one function is dominant, with a second just a little less so, and the other two discarded to the background, thought inferior by that particular person.

He found that his psychiatric patients unconsciously drew mandala images but could not explain what they meant. Jung's studies found him delving into every recorded religion and then travelling all over the world in search of these mandalas, and his intuition about them was confirmed. Even in the remotest tribes of Africa, he found such depictions as an essential tool in their religions.

The woodcuts from the text are such mandala depictions, full of meaning, and in this text, Jung carefully and patiently unfolds the meaning from each one. The men are simply enthralled. Here are the directions and depictions necessary for the unfolding from ego consciousness of the human soul; the core from which our existence takes its power. 'Time' now begins to take on a new meaning; inextricably bound up with the four-functioning, human mind.

Brandon

There is a strange and uncomfortable feeling of dizziness, followed by faint nausea as the two men return to consciousness. Dr Fellings has never felt the like before, and he looks queasily across at the face of his son. Brandon too, is just returning to full consciousness, aware that what he feels is the result of passing through the Curtain. He is becoming used to these effects.

"How do you feel, Dad?" he asks.

"Very strange," Fellings senior replies, "I can't say I am enjoying it either!"

"These are the effects of passing through the Curtain; I am getting used to them."

"Well, I sincerely hope I don't have to get used to them too!" Fellings replies testily, "What do we do now?"

"We have to find out where and when we are, Dad, and it is impossible to know from the coordinates I set; as I said, this machine is not behaving in any ways as it should, so we will have to get to the surface, and hopefully there won't be anybody around when we do!"

"Give me a few minutes, will you Brandon? I need to get this dizziness under control before we have to move."

Brandon looks to the console, checking that everything is as it should be after the re-emergence. He begins the shutting down sequence while he waits for his father to gain his wits.

Several minutes later, Fellings' nausea and dizziness begin to ease, and he signals Brandon to allow the submersible to rise to the surface. They are immediately met by the dark, star-strewn, night sky. Waves roll in towards a dark shore, and both men screw up their eyes in the effort to see more. There is nothing to gauge where or when they are; the submersible is carried slowly on the waves, heading towards the shoreline. Both men watch and wait with trepidation. There is simply no way to tell what they are moving towards. Soon they can hear the breakers as they pound the shoreline, they must be getting close. Brandon releases the seals around the dome and allows the dome to rise. There is a distinct smell associated with the air here, and Brandon at first cannot put a name to it. Fellings has no such problem.

"I smell sulphur in the air, Brandon, can you smell it too?"

"Yes, Dad, I couldn't place it for a moment. What do you think it means?"

"I hope I am wrong, but this reminds me of natural histories I have read, about the Cretaceous period."

"I hope you don't mean the dinosaur era, Dad!"

"I certainly do, but by the air quality, I believe we have landed after the dinosaurs, at least a million years after, or we would be unable to breathe the air at all. If I remember correctly, there was an asteroid collision with the earth in a geographic region rich in sulphur. The resulting sulphur-filled atmosphere is believed to have been the reason the dinosaurs died out. The fact that we can breathe means that the atmosphere has had a substantial period of time to clear, so we are unlikely to be bothered by any giant sauropods. That said, there could still be instances of megafauna."

"How will we be able to survive here do you think?" Brandon is fearful of such an unknown and unknowable place and time. If only they had stayed in Maui! At least it had been a contemporary time; now what were they going to do?

"We will just have to make the best of it until we can move on," Fellings replies, "at least we don't have to worry about people; human beings have not evolved yet!"

Brandon laughs loudly, his voice verging on hysteria. After everything he has already been through, this takes the cake! He imagines what will be his mental state if they can ever return to Kettering. His past life seems like a dream from the present, and he knows only too well, that it should be the other way around.

"Let's make for the shore, Brandon, and see if I am right. We may find a place to hunker down for a while, and at least we have enough supplies for now, thank goodness."

"I think we should wait until it is light enough to see," Brandon pulls himself together, "it's not as if we need to worry about being seen, is it?"

"Yes, that's a good idea. Let's prepare our packs, and perhaps if we eat now, we can concentrate on the environment when we actually land. I guess you know how to put the submersible on standby in case we need to leave here quickly?" The question is largely rhetorical, and Brandon does not bother to reply. He quickly helps his father to prepare their packs and then they put together a quick, cold meal, after which, both men doze waiting for the dawn to break. As the light begins to become brighter, Brandon and Fellings jump into the last of the breaking waves and wade ashore. Brandon reseals the dome and sends the submersible under the waves a short distance from the beach.

The beach is sandy and curves away as far as their eyes can see. The weather is abnormally cold; tree ferns indicate that this should be a warm place, but both men are wearing tracksuits and sneakers. There is a cold breeze that makes standing still with wet legs uncomfortable. The men begin to walk towards the landside. Smaller bushes give way to giant, fern-like shrubbery, so Fellings senior is able to deduce around about the era they are in. Trees did not reappear until long after the dinosaurs became extinct; this means they do not need to worry about the gigantic type of predator. All surviving bird species were ground dwellers, so maybe they will be able to supplement their supplies with post-Cretaceous chickens, whatever they may be like! Or just maybe, they, themselves could be on the menu for some sort of mega chicken varieties! Brandon and Fellings move beyond the beach into the surrounding fern forests, carefully and deeply marking the trunks of tree-ferns as they go, to guide them back to the beach. It does not take many minutes before there is rustling in the undergrowth and the fleeting glimpses of movement, too quick for their eyes to catch the sight of whatever the creature was. The forest gives way to a high, rocky expanse from the top of which, water flows steadily and fast. The natural waterfall appears to enter a basin, from which it flows into a river, also fast-flowing through rocky rapids, away into the forest. Strange footprints appear in the soft ground around the edges of the flow; neither man is able to name what creature made them, or if they were made by four-legged creatures at all. Perhaps large birds inhabit this forest.

Brandon squats down on the riverbank ready to take a drink from the flowing water, but his father stops him.

"Let's make sure the water is clear enough to drink, Brandon," Fellings says, "we have no idea whether there are poisonous compounds mixed in here."

"How will we know anyway?" Brandon asks, "We have no way of telling other than the taste."

"Aha," Fellings replies smugly, "I took the opportunity to buy some water purification tablets just in case we needed them." He quickly takes his pack from his back and opens the front zipped pocket. He takes out a foil pack and a plastic bottle just big enough to hold a half liter of water. He dips the container into the river and sets it aside. Breaking open the foil, he drops a tablet into the water, and they wait the required ten minutes before they both drink from the bottle. The water is crisp and cold, and Brandon is thankful that his father has thought about what they may need.

Henry

The sixteen men file onto the second helicopter along with two armed soldiers. The seating is crude and uncomfortable because the usual interior of the helicopter has been stripped out to accommodate a larger number of men than normal. Seating is nothing but iron decking along the sides, and Peter and his men sit along each side of the seating. Nobody says a word; they are all too cold and worried about what is to become of them to speak. As the helicopter begins to lift off, the men look out once more, hoping this is not the last glimpse of their freedom they are looking at.

It takes about two hours flying time to get to the island of Nunavut, and there is little to see. The weather is now closing in as a late spring blizzard drops snow at a rate not seen in England. The helicopter lands on a beacon lit from within the helipad, and the men notice a low building that could be a warehouse by its size but is actually the barracks for the soldiers accompanying them. Shivering in the snow, the men jump down from the helicopter and are quickly led into the warmer interior of the building. The interior is lighted, and a long passageway leads into a large, central space heated by two open fireplaces, one at each end of the room. The soldiers order them to sit, and one leaves to find the commanding officer. Peter looks around him, wondering how they will fare here. He looks up as a tall, thin, middle-aged man enters the room. The soldiers stand to attention and salute him; he returns the salute and comes to stand in front of Peter and his comrades. He looks at each in turn and then takes a seat across from them.

"You know where you are and why," the man begins, "I am not here to question you; that will be done back in England, but I must warn you, things do not look good at all. If you cooperate with the doctors here and do not cause any problems, we will get along fine. Should you think you can escape, or shoot your way out of here, then I will have you all confined to our cell block. Do I make myself clear?"

"Yes," Peter can find nothing else to say and knows it would be pointless anyway. This man's job is to check for any medical or psychological problems and then send them on their way again. At least being cooperative will afford them the luxury of beds and food, and right now, Peter can think of nothing else. He is tired and worn out from the experiences suffered since they landed on the Greek shore.

"Good!" the man replies, and his tone softens slightly. "You will all be allotted rooms, and as soon as the doctors have examined you, I will organize a hot meal for all of you. Tomorrow morning you will continue on your journey to Quebec."

With no further ado, the man stands and leaves the room. There are soldiers left to guard Peter's group, and they stand watchful but relaxed, or as relaxed as soldiers on duty can be.

The next men to enter the room are dressed in blue scrubs; one is pushing a trolley with medical equipment. The senior doctor by his demeanor sits next to Peter.

"They tell me you have a burn on your hand," he says, "please show me."

Peter rolls up his shirt sleeve and places his hand palm up on his knee. The doctor examines the burn, doing his best not to cause Peter any further pain.

"I will dress this for you later," the man says, "but first we need to take blood samples from all of you to check for any viruses or problems from your journey."

"I'll go first." Peter rolls his sleeve up further and allows the trolley person to take his blood. The tubes are labelled, and each man is asked to supply his date of birth.

"OK, next I want to examine each of you; just a routine health check and then you can all eat."

The senior doctor leaves the room, giving orders for the trolley man to bring the men to him one at a time. Peter goes first and returns to the room with his hand bandaged. Each man takes his turn and afterwards, returns to the warmth of the central room. All told it takes about ninety minutes, after which one of the soldiers escorts them to the mess. There is a long hot cabinet with various dishes on display. Each man is given a large plate and moves along the cabinet front, signaling his choice from the dishes. There are steaks and sausages, fish, chips and vegetables, all looking inviting and fresh and for the first time in two weeks, the men take great delight in sitting down and eating. Nobody stints his serving, and soon the men are talking and relaxed. This is a vastly better meal than any of them has seen since they arrived in Athens.

"What did you find?" The senior doctor looks up as one of the laboratory scientists enters his office. The scientist pulls up a chair and sits, looking decidedly stressed.

"It is exactly as you expected," he says, "all of their blood is changed in ways that I don't understand. The only consistency in this case is the fact that each of them has passed through the Curtain, so this must be an effect of that and, as yet has not been recognized. Their blood does not look like human blood should, and I suppose the extra molecules — which as yet I have no idea what they are — could only be instilled when the human body is sent into a state of diffusion, as apparently is the case with the Curtain. Just how this happens, I have not been briefed on, but one thing is for sure, you cannot break the body down into its constituent molecules and reconstitute it again without the possibility that something else will be reconstituted with it."

"This is just what I feared when I heard what Kettering aerospace was doing," the senior doctor leans back in his chair and rests his chin on steepled fingers. "Well, it is not for us to decide what should be done now, nor can we take it upon ourselves to order further tests. That will have to be done under the auspices of MI6. Please write up your report and send it in the usual encrypted manner. Thanks for your help and let's hope we can contain this ludicrous experiment before something more dire occurs."

The scientist nods, stands and leaves his commanding officer deep in thought.

The Family

"Can I please have all your attention," Canath taps his spoon on his cup.

"I am sorry to break up this family time, but there is something I must tell you all, and especially you, Aletheia."

The family quieten and look to Canath; the look on his face sobers their merriment.

"As I told you when we met last, each of you has been born to a task that is so important, that all life as we know it will cease should we not take up the burden placed on us." Canath looks at each of them in turn.

"Ladon is now mortal and will be unable to stand as guardian between the finite realm of cause and effect and the infinite plenum until he attains adulthood. We don't know how long that will take." Canath repeats what each of them already knows.

"While he is growing, it is essential that Aletheia now take her place as that guardian; at the moment there is no guardian, so the Universe is at dire risk."

"I am ready, Father," Aletheia smiles at Canath.

"My beautiful daughter," Canath addresses her, "that is not all. I must now tell you what has to happen before you can take up your role."

Canath stands and begins to pace.

"You cannot know how hard this is for me," he seems to be deep in thought and paces backwards and forwards to ease the strain.

"Before you take up your role, I must do something that no father could countenance, and let me tell you, if I were sure that there was even a slim chance that we could accomplish everything without this task, I would gladly take it."

"What is it, Father?" Aletheia looks worriedly at her father's strained demeanor. "What is so awful as to make your whole countenance pale?"

"You have visited the Oracle at Delphi, Aletheia. What did you see?"

"I saw a blinded girl child sitting in the Oracle's sacred place, Father."

Suddenly, it hits Aletheia just what is troubling her father so deeply. She looks up at him and knows from his face what must be done. Can she face this enormity? Is she strong enough to go through the ritual that accompanies her task? A deep shudder wracks her whole body, and she sits down before her shaking legs give way. Her thoughts scramble over each other, and she has to use her whole soul to calm herself. She wants to ask Canath if there is another way, but she already knows the answer. He would not be so deathly pale if there was.

At last, gaining control over her body, she steels herself and looks into Canath's eyes.

"I will do this, Father, if I must. Do not trouble yourself further. Just tell me how it must be done."

Canath steps around the table and takes his daughter in his arms. She feels his tears run over her face. She could not love him more than at this moment; his tears tell her of his absolute sorrow at what must be done.

"It must be done in the archaic way and by my own hand, darling girl," he whispers to her.

"What is going on, Father?" Phoenix asks sternly; he doesn't like the way his sister has been shocked. Something terrible lies between them, and he is frightened more than he can say.

"Tell them, Canath," Florence looks at the three concerned faces of her other children. This is when resistance may rise up between them, and the sooner Canath speaks, the sooner they can deal with the information together.

Canath sits back down and takes a large swallow of his cup of brew.

"There is one task left me before Aletheia can take up her role as guardian in Ladon's stead. I must, by my own hand, blind my daughter in the archaic manner of the ancients."

"No, Father, you will not!" Phoenix stands up so abruptly that his stool clatters to the floor. "How can you even think to do this? I will do everything in my power to stop you!"

"Phoenix, listen to your father; do you think he will do this without great cost to himself?" Florence tries to calm her oldest son, but he is glaring at them with absolute fury.

"Phoenix, my beautiful and courageous brother," Aletheia speaks calmly now, "please do not blame father for what must be done. Remember, we were born to this, and I will not forego my duty simply because I must go through some pain and anguish. There will be times in your own tasks when you have to be immolated, and I do not want that either, but we are foresworn. Remember, the gods do not give us tasks that are impossible for us to bear. They give them to us, precisely because we are strong enough, where others might fail."

Phoenix sits back down and stares at the tabletop. He refuses to meet his father's or mother's eyes, and his knuckles are white in the fists formed from both hands.

"Then I must be there when it is done!" He does not ask; his voice brooks no dissent. This is a demand of the highest order, and Canath recognizes the man in his oldest boy's body.

"Then you shall be there, my son," Canath assents immediately knowing full well that arguing with Phoenix will not be successful. The man, Phoenix, has spoken.

"When and where, Father?" Phoenix asks.

"As soon as we finish breakfast, I will take Aletheia to the sacred site here on the island. It has been used for centuries for pagan sacrifices and rituals of all kinds by many, but the Druids were the last. The place was sacred long before they arose here in Britain.

"This site has been re-sanctified by the Rift Spinner, the successor of all those from whom our own line has evolved. When Ladon reaches his maturity, he will also have to go through a ritual of re-immortalization. Only here can these rituals be undertaken. Tried anywhere else on earth, and the person undergoing the test will most certainly die." Canath stands and leaves the room; he cannot stay longer knowing what he will have to do next.

"Children, you must know how much your father and I love you. We could not do what is necessary unless our love was absolute and unconditional. Please try to understand. Do you think Canath would allow anyone else whosoever to do this to his beloved daughter? No, he must do what needs to be done himself and that smacks of the greatest love." Florence looks gravely at each of her children in turn, and Phoenix at last looks up and meets his mother's eyes. He knows it is the truth. He wonders if he will be as brave as Aletheia when the time comes for him to be burnt alive! Their futures are now arrived, and he must bear an unbearable witness to his sister's suffering and stand beside his father as he undertakes this horrific task. He stands up to leave; he needs to apologise to Canath and lend him support before he has to undertake the gruesome ritual, and he will do the same for Aletheia very soon as she undergoes the unthinkable.

Greg and Tim

The reading has progressed, and now, after completing Jung's text, all four men are taking a break in separate places throughout Felix's house. The thinking is also progressing to the point that each and every one of them sees themselves, and their place in universal terms much differently than when they began. It is most obvious to them all that what we call time is purely a condition of the way of being that we name human. Heidegger's notions of the ecstasies of being, or the temporal horizon of being human sets us apart from the animal kingdom in one important sense. Past and future hold open and condition the space which we call 'now'. This space is itself a temporal effect, of both past and future, and the resulting 'time' we name is nothing but the countenancing of our inner being. Counterpoised with this is the eternality of universality. Only a being intrinsically finite can understand its being as 'time'; for it has in a certain sense, a beginning and an end. For everything else, there is no 'time', rather there are the eternal movements of the infinite power of existence.

"Felix, do you think we should tell the others about the orb now?" Gavinar, like the rest, has come to the understanding necessary to see his life clearly. His need to amass wealth has shifted, without his knowledge, and as his understanding has grown. He remembers clearly the precepts of Gutama Buddha; that we should free ourselves from attachment to the world. This has always seemed to him to be a task that required a supreme, herculean effort, but now Gavinar sees it from the Buddha's perspective. There is no struggle, it simply happens as our focus changes from egocentricity to selfhood. The amassing of wealth was but a veil covering a need that was not clear. Understanding proved to be the veil remover, like scales falling from the eyes, that shone the focus on the real need of being human, the breaking open of the narrowed perspective of ego consciousness. Once that was achieved, then amassing wealth could be seen for what it was, a useless enterprise.

"Gavinar, I think it is now time as you suggest." Felix has also seen the light, so to speak. "Let's go find Greg and Tim and show them what we did."

The two friends leave together to find the others and to tell their real truth. Now perhaps they can take the journey to Kettering together and discover what lies at the centre of the orb.

"Greg, do you see, as I do, why we must return to Kettering?"

"I do, and yet I don't if that makes any sense at all. I'm not sure we can physically do that anyway." Greg is still deep in thought and tries to focus on Tim's question.

"I am not sure if returning will be of benefit now that we are so much more aware of the reality of things. I for one, need to think about the meaning of passing through the Curtain, and how that gels with everything we now know about what and who we are."

"What is the point of staying here? We can't do what we set out to do in this part of the plenum, and God only knows what Henry and the rest are up to."

Gavinar and Felix enter the room just at that moment and Greg and Tim look up in surprise. They had all agreed to meet in the lounge room at four p.m.

"Gentlemen, we have a confession to make." Gavinar addresses Tim and Greg, and Felix looks chagrined.

"Does it involve the orb?" Greg asks. Gavinar is stunned at Greg's perception and is not quite sure how to proceed.

"Er, well, yes it does," he replies, "but how could you know that?"

"I did not believe the story you and Felix came up with; it was just a little too coincidental for my liking. I am not saying it was fully fabricated, but you did not tell us the whole truth, did you?" Greg looks each of them in the eye. Both men have the decency to look down.

"We wanted to get you both to take us back to Kettering," Gavinar sighs, "but we did not want to tell you that we already knew how the orb works; we are willing to tell you both now however."

"Why should we believe you now?" Greg asks.

"Because I can show you how we know." Felix answers this time. He rises to his feet and leaves the room, while the other three look at each other.

"Felix has gone to fetch the orb and something that we did not show you last time." Gavinar explains, "Let's go to the lounge, because this is going to take some time."

The three men settle themselves comfortably, and Gavinar summons the servants to fetch some wine and four goblets. Soon Felix returns with the wooden box and what looks like an old book. He puts the box on the low table but keeps the book in his hands.

"When we opened the box after returning from Kungsbacka," he begins, "this book was also in the box. It is an instruction manual of sorts, but not only that. In here are the instructions for mesmerism; as yet unheard of by most, since it was only developed in 1744, but quite understandable once the Latin text is translated. I began to study this text, and within a few months, I began to experiment with this new kind of mind control. It seems I have a knack for it; I became very good at it indeed! Hence how I was able to hold you both without your permission. All I had to do was mesmerize you, and I am adept at several methods, some that are not able to be seen as I undertake them. That is the first thing we did not tell you."

Greg and Tim are now enthralled, and past events begin to make sense.

"Please go on." Greg asks Felix politely.

"The text also explains how the orb can be used," Felix begins again.

"It is a kind of focus that when introduced to a person, is able to divine from his or her very mind, what or where their thinking lies. I only had to get you to tell us about your home-town to get the projection to play out in the surface of the orb."

Greg begins to ask a question, but Felix holds his hand up to stop him.

"Let me tell you what I hypothesize about how this works, and why it may solve our problem; then you can ask questions to your heart's content. The men remain silent while Felix gathers his thoughts to begin again.

"If as is already proven, this object can garner one's thoughts and project them, I think it may also be able to somehow project the person into the place displayed on its surface. I have been working on this, but so far, I have not made much headway. My intuition, however, points me to just this process and I wonder from your description of the Curtain and the sigils that work as entry points, whether this may not work in exactly the same fashion. I had this intuition before you arrived here, so your arrival almost acts as proof; I just have to work out how that could work."

Greg and Tim are now completely absorbed by Felix's tale; they know now that time as they know it is a condition of the human mind. If Heidegger is right, and there is no reason to suggest he isn't, then what Felix suggests is cogent and very likely, possible. Both men are scientists and the physics of the Curtain, they know in a rudimentary form. The men sit back, their faces exhibiting their excitement. This may be a real chance to return to Kettering or go anywhere else in the world that they can visualize, especially if they are able to transport the orb along with themselves! Felix sits down and watches the men closely.

Brandon

Their thirst slaked, Brandon and Fellings senior look about them, trying to gauge what to do next. The noise of the waterfall covers any other sounds, and the rocky height from which it falls is too high for them to see what lies beyond, without making the slippery climb to the top. The river rapids fall away through the fern forest as if the forest floor slopes quite sharply downwards up ahead.

"Which way do you think we should go, Dad?" Brandon asks his father to make the decision. He is still suffering from exhaustion and has had enough of trying to decide what to do next.

"Brandon, I don't know if we should go anywhere else here; perhaps we should recall the submersible and get out of here."

"Do you want to go back to the beach then, Dad?"

"I do. I don't like the effects of passing through the Curtain, but I surely can't see the sense of staying here. Let's go back and check the console out. If you show me how this thing works, perhaps I can figure out how to go where and when we want. What do you say?"

"Let's do it, Dad, I just want to get back to some sort of normality, whatever that can mean after everything that has happened."

The two men retreat to the beach with the help of the marks they made earlier in the tree-fern trunks. The sun is now fully risen, and they can see where the breakers brought them into the cove. The odour of sulphur still taints the air; another good reason to leave as soon as they can. Brandon pulls out the transponder, connects to the satellite and recalls the submersible. Soon they spot the dome just beyond the breakers. Again, Brandon sheds his pack and tracksuit, hands the transponder to his father and wades into the surf until it is deep enough to swim. Fellings watches as his son makes strong strokes towards the dome.

He is almost level with the dome when the water around him starts to boil with bubbles and a dark shadow passes directly under his body. Brandon starts to panic, kicking with all his strength as he reaches out to grasp the rim projecting from under the dome. Suddenly the water parts, and a gigantic, black body heaves itself clear of the depths. The thing continues to rise until it is as tall as a ten-storey building and a great maw opens showing row upon row of gigantic, serrated teeth. Brandon has time only to scream before the maw reaches over and entirely swallows up his body and the submersible. With an almighty splash, huge enough to send a wall of water towards the shore, the creature dives back into the depths, taking Brandon and the submersible with it.

Fellings senior is frozen to the spot, unable to move and scarcely able to breathe. He cannot believe his eyes, then the incoming wall of water hits him and lifts him clean off his feet. He tumbles underneath the wave, swallowing sea water, spluttering and trying to claw his way back to the surface. His feet touch the sand as the wave begins its withdrawal, and he sits in the sand left behind, shocked beyond sensibility. The packs and the transponder are nowhere to be seen.

Henry

It is still dark when the soldiers wake the men and ask them to dress quickly. As they pass from their rooms, the soldiers check they have left nothing behind, then escort them to the mess again, and they file past the counter to fill their plates with a hot breakfast. Seated, around the tables, they remain silent and concentrate on eating, each absorbed with his own thoughts. The commanding officer enters the mess and calls for their attention.

"Men, it is four a.m., and in precisely one hour, you will be escorted to a military aircraft for your flight to Quebec. I hope you all manage to return to England unscathed, and I wish you the best for you onward journey." He leaves as quickly as he entered, and the men return to their breakfast.

"Do you have any idea what is going to happen next?" John whispers to Peter. Peter gives him a withering look and ignores the question. John looks around the tables at the other men, but only Steven shrugs his shoulders in an "I wouldn't have a clue" kind of response. John resumes eating.

"Have you sent your report to England?" the C.O. asks. He will be glad to hand the party of men over to the British authorities and be done with them. There are other tasks that call for his attention here.

"I sent it late last night so that if there are any changes to the plans, we can be alerted before the men embark." The scientist is also aware that with the anomalies in the blood work, they may be asked to keep the men here for further tests. This is a remote outpost, so poses no health threats to a large-scale population.

"Do you think that may happen?" the C.O. asks, looking up from his paperwork, wondering why the scientist mentions a possible change of plan.

"Well, I wouldn't be surprised," he replies, "if I was looking at it from a safety point of view, keeping them here in an isolated situation would reduce any health threat that they might pose."

"Let's hope you are wrong." The C.O. does not want to be babysitting this group when he has other schedules to meet. "Have you made any headway in working out what the anomalies mean?"

"Not at all as yet," the scientist knows the C.O. does not understand enough about the secret project as a whole and has little interest in knowing more, but he, on the other hand, is fascinated with this unknown occurrence and would like to work with the men to solve the enigma.

As he makes his way back to the section where the laboratories are housed, the scientist is already thinking about the unknown molecules. So far, all tests have revealed that although similar to many common compounds, there are miniscule differences in the bonding such that the electron fields of each don't correspond to the known. He has never seen anything like this anomaly that seems to defy the laws of physics as we know them. Using his electronic keycard, he enters the outer door and releases the seals to enter the inner door into the laboratory.

The C.O. has just returned to his paperwork after the interruption by the scientist when his private phone rings. He sighs deeply, irritated now, because a task that should have been completed some time ago is still unfinished.

"Major General Robbins," he says a little too forcefully.

"Ah, General, I have just returned from an all-night meeting with the Thames House boys; as you know the report sent yesterday by Dr Higgins was unexpected and of grave concern." The speaker takes his time with what he has to say, and the General shifts impatiently in his chair.

"We want you to keep them there and continue with testing. Has Higgins come up with anything yet, or a reason for the anomalies?"

"Sir, do you really think they should stay here?" General Robbins ignores the question, trying not to appear rude. "We don't have the facilities to deal with a pandemic, if that is what we are looking at."

"This was a joint decision, and MI6 were very insistent that they remain with you for the time being. They are sending their own medical team, along with two agents to question the men. It seems the whereabouts of Henry Bonnington is in question, and we must find him to complete the picture of what happened."

The General knows there is no point in arguing further, so with resignation clear in his voice, he assents and ends the call. He remains sitting, thinking about the turn of events and with great reluctance, he lifts the phone receiver and calls down to the lab to alert Higgins to the new plans. He then rises from his chair and makes his way back to the mess. Having not eaten yet himself, he helps himself to a mug of coffee from the coffee maker and heads over to the front to address the men one more time.

"Men, there has been a change of plan," he starts speaking, "you are to remain here for the time being, the authorities want us to administer a more thorough testing regime before you leave. As soon as you have finished your meal, the soldiers will escort you back to your rooms. I will get the quartermaster to dig up some fatigues so that you can all take a shower and change your clothes. Please bear with us, we must follow the orders from the brass back in England. Are there any questions?"
    Peter looks thoughtful and stands to address the C.O.
    "Sir, what has caused this need for more medical tests? Has something come up from the blood work?"
    The C.O. looks down and thinks carefully before speaking.
    "There were some anomalies, yes, and until we know more about what they mean, you will be staying here. It is safer that way. The British authorities are sending a team to work with Dr Higgins to find out what has caused the glitch. You do not have any known diseases, so you don't need to worry about getting sick."

Peter sits down again, his mind turning on the news. At least they will be in warm, comfortable conditions, and they can rest. It could be much worse!
    When there are no further questions, Robbins turns to refill his cup and return to his office. Outside the door, Higgins is waiting for his return. The C.O. resigns himself to the fact that his schedule for today is now thrown out the window, so to speak, so he lets his irritation drop away, rather than carry it around with him all day. It would only be hurting himself after all.

The Family

Canath stands before the Calainth Stone, his eyes closed. He is dressed in a cloak of a white fur; his golden beard and hair stand in stark contrast. Before him stands Aletheia. She is dressed in what appears to be another unusual kind of long, silk robe, but this time, black with red striations running in zigzagging lines from the neck to the hem. Her feet are bare, and her hair falls in a fine, golden stream around her shoulders. She, too, has her eyes closed, and if one looked closely, they would see a slight, well-controlled shivering in her limbs. Phoenix stands at his father's shoulder and just behind him, his eyes are wide open, dark and intense.

On the Stone lie two masks, one with holes where the eyes appear, one is a half mask. Near the stone, there is a brazier; red-hot coals simmer in the bottom, and there are two long rods leaning into the brazier, their metal ends glowing cherry red. The silence is broken only by the crackling of the coals.
    Canath begins to speak in a strange tongue; his deep voice projected so that it bounces off the few trees and the stone walls of the tower. Just as soon, he stops again, and the silence seems ominous.
    Slowly at first, and then with increasing volume, Canath begins to chant; the chanting seems to fill the whole Universe, and its strange notes linger in the air, like fine mist. There is no bird song and no flitting of small bodies amongst the trees and shrubbery. At last, Canath opens his eyes, and his face is set like steel. He takes three steps towards Aletheia and she, too, opens her eyes. They betray nothing of what she feels.

Canath places his right hand on top of Aletheia's head and begins to chant again. This time, the notes cling to Aletheia's hair and face, granting her an unending feeling of peace. She once more closes her eyes. Canath reaches for the two masks, placing the one with holes over Aletheia's head, and the half mask on his own face, chanting all the while without missing a beat. The chanting reaches a crescendo now, the notes flying into the Universe as Canath reaches with his bare hands for the two rods. There is a sizzling as the metal connects with his hands, but again he does not miss a beat. He is about to insert the rods into Aletheia's eyes when there is a loud thunderclap, the reverberations bouncing echoes off the rocks of the tower and around the grove in which they stand.

Canath opens his eyes as a shimmering appears and then forms begin to move and take shape. There stand Marcom and the Rift Spinner, and Canath drops the rods and bows.

"You have done well," the scratching voice of the Rift Spinner addresses Canath and Aletheia. "There is another way, Canath, and I will administer it; you have been granted this boon by the power of existence itself."

"I submit to your authority, Mighty One," Canath breathes a sigh of absolute relief. The Rift Spinner moves on its eight, huge legs to stand before Aletheia; she does not shrink back from the horror before her, rather she smiles in greeting.

"Daughter of the Universe, you have shown yourself to be worthy of mercy; your greatness will be sung by the heroes of the future. I bring you the sting of poison that will give you second sight. Do you submit willingly?"

"I do, oh Mighty One." Aletheia replies.

"Then hold out your hand." The Rift Spinner demands.

The spider-human takes Aletheia's hand with two of his legs and places it over his abdomen, from which a long, thin spike is ejected. The spike is so sharp, she barely feels it pass right through her hand, but she feels the sting. The effect of the sting renders her immediately unconscious, her body slumps seemingly unbreathing, to the ground.

There is another loud booming and the Rift Spinner and Marcom begin to shimmer and then disappear completely before the echoes have died away. As soon as the air is still again, Canath and Phoenix rush to Aletheia's side, their consternation making their hearts beat faster. Canath reaches down with his terribly burnt hands and feels for her pulse. He sits back on his heels, relief flooding his system, she lives, and the task is complete. Thank the gods! He removes the masks, tossing them both into the brazier. Bright green flames jump up and quickly reduce them to ashes.

Ladon lifts his head, his green eyes shining. He hears the sonic booming of the Universe and smiles. It is done! In his baby voice he begins to sing in the archaic language only he and Marcom understand. He sends his thanks to the Power and returns to sleeping again, his tiny hands wound tightly into his mother's hair.

Florence lies waiting; her heart is beating like a drum. She cannot sleep and she cannot think; all her energy is centered on Aletheia and the terrible ordeal she will even now be undergoing. She hopes her daughter will be strong enough to withstand the horror and the pain. She thinks of her husband, Canath, and hopes he can do what must be done to protect them all. Suddenly, she experiences the shaking of the walls as the sonic boom reverberates, and she knows it is done. She thanks the gods that it is over.

She quickly rises and dresses. Moving quietly, she descends to the kitchen to prepare brew strong enough to allay the horror of those outside. She sips from a cup herself, ready to help as soon as the others appear. There is the sound of heavy footsteps and she opens the door just in time for Canath and Phoenix to enter. Between them they carry the prone Aletheia; Canath instructs his son to continue up the stairs to Aletheia's room. Florence follows close behind. As they lay her on her bed, Florence gasps; her daughter's face is whole. There is no sign of her eyes having been damaged at all. She looks questioningly at Canath.

"We had a visit from the plenum," he speaks quietly, "the Rift Spinner completed the task without the need for my brutality. I need to sit down, Florence."

"Come with me," she immediately takes Canath's arm, and Phoenix takes the other. Carefully they lead Canath down to the kitchen, and he sits heavily. Florence reaches over to the sideboard and places a cup in front of him.

"Mother, Father has terribly burnt hands," Phoenix crosses to the water bucket and reaching for a bowl, fills it to the brim with the cold water. He fetches it to Canath's side and helps him place his hands into the water. The relief is writ large on Canath's face, and he nods his thanks to his oldest son. Phoenix lifts the cup so that Canath can take a large swallow; meanwhile, Florence sends for the midwife to come and tend to the burns.

"I am so glad you did not have to complete the task," Florence runs her hands through Canath's hair in an obvious sign of soothing and affection.

"You have no idea how glad I am also." Canath answers, the pain from his hands evident in his voice. "It is done, and our girl may take time to recover, but her pain will be much less this way. I think we have Marcom to thank for the intervention."

"Then we will give him our sincerest thanks when he returns to us." Florence sits next to Canath, making sure to feed him the strong brew at short intervals and keep physical contact with him.

"Phoenix, you should go and rest, dear boy. Thank you for supporting your father and sister, and please take a cup with you to help you sleep. We will wake you in time for a late breakfast." Florence smiles at her son, and he nods and turns towards the stairs.

Greg and Tim

"Gavinar, we need to study this text together!" Greg is excited now, and his excitement infects the others.

"Do you think it is a possibility?" Felix asks, his own excitement ratcheting up a notch.

"Well, we won't know until we understand the way it works; but yes, I see it as a possibility. Is there any indication of who constructed the orb, or from what time it came to be here?"

"Nothing that I could determine except Mesmer's description," Felix replies, "but I was not looking at it from the perspective available to us with you both here and from the readings we have carried out."

"Then let's get to it," Greg replies, and the men settle in to read; the text propped up in a position in which they can all see the pages clearly.

There is a foreword and a distinct warning in the first words of the page written by Franz Mesmer. "The method written herein should not be attempted without the close study of animal magnetism. The dangers inherent may cause great harm if not applied in the correct way."

"So, the forerunner of modern-day hypnosis." Greg speaks aloud.

"I have managed to use the method in a certain way, as you well know," Felix replies, "but I know nothing of this, 'hypnosis' that you mention."

"Not to worry, Felix, let's just continue our reading." Greg determines not to speak aloud again while they undertake to read the text.

At first, Mesmer explicates his new method calling it 'animal magnetism', and as the explication leads on, he writes in his own name as the final indicator. Mesmerism, it seems works by tricking the rational conscious mind to relax to the threshold point that separates consciousness from the unconscious mind. Later this would be called the subconscious. It is at this point that one can make suggestions to the subject, and the subject react to those suggestions in whatever way the mesmerist requires. The 'state' requisite for this to occur is similar to sleeping but yet retains a shred of consciousness into which the mesmerist works his projections. Franz Mesmer hypothesizes that his method of subconscious suggestion could be used to cure social ills and even perhaps physical and mental illnesses if used correctly. At this point, Greg recollects reading the work of Freud and Jung, written more than a hundred and twenty years later than this text, and their understanding of the collective unconscious from which our conscious ego has arisen. He remembers Jung's suggestion that ego consciousness is akin to an orange floating in the Pacific Ocean, the ocean being the collective unconscious of all humankind. They continue with the reading until this section is finished.

The next section of the text refers to the orb, and this one, Greg and Tim read carefully. The orb, so the text relates has been finely hand finished, constructed from a crystalline rock that Mesmer calls 'robelite'. He does not say where or how he came by the 'robelite'; just that it can project the thoughts of anyone within the necessary proximity for it to work. Greg wants to follow this up by himself, so he speaks to the others,
 "I think it is now time to take stock before we continue further. What do the rest of you think?"
 The men decide to take a break and to eat, and Greg suggests that they then separate again to think on what they have just read. The servants are called to fetch food and wine, and the four retire to the sitting room floor cushions to wait to eat together. Nobody speaks further; they are all tied up in their own thoughts. Soon enough Petyr and the maid appear with a jug of wine and a platter of flatbread and cold meats, and the four men tuck in. As soon as everyone has eaten his fill, the four men go to their rooms to think. As they are leaving, Greg indicates to Tim to follow him. The two men go back to Greg's room, and he lifts his laptop from his pack and places it on the small desk next to the window.

"I want to try to find out what this 'robelite' might be," Greg speaks quietly. "The mesmerism is quite obviously the forerunner of hypnosis, so we don't need to wonder about that at least."

"I am more interested in the globe, too," Tim replies, "and how we might use it to return to Kettering."

"Let's start with what it is made from," Greg says, and the two men watch the screen as Greg connects to the satellite and brings up a university search engine.

He types in the words 'robelite' and 'minerals' to start the search. In no time at all, a web page pops up, asking whether the searcher means 'riebeckite'. Greg clicks on the 'riebeckite' and a full page comes up with relevant information; what kind of mineral it is, its chemical formulas, properties and how many variants occur naturally. The men read with great interest and type the question: 'where in the world it is found.' Portugal is one place, and this being the closest to Gothenburg, it is the one of interest to Tim and Greg. The properties and physical environment in which riebeckite is found makes it a very likely candidate. Greg and Tim continue to search the known minerals that have a similar sounding name to 'robelite', but nothing occurs that has the distinct properties necessary to construct the globe. After an hour, both men agree the globe must be made of riebeckite, discovered and named as such by Emil Riebeck after 1853, but obviously known to the Alchemists in their present time as 'robelite'.

"I just don't see how something that was not discovered yet could be found by our searching for a mineral that sounds similar." Tim is confounded by this fact and not a little dubious about what Greg has found. "Can you please explain that if you want me to accept that this could be fact?"

"What have we been doing, Tim?" Greg replies with a question of his own.

"I don't know what you mean."

"What have we done since starting out with Henry?" Greg tries again.

"Oh, you mean passing through the Curtain." The question is rhetorical.

"Precisely!" Greg replies.

"Well, I guess what you are alluding to is the fact that we are here, about two hundred and twenty years before we are actually born, yes?"

"Exactly, Tim, and how can that be?"

"Because time as we know it does not exist except in the human mind beholding what is before it." Tim is starting to get the fleeting edge of an idea that he is not quite grasping; it seems to refer to what all this could mean in terms of their present search.

"I get, in essence, what you are saying, but how could the name 'robelite' sound like a name of something not yet discovered and so named?"

"From reading the letters written between Jung and Wolfgang Pauli," replies Greg.

"I still don't get it." Tim replies.

Greg sits for a few seconds, collecting his thoughts before beginning:

"Well, Jung researched meaning and came to understand that there are events that happen when the human mind is concentrating deeply on some idea. He called these events synchronicity. To cut a long story short, when you concentrate mentally and deeply, sometimes a physical emanation occurs that cannot be linked in any way as a cause-and-effect relationship to what you are thinking about, and yet it is full of meaning in just those terms. This happened to Jung many times, and that is why he and Pauli talked about a plenum; an underlying substratum in which everything that was, is and ever can be, already exists. This explains how telepathy at a distance is possible. It means that there are no miracles, no supernatural events, but rather an emanation pops through the veil between human consciousness and the plenum. Heidegger even named this 'the between' in his work.

Jung re-conducted the experiments of J.B. Rhine, who devised a set of twenty-five cards, all with different markings, like a star or wiggly lines. He then asked students to try to discern what was on a card held in one room, with the student sitting in another. The upshot was that the number of correct guesses in most cases was beyond the mean for it to be coincidental. This testing was carried on over several years, and the distances between the cardholder and the guesser was increased to two thousand kilometers. The distance did not make any difference to the results, but one factor weighed heavily on the results; the interest of the guesser. Once their interest in the experiment started to wane, the number of correct guesses waned also in proportion. This is one of the results that led Jung towards his theory of synchronicity — that when one is highly interested in an idea, the interest can actually have the result of manifesting a physical appearance that is deeply meaningful to what the person thinking is interested in."

"But how does that relate to what we are talking about here?" Tim is still mystified.

"One of the things that Pauli suggested to Jung was to establish a lexicon of terms that combined the concepts of both physics and psychology, because he found that the scientists working in particle physics at the time, began coining terms already in use in psychology, but that fact was unknown to the said scientists. They thought they were introducing new terms, when in fact, the terms were already in use in a science that they had never read. This fact consolidated Pauli's understanding of an underlying plenum and enabled him to make the discovery of the 'exclusion principle'. He hypothesized the 'neutrino' on the basis of his understanding of the plenum."

"So, what you are saying," Tim states, "is that the plenum, through which we have both travelled twice, holds the answers to any question that can be asked, and that this can be wholly diachronic since time as we understand it, is our own finite illusion."

"Exactly." Greg replies. "And if this is truly the case, then anything that can focus human attention into a projected form, can also behave as a physical manifestation of that projection. Now do you get it?"

"Oh my God, yes, now I get it!" Tim is awestruck.

Brandon

For a full minute, Fellings senior sits in the sand, trying to settle both his mind and body. Could there be anything more catastrophic or horrific that what he has just seen and been through? He thinks not. As the shock subsides, he begins to understand his awful position. He has no food or water, the transponder is gone along with his son and the submersible, and he is stuck in a time-warp of his own choosing. If only he could wake up from this freakish nightmare! He should have remembered that the Megalodon survived the mass extinction; he just let his son swim out with no thought whatsoever of the possibility of an underwater attack from this, or one of many extant giants of the deep. With a supreme effort, he shakes himself out of the daze he feels and looks around him. What to do now or even first? Well, first things first, what can be salvaged from the situation? The first thing to be done is to search the shoreline and the shallows for any sign of the backpacks or the transponder. If he can find those, at least he will have a few supplies to go on with, and perhaps if he can find the transponder and work out how it works, there could be a slim chance that he could recall the submersible, provided it was not actually swallowed or shredded by that massive maw! He begins to look along the immediate shoreline, searching carefully for anything that shines or looks unusual; when he has covered several hundred yards in each direction, he moves further up the beach towards the forest, remembering that the wave that broke over him might have carried the articles along with it. There is still enough moisture in the sand for him to see the full span of the wave's inland incursion.

There is nothing evident in the sandy tract, so he moves further towards the fern forest carefully searching in a grid and slowly moving towards the ferny edge of the forest. Adrenalin keeps him moving, and the necessary mental focus eases his mind from the horrors of the last several hours. Soon, he becomes aware that he is very thirsty, so he looks around him to remember where he is in relation to the area searched, then moves through the forest, using the marks in the trunks made previously to reach the waterfall. With little thought for his own safety, he squats quickly and slakes his thirst with the fast running, cold water. He dips his head in the water to keep his focus clear. At least it is cold here, not hot and steamy like it will be in another million years or so! He stands and stretches his back and arms, aware of the ache from bending to look for so long.

He searches with his eyes for as far as he can see ahead but notices nothing untoward. He is just about to return to the forest edge when a movement catches his eye. He stands stock still, not wanting to scare whatever is moving through the ferns; he waits and is rewarded after a few seconds by the brushing sound of a body moving against the foliage. The sound seems to be coming from about shoulder height and moving slowly and carefully as if it is foraging. Suddenly, a bright blue head with a bony ridge and red wattles emerges from the ferns, and the heavy body of the bird follows. It squarks in fright as it spies Fellings standing there, and turns tail, crashing back through the forest with no thought for the noise it is making. Fellings remembers having seen a cassowary at the London Zoo when he was a boy; the startled creature resembles the bird he saw, perhaps this one a little taller than its modern relative. The sight of the bird somehow eases Fellings' mind; he is at the least not totally alone here. If he cannot find the backpacks, perhaps he can work out some way to trap a bird like the one he just encountered. The thought of killing such a creature is not in the least appealing, but he knows he will need to eat if he is to survive.

It takes him all morning to search through to the forest proper, and by then he is starting to lose heart. He knows it is highly unlikely that he will find the lost things amongst the ferns, and he must try to make a shelter for himself before the night falls. He is tired, hungry and despondent; the thought of giving themselves over to the British authorities now seems like a sweet dream compared to the situation he now faces. He sits down on the sand to think, but his mind will not obey, and he falls into a daydream of self-pity and remorse. He can see that the sun is past its zenith and will soon begin its descent towards the horizon.

He already feels the chill of night in the air. He huddles down in the sand, at least his tracksuit is dry now.

A loud cracking sound wakes Fellings out of a deep sleep; it is pitch black, and only the darker shadows of the ferns are visible. He is very cold and stiff, and it takes a few minutes to work the numbness from his limbs; it must have overtaken him while he slept. He tries not to make any noise and listens intently. Something woke him and it must have been loud because the sound of the breakers is quite loud.

He can see nothing, but he regulates his breathing so that it cannot be heard. His heart is beating loudly in his own ears, and he hopes it cannot be heard through the ferny forest. He is so cold now, that he begins to dig out the sand around him. It takes some time, but soon enough he has dug a burrow, deep enough that he can sit in it and just look out over the top. He tries to make himself comfortable and huddles back down, his head resting on the side of his sandy hide. Exhaustion and shock overtake him again, and he soon falls back into a troubled sleep. He dreams he is chasing Brandon through a dark tunnel. He cannot quite reach him when the tunnel becomes the giant maw of a Megalodon, the teeth four inches wide and seven inches high, serrated along the edges. He tries to grab onto a tooth to stop from being swallowed and it slices his hand open. He screams and wakes himself up from the nightmare. The utter darkness has given way to the twilight shadows of pre-dawn. Although it is cold, Fellings is sweating from the nightmare visitation and lies unmoving until the nightmare has totally receded. His heart is beating like a drum, and his breathing is shallow and rapid. He slowly calms himself and brings his breathing under control.

His first conscious thought is that he is ravenous and thirsty. He stands and steps out of his burrow, brushing the sand from his clothes, hair and hands. He stretches himself and feels his back crack as his spine unwinds from his awkward sleeping position. He will surely have to try to construct a better shelter today! He returns to the waterfall to drink and take a cursory wash, just his face and hands will do. He searches the rapids for any signs of living creatures, but the water is boiling and bubbling such that anything in there could not be seen anyway, even in broad daylight. What to do now? He decides to follow the river edge for a while and searching around on the ground, he eventually spots a sliver of broken rock, the edge of which is sharp enough to mark the tree fern trunks. The last thing he wants is to be lost in the forest! He pockets the makeshift blade and sets off along the water's edge.

The rapids continue for several hundred yards and the ground slopes downwards. Soon, however, the ground levels out and the rapids slow, to the point that he can see to the sandy bottom of the clear water. He stops and squats down, the better to see if anything is crawling or swimming in the water. He is so engrossed in trying to see what is in the water that when he eventually looks up, he is startled to find himself under intense scrutiny by a pair of enormous, beady eyes. He is careful not to make any sudden movement as the head of the huge, python-like snake dangling from the fern fronds above his head stares back at him, its large tongue testing the air for his smell. Very slowly, he inches away from the head, backing into the ferns alongside the river. Slowly he withdraws the sharp stone from his tracksuit pocket, making sure to keep his eyes on the snake. It seems to be curious rather than aggressive; it has never seen a human being before, and it obviously feels no danger from the creature in front of it. Its whole demeanor seems to be one of a top predator, hunter rather than hunted.

Fellings backs into the immediate forest and tracks a wide arc around the tree ferns containing the body of the snake. He breaks out of the forest again, some twenty yards ahead of where the snake's head dangles lazily. Although the creature gave him one hell of a fright, he is also delighted to see it here, because it means that there must be enough small game or birds to keep it fed. If that is the case, then he might be able to feed himself too.

Henry

Peter settles himself on the bed in the room provided for him and waits for the quartermaster to bring him something clean to wear. The thought of a hot shower and soap is like a dream after the last week or so; he daydreams about it while he waits. The others wait in their allotted rooms also, but Derek, as usual, cannot contain his fear and impatience. He walks out of his room to complain, right into the arms of two soldiers.

"I want to know why we are being kept here," he speaks petulantly to the shorter of the two guards, "you can't just keep us here against our will!"

"Step back into your room." The soldier stares at Derek and his face assures him that he will brook no disobedience.

"Why can't you tell us what is going on?" Terrified, Derek continues to harangue the soldier. The two guards take him by the arms, and when he tries to shrug out of their hold, he realizes he does not have the physical strength to free himself. Fear immediately sublimates to anger, and he rages at the two guards to little avail. The shorter guard speaks quietly into his headset, and within seconds, a man dressed in scrubs hurries towards them a hypodermic syringe in his hand. Derek struggles relentlessly now, but soon the doctor injects him, and within seconds, his full weight slumps forwards, and the two guards carry him between them and lay him gently on his bed.

"Will you please let the commander know that we can't keep these men calm for too long. They are intelligent enough to understand something is amiss, and without an explanation that makes sense to them, I think we may be in for more of this." He points towards Derek.

"I will speak to the General immediately. Good work and you showed great restraint men." The doctor turns and takes his leave. He does not want to chemically restrain the men if possible; he does not want to introduce anything into their physical systems until he has a chance to do more tests, and he knows that the team from MI6 will not like it either. He makes his way to the General's office and knocks.

"Come!" the General looks up from his paperwork as the doctor enters and bids him sit down. Higgins settles himself before beginning.

"We are in an untenable position with the visitors, and I have just had to sedate one of them. Can't we reason with them and let them know what this is about? I really don't want to use any chemicals on them at this point, or our tests may be skewed."

"I have to follow orders too, Doctor, but I will check when the team from England are due to land. We may have to think of something else if we have to wait any length of time."

"Thank you, sir," the doctor replies, "I think we need to keep the situation as calm as possible, even if it means finding something for the men to do until the team from MI6 get here."

The doctor rises to leave, and the General assures him that he will let him know how long it will be as soon as he has that information. He picks up his phone and asks his adjutant to get Thames House on the line. There is little point trying to get paperwork done while the base is so unsettled; the General decides to try to find out more about these strangers and why they came to be in his proximity. He knows only that they are academics from Kettering, that they are part of a secret mission of some kind, and that the English authorities have been looking for them, but that is as far as his intelligence on the situation goes. Perhaps if he can find out more, he can make decisions based on facts and not on half-truths coming from England.

His phone rings, and he picks it up impatiently.

"Robbins." He says and waits for the caller to speak.

"General, what can I do for you?" the same unctuous voice answers as spoke previously.

"We have a problem, sir, and I need to know the ETA of your team."

"What seems to be the problem?" the man replies with his own question.

"The men you sent here are becoming fractious, and one has already had to be sedated by my men. Higgins is concerned about using sedation before he can run the more intensive testing, so I need to know how long before your team gets here."

"They will be with you in about four hours; they left immediately after my call to you. Do not use any further sedation under any circumstances, and that is an order."

"Yes, and thank you, sir." The General ends the call; his frustration with being kept out of the loop at boiling point. He is fed up with orders that are irrational at best and dangerous at worst. The suits in Thames House have no idea how things work on the ground and how quickly a situation can go awry.

Steven sits down on his bed again; he has just witnessed what happened to Derek, and his mind is working overtime. Something is very wrong, but what? He reflects on what has happened since they arrived here. The reason given for why they are being kept here is that something has shown up in their blood, and that obviously has the authorities in a spin. So, what is the common factor in the case that all their blood tests are anomalous? That is the mitigating question, and the only thing that they all have in common, is passing through the Curtain. Has this caused their blood work to be affected? He falls back into his philosophical mode to try to reason it out. What are the known premises? Premise one: all the blood taken from sixteen individuals is showing similar anomalies. What are the commonalities that could cause this to occur?

Premise two: they have all passed through the Curtain at least twice. What does passing through the Curtain entail, as far as he understands?

Premise three: the mode of passing through the Curtain is aligned to breaking the body down into its constituent molecules and reforming the body at the other side. What is the most likely thing that can go wrong?

Premise four: the reforming process has not been fully successful, complete or contains something other than the original molecules.

Conclusion: there is something in the blood work that does not belong there, or there has been a change in the reconstituted molecules. Steven punts for the latter; there is a change that does not appear in normal human blood, and if this is the case, then more testing would be needed to find out what it is, or why it is the case. Steven sits and ponders what this will mean for each and every one of them; obviously, their bodies have completely reconstituted, or they would be physically aware if this was not the case, so the reforming is both complete and successful, which leaves a change in the blood molecules of each of them. No wonder they are being kept at this isolated location!

The Family

Antheia is woken by the chanting of her son, Ladon. His bright green eyes are focused on her face, and he smiles as she opens her eyes. She returns the smile and kisses his sweet face making him giggle with pleasure. She props herself to a sitting position and puts Ladon to her heavy breast. He begins to gulp as the free-flowing milk floods his mouth. As he feeds, Antheia remembers her sister's ordeal, and she wonders how she is faring. She decides she will rise and visit her room as soon as the baby has drunk his fill.

Aletheia wakes from her drugged sleep and immediately puts her hands to her eyes. She sighs deeply as she feels the normal contour of her face, and her heart begins to slow its drumming in her chest. She opens her eyes as she normally would, but there is no sight. She reaches out with her mind and feels the ragged edges of what once was her field of vision; the field is no longer there. It is as if, like a piece of paper, it has been torn away by the Rift Spinner's sting. She lays quietly, thinking about what this now means for her lived experience. Without extending any effort of her own, and as she lies thinking, an inner sight begins to develop. There is a shimmering behind her eye lids, and a glimmer of light starts to shine, just around the edges of her mind at first, but as she waits patiently, the light begins to spread towards the centre of her mind, a warming feeling accompanies this growing insight. The message of the Oracle replays in her mind and now makes perfect sense. "You must be blind like me…" And she is! Just like the oracle, Aletheia has been gifted with second sight, by losing her primary physical vision. She thanks the gods that she will not have to live in darkness, and as the insight develops with no effort from her, and beyond her control, she understands that anything truthful will be filled with light. This is how she will recognize truth; the light of it will shine brightly for her. With this understanding comes the memory of her responsibility, and she determines to stand as guardian in Ladon's stead and never allow falsity to pass her scrutiny. She will fulfil her destiny and freely vows to do so.

Ladon lies back milk-drunk and sleepy, his face rosy and his eyes closing. Antheia clips his silver locks again, and using the wooden box given to her, she places them inside, and closing the lid, turns the key. Gently she lays him in the bed next to where she herself lays, and rises quietly, donning a woolen robe as she steps out into the passage leading to Aletheia's room. As she enters, her sister smiles and holds out her arms. The two embrace and Antheia stares at Aletheia consternation written on her features,

"Lethi, did Father not carry through the ritual? Was he unable to hurt you?"

"It was not necessary, Antheia; we had a visit from the plenum, Marcom and a creature called the Rift Spinner. Just as father was about to blind me, the Rift Spinner called a halt. He said the gods had granted father and me an intercession. If I was willing to submit to his sting, then my eyes would remain whole."

"Oh, Lethi, how wonderful! How do you feel, and can you see anything at all?"

"At first there was only darkness, but as I lay thinking, a light began to appear. At first it was just a glimmer on the edge of my consciousness, but as I waited, it began to fill my whole mind. Now it is there constantly, and while I cannot physically see you, the glow of you is present to me."

"This is how it must be for the Oracle; I could never work out how she knew when someone approached her, but this must be the way."

"My thoughts exactly, and her message could not have been clearer." Aletheia considers all that has come to pass since that last visit.

"We must all fulfil our destinies now." Aletheia voices what she and Antheia already know; they have both made a start along their allotted paths.

"Let's both go down for breakfast," Antheia suggests, "while Ladon sleeps."

The sisters go arm in arm, down the stairs, Antheia leading Aletheia until they enter the kitchen. Canath and Florence are already seated along the benches in deep discussion. There is no sign yet of the boys, but their parents look up and stand to welcome both girls with a hug. Canath's hands are heavily bandaged, but this does not stop him reaching for each of his daughters in turn.

"Today you will take up your guardian role, Aletheia. I will accompany you into the plenum until you feel strong enough to remain there alone. The universal unguarded state can go on no longer." Canath immediately comes to the point; the urgency in his voice reminding the girls that the danger of the situation is still critical. Any respite from their duties is over, and each of them sighs; at least they have been a family here for a short time, and each knows that there is much to do before they can be together like this again., and only then, if everything goes to plan.

"Father, thank you for your kindness and consideration earlier," Aletheia speaks, "I know by your burns, how much the thought of blinding me was a torture to you. I will not let you or the Universal Power down."

"That is why you were chosen for this onerous task, child." Canath replies.

The servants arrive with the breakfast platters piled high, so the four of them begin their last meal together with no further talk of duties for the moment. Blindness does not seem to hamper Aletheia; she reaches deftly for the plates of food and serves herself watched on by the others. It is as if a second kind of sight directs her hands, as is the case.

Phoenix stares at the ceiling seeing nothing. His mind is replaying for the umpteenth time the horrors of earlier that morning. The arrival of Marcom and the Rift Spinner brings with it many questions and no answers. Who is this creature? What is his part in this odyssey? What about himself and Kenny? What is to become of them? No longer able to control his tumbling thoughts, Phoenix rises and dresses quickly. Perhaps a drink of water will help. He quietly makes his way to the kitchen, only to find his parents and sisters already enjoying a delicious looking breakfast. He kisses each of them on the cheek and quickly takes his place at the table, his stomach growling at the delicious aromas. He piles his plate high and drinks from the cup set next to him.

"Good morning, Mother, Father, Aletheia, Antheia," he says before tucking in. The others laugh at his haste to fill his mouth; the sure sign of a boy growing quickly into a man.

"When you have eaten, Phoenix, will you please wake your brother and send him directly to me?" Canath looks at his hungry son and smiles; the boy is certainly able to hold his own in the most horrendous of circumstances. All to the good, for he has many ordeals to go through!

"Certainly, Father, I won't take long." Phoenix stuffs another large mouthful in, chewing with relish.

"And how is my grandson this morning?" Florence asks Antheia.

"Eating and growing like a horse," Antheia smiles as she replies, "I have to cut his hair every morning now, just so that it does not tangle him up."

"Aletheia and I will take what has been cut with us today," Canath says to Antheia, "we have need of it where we are going."

"Surely, Father, and you are welcome because soon I will need another box to put it in. Do you know why it is growing at such a rate?"

"For the precise reason that we need it, Antheia," Canath carefully replies, "and I will need the constant supply for Aletheia until Ladon is grown."

"Then please take it and may the gods bless Aletheia as she takes her place today as the guardian."

There is little more to say, so the family continue with their breakfast until Phoenix excuses himself to wake and fetch Kenny. Florence and Canath exchange a knowing look while the girls chat happily about the baby.

Greg and Tim

As the four men return to continue their study and before they sit down again, Greg holds up his hand and speaks.

"Gavinar and Felix, Tim and I have been brainstorming the use of the orb, and we would like to find out if we are right about how it operates. Could you fetch the box, please, Felix?"

Felix looks puzzled; how could this be when he and Gavinar have tried without success for the last two years to understand how the object works? Is this some kind of trick? He looks askance at Greg, and Greg reads his suspicion.

"It is just that Tim and I have access to much more advanced physics and psychology than you two," he starts, "and so we are not as bemused by it as both of you. There are many newly discovered devices that would blow your minds if you were exposed to them without knowing the science behind how they work. My laptop and the fact that I can power it from a device orbiting the earth and in a diachronic situation is just one."

"I take your point, Greg, apologies, I will get the box." Felix leaves the room.

Greg, Tim and Gavinar sit down to wait; Gavinar has an inscrutable expression on his face, and he studies the other two men as surreptitiously as is possible. Could they really have the answer? He wonders what the result will be if as he now believes, they can really travel through time. The men have talked of a Curtain of some kind, but he realizes he did not pay much attention to their fabulous story when they first appeared at his door. Well, maybe they will soon find out!

Felix reappears, the box in hand and he carefully places it on the low table. With deft hands he opens the box, and using what he has learnt from the text included, he raises his hand for the orb to rise from its nestled position. As it rises, it begins to spin as it did before, but there is a distinct difference. As soon as it has cleared the top of the box, it makes its way over to Greg and rotates in a position just above his eyes. Greg thinks, and the orb transmits. Once again, the scene from Kettering appears in the surface of the spinning sphere, then just as suddenly, the orb goes black. The surface of the orb lights again and displayed now is the scene from Athens. The house in which Tim and Greg stayed is now displayed. It is empty; there is no sign of anyone, anywhere. The scene changes again, and now there is shown a man sitting in a room wearing military fatigues; outside the open door stand two British soldiers. Greg gasps, the others have been captured somehow, but at least they are back in their own time. He takes the orb through the door displayed using only his mind and by summoning up the faces of the other fifteen men. He soon finds that the sixteen men are all accounted for, confined in what appears to be a barracks, but the outside scene is not England. His mind is tiring now, so he sends the orb back to its box and sits back musing on what they have seen.

Felix and Gavinar sit spellbound, staring open mouthed as Greg directs the orb. Nobody but Felix has been able to control the device and only then, after his long hours of study. Perhaps Greg is right; the future holds secrets not yet available to Felix. What can they glean from what they have just witnessed? Firstly, it works by some sort of mind control, but not just in the ways described by Franz Mesmer. Greg also seems to be able to control what is displayed, and this must also be by using his mind. So, what does this mean for them all?

"Would you care to explain what you just did?" Felix asks somewhat put out with this turn of events.

"Don't stress, Felix," Greg responds, "I was pretty sure that the thing works in the same way as animal magnetism, as Mesmer describes, but with the added dimensions that we know of how hypnosis and mind control work. Would you believe it if I told you that in our own time, scientists have discovered how to build a false limb that works as the real thing, just by the wearer learning to control it by thinking about what he wants to do? So, you see, it really made sense to me that the orb works in a similar fashion."

Rather than question Greg further in relation to the orb, Gavinar now asks Greg,

"What does this mean, do you think, about whether or not we can use it to travel through this Curtain thing you told me about when you arrived?"

"Now that is the real question," Greg replies thinking, "I am not sure, but Tim and I now need to do some research of our own to try to answer it."

"Do you need the orb to test any findings?" Felix asks, relaxed now.

"Not at this stage, thanks, Felix," Greg stands up and Tim follows, "we need to look up and read some scientific articles, then we may be able to answer your question."

"Would you mind if Gavinar and I look on?" Felix is anxious to be included in the knowledge gathering process.

"That's fine, Felix, as long as Tim and I do not have to stop to explain what you may not understand. I want to find the answers as much as you do, and I don't want to waste time with teaching the both of you. Is that OK with you?"

Greg looks at Gavinar and Felix in turn, and both men nod their assent.

"That is fair," Felix replies, "we both want the answers too; we have had to wait two years so far, so please let's just get on with it."

Brandon

Fellings heads back towards the beach, following the marks in the tree fern trunks. As he walks, he is thinking. He is very hungry, but he must, first of all, take care of his shelter needs before the day is through. He is still stiff and sore from his night in the sand, and has no wish to repeat the experience. If, as he considers, he builds a rudimentary shelter near the edge of the fern forest, he only has to worry about anything approaching from that direction. As far as he can remember, there is nothing else in this time period that can approach him from the beach side. As he walks, he gathers a few dropped fronds and anything else that might be useful. Near the forest edge, he looks for a flat stretch that is high enough that a high tide cannot wash him out. At last, he settles on a small knoll just inside the forest proper; this will afford him shelter from the wind and the sun, if that becomes a problem, although the ambient temperature says otherwise. There are tree ferns sparsely distributed on the knoll, and he looks for two that are about two metres apart; he spies just what he needs. He begins by digging down through the sand to about ten centimetres around a perimeter that includes the two ferns as the end points. He wishes he had a shovel or some kind of implement rather than just his bare hands and a piece of sharp rock; this is going to take a long time!

It takes more than two hours just to clear the base of his shelter to an approximate size of two-by-two metres and to a depth of about ten centimetres. Sweating and tired, Fellings sits down to survey his work. Paltry by any standards! He sets off back into the forest to drink again, wondering if he can survive at all. His thirst slaked at the waterfall; he trudges back to his unmade shelter. There is almost no point to his continuing with no tools, and he now knows that the story of Robinson Crusoe is so far from the truth that it hardly matters. Despondent, he sets off down to the water's edge; perhaps he can look in any rock pools for a small fish or anything that may be edible. It is more than twenty-four hours since he last ate, and he is weakened from shock and lack of food. There is a shallow rocky outcrop that he can see just around the curve from where he and Brandon came ashore; he carefully makes his way in that direction.

He clambers up onto the outcrop, checking for any shellfish that may be attached. There are rock pools and before long he spies a strange-looking crab scurrying along the bottom of the deepest. The crab looks to be about ten centimetres across and without thinking, he plunges his hand in to pluck it out before it can escape. For the first time in many hours, he smiles. Maybe there is hope after all. Looking around, he spies a flat rock, and using only his hands, he slams the crab down onto the surface several times, with as much force as he can muster. The shell of the creature splits open, and Fellings falls on the flesh and innards with gusto. It will not fill his empty stomach, but it will go some ways to helping him stay alive. Just the tiny triumph of catching the creature lifts his mood. With this instant success, Fellings concentrates on searching the pools thoroughly; there is a rough kind of seaweed in most, and he gathers a handful, testing a minute piece of it in his mouth. He waits several minutes for any reaction, but when none is apparent, he eats the handful. It tastes like sea water and agar, but if it does not make him sick, he will gather and eat more tomorrow.

Before he steps back down from the outcrop, he looks around at the vista; he can see slightly further from this shallow elevation. He turns around to step down to the sand to return to his side of the cove. As he steps around the curve towards his former position, he notices the end of some black object sticking out of the sand between a jumble of several fallen fronds. He nearly walks on, thinking that it is a rock or pebble washed up onto the high tide line. Still, there is no harm in taking a closer look, so he ambles towards it and stops. He stoops down and grasps the bottom end of the transponder, pulling it free of the fronds and sand. Carefully, he wipes off as much of the sand as he can with just his hands and turns it over. It appears to be dented in one place and several scratches have been made by tumbling in the sand as it washed ashore. Renewed hope washes through him and he sits down, his legs wobbling and almost unable to hold him up.

Henry

Given what he has just worked through, Steven decides to ask the guards if he can go to Peter's room to speak with him. He stands at the door jamb and signals to one of the soldiers. The man walks forward.

"Is it possible for me to go to my friend Peter's room for a few minutes," he asks politely.

"We can't let you leave your room, sorry," the soldier replies, "when the team from England gets here, I am sure they will make arrangements for you all to fraternize, but until then, we have our orders."

"OK, thanks." Steven returns to his bed and lays down again. He might as well get some rest while he can, and he is comfortable here. Before long, he is napping.

In the meantime, the General has opened his laptop and connected to the university website in Northampton. He sets a search for the scientific principles of astrophysics and opens a page. There is so much technical jargon interspersed with mathematical formulae, that he soon shuts it down again. There is no way to interpret any of this without years of groundwork study. He sits thinking pensively when a knock at his door breaks his reverie.

"Come," he says. The door opens and Higgins pops his head around the door.

"Can I have another quick word, sir?" he asks politely

"Sure, Higgins, what can I do for you?"

Higgins comes in, shuts the door and sits down.

"Well, I know it is irregular, sir, but I would like to take more blood from our guests if you will authorize it. I don't know whether we will be kept in the loop once MI6 take over, and I really want to try to find out what is going on. "

"I don't like this any more than you do, Doctor," the General replies, "and I want to know what we are dealing with too, so if you date stamp the blood samples with yesterday's date, you can go ahead. Realise though, if there are changes from yesterday, the blood will have to be destroyed before MI6 get here, or it will be my head for the chopper."

"I agree, sir, and I will be very careful to hide any signs of going ahead after the orders were received and thank you. I will report to you as soon as I have had a chance to look at what today's tests show."

Higgins leaves quickly as if he is worried the General may change his mind. He takes out his mobile and orders his staff to immediately take blood from the strangers again. He reminds them not to say a word to anyone about what they have found, or why they need to repeat the tests.

"If the men ask you," he says, "tell them we are rechecking to make sure they have contracted nothing while in Greenland. Tell them that they need to be in good health to return to England, so this rerun is precautionary only. That should allay any concerns and get their cooperation."

Higgins makes his way back to his laboratory to prepare the necessary equipment to get to work as soon as the samples arrive back. When everything is ready, he re-examines the blood from yesterday, carefully scrutinizing for anything he did not pick up in the initial screening. The only thing he notices is that in each sample, the unusual molecules are now grouped together, when yesterday they were dispersed throughout the plasma. Today's samples will confirm if this is the case, or if it is just an anomaly of these samples. Perhaps because of a slight difference in weight, they may have been trapped in a sedimentary fallout in the test tubes.

Peter sits up as the medical orderly enters with a cart. It looks like they need another blood sample. Peter rolls up his sleeve and lets the orderly get to work.

"Is everything OK?" Peter asks nonchalantly.

"Sure," the orderly replies, "we just need to make sure you are fit before you return to England. Some viruses take a few days to show up in the bloodstream, so this is just a precaution."

"Thanks," Peter replies and lays back down. He is not at all sure that he is being told the truth, but what can he do about it if the orderly is lying? He wishes he could speak with the others, but he has seen what happened when Derek tried to leave his room by force. He hopes it is not too much longer before MI6 arrive; at least then things will start moving along again.

Steven looks up as the orderly enters, recognizing that more blood is going to be taken. He thinks about what he has concluded and then when the orderly is nearly done, he speaks softly,

"Do you think the anomalies in our blood are the result of our passing through the Curtain?"

The orderly frowns and does not reply for several seconds.

"I am sure there is nothing to worry about," he replies, "all of these tests are purely precautionary. We don't want to send you home with any viruses that you contracted in Greenland."

"But the C.O. told us this morning that our blood contains anomalies, and that more tests are required to find out what they are. This does not sound like precautions against viruses to me."

"You will have to ask the doctor or the C.O. for more information. I just do the blood sample collection." The orderly looks sheepish and will not meet Steven's eyes, a direct tell that he is lying. He finishes up and quickly leaves the room. Steven is thoughtful; he does not believe a word of it.

Higgins sits with a cup of coffee and thinks about the anomalous molecules; why would molecules that are freely interspersed throughout the Universe suddenly rearrange themselves in the way evident in the blood samples? It must be something to do with the top-secret experiment, or this would have occurred and been recorded before, and he has checked for any scientific precedent to what he has seen. There is none. The whole enigma denies the known laws of physics as he understands it. He desperately wants to be part of the solution, but he knows that it is highly unlikely under the circumstances. How can he make sure he has access to the blood without MI6 knowing? That is what absorbs his mind while he waits.

Outside, a large military aircraft circles the base, its landing lights flashing. On the ground the technicians send the 'good to land' signal and turn on the runway lights. The snowstorm has eased slightly, but there is still enough falling to obscure the pilot's sight, and it is still dark. Luckily, he has trained and seen action over many different terrains, so he manages to land with nothing worse than a few bumps from the wheels. As the aircraft taxies to the waiting ground crew, the team prepares to disembark. Most of these men are doctors or scientists, with just a handful of MI6 agents accompanying them. The agents wait for the others to leave first, then they unpack their own hand luggage from the lockers overhead. As soon as they are on the ground, they cross quickly to the barracks and enter. A soldier at the door directs them to the CO's office, and they make their way down the long passage. Without the courtesy of knocking, they enter, and the General looks up scowling.

"Why don't you knock like any rational person would do?" he asks angrily; he already dislikes these bastards in suits, and he hasn't even exchanged a word with them yet. "As far as I am aware, I am still in command here and you need to remember that if we are to get along. Now what is it you so desperately want?"

"General, you are relieved of your command," one agent is obviously in charge and brooks no sarcasm from the General.

"Well now, let me see," the General leans back in his chair and scrutinizes the speaker. At length he continues. "Unless you have orders signed by the P.M, you are out of line, young man, and I don't like your attitude one little bit." He leans forwards quickly and the agent almost takes a step back but is able to stop himself in time. "I think you had better put up or shut up!" The General stands and faces off with the agents. He is at least two inches taller than the tallest, and although slim, his stature is such that most rugby fullbacks would treat him with respect. He walks around to the other side of his desk to stand toe-to-toe with the four agents. "Now, let me see the orders."

The agent reaches slowly into his inside suit pocket and hands the General a white envelope. The General opens it and reads the contents.

"I am afraid your boss does not have the power to remove me from my command," the General smiles. The smile does not reach his eyes. "I am sorry, gentlemen, but you will not be running this little show. Now, I will call your boss and put my phone on speaker so that you can have no doubts as to who is in charge here."

The General orders his adjutant to get Thames House on the line, then replaces the receiver. He leans his bottom on the desk top and folds his arms, all the while staring at the four men in front of him. The arrogant agent returns his stare.

The phone rings, and the General lifts it and sets it to speaker mode.

"Good morning, General," the unctuous voice says, "I assume you have my letter by now?"

"Yes, I do," the General speaks brusquely, "and I want to know what the hell you are trying to pull?"

There is silence for a moment and then the voice replies. "I see you know your statecraft, General, but surely you don't intend to run my show for me, do you?"

"I do, and I do," the General replies, "so you had better call off your hounds here, or I will have them put in the cells to cool their heels."

"You can't do that, General," the voice splutters with indignation.

"Oh yes, I can, and you know it. I have been very patient with your side of the business, but you are now overstepping your authority, and if I need to, I will take this up with number 10!"

"There will be no need for that, General," the voice coldly and quickly replies, "I will send my boys the message to step down. Can you please let me know what happens out there as soon as you know anything?"

"Of course, sir," the General replies, and smiling puts down the phone. The arrogant agent has turned very pale and is quick to offer an apology. The General asks his adjutant to show the agents to their quarters and to then take them to the mess. He turns to them again and asks, "Is there anything else gentlemen?"

The agents leave without answering, their heads down, and as soon as the door shuts behind them, the General smiles a genuine smile for the first time in this encounter.

The Family

Yawning widely, Kenneth follows his brother to the kitchen. He has dressed, but his hair is still wild from sleep, and he looks a little bleary eyed. Canath and Florence smile, and Canath addresses his youngest son,

"Kenny, good morning, you look like you did not sleep too well. Are you all right, son?"

"Dad, I had some strange dreams, and I thought I heard some screams, but when I woke up, there was nothing there. I could not get back to sleep, sorry for yawning."

"Let's get you fed, young man," Canath answers and he fills a plate for Kenny to eat.

"Thanks, Dad, I'm really hungry," Kenneth sets to with relish, now that he is properly awake, he realizes how hungry he is.

"Today, boys, I am giving you both over to Brian Boru; he knows what needs to be taught to you, and he is the best person to instruct you, so please mind what he says and try to perform the tasks he sets for you. It is essential that you are ready to go in a few days."

"What are you doing today, Father?" Phoenix asks, he is unsure of the road ahead, and he hopes his father will be around for the foreseeable future.

"Today, Aletheia and I will enter the plenum. I will stay with her until she is at home in her role as guardian."

"Can we spend some time with her first?" Phoenix asks.

"You can have an hour together now, then we must go; the Universe is unguarded right now and that cannot continue, so make the most of it because you may not see your sister again for some time."

Aletheia holds out her arms, and Phoenix rushes to her embrace. Kenny continues to eat.

"Don't worry, Phoenie," Aletheia whispers, "I have the feeling that I will be able to keep in touch with you. The guardian 'sees' everything, after all, so listen with your mind and send me messages if you need to ask or tell me anything. I love you so much, both of you."

"Can we go for a walk, Lethi?" he asks, and his sister rises. He takes her arm and leads her to the door. Looking back over his shoulder he says, "Kenny, come when you are finished, OK?"

Kenny nods, his mouth full of food, and Phoenix leads Aletheia to the outside door. They take the path to the grove, Phoenix thinking about how to say what he needs to say.

"Lethi, I want to thank you for being such a good mother to me and Ken," he begins, "without you I don't think I would be able to do what I have to do. I am scared about the future, and I only hope I can go through the immolations with courage."

"Oh, my darling brother," Aletheia replies, hugging him to her, "remember, the Universe does not set us tasks that we cannot bear. That I know; even when father was going to blind me with the rods, somehow, I knew it would be all right, somehow, I knew I could bear it, and in the end, it wasn't necessary. So, you see, perhaps what you need to go through will end up differently than what was proposed to us. Take heart from what happened to me."

"You are right, Lethi," Phoenix already feels better, "I will be sad to see you go, but I know it is necessary. Please let me know you can still contact me when you are settled. Then I will feel better, knowing that I can still speak to you when I need to."

"Count on it, Phoenie," Aletheia replies, "and take care of Kenny; he is still so young, and he needs you."

"I will, Lethi, I promise." Phoenix replies.

As soon as the boys have bidden Aletheia goodbye and God speed, Brian takes them into the grove. He asks them to kneel on the ground near where Canath was to complete the ritual with Aletheia. He looks at each of them and says a silent prayer for their strength to do what is necessary.

"Young men," he begins, "you have been born and chosen since before the beginning of time for the tasks that are now to be undertaken, so I ask you to bow your heads and pray to the gods of the grove for strength and courage."

Both boys do as Brian asks, and soon they raise their eyes to his.

Their faces are fraught with worry and trepidation, especially Kenny, who still does not quite understand what they are meant to do.

"We are going on a journey, you and I," Brian says, "but this journey does not include movement through space, so come with me, please. Marcom and I have been travelling in this manner for centuries; there is really nothing to it, and I think you are going to enjoy this part of your training."

Kenny looks at Phoenix, and Phoenix raises his eyebrows. He does not have a clue what Brian means, but a sense of adventure overcomes his trepidation, and he winks at Kenny. Both boys have passed through the Curtain, but if this was what Brian meant, he would have said so. Both boys hurry along in Brian's wake.

The three figures pass from the tower precinct and down to the lakeside. There a small rowing boat is tied to a cleat. Brian signals for the boys to jump aboard, while he unties the rope and settles himself in the scull position. With no words spoken, he rows out into the lake, then turns towards a bend, hidden by large overhanging willows. As he nears the bend, the boys spot a large mound of earth covered in grass, with what looks like a small door near the bottom. Brian rows as near as he can to the mound, then jumps ashore and ties the boat to another cleat, just now visible to the boys. The whole area is dimly lit; trees surround the mound on all sides except the lakeside, but the willows provide a curtain here, so it is hidden from everyone except those coming across the lake by boat. Brian signals for the boys to follow him, so they scramble ashore and set out behind him. He stops at the small entrance to the mound, and crouching down on his hands and knees, crawls forwards and disappears from sight. At first the boys are shocked, but they do as Brian has done, and soon find themselves in a narrow passage that quickly leads to a cavern hewn out of the hillside. The roof is just high enough for a tall man to stand upright, and there set before their eyes is a very strange scene indeed.

Greg and Tim

The two men, with Gavinar and Felix looking on, access from the university library and read two specific texts. The first is Jung's work called 'Synchronicity', the second, 'Atom and Archetype'; the book of letters exchanged between Jung and Pauli over a twenty-year period. As they turn to the last page, Greg decides they need to break for thinking. It is now dark, and the men become aware of this fact for the first time. The whole day has disappeared with the reading; and they have disappeared into the reading too. Felix stands, stretches and rings from the bell pull, for the servants to come and light the lamps and prepare dinner. He suggests they all could use a glass of wine, and the others agree with alacrity. What they have just read and absorbed over the last several hours is mind boggling.

Nobody speaks further; they are all still too absorbed in the ideas and evidence presented. Soon Petyr arrives with a decanter of deep red wine and four crystal goblets; how did he know a celebration was called for?

At last, and after several large sips from his glass, Greg speaks.

"When we have eaten, Felix, I will need you to bring the box back in unless we all decide to sleep on what we have learnt and resume in the morning, what do the rest of you think?"

"I think we should sleep on it for now," Gavinar is tired and well as wired.

"I agree," Tim speaks for the first time, "we need to think about all of this before we do anything else. You know how facts can be lost when we move too quickly."

Felix and Greg both nod their agreement, so the men relax and wait for the food to arrive. Only now do they realise they are all very hungry; lunchtime went by unnoticed along with the rest of the outside world.

As they eat, the men speak of frivolous things, the weather, and the time period. Greg and Tim are interested to hear about everyday life in this time and place, and Gavinar and Felix are happy to answer their questions. It is only when the clock strikes midnight, that the men decide to retire for the night. Felix instructs the servants to prepare a late breakfast, and the men all retire to their rooms.

Tim lies awake thinking; he is very tired, but his mind is still working overtime. How will they use what they have discovered to get back home? This is the question that he cannot quite fathom. Soon sleep begins to overtake him and at last, he succumbs. Tomorrow they will start again.

"Ah, good morning, Greg and Tim," Gavinar stands as the two men enter. It is just eight o'clock, but both Gavinar and Felix are already dressed and waiting for the breakfast to arrive.

"Did you sleep well?" Felix inquires, "Gavinar and I slept like the dead, but this morning new ideas surfaced for both of us. I think, like Tim said last night, that when we think on things, they become set into our understanding and sometimes in new ways."

"I found it difficult to get to sleep at first," Tim replies, "but then I woke, and it seemed like I had only slept for a few minutes, but it was nearly eight o'clock."

"I slept well, thanks." Greg replies.

Soon breakfast arrives and hot coffee. All four attack the food, and the coffee is drunk down to the last drop. Eventually Greg speaks again.

"Felix, bring in the box; I want to see if what I suspect is in fact the case."

Without questioning Greg further, Felix leaves to get the box. The faces of the three men left in the room are filled with expectation. It only takes a minute and Felix reappears, the box in hand. Before he has a chance to open it, Greg speaks.

"I want you all to consider what Jung writes about synchronicity or the physical manifestation of something when the human mind is absorbed with a deep idea."

"OK," Tim says, "please explain what you mean by that."

"Well, I expect to be able to show you something relative to the discovery of the orb, but to do so, I just want you all to bear with me." Greg asks them all to wait on an explanation until he has the chance to test his theory. The three men remain silent and watch Greg with rapt attention.

"Felix, please open the box." Greg asks politely. Felix does as instructed, and then sits down again, waiting. Greg closes his eyes, and the orb rises and begins to spin but does not move away from the vicinity of box this time. As the surface begins to light, Tim gasps aloud. There in the surface is a sigil, exactly the same as they found in the basement of the house in Athens. Greg remains with his eyes closed, and the sigil in the surface seems to move away into the background; in the foreground, the surrounding area becomes visible and this time, Felix and Gavinar gasp. The scene is of the cliffs near Kungsbacka; the field where they found the box containing the orb in full view. Greg opens his eyes, and the surface of the orb goes dark again, then gently drops down into the box. Nobody speaks for several minutes.

"Now do you see?" Greg asks, looking at each of the other three men in turn.

"I don't understand," Felix admits, "how did you do that and what does it mean?"

"It means that if we understand the work of Jung and Pauli, then the orb and the way it works makes perfect sense, as I have just demonstrated."

"But how did you know about the scenery around Kungsbacka?" asks Gavinar.

"I didn't," replies Greg with a grin, "but I surmised that wherever the orb was found, there too would be found a sigil. It was the sigil that I concentrated on, then just moved it back towards the background. The scene around it appeared that way, it was the sigil that gave the tell of the where."

"What on earth does all this mean, Greg?" Tim asks incredulously. It seems to him that Greg is several steps ahead of the rest of them as far as understanding this thing goes.

"It means, Tim, as you should well understand, that we can locate any sigils with this thing by purely thinking them into the projection, and the orb itself can then direct us as to where the projected sigils are located. With this orb, we can travel through the Curtain at will. Now do you understand?"

"Oh my God," Tim is gob smacked, "oh yes, now I get it! You are so clever, Greg, I could never have come to that understanding in a million years."

Gavinar and Felix look between the two men, startled expressions on their faces. Greg laughs out loud; he is so relieved and delighted with what he has discovered.

"Gentlemen," he says at last, "it looks like we are taking a trip to Kungsbacka."

Brandon

Fellings looks at the transponder in his hand as if he cannot believe his eyes; he had all but given up any hope of finding it or the backpacks. With the thought of the backpacks in mind, he rises to his feet, his legs still shaky, and putting the transponder in his pocket, heads towards the forest above the high tide mark. Slowly and carefully, he begins to search the surrounding area resuming as much of a grid formation as is possible in amongst the ferns. He lifts up any detritus lying on the forest floor, making sure that he has checked everything in each section. As the time goes on, he begins to lose heart again; anyway, there is no surety that the transponder and the backpacks took the same course in that overwhelming wall of water! But then again, if something as small as the transponder arrived back at the beach, could the backpacks, logged with water, have lodged in the sand or rocks closer to the water's edge? With this thought, Fellings hurries back to the water, looking in each direction as far as he can see. He decides to check farther along the beach, away from where he and Brandon first came ashore, around this side of the cove. He will give it twenty minutes or so before turning back. The slightly sulphureous air is beginning to take a toll on his breathing, and he has to slow his pace to get his breath. There seems to be nothing here, on this side of the cove, and he is just about to turn back when a glint catches his eye. He turns towards it, but it is gone, and he cannot make out where it came from. He waits. Surely it was not his mind playing tricks on him, or was it? Suddenly, it comes again, about five hundred metres further up the beach. He sets out at the fastest pace his breathing allows, watching carefully for the gleaming spot to reveal itself again. Soon, there is the shadow of a shallow indentation, in which appears to be a large, strangely shaped object----, lying in the shallows and washed over continuously by the wavelets coming in from the sea. As he gets nearer, the shape becomes ominously and obviously humanoid, or at the least, a set of humanoid bones and rags, and he sets out at a run, regardless of his ragged breathing. He stops about fifty metres from the ragged mass and bends over to regain his breath, his heart thumping painfully in his chest. Walking with trepidation now, he sees what he thought he would never see again; the body of his son, Brandon, recognizable only from the watch still attached to the wrist of his right arm. This is what the sun was glinting on and which he caught sight of by pure chance.

Bending down he gently runs his hands over the ragged body, feeling for breaks in the body form itself, or the underlying bones. The body is intact, but there are at least two breaks evident, and with great care, he turns the body over onto its back. Pieces of tracksuit cloth come off in his hands, and there is blood and some other kind of body matter clinging to the chest. Brandon's face is scratched and torn, his right cheekbone showing through a huge gash. Fellings carefully places his hand on the battered neck and recoils in fear. There is a faint pulse here, he is still somehow alive, although only just. How could this possibly be? He saw the great maw of the beast come down over the top of Brandon and the submersible before he was hit by the wall of displaced water. What to do now?

As gently as he can, he grasps what is left of Brandon's top and slowly drags his body up onto the dry sand. He opens what is left of the jacket and begins to massage Brandon's heart. Looking around desperately, he sees nothing with which he can bind the broken bones or sew back together the torn cheek, and he collapses down next to his son, tears of frustration streaming down his face. How on earth is he going to get Brandon back to the other side of the cove so that at least he can give him some water? Gradually he regains control of himself; panic and despondency are enemies to action, and he must think. There is no going back; he will just have to improvise here and try to get Brandon back to the fern forest, but first he needs to find some large fern fronds with straight branches. These will have to do as makeshift splints for the one arm and one leg with broken bones. If he can secure these, he can then perhaps move Brandon. He must leave him here to search for what he needs, and he sets off quickly, the sooner to get back, and all the time praying that he can somehow keep his son alive.

Henry

Higgins looks up as the team return with the new blood samples. He quickly removes the test tubes from the trolley and sets to work. With a sterile pipette for each sample, he settles one drop from each tube into each of the electron microscope's containers and numbers them. Then, turning to the machine, he loads the first sample onto the copper grid inside the main tube, and turns the machine on. He taps his fingers on the desk as he waits for the frequency to reach the point where the first sample lights up on the monitor screen. The tubes have been labelled and numbered by his staff, and they have returned the tubes to the cold room cabinet for further testing alongside the samples from yesterday, but as yet, they are undated. At last, the image appears in high resolution, and what can be seen on the screen leaves Higgins open-mouthed. As he stares at the screen, a cold sweat breaks out along his hairline, and his face turns ashen. What on God's earth is he looking at?

Without hesitating, he sends his staff to the canteen for their meal break, and alone in the lab, he unloads and reloads the microscope's tube and repeats this process until all sixteen samples have been viewed. He then sits down and mops his brow, his mind tumbling as he thinks about what he has just witnessed. What to do next? He lifts his office phone and pressing just two digits he waits.

"Robbins," comes the answer from the other end.

"Sir, could you please come down to the lab immediately?"

"On my way," the General replies, and ends the call, understanding by the tone of Higgin's voice that something dire has come up.

Higgins sits dumbfounded and waits for the General to arrive.

"Please lock the door, General," Higgins says as the General appears, "we can't let what I am going to show you become known to anyone else."

"This sounds ominous, Higgins, is there something wrong?'

"Oh, yes there is, sir, and I have no idea what is going on. The only thing I can say is that if I did not know that the blood was taken by my own staff, I would say someone was playing a trick on me. The blood you will see looks nothing at all like human blood."

"What do you mean?" the General frowning now, searches the doctor's face.

"I mean, the blood does not only contain anomalies today, but it is also totally different."

"How can that be, and what does it mean, Higgins?"

"I have absolutely no idea," Higgins replies, wiping his face again, "here, let me show you what I mean."

Higgins goes to the cold room cabinet and removes two tubes; one from yesterday and one from today, both are blood from the same man. Quickly he repeats the loading procedure, and first of all, loads the sample from yesterday.

"Look at the screen, General," he points to the grouping of molecules that are not as they should be, "do you see here, and here; these are different from this one and this one, yes?"

The General looks closely at what Higgins has pointed out, and he sees what Higgins has discovered. The difference does not appear to be significant to him, but he is, after all, not a scientist, so he bears with the doctor.

"Now this I can't explain, but at least the sample is recognizable as human blood."

He removes the sample and loads the second.

"This, however, is totally different, can you see what I mean?"

This time the difference is significant, and the General looks on for some considerable time before facing Higgins again.

"What the hell is going on here, Higgins, do you have any ideas at all?"

"Not the remotest sense of what is going on!" Higgins replies immediately.

"Have MI6 been here yet?" the General asks.

"No, sir, do you want me to hand over these samples when they do come?"

"No, Higgins, I want you to destroy all the samples from both today and yesterday. Photograph what you have seen in each case and bring the printed resolutions directly to my office as soon as you can. In the meantime, I will try to keep MI6 busy somehow. Is that clear?"

"Yes, sir," Higgins responds and sets about preparing the microscope to revisit all samples, from yesterday and today and photograph each as quickly as he can.

The General goes to the door, then stops and turns back to the doctor.

"Lock the door when I leave Higgins and admit nobody, your staff included, is that clear?"

"Yes, sir," Higgins replies without looking up from what he is doing.

The General moves directly to the mess. He picks up a cup and helps himself to coffee. The medical staff from the base, the team from MI6 and the four agents are all seated at tables enjoying breakfast; the team of scientists are talking quietly together but at different tables from the base scientists. The agents sit together, stony faced saying nothing. The General walks up to the table at which the agents are sitting and asks politely if he can join them. The surly agent indicates with his hand for the general to sit down.

"Gentlemen," the General speaks, "I hope you find our rations here to be adequate?"

"Very," the agent leading the mission replies without saying anything else.

"Good," the General responds, sitting watching the faces of these four men as they eat. "May I suggest a tour of this base when you are finished eating? I would be glad to show you around. We are strategically placed here to examine all the life forms presenting, and just across the coast in Greenland, we have a scientist from Leeds researching the changes in the earth's magnetic core and how these changes affect the magnetic pole. There have been signs of interference in the two magnetic systems."

"Very kind of you, I'm sure," the lead agent replies, "but we would like to question the men picked up in Greenland as our first priority."

"Of course," the General replies, "I will have rooms made available to you as soon as you finish up here."

"Thank you, General," the lead agent says and without looking up, continues to eat.

The General returns to his office, thinking. After a few minutes, he asks his adjutant in the outer office to get Higgins on the phone again. An idea is morphing into a plan, and he lifts his phone when it rings.

"Higgins here, sir, I have nearly completed the tasks," he states without waiting.

"Please come to my office as soon as everything is finished and sanitized there."

As he waits for Higgins, he finalizes the details of the plan, and when there is a knock at the door, he is ready to instruct Higgins on what to do next.

"Is everything taken care of as we discussed," the General asks.

"Yes, sir," Higgins replies, "and here are the printed resolutions. I did not name them, but the numbers I have added allow me to distinguish between them."

"Good work," the General replies, and rising from his desk, he uses his index fingerprint to open the safe and deposit the resolutions inside. "This is the safest place for them for now," he says as he closes the safe and returns to his desk, "you are the only one who knows about this, so let's keep it that way. Should anything happen to me, you will need to remove my right index finger to open the safe."

The doctor pales again but does not reply.

"Now, we need to go into damage control before MI6 want access to your laboratory. What I have decided is for you, alone, to take blood from me, yourself and fourteen other people from the regular staff here. I want you to name and number each as if they came from the strangers, and I want these samples stored in the cool cabinet ready for MI6 to access. Take enough that there are two samples for each person named, and date them yesterday and today, just in case your staff are asked about the number of times blood was taken, and let's hope there is no need for further samples to complete any testing."

"That is a great idea," Higgins looks better, "but what are we going to do to retain the sixteen men here?"

"Leave that to me, Doctor; you just get that blood as quickly and quietly as you can."

The Family

Phoenix and Kenny look around them stunned. The earthenware walls and floor are covered in patterns that look like sworls. Along the edges, are carved knots with what look like plaited ropes between. There is, in the centre of the floor, a large design with interwoven plaited ropes and knots interspersed with what looks like an oak leaf design. There is not one square centimeter of the cavern that is not etched.

"This is a sacred place," Brian whispers, "used for centuries for the most important rituals and known only to those of the priesthood of whatever religious group came here. The last were the Druids, and it is their etchings you see all around you here."

"The etchings all seem to move when you look at them for more than a few seconds," Phoenix exclaims in hushed tones, "is that the case, and if so, does it have anything to do with what you are going to teach us today?"

"You are very observant, Phoenix, and yes, we need the movement to aid in taking your mind to the next level."

"Phoenix, the patterns are making me feel sick." Kenny has turned quite pale, and Brian squats down and takes him by the shoulders.

"Look at my face, Kenny," he says, "the effects can be very powerful; this is indeed a powerful place, and you need to tell me when you become nauseous or dizzy, OK?"

"Thanks, Brian, I feel better now." Kenny keeps his eyes on Brian's face and the disorienting feeling subsides.

"Good boy, now I want you to keep your eyes closed while I explain what I want you both to try to do, OK?"

Kenny shuts his eyes and clutches his brother's hand.

"Now, Phoenix, I want you to think carefully, then tell me the most unusual thing about this place. Take your time."

Phoenix stays silent for several minutes before he replies to Brian's question.

"I think that what is highly unusual is that we can see clearly in here when there are no windows or lights."

"Well, done," Brian smiles. "Can you give me an explanation for this phenomenon?"

"Is it because Kenny and I are fire-born? But if that is so, then you must be fire-born too, Brian."

"Right again, Phoenix, although my training has enabled me to see as you do down here, I am not fire-born as both of you are. Do you know what today is, Phoenix?"

"No, except it is the day we are to learn from you," Phoenix replies.

"Today is your thirteenth birthday, and you have now entered an important transition phase of your life. You are now directly between childhood and full adulthood, and today you will be able to do what you could not do yesterday."

Phoenix thinks on this; he has never known when the day of his birth was, nor exactly how old he was. Now he understands why today they are working with Brian.

Back at the tower, Aletheia is taking her leave of Antheia, Ladon and Florence. Her mother hugs her tightly to her and whispers in her ear.

"Just as last time, darling girl, you must leave me now, but it won't be forever. When Ladon has grown, he will relieve you of your task and you can return here. I will be waiting for you. God speed, until we meet again."

"Thank you, Mother, I will not let you down." Aletheia now takes her sister in her arms and hugs her tightly.

"Antheia, take care and stay well; I will tell you everything that happens when I return."

"I love you, Lethi," Antheia's eyes are brimming with tears; for her sister has also been her mother for a long time now, and she will sorely miss her.

Lastly, Aletheia scoops up Ladon and hugs his tiny form to her. He places his hands over her eyes and begins to chant in the Archaic tongue. At first, the sound is all Aletheia can hear, then suddenly, the deepest voice in the Universe breaks in and Ladon says, "Go, my child, you are my guardian and soon I will return. You and I cannot be overcome except by the Power of existence itself. Until we meet again."

Alethiea becomes aware of those around her again, Ladon has stopped the chanting and lies quietly in Aletheia's arms, asleep. At that moment Canath enters the room.

"It is time to go, my daughter," he says, "we need to hurry."

Aletheia hands the sleeping child back to Antheia, takes Canath's hand, and they both begin to shimmer, then they disappear. The room is empty of all but the three family members. Florence puts her arm around Antheia's shoulder, and the two women leave the room. They are now in charge here until Canath returns, and Florence must start Antheia's instruction soon.

Greg and Tim

"Take only what you absolutely need." Greg is speaking to Felix and Gavinar.

"We hopefully won't be coming back here, so you both need to tie up any loose ends and sort out what you need to tell your servants."

"Are you sure about this, Greg?" Gavinar has set plans for his household should he be away from home for any length of time.

"I am sure of nothing, but I am very hopeful that in Kungsbacka we will find the sigil we need to move through the Curtain. You don't have to come with us unless you want to; Tim and I need to try to get back home."

"No, we want to come with you," Felix replies quickly, "I assume you want the orb with us, yes?"

"Most certainly; with the orb we may be able to travel through the Curtain at will, so if we end up, somewhere or sometime we don't want to be, we can move on again. You have no idea what a boon that may be."

"Do we need to take money with us?" Gavinar asks.

"No need," Greg replies, "we are hardly likely to end up anywhere your currency would be in use. If you have any gold, perhaps a small amount may come in handy."

Gavinar takes his leave and summons his servants to return to his house. Felix sets about looking for something suitable in which to carry his belongings. He returns to the two men with what looks like a large, soft carpet bag. He has changed his clothes, and carefully, he removes the orb and its nest from the box and places it in the large bag. Greg and Tim change back into their own clothes; both have carried them in their backpacks for just this event. These three men have arranged to meet Gavinar at his house, but first they must go to the stables to hire a carriage and two horses to make the trip to Kungsbacka. On the way to Gavinar's house, they stop at several market stalls to buy food for the journey, both for themselves and the horses. Felix has told his servants to shut up the house until his return with the exception of the housekeeper and her daughter; they will remain and keep the house in good order. He has left them with sufficient funds should he not return.

As they near Gavinar's house, they notice a commotion going on, with people shouting and gesticulating in the street. They hurry forwards to find out what the problem is. At the front door of Gavinar's house, a small crowd has assembled to watch the scene being enacted just inside the doorway. Petyr is trying to stop two men from entering, and one man is attacking Petyr with a stout walking stick.

"What is going on here?" Greg shouts, and the crowd quietens somewhat when they see the horses and the speaker's strange clothes.

"What business is it of yours?" one of the men turns to them and speaks in accented English.

"We are making it our business, so speak up, man, tell us what the problem is." Greg brooks no dissent, and both men now turn towards the carriage holding the three.

"We need to speak with Gavinar, and he won't come out," the older man says, "he must pay for what he has done to my daughter."

"And what has he done?" Greg asks.

"He has ensorcelled her," the man replies, "and she is no longer in her right mind. He told me he could help her, and all he has done is make her worse."

Greg, Tim and Felix step down from the open carriage, and Damon appears to lead the horses through the gate and around to the back of the property. Greg motions to Petyr to let the men and themselves into the house. He does not want this to turn into an affray in the street and thereby attract the attention of any local authorities. Once inside, Greg sends Tim to find Gavinar; he sends Petyr to fetch some coffee, and he bids the two men to sit down and calm down.

"Now," Greg begins, "please tell me the whole story so we can come to some decisions about what is to be done."

"The man who lives here has been advertising his services as a mesmerist," the older man begins, "and my daughter has been suffering from a kind of lack of interest in everything, including food. I consulted this man, and he told me to bring my daughter to this house; that he could help her. I left her here as he requested, and when I came back to take her home, she was in some sort of trance. She is still in this trance, and nobody knows how to bring her back. I need this Gavinar to compensate me for the damage he has done to her."

"Where do you live?" Greg asks.

"The next street over," the man says, "but I must speak to this Gavinar."

"I want you to go home and bring your daughter back here immediately," Greg responds, "I believe I can bring her out of the trance without any further damage being done to her. Can you trust me to do that?" Greg waits for the man to reply.

"I will do as you ask, but I warn you, if I am not satisfied with the outcome, I will call for the konstaapeli to arrest you and the man who lives here."

The two men leave to fetch the daughter, and Gavinar comes into the room; he has been listening from behind the door. Greg looks at him and shakes his head.

"What on earth did you think you were doing with this woman?" Greg remonstrates, "You have no real idea how hypnosis works, and yet you try it on an innocent person with no supervision. You must be mad, Gavinar!"

"I did not mean any harm, Greg," Gavinar looks chagrined.

"But harm is exactly what you did; why did you do something so stupid?" Greg is angry and does not hold back in his condemnation. "You had better hope I can reverse your work," Greg says, "and I wonder whether you and Felix deserve to come with us. Perhaps Tim and I should go on alone. We do not want to take idiots with us!"

"Oh, please don't say that," Gavinar begs, wringing his hands in despair, "I promise we will not hamper you."

"Well, let's see what I can do with your disaster," Greg replies sternly, "then Tim and I will decide who goes and who stays."

Just as Petyr arrives with the coffee, there is a knock on the door, and he leaves again to answer it. Gavinar rises to absent himself, but Greg demands he stay and face the people he has harmed. He sits down again, nervously. Soon, Petyr shows the two men and a young woman into the room, and Greg bids them sit. He scrutinizes the woman carefully; her eyes are fixed, and she is indeed in a trance. The older man must lead her to a chair and push to make her sit down. There is no sign that she is aware of where she is. Gavinar has turned pale and drops his eyes. Greg rises and squats down in front of the woman; she is unaware of his presence. He stands again and addresses Gavinar.

"How did you engage the trance state?" he asks, ignoring everyone in the room except Gavinar.

"I did what the book advised on page seventeen," he replies.

Greg looks towards Felix and asks him where the book is now. He is hoping against hope that Felix has secreted the book into the carpet bag along with the orb.

"Why, I have it here," Felix replies, and with deft hands, he reaches into the bag and extracts the book, handing it over to Greg with a flourish.

"You are both very fortunate that I have studied the modern methods of hypnosis," Greg says, "or there would be nothing I could do. Now sit and pour the coffee for these two gentlemen while I read what Gavinar has done."

There is silence in the room as Greg reads, then after only a few minutes, Greg shuts the book and hands it back to Felix.

"I won't be needing this again," he advises Felix, and Felix replaces it in the bag. Greg steps towards the woman and asks the older man to make room for him to sit down just behind her head. When he is very close to her head, he begins in a soft, calm voice.

"You are feeling sleepy now, so rest," He waits several seconds then resumes. "I am going to count backwards from twenty, and when I get to three, you will begin to wake up. You will remember nothing."

Greg begins to count backwards slowly and calmly. When he enunciates three, the woman gasps and opens her eyes. By the time Greg has said one, she is wide awake and looks around her. She jumps when she sees the strangers, but the older man comes across to her and takes her hand.

"How do you feel, Agnes?" he asks gently.

"Well, I feel fine, Father," she answers, smiling at him, "is that coffee I smell? I am so hungry and thirsty!"

The old man looks at Greg with tears in his eyes but immediately pours Agnes a cup of coffee, stirring in three spoons of honey to help with any residual shock. He hands the cup to her, and she sips appreciatively. Gavinar looks on but says nothing, and the two men ignore him, and after drinking their coffee, they turn their attention to Greg.

"Sir, I don't know how to thank you for saving my child," the older man begins, but Greg puts a hand up to stop him.

"Please do not concern yourself with us, just take your daughter home now. She will have no more trance states." Greg stands to show the three people out, then closes the door and returns to the room. He looks at Tim, and Tim nods his head.

"Looks like you can come, with us," Greg begins, "but any interference with anything we say or do, and we will leave both of you to fend for yourselves. Am I making myself clear?"

"Thank you, both of you, and thank you, Greg, for saving that girl. Without your help I would be in jail by tonight. You won't regret it." Gavinar says fervently, and he and Felix both look relieved. Tim looks puzzled and says to Greg.

"When did you learn to carry out hypnosis? I would think it is far removed from your IT world."

"It has been an interest and a passion of mine since I was a boy and saw a show put on by Dave Hill. Since then, I have read and studied the relevant works of the famous men of hypnotism, taking courses at the same time as I was studying for my Masters in IT. I have become competent but not an adept at the methods used today."

"Well, thank goodness for your side work!" Tim replies smiling. All four men begin to relax, and Petyr pours more coffee for them. Greg begins to contemplate and plan their journey as they sit.

Brandon

Hastily, Fellings begins searching for what he needs, throwing aside the fronds that are too small or those whose stems are too bent. He comes across one with withered fronds but a straight, thick stem, so he strips off as many of the dead leaves as he can with bare hands, then puts the stem in a cleared spot to take back to the beach. Soon he has several others that will suffice, and he lofts them all onto his shoulder and sets off back towards where Brandon lies, unconscious. He is almost at the edge of the forest, and he can see Brandon, when he trips over something hidden under the forest floor detritus and falls flat. He stays prone until he gets his breath back; he must have fallen on his breastbone, and he is badly winded. At last, he stands up, brushing dirt, sand and dead frond leaves from his clothing and hands. His hands have both been grazed, but he takes no time to worry about that; he picks up the fern fronds again, lofts them onto his shoulder and starts to take a step away from the forest again; he stands on something and nearly trips again.

Putting down the fronds, he digs below the surface detritus and sees a flash of blue. He clears the floor around the flash and makes out the shape and size of one of the packs. Excitedly, he uncovers the rest, and standing up, shakes it free of sand and detritus. With shaking hands, he puts it down again and kneeling, opens the front zipped pocket. The contents have all been saturated with sea water, but most of what is in there is wrapped or sealed in plastic, so the damage is purely external. He checks each pocket for damaged contents, then with surging hope, he dons the heavy pack, shoulders the frond stems again and sets off back towards Brandon at a trot.

Using the pocketknife from the pack, Fellings can now strip the fronds easily and soon has four, straight and strong stems, all cut to the appropriate lengths, with which to secure Brandon's broken arm and leg, but first he must realign the bones so that they can heal as best as is possible under the circumstances. With Brandon unconscious, this task is quick and relatively easy, and soon, Fellings has the limbs encased in the stems, each of which is wide and curved enough to act almost as a plaster would. Now all he has to do is find something to use as binding to keep the frond stems in place. He searches the pack hoping against hope that this is the one he thinks it is. He shouts aloud when he sees the reel of nylon cord, at last his luck is on the turn. Soon, he has the job done to the best of the improvised conditions he has to work with. Now he needs to get Brandon back to the forest edge. He checks his condition and feels a slightly stronger pulse now, so slowly and carefully, and with the precious pack on his back, he drags the prone body towards the forest edge. He stops every few metres to check Brandon's pulse before resuming. It takes him nearly an hour of back-breaking effort to get his son to the site he considers to be the best. They are sheltered from the tides and wind but close to the forest edge so that anything coming through the forest will be instantly noticed.

Not wanting to use the supplies from the pack, Fellings decides to search further into the forest for water. He has used a bottle from the pack to wash out Brandon's gashed face and to get some into his mouth and swallowed without him choking, so he can use it to carry water back to the site. He looks around him for landmarks to orient himself by, and taking the knife, he deeply marks the tree fern trunks as he and Brandon did at the other side of the cove. He stops to listen at regular intervals just in case there is another waterfall in the vicinity, but he hears nothing. The ferns become nearly impenetrable, but still, he moves resolutely into the forest, making sure to mark his way well.

There is a thinning of the ferns at last, and soon he can see a sandy tract up ahead. As soon as he steps out of the ferns, he hears and sees the fast-flowing river, probably the same one that had the waterfall further along the forest. He squats down and drinks, slaking his thirst and then drinking more. He must try not to leave Brandon too often; he wants to be there if and when his son regains consciousness. With returning vigor, he fills the water bottle, caps it and stands to look around him. Next on the agenda is to try to find food, so that he can feed Brandon from the pack supplies without needing to eat them himself. That will alleviate the need to worry about Brandon's diet for the time being at least. Suddenly he realizes that he is feeling quite chipper, not so exhausted and definitely not so defeated as he did, before finding Brandon. He vows to keep positive and not let himself get down again, regardless of what happens.

Before returning to the rudimentary camp site, he searches the riverbed for anything living in the water. He is still squatting down but not moving when he notices movement through the undergrowth. Being careful not to scare what is coming, he slowly and carefully removes the pocketknife holding it in his right hand. Before long, the body of a snake crawls into view. Without thinking about it, Fellows leaps towards the snake and manages just to grasp the tail as it retreats hastily. The head rears backwards, over its back, and Fellings manages to swing the pocketknife in an arc that almost cuts the snake's head off. The creature thrashes about, but Fellings is able to stand and lift the whole body off the ground so that no matter how the snake thrashes, it can go nowhere. Careful to remain at a distance from the thrashing head, Fellings drops the snake down until only its head is on the ground, then stands with his full weight just behind the head. He bends down and quickly removes the head totally. He feels like roaring like a lion; the feeling of exhilaration takes him by surprise. He has just found and killed enough meat to fill his belly tonight. He sets off back towards the camp site, the full water bottle in his hand and the body of the snake slung over his shoulder. With luck, there will be a packet of safety matches in the pack, and he will be able to light a fire to cook the snake and keep them both warm through the night. He smiles widely.

Henry

As quickly as he can, Higgins collects the blood required to satisfy the MI6 scientists, making sure to tell each of the donors that they are to say nothing about having their blood drawn. He leaves the General and himself until last and knocks on the General's door.

"Come," the General is expecting him and quickly rolls up his shirt sleeve ready for the doctor to draw his blood. "Is everything else secured, Higgins?" the General asks.

"Yes, General, you and I are the last; then all I need to do is get the samples back to the cooler. I have taken twice as much as normal, so I don't have to waste time splitting the samples. I need only name and date them, and that will take me all of ten minutes."

"Good work," the General says, "is there anything else you need from me before the team gain access?"

"Sir, how do you want me to deal with the fact that we sent a report stating anomalies with the first test?"

"I have given that some thought, and I would suggest you claim a mistake was made when the samples tested were mixed up with animal samples. There is no evidence to show what the anomalies were, and you did not send photographs, so you will have to look suitably chagrined that a staff member was silly enough to take the wrong tubes from the cooler. Do you have enough animal blood for this to ring true?"

"Yes, that should work provided my staff are aware of the need for this subterfuge. What do you want me to tell them?"

"Tell them that we need to retain the sixteen men here, and the only way we can do that is if MI6 believe that a mistake has been made. Tell the other scientists that you have new samples that show no anomalies, and to keep their mouths shut if they don't want to be sent back to England in the charge of MI6."

Higgins takes the samples and hurries back to the laboratory. As soon as he has them dated, labelled and in the cooling cabinet, he sends a text message to each scientist ordering the whole team of six to come immediately to the conference room, making sure they understand the urgency. He then walks directly to the room and checks that all the locks are in place excepting the main entrance. He does not want anyone to be able to walk in without an invitation. He sits at the head of the conference table and waits, going over in his mind the plan he and the General have put in place so quickly, making sure that there are no unforeseen problems with what they are now going to do. As the six scientists wander in and take a seat at the table, Higgins brings the meeting to order.

"Gentlemen, we have a problem, and I am going to tell you now, how we are going to handle it, so listen up."

The team looks surprised and curious. They give their full attention to Higgins.

"I have on the orders of the General, destroyed all the blood samples taken from our sixteen visitors and replaced them with samples collected from various staff, myself included. I have labelled and dated these as if they are the samples from the sixteen. You will obviously be questioned by MI6 as to how many samples were taken and what those samples showed. You will claim a mistake was made. Does anyone want to ask a question before I continue?"

"Why are you doing this?" one scientist immediately asks.

"I will get to that later, for now you need only follow the orders given to you." Higgins shuts down this kind of question.

"You will say that one of you, and you can decide who right now, removed the wrong samples for testing. The mistaken samples were animal blood. Do I have a volunteer willing to be the scapegoat for our little subterfuge?"

Nobody raises their hand, so Higgins chooses a man he thinks can stand up to the questioning that will ensue for the mistake maker.

"David, not only are you the junior here, but I think you are the most assertive of all, so I call on you to do this for all our sakes. Can you do that?"

"If you feel it is absolutely necessary, Doctor," David replies, "But I am totally mystified by what you are suggesting. Can you please explain why we have to prevaricate like this?"

"It is extremely important to make MI6 believe a mistake was made," Higgins answers, "because the anomalies that you all witnessed yesterday are now more advanced, and the General and I want to keep the sixteen men here without any interference from the authorities. The General is working on a plan to put to MI6 to that effect. Anyone of you who wants to disobey the General's orders will find himself travelling back to England under the auspices of MI6. Do I have any dissenters for what I have ordered you to do, gentlemen?"

Again, nobody speaks so Higgins continues.

"What we need to happen now is for MI6 to complete their testing and questioning and then leave us the hell alone. There is something very much amiss, and we will get to the bottom of it if we can manage to keep the sixteen men here. Does anybody not fully understand what they are ordered to do?"

Everyone seems to be on the same page, so now Higgins allows questions.

"So, Doctor, what you are suggesting is that we let the MI6 scientists into the lab to carry out their own tests on the blood samples, yes?"

"That is correct, Geoffrey; they came here to do just that, and they will find the samples are all within normal parameters. This will enable the cover story to ring true, especially when they want to see where we store the animal blood, which you are now going to shift into the cooling cabinet adjacent to the sixteen samples. When that is done, all you need to do is remember that if MI6 is not satisfied with our story, then someone's head will roll, and this place may well be shut down. So, if you like your jobs and the conditions and pay that go with them, let's rid ourselves of MI6 as quickly and quietly as possible. Are you all in agreement with the plan, and does anyone foresee any problems with what has been decided?" Higgins gives them a minute to decide, and when there is no dissent, he continues.

"The General and I had very little time to come up with the plan, so any thoughts about what could go wrong would be helpful. Please resituate the animal blood samples and then resume your work, men, and if you can see a problem and need to speak to me or the General, feel free to knock on our doors. The sooner we can get MI6 to leave, the sooner I can fully divulge to you what is going on. Lastly, men, realise that what we are doing is imperative to our wellbeing here; we would not attempt to do this otherwise."

Hoping that he can rely on the six men, Higgins leaves with the team and makes his way back to the General's office. He knocks and enters without waiting for a response, only to find the lead agent from MI6 sitting across from the General. He makes to excuse himself, but the General waves him in and to the second chair across from his own. Higgins sits down, watching and saying nothing.

"Higgins, this is Agent Perkins; he and I were just discussing the questioning of the sixteen visitors and the re-testing of the blood samples. Is there any reason why his team cannot get on with the testing?"

"None whatsoever, General," Higgins answers, "the blood samples are all still in the storage area, labelled and dated, so I am happy to introduce the team to my men and let them get going."

"Good, then perhaps I can ask you to collect the scientists and take them to the lab and let them start?"

"Certainly, sir, I will get right on it." Higgins stands and nods to the agent, then leaves, shutting the door behind him. The General returns his attention to the agent sitting across from him.

"Now, Perkins, let's get you and your team set up with interview rooms. If you would be kind enough to come this way?"

The General walks around from behind his desk and holds the door open for Perkins to exit before exiting himself, he leads the agent to a set of four comfortable rooms equipped with table, chairs and recording equipment. There are coffee makers, cups and biscuits on sideboards against the walls of each room. Perkins inspects each room and then merely nods. The General leaves him to get on with his job and makes his way to the mess to get himself yet another cup of coffee. Now is the time to hope that he and Higgins have thought of everything and anything that can go wrong.

The Family

There is a slight buzzing and the sensation of falling as the two figures of Canath and Aletheia begin to coalesce back into human shapes. They find themselves in what looks like a large room with very high walls of pale grey. The whole vista has a two-dimensional greyness such as is seen in an old, slightly unfocussed, black and white movie. Both look around them while their disorientation begins to fade.

"I can see here, Father," Aletheia says, surprise evident in her voice.

"Yes, child, I suspected that would be the case. We are in the between zone; the twilight of becoming in which time as we know it no longer holds sway. This is the cross-roads of the eternity that we call the Plenum, my dear, and this is your 'house' for the foreseeable future. Everything that has been, is and ever will be is already here, and you will see for yourself the truth of being in this place, if place is the right word. Here you guard the infinite becoming of world-time and space. Here you must only allow the truth to pass through, for only in this way can the Universal Power release from out of itself, the infinite becoming and dissolution of finitude. Here you cannot age. Here you cannot fall ill. Here you will remain exactly as you are now."

"How am I to do what needs to be done, Father?" Aletheia asks.

"We are going to determine that together, and before I leave, everything will be clear. You must be accustomed to this 'place' and how it works before you can take up your task, so firstly, we need to take a wander through the whole horizon available to us and see what lies within its parameters and find the limitations of our humanity that will define you here. You see, even as an immortal, I still retain my human side as do you. We are not infinite but merely immortal. We still need the Power of existence to exist at all. Let us go now, and I will explain as we go why you have been chosen for this task."

The pair move without taking a step; they merely think what they want to do, and their bodies act accordingly. As they meander through what appear to them to be unadorned hallways and rooms, there is the manifestation of whatever enters their mind. Think of a table and a table appears, think of green fields and green fields appear; their very thoughts are unbounded by anything other than their human consciousness. As they become accustomed to using this power, Canath decides to think 'Plenum.' There is a sonic booming, and a portal opens into an altogether different, black expanse. The portal shimmers with the threshold between the two realms clearly demarked and clearly visible as the shimmering. Within it is the pulsing of infinite heartbeats and infinite stars, planets and comets appear and disappear like colours in a soap bubble. Canath stands well back from the threshold and ensures Aletheia does the same.

"You cannot nor must you try to cross through the shimmering," Canath warns, "for the threshold will annihilate even the idea of you."

"I don't understand, Father," Aletheia looks bemused and frowning, turns to Canath.

"We can see the threshold, but no mortal can," Canath answers her bemusement, "for immortality holds us, but beware, for the Power is absolute. You are looking at the birthplace of life itself; without which nothing could or would exist. This you must guard with your life."

"I understand, Father, please close the portal, for it makes me swoon to look at it." Aletheia is beset by a feeling of disorientation, and her sight flickers with the feeling. Her ears feel like they are under extreme pressure; much like being deep under water, although how this thought comes to her, she does not know. She has never been deep under water. Canath notices her discomfort and taking her hand begins to move again without actually moving.

"Let us continue with our reckoning, Aletheia, then I will tell you about your life in Athens. You must by now be wondering why your mother and I left you and the others there for so long. There is a reason, a very important one."

As they traverse the hallways and rooms, their presence is felt, acknowledged and welcomed. They are led and they are acclaimed by the Power. Soon understanding breaks in, and both find that they know this place like the backs of their hands. This knowledge comes upon them without any effort on their part. Suddenly, Aletheia breaks into a smile; she recognizes her task, her surroundings and her powers. Now she understands everything she needs to undertake the task; how to be, how to ensure nothing but the truth passes and how to communicate with the Power of her own existence. This knowledge has lain hidden within the depths of her human soul, awaiting the right 'time' to emerge. She is at last, at one with the Universe.

She thinks a table and chairs, at which she and Canath sit down to talk. Wine appears and two crystal goblets, so she pours the wine and sits back ready to hear what her father, Canath, needs to explain.

"Do you remember the day your mother left you?" Canath asks.

"Yes, Father, and her last words to me I used as a comfort in the hard times."

"You were aware of me, but you were told I had been killed by Henry Bonnington and the Ketters, yes?"

"Yes, Father, although I could never make sense of the fact that you died before I was born and yet, you fathered the three younger ones. I often wondered about this enigma, but I was not able to solve it."

"It was important for you to remain ignorant of my identity, so that no intruder could ever learn who and what we really are." Canath speaks ruefully. "It was essential, in fact, for there have been assaults on the Power from those who have little or no understanding of what they are doing."

"But why was it necessary for us to remain in Athens, Father?" Aletheia asks.

"The Athens of your birth and that you know from living there, Aletheia, is not as it should be. Damage was wrought by a very powerful force that challenged the Power; this damage has remained and can only be rectified by our family, especially the man Ladon is becoming as we speak. There are two cities of Athens belonging to the same 'time'. Each is the real Athens, but they do not and cannot coincide, because both are the modern day and yet one is the ruins that held sway at some other time. The 'time' of which I speak is one and the same. Does that make any sense to you at all?" Canath scrutinizes Aletheia's face to see what if anything she can grasp of what he is saying.

"Please, can you tell me this in another way? I can't seem to grasp what you are trying to tell me, Father."

Canath sits for several minutes, thinking, before he starts again.

"The Athens of your birth should look like this." Canath thinks about the Athens of 2020, and a vista appears in front of Aletheia's eyes that she has never seen before. If it were not for the Acropolis and the familiar landmarks, she would not recognize it as Athens at all. She stares in consternation at the houses, the street lights, the people and the bistros. She stares open-mouthed as cars and motor scooters traverse the narrow streets.

"How can this be, Father?" she asks startled at the scene.

"This is the same Athens in which you were born and grew up." Canath explains, "Although you have never seen this dimension, it is the exact same place and time. The reason you do not recognize it and have never seen it, is because of the damage that was done when someone tried to breach the portal to the Plenum. The Athens you know is the result of that damage; the reason why you had to stay there while your mother and I left to work through the problem, and find a way to restore the Athens I just showed you. Without the presence of the fire-born to hold the Athens of your birth in a stable form, the damage could have been absolutely catastrophic for all life as we know it. We had to leave you there to protect the universal order from further damage."

"Is that why Antheia and I had to visit the dragon's lair, Father?"

"Precisely why, child. Your brothers were fire-born from birth, thanks to your mother's ordeal in Ladon's lair, and she could not leave until they were old enough to hold the Athens of your birth into stability. With their coming into their powers, and especially Phoenix, the time was right; she was then able to instruct you how to find Ladon. Only then could she leave. Your visit to Ladon ensured the stability of Athens in both juxtaposed forms, and of course, Ladon had to choose the purest soul in the Universe to impregnate with his human counterpart. We did not leave you willingly, but the problem is enormous, and we both had much to learn and develop before it was safe for the four of you to come to us."

"Who is holding the Athens of our birth now, Father?" Aletheia is worried.

"Why, your mother, dear girl; her development under the tutelage of Marcom and Brian is now complete. She is the strongest fire-born human of universal proportions. She alone can hold Athens for as long as it takes for Ladon to reach his maturity as an immortal human."

"When he does, Father, will he be able to repair the damage?" Again, Aletheia is concerned.

"Not without our help, Aletheia, and as he grows, we grow stronger also. Your task is difficult because you must be constantly aware of all that passes. When you grow weary, you must use your strength and goodness to go on. There is not another who can assist you here."

"I will do what must be done, Father," Aletheia replies, and Canath knows this is the truth.

"You can summon whatever you need as you have seen, Aletheia, but it is not essential to eat, drink or sleep in this place. The most important task is not to lose concentration, for that is the only way to fail at your task. Do you understand what must be done to deny entry to everything that is not true?"

"Yes, Father; as we were moving around, the Power gave me all the knowledge and power necessary to the task."

"Then I must leave you now, Aletheia; may the gods give you the strength and resolve to carry out this onerous task. I will see you again when it is time. Know that I love you and that I am so very proud of you, my child."

Canath's form begins to shimmer, and soon, Aletheia is alone in the greyness. She sighs deeply, then begins the task that will preserve the universal order.

Greg and Tim

The men, packed and ready, gather at the front door, and Gavinar directs his attention to Petyr.

"Please do as I have instructed and stay here until you hear from me. I may be away for some time, so you know what to do if you need funds for living."

"Do not worry, master, I know what you have put in place, and I will action what needs to be actioned if the time comes. I wish you all a safe journey."

Having taken their leave of Gavinar's household, the men climb aboard the coach, and Damon gathers the reins and gees the horses. He will go with them to Kungsbacka, and if they no longer require the coach, he will return it and the horses to the stables. Greg remains silent, watching as the city begins to recede and the countryside rolls towards them. He is deep in thought and does not notice much of the scenery. Tim, on the other hand, engages both Gavinar and Felix in questions about the region they are passing through and the crops that are evident in the fields. He was not expecting a country like Sweden to have a summer hot enough to grow grain, but the fields give the lie to this notion. The wind is still very cold, but the sky is clear, and there are patches of verdant green and fields of what looks like wheat or barley.

"What is that crop with the large green leaves?" Tim asks, his interest piqued by the unusual shape and colour of the leaves.

"That is our famous horseradish," Felix answers, "we grow the best in the world here. When we stop for the night, I will ask the hotelier to let you try some."

As the horses settle into a steady gait, the coach rocks gently on its springs, lulling the men and soon they are all yawning. There is a long way to go, so they make themselves comfortable and soon their eyes begin to droop, and they nap.

Greg is not napping, nor is he sleepy. His thoughts are centered on how the orb works and what the effects of taking it through the Curtain might be. He is not at all sure if it is such a good idea. What if it has some unknown effect on the Curtain? Could it be dangerous to try to take it through? What do they actually know about the orb or the Curtain for that matter? These questions are bothering him, and he knows that the only way to find out the answers is to attempt to go through. This does not make him feel any better because there is something nagging at the back of his mind that he can't quite bring to consciousness. Something important, or so he thinks. What is it that he can't quite remember? As the time passes, he too succumbs to the rocking of the coach and allows himself to drift towards sleep.

The sun has fallen well below its zenith when the coach stops outside the same hostelry that Gavinar and Felix stayed at on their last journey to Kungsbacka. Damon alights and enters the inn to secure rooms for the men. Although it is two years since they have been here, the host remembers the names, Gavinar and Felix, and sends his daughter to ready the rooms and light fires. Damon wakes the sleeping men, and they stretch, then alight from the coach. Gavinar and Felix enter the inn, and Greg and Tim look around them, taking in the surrounding countryside.

"You look like something is bothering you," Tim speaks quietly.

"Something is. At least something is nagging at me, but I can't for the life of me remember what it is."

"Do you think it is important, Greg?" Tim asks.

"Yes, and that is what is bothering me. Hopefully if I sleep on it, it will come to me. I am sure I need to remember before we try to use the sigil"

"Then let's get inside and relax so your mind can work unhindered." Tim suggests.

At this last remark, they too enter the inn and find themselves in a large room with a flag stone floor and low, oak beams. A massive fireplace cheers the gloomy interior, and they settle themselves in large chairs set out around the fire. The room is very warm but cosy, and Gavinar signals to the hotelier to fetch food and drinks. Soon a kitchen maid appears with a tray holding four large earthenware mugs of foaming ale. She sets them down on the small tables in front of the men and returns to the kitchen to fetch their meal. There is a savory smell coming from that direction, and the men wait with anticipation and appetite. Large wooden bowls brimming with a meaty stew soon arrive and several loaves of fresh, dark bread. The men set to with relish. The stew is very good.

Although the men have napped, they all still feel tired from the day's excitement and exertions, and soon, they decide to turn in to their rooms. They have decided to make an early start, before daybreak, so sleeping now will suffice. They agree to meet downstairs before dawn, and all four men retire and fall quickly asleep. Damon alone, sits by the fire downstairs, nursing a mug of ale and thinking about what is to happen tomorrow. He will sleep in the stables with the horses, and soon he turns in also; he tends to the horses, brushing them down and putting on nosebags before he settles himself into a blanket in amongst the bales of hay inside the stable proper. He considers once more what tomorrow might bring.

The morning is cold and dark as the men leave the inn. All four have slept well and woken well before dawn. The sky is clear, and a crescent moon lights the way. The coach is set with two large gas lamps on the outside front, and these help Damon to see the road ahead. They set a good pace because the road is empty of vehicles except for theirs, and they want to get to Kungsbacka in daylight. Greg now voices his concerns to Tim and the other two men listen intently.

"There is something about the orb that puzzles me," he begins, "I know what you both related to us about where and how you found it, but I am wondering how it got there in the first place. Do either of you know anything about the area?"

"What kind of things?" Felix asks.

"For instance, do ships dock along the coast anywhere? Who uses this road and what for? What is Kungsbacka known for?" Greg searches their faces hoping for a clue to what he needs to remember. He still cannot bring it to consciousness, but there is an urgency to his nagging intuition today.

Felix sits back and thinks for a moment before answering. He looks at Gavinar, but Gavinar merely shrugs his shoulders in an "I don't know" kind of gesture.

"Kungsbacka is an agricultural area known for its crops and meat growing," Felix begins. "Pigs, sheep and cattle are farmed along with horseradish, wheat and barley. The coastline is rugged with cliffs; most are inaccessible, and seabirds breed there in the spring and summer. As far as I know, there is no commercial port, but it is renowned for smugglers, who bring contraband ashore. It is not easy to police because of the ruggedness of the shoreline." Felix waits for Greg to process the information.

"Something is wrong, yes, Greg?" he asks.

"Yes, something is nagging at me, but I can't for the life of me remember what it is, and I know it is important." Greg's concern is written on his face, and the others hardly know what to suggest to help him.

"Do you think it will be a problem?" Gavinar now joins the discussion.

"That is what concerns me," Greg replies, "and we really don't know enough about the orb to be sure of anything." Greg looks at each man in turn. "We may well find that the orb affects the Curtain in ways we can't understand, and if that should be the case, we might find ourselves in a great deal of trouble."

"But what else can we do?" Felix asks, "We have no idea where the orb came from, or how it got here. I can't see how Franz Mesmer came by it either. It seems to be too intricately made to be of this particular time period."

"That is my thinking too," Greg says, "what if it is a relic of another group of time-travelers; people who came as we did though the Curtain? Can we be sure that this place with its sigil is unknown to the locals? What if the sigil has been breached here, and we are not the only ones trying to pass through?"

"I don't get what the problem would be anyway in that case, Greg," Tim speaks for the first time, "we know that Henry found the Curtain by accident, but we also know that a group of astro-physicists at the university were designing the submersible stolen by Henry, to travel through the Curtain. So, there must have already been forays into the plenum; and if that is the case, then it is not unlikely that others have been here and are now gone."

"Something is not right with that assumption, Tim, and if only I could remember what is bothering me, perhaps we would have a better idea about the whole dynamic."

"Then what do you want to do, Greg?" Tim asks.

The other men wait silently for Greg to think about this question.

"Leave me to think about it again, and I will try to go back through everything that has happened since we landed in Athens. Perhaps something will jog my memory. Unless I can recall that something, then we really have no choice but to get to the sigil and try to use it. We cannot get back home any other way, Tim."

"Yes, I agree with you, Greg. Do your best, and when we get to Kungsbacka, then we all have to decide on what we are going to do. For now, I suggest we leave you to reminisce and hope for the best."

Gavinar and Felix nod their agreement, and each man brings his mind to the problem. It is a good idea to retrace their own steps in this whole journey; Felix and Gavinar to the time they found the orb and what has happened since, and Tim, like Greg, to think back on everything that has happened since Athens. Silence, except for the clopping of the horses and the occasional creaking of the coach, enjoins the rest of the journey.

Brandon

Fellings sets about collecting dead fern fronds and any woody growths that he can see. After digging down in the sand to make a fire pit, he carefully sets a fire, hoping that the dry foliage will burn without too much smoke. He is concerned about the sulphureous air too; he hopes the oxygen levels will be high enough to allow a fire to burn. After checking Brandon again, he opens the pack and takes out the box of safety matches brought with them from Maui. The box feels slightly damp, but the plastic wrapper has protected it from the worst of the drenching sea water. Carefully he strikes a match and shielding it from the breeze, he sets the flame beneath the driest of the fern fronds. There is a crackling and spluttering, and at last, the dry fronds catch alight, and the flames grow steadily in intensity. There is a blue tinge to the flames, but at least the fire takes hold. Soon there is a bright fire, and Fellings feeds the flames with more fuel, taking care not to overload it and extinguish it. After several minutes, he rises and makes his way back to where Brandon lies, still unconscious. The snake he managed to kill lies there too, and he takes the pocket knife and slices the snake into several thick pieces. He places these in the fire pit around the edge, on flat stones he found near the rocky outcrop at the shore's edge. He has placed these stones around the back of the fire from where he and Brandon are, just in case they explode from the dry heat of the fire. He remembers at least some of the bushcraft taught him when he was a boy scout.

There is little more to do now but wait for the snake to cook and hope it is edible. He has filled the empty bottles with water from the river, and his concern now is to try to stitch Brandon's face before he regains consciousness, if he does at all. There is a sewing kit with needles in the pack but not thread strong enough to use as sutures for the slash on Brandon's cheek. He thinks about what else he could use. Suddenly, he has an idea, and carefully, he looks through the clothes in the pack. He finds a pair of Brandon's army surplus pants made from a sturdy, hard-wearing canvas type material. This should do the trick! Taking the pocket knife, he cuts off one leg of the pants just above the hemline. Carefully he teases the thread of the fabric until it begins to unwind from the cut edge. Taking care not to do more than unwind it, he cuts off several good lengths and carries them down to the sea, dipping them in the salt water until saturated. Carefully, he carries them back to their camp site, and sets them on Brandon's clean shirt from the pack. Sea water has saturated the clothes, but they have now dried out, and although somewhat stiff with the salt, the shirt will do as a sterile site to lay out the rudimentary tools. The needles are in a plastic packet, so Fellings does not open them until the thread is fully dry and he is ready to try to stitch Brandon's face. He thanks God that he trained as a doctor before changing track to astrophysics. Without his medical training, Brandon could not have survived. He does not relish what he needs to do next.

Heating the knife in the fire to sterilize the blade, he then takes it and begins to trim the dried edges of the cut flesh, making sure to remove any that has begun to heal. He must have fresh edges if the slash is to heal cleanly and without becoming infected. He washes the cut out with sea water, then fresh bottled water, lastly tipping in a liberal amount of iodine from the first aid kit from the pack. At last satisfied that he has done all he can, he opens the needles, takes out the largest with a sharp point, and threads it with the thread from the army pants. He dips this and the needle in the iodine before starting. Slowly, and carefully drawing the edges together, he begins to put in the individual stitches that will hopefully hold the slash closed so that it can heal. It takes quite a while and eleven, well-spaced stitches to finish the job. Fellings sits back on his haunches to inspect his work. It is the best he can do given the conditions, and at least, Brandon remained unconscious while he worked. He cleans everything throwing the small slivers of flesh into the middle of the fire. Exhausted now from his endeavors, he checks the pieces of snake, removing them from the stones with the blade of the pocket knife. They are blackened and not very appealing, but he is very hungry, and as soon as they cool, he lifts one and breaks it open. Inside there is white steaming flesh, and he tentatively puts a small piece in his mouth. He is surprised that it tastes very much like chicken, and he sets to with gusto, his hunger overcoming any reluctance. Lastly, he bolsters the fire and lays down next to Brandon. It is not yet dark, but tiredness overcomes him, and he falls into an exhausted but troubled sleep.

There is movement and Fellings wakes with a jolt. It is pitch black except for the glow from the fire pit. He quietly stands and searches the area with his eyes before moving to the pile of fern fronds collected to keep the fire going. As quietly as he can, he drags several across to the fire pit and pushes them into the glowing ashes. It takes hardly any time at all before the fire breaks out into flame again. He turns back towards Brandon, his eyes searching as far as he can see, and he jumps when he notices Brandon's eyes watching him. His son has woken from his unconscious state, but there is a staring quality to his gaze; his state of severe shock is evident in his glassy, staring eyes. Fellings walks slowly and deliberately over to his son, and squatting down next to him, speaks slowly and calmly.

"You are going to be fine, Brandon," Fellings begins, "I found you yesterday. You were washed up on the shore. You have a broken arm and leg, and I have stitched up a large gash on your face. Rest now, son, you are safe, and I won't let anything happen to you."

Fellings opens the pack and reaches for a sealed bottle of water. Breaking the seal, he gently lifts Brandon's head and dribbles some of the water into his mouth. Brandon coughs and then swallows thirstily, but Fellings allows him only a little more.

"I will give you more in a few minutes, son," he says. He watches as Brandon's eyes droop again, and he falls into sleeping once more. This time Fellings recognizes it as normal sleep, not unconscious coma. The worst is over. If Brandon can hold his own over the next seventy-two hours, he will survive. Fellings sits back down but does not allow himself to sleep again. He will have to make do with what he has just had until he knows for sure Brandon is going to be OK. As he sits, he lets his mind wander over the events that brought them here. If only he had not made the phone call in Maui, if only he had thought of a different way to escape the clutches of MI6. Given their time over again, he would never countenance using the submersible. The submersible! Suddenly, and with some consideration, he remembers the transponder he found before he discovered the unconscious body of Brandon. Where did he put it?

Reaching into his zipped, left, tracksuit pocket, Fellings draws out the transponder and looks it over again, this time he takes time to scrutinize it properly. He understands the basics of this kind of instrument; how it connects with an orbiting satellite, from which it is powered and from which it sends signals to the submersible. Could it be possible, he wonders, that like Brandon, the submersible somehow remained intact? Could it be that the megalodon did not in fact swallow them, but somehow, they were washed out of that giant maw by the massive displacement of water? For the first time, a tiny trickle of hope teases at Fellings; he begins to believe that they may yet have a chance to escape this primordial beachhead. He watches the flames of the fire, and his hope grows with the dancing flames. First and foremost, Brandon, then with a glimmer of luck, perhaps they can try the transponder. He dares not allow his hope to grow exponentially; there is, after all, only the glimmer of a chance. What would he do if he could get Brandon back to Kettering he wonders? It seems like a lifetime ago that he flew to Maui, let alone was at home in Kettering. He wonders what his wife and daughter are doing right now. He wonders if MI6 have left them alone, or are even now trying to get information from them. It is another world and another time and not for the first time, he wonders if he will ever see it again. As the night gives way to the greyness of dawn, his meandering thoughts allow a kind of rest to his weary body. Sleep would be preferable, but inaction is good too right now.

As the sun touches the horizon, Fellings stands and stretches the stiffness from his body as best he can. The fire has burnt low again, and he fetches more fronds to keep it burning. The less he has to use of the meagre supplies in the pack, the better; he does not want to think about what happens when they are completely depleted. But then, it was only yesterday that he had nothing, not Brandon nor the pack. He will do what he must to keep them both alive, resources or not. There are several pieces of the cooked snake left next to the fire pit, and he breaks his fast with one. The flesh is quite palatable, and he decides to hunt for more today when he has had a chance to check Brandon. It would be best if his son woke up before he left, so he waits patiently for the sun to rise above the horizon. He barely notices the sulphureous tang in the air now, but he does notice that breathing this air restricts his physical abilities. He cannot do what he normally would be able to without getting puffed. Best to reserve his energy for when he needs it.

Henry

A few minutes later, the team of scientists from MI6 have been collected and taken to the lab to retest the blood samples. Higgins introduces them briefly to his team, then leads them to the cool room and shows them where to find the samples. He explains what happened with the samples that produced the original anomalies; that the human samples had been mixed up with samples of animal blood. He apologizes profusely for the stupidity of David, one of his scientific assistants. The MI6 team begin their own testing without further questions; they will check for themselves before interrogating the rest of Higgins's men.

The two agents have finished questioning the sixteen men, and all tell a similar tale. There seems to be no way to prove that these men knew about Henry's machinations; as far as they were concerned, they were recruited and paid an exorbitant amount of money to take part in what Henry declared to be a two-week experiment. Each man has told of how the invisibility cloak was used to shield them when they landed from the submersible but also to keep them from seeing the vista that eventually met their eyes. Each tells the same story of searching, from a map they were made to memorize in Kettering, the shoreline and caverns of Athens for the sigil shown to them only when they had landed. Each tells of the night that Henry escaped his guards and followed the party to the cavern and how he was immolated when he inadvertently stepped on the alien footprints outside the cavern. All the men explained how they used the sigil found in the cavern to pass through the Curtain. Peter showed them the burn mark from holding the rod as it contacted the sigil. There seems to be no point in further questioning or searching further for Henry Bonnington. If he is alive, he will still be in Athens, at far removed from their clutches.

Brandon Fellings, however, is another matter altogether. The men have described how Henry left to follow the missing men, Greg and Tim, how they slept and when they woke, Brandon had disappeared. All assumed he had taken the submersible and left them to Henry's machinations. Each man felt he had abandoned them because he was frightened of Henry. Each of them tells of Henry's temper and his single-mindedness regarding the sigils. Each man has related that he had no doubt that Henry was capable of killing when angry. Each man had been very wary of him, and each man told of the fact that they had met away from the cavern, and all were sure that Henry had lied to them about what was really going on.

The details, related by the sixteen men, as the agents from MI6 are acutely aware, are top secret. The problem will be how to deal with these people. Taking them back to England would require that they be kept in isolation or detention. But to imprison them would cause an uproar in the university, as well as their families and the wider community. Sooner or later, someone in power would demand that they be released. With this is mind, Perkins has contacted Thames House and asked for advice about what to do with the sixteen. Of course, the blood tests could show anomalies, and if this is the case, there would be a legitimate reason to keep the men here, in this isolated outpost. Suppose the tests look normal? Then the report submitted by Dr Higgins could still be used to keep the men here. Would the General be amenable to this plan? The suggestion from Thames House is that Perkins needs to talk to him and gain his compliance.

"I think the only way to now deal with this situation is to demand that General Robbins keep the sixteen men here for the duration. What do you think?" Perkins, as the lead, asks this question only to find out if his second will be compliant.

"Yes, sir, I agree." Good, no problems from that quarter.

"Why don't you go down to the lab and see what the medical team are doing. Ask them to come here as soon as they have finished the tests, and tell them no written report will be necessary, nor are they to question the scientists."

"Yes, sir." The second agent moves quickly to do as he has been ordered, and Perkins makes his way back to the General's office. He knocks and then, without waiting for a reply, enters. His lack of respect, as the General is well aware, is not unintentional. Perkins is still fuming about his earlier embarrassment; the General does not rise to the insult and stops writing as soon as Perkins takes a seat. He now has a very careful game plan to play, or so he thinks, if he wants to keep the sixteen here.

"General, we have finished questioning the sixteen men, and we are satisfied that they have committed no crimes. The man responsible has either been killed, or is at large in a place and time inaccessible to us."

"What do you need from me now then, Perkins?" The General asks politely.

"What we need is for the blood testing to be completed, but by the sound of things, the earlier anomalies appear to be the result of your lax procedures here. However, I do not intend to make a report to that effect. We will leave you to deal with the situation, but I recommend you advise your scientists to take more care."

"Thank you, Perkins, I appreciate that and your candor. I certainly will be taking measures to ensure nothing of the kind happens again."

"We do have one favour to ask, General," Perkins begins, "we would like you to keep the sixteen men here for the foreseeable future, since the information they have regarding the submersible and the work being done is top secret. It will be very difficult for us to keep a lid on them back home; their families and the university community are not likely to brook our detaining them for long."

"Ah, I see," the General is ecstatic with this turn of events but is very careful now to make his response a guarded and convincingly reticent one. Now is the time to snap the trap closed.

"I don't really have the room here, and I don't need this added responsibility, Perkins," the General begins. "Besides, surely they have the right to return to their families and jobs if as you say, they have done nothing wrong."

"Not now, they don't," Perkins begins to argue his case. "We cannot allow the critical work to be breached again; already, with the theft of the submersible, we have been lucky not to have an international inquiry into what we as a government have been doing. If even that information gets out, the PM could be toppled along with the agencies that have had a hand in keeping this under wraps. Do you want our traditional enemies to have free reign into our most secret, developing defence capabilities? I ask you as a serving General to help us with the damage control; damage caused by an unscrupulous and egoistic man. There is really no other way to shut down the problem quickly. What do you say, General?"

Robbins does not miss the surreptitious, intended threat in the argument, and so, after waiting several minutes, appearing to be deep in thought and without in the least appearing to be eager for the men to stay, he at last replies to Perkins.

"If this is the only way to ensure counter measures, then I suppose I don't really have any choice. I can find work for the sixteen, so I agree to keep them here for as long as you feel it is necessary. Do you need me to contact Thames House, or will you deal with them?"

"I will deal with the authorities in England, General. Believe me, you have made the right decision, and for all concerned. As soon as the blood testing is done, I will be leaving with my team, and I wish you all the best. Thank you for your hospitality and good luck."

Perkins stands and offers the General his hand. The General takes it and gives it a perfunctory shake, making sure it seems as if he feels he has been taken advantage of and is not at all happy. Perkins smiling, heads to the door. He turns back just before he leaves saying, "No hard feelings I hope, General?" and closes the door before the General can reply. Now it is the General's turn to smile.

The Family

Brian prepares for the rituals that must now take place. His own powers will now be tested, and he must not fail, for he has one chance only to complete what must be done. He is ready, and he turns and stares into the faces of Phoenix and Kenny, holding their eyes with his own and begins to chant. The chanting is in a foreign tongue but not the alien tongue used by Marcom and Ladon. As the chanting rises in pitch, the internal room of the barrow begins to spin, slowly at first, and then gaining in speed, and both boys feel dizzy and faint. Slowly, and with great care, Brian leads first Kenneth and then Phoenix to two mounds spread with a cloth embroidered with the same swirling knot work as the walls and floor. The cloths are the exact same colour as the walls, so they went unnoticed when the boys first entered. As each head touches the embroidered cloth, the boys lose consciousness, and Brian checks each boy's eyes by lifting their lids before he ceases the chant. Their eyes are fixed; they are in the trance state.

Brian takes two, long breaths to steady his nerves, then raises his arms above his head, and touching the patterned roof, begins to speak a homily to the spirits that guard this place. He closes his eyes and waits. Suddenly, his eyes spring open, and from his mouth, a very different voice begins to speak. Brian is no longer in charge of his body. The voice commends him for his work and then begins the words and actions that will take each boy on his own inner journey.

"Phoenix," the voice begins, "what do you see?"

"I am standing in a grove of oak trees," Phoenix begins, "there are people here dressed in white robes, and they have bound my hands in front of me with vines."

"What is your name?" the voice intones.

"My name is Fhionn, and I am to be sacrificed. I am the oldest son of my family, and we have been awarded the honour of this year's sacrifice. I will become immortal, and my family will live on for a thousand years."

"Who commands this sacrifice?"

"It is Tine, our sacred father."

"Look around the grove, what can you see?"

"I see a wicked man."

"Describe this wicked man."

"It is a massive man, woven from the small branches of the linden tree. It has a door at the top of the head."

"This, my Fhionn, is a wicker man. Do you understand what you are to undergo?"

"Yes, I must climb the bank to the top of the wicker man and enter the small door at the top. I must be brave enough to ensure my immortality and my family's continuance."

"What will happen when you enter the door, Fhionn?

"A bough will be taken from the eternal fire that burns under the sacred oak tree. This bough will light the wicker man, and I will be burned alive."

"Are you willing to do this?"

"Yes, I must. My own and my family's futures depend on my actions here and now."

"Then go, Fhionn, and may the gods go with you and grant you their eternal peace."

Phoenix lies restless and sweating on the embroidered cloth and again the voice from Brian's body speaks to him.

"Are you ready, Fhionn?"

"I am ready." He kneels before Tine and kisses the hem of his robe, then he bounds up the bank of the valley wall, regardless of his bound hands and enters the head by using his bound hands and swinging his legs over the edge of the cage door. He is ready.

"Tine, light the wicker man!"

As Phoenix watches on from his unconscious state, the wicker man is lit, and the flames travel quickly up the centre of the body. Soon the flames begin to lick his feet and with all his strength he tries not to cry out. As the flames take hold, the prone Phoenix screams a heart-rending scream and then lies still again.

There is smoke, lots of smoke. There is a silence so profound that the flames around him do not make a sound. He floats above them, his body already well alight, but the flames do not eat him. A serenity overcomes him, so sweet, it seems that he floats on the clouds. He sees the people down below, his family among them, and yet he feels no pain, no burning heat, just the profound silence of the eternal Power. Then he speaks.

"I am the Phoenix. Immolation cannot annihilate me. Out of the ashes, I rise again. Oh, behold the beloved Power; this is my victory, this is my destiny, and this is my duty."

Phoenix sleeps as the body of Brian and the alien voice now turns its attention on Kenneth.

"Kenneth, what do you see?"

"I am in a dark wood; I think the trees are oak trees. There is a dim green light, but I can see clearly."

"What is your name?" the voice again intones to Kenny the same questions it asked Phoenix.

"I am Slanaith Dealan-De, I protect the souls of the dead, and I am the keeper of powers."

"Look around the forest, what else do you see?"

"There are beautiful butterflies in here, even though it is dark and green, and they are speaking to me."

"What do they say?"

"They are saying that I have an onerous responsibility to care for the dead and to bring faithfulness to bear on all the powers. I am to be their keeper and not allow them to be squandered on frivolous desires."

"Do you see the powers and the souls of the dead?"

"Oh yes, they are so beautiful. The butterflies carry them on their wings."

"Will you take them all and keep them all?"

"I will."

The body of Kenneth lies still, a beautific smile adorning his face.

"Are you ready, Slanaith Dealan-De?" the voice asks.

"I am ready," Slanaith Dealan-De replies.

The butterflies approach him fluttering his face with their fragile wings, and the powers and the souls transfer to the body of Slanaith Dealan-De. He feels the weight and gravity of each one of them. He bears them with insouciance, and with the greatest of gentleness, he kisses each butterfly as it reaches out to him. He speaks,

"By the Power of all that lives and dies, I am Slanaith Dealan-De, keeper of the powers and savior of souls. I will endure. This is my great, joyous victory, this is my destiny, and this is my duty."

Kenneth sleeps and the body of Brian slumps to the barrow floor. He lies unconscious as the boys sleep on in dreamless sleep.

Florence has cooked breakfast for herself and Antheia. The child, Ladon, watches his mother and grandmother with his large, bright, luminous eyes. The two women are lost in their own thoughts, so it is some time before one of them speaks.

"Mother, will Aletheia be able to undertake her duties without her sight?"

"Oh, Antheia, yes, my dear, for our human sight is but one kind of seeing. Have you not already experienced another sight, an insight with the imprinting done while you carried Ladon inside you?"

"I had thought it was only due to that, Mother," Antheia replies thoughtfully.

"There is so much yet for you to learn, and we are going to start this learning today and together. The reason I had to leave you all in Athens was to prepare for this learning that you now need to undergo." Florence gently chides her second daughter.

"What of Ladon, Mother?" Antheia asks. She is worried about the child; he has grown so quickly she hardly recognizes him from one day to the next. As she has done since his second day, Antheia cuts his silver hair every morning and yet every night it seems to grow thicker and longer. This morning she noticed teeth in his mouth, and although she feeds him on demand, he seems to need more than her milk can provide. Just as this thought reaches her consciousness, Ladon reaches out with his tiny hand and catches a piece of bacon in his fist. He has it in his mouth and is chewing before Antheia can move to take it from him.

"Well, little one, it looks as if you are ready for real food!" Florence smiles at him and reaches out to stop Antheia's hand from reaching to take it away from him.

"We do not know how he will develop, Antheia, but I suggest you allow him to choose what to eat. He is, after all, Ladon, and we must trust that he knows what he needs."

Both women watch him thoughtfully, and as soon as he has devoured the bacon, he reaches for a second piece. Ladon eats and Ladon grows.

Greg and Tim

The coach slows at the entrance to the muddy track leading to the lodge in which Gavinar and Felix stayed previously. This time all the men are awake, and Tim looks around with curiosity as they get closer. The lodge is a rough but solid-looking, wooden construction, obviously able to withstand the gales arising from the sea. There is the salt tang of the sea in the air here, and he can hear the faint screeching of gulls or other seabirds, so they can't be far from the ocean. It is late afternoon but still light enough for the men to enter and begin the preparations for their stay. As before, Felix sets to building and lighting a fire in the stone fireplace and Gavinar sends Damon to hobble the horses under the cover of the lean-to at the back. Hopefully, this time, there will be no storm winds to blow it down. Gavinar looks around the storeroom and brings in their supplies to begin preparing a meal. Greg speaks.

"Gavinar and Felix, do you mind if Tim and I take a brief walk outside to look around?"

"Of course, make yourselves at home. Dinner will be about an hour, so you have time for a reasonable walk." Gavinar does not even look up from his task.

Tim and Greg head for the door and closing it, set off across the open fields towards the ocean. When they are several hundred metres from the lodge, Greg speaks quietly.

"I have remembered what was bothering me, Tim, and we need to decide what to do about it."

"Tell me," Tim replies.

"Do you remember when we were first told about how Felix and Gavinar found the orb here?"

"I remember most of it, but what has that got to do with your gut feelings?"

"Do you remember why Gavinar said Felix needed to come here?"

Tim stops walking for a moment, trying to recall the story as related to them by Gavinar.

"Wasn't it something to do with the Alchemists, Greg?" Tim asks.

"Yes, Felix said he needed to check for certain minerals in the cliffs here, or so he claimed. But they did not do that after they found the orb, and as far as we know, they never returned again to do so."

"Again, I can't see the relevance to what we have come here to do?" Tim still can't grasp the significance of what they were told back in Gothenburg.

"What if the reason given to Gavinar for their journey was false? What if Felix already knew about the orb and that was the reason he needed to come here; to come back and search for it?"

"But how could he have known, Greg? Have you thought about that?"

"He could only have known if he already had it in his possession at some stage. I have been thinking about it since I remembered at about half-way here, and the only sense I can make of it, is this. What if Felix travelled here with the orb and some mishap caused him to lose it here?"

"Like what?' Tim asks.

"Smugglers are known to use these shores to unload their booty; if Felix travelled with such a group, then perhaps there was a shipwreck, and he survived the wreck but lost the orb."

"But then, how could he have known Gavinar well enough and for long enough to return here without Gavinar suspecting something of the kind? You know as well as I do, that Gavinar is far from stupid. In fact, I would suggest that Gavinar is the brains of the two."

"I would too, except recall how Felix was able to hold us easily with his mind, and don't forget the feeling induced by the clock near the door to his house. What if Felix is using Gavinar as he is trying to use us? Gavinar could have been hypnotized into believing that he has known Felix for years, by being subliminally given knowledge appropriate for the suggestion to stick.

"Another thing: remember we looked up robelite — which Felix showed us the orb was made from — and found it to be what is now known as riebeckite? What if Felix came here to look for minerals necessary to construct another orb, since he had lost the first one? I think there is much more to both of these men that we don't know or understand, and I intend to find out before we even try to find the sigil. As far as we know, neither of them knows what to look for; what the sigil looks like, but this assumption might also be premature."

"What do you mean, Greg?" Tim is now more confused, "you did show them the sigil, don't you remember? When you took control of the orb, you pictured the sigil and then widened the image to take in the back and foreground. That's how we knew to come here."

"I had forgotten, Tim, thanks for reminding me; but that still makes no difference to what I propose, in fact, it is directly related to it." Greg thinks before speaking again.

"What I mean is this: what if Felix already knows about the sigils because he has already used them to travel through the Curtain? It seems just as likely, given his possession of the orb and the fact that it is constructed from materials unknown in this particular time. The book by Mesmer may be a red herring to trick us into thinking he is oblivious to what we know in our time. If you were going to try to enact subterfuge without being discovered, what would you do?"

"I must admit now, Greg, that I tend to agree with you, but how are we going to get to the truth of all this?"

"Leave that to me for now," Greg replies, "I think I have a plan forming, but I need to think about it further. The less you know about it, the better. You will then be genuinely surprised, and that is what I want you to convey."

The two men turn back towards the lodge; neither man has taken the slightest notice of their surroundings, so engrossed in discussion have they been. There is now a wisp of smoke coming from the chimney as they near the door, and both men can smell the scents of cooking. Now that their noses are assaulted, they both realise they are very hungry. Stamping the sandy dirt from their shoes, they open the door to a cheerful scene. Felix has lit several oil lamps, and the room is bright and warming. The fire is burning brightly, and Gavinar is stirring a pot hanging from a hook over the fire. For the first time since they set out, Greg starts to relax and let the ambience work its magic. There are two armchairs set on either side of the fireplace and several high-backed wooden chairs set around a small table, at which Damon is sitting. Felix fetches a bottle of wine from the storeroom and opening it, pours it into five beakers set out on the table. With a flourish, he hands each of the others a beaker and makes a toast, "To the Curtain and all who travel through!"

The men drink, and Felix replenishes their beakers. Damon looks on but says nothing. He is smart enough to know that he will learn more by listening than by taking a part in any conversation.

As soon as the stew is ready, Gavinar ladles it into earthenware bowls, and the men all sit down at the table to eat. When the food is eaten, the men stay seated and begin to discuss what tomorrow may bring. Damon bids the others good night and retires to the lean-to; he will sleep with the horses, and he wants to rise early enough to get his chores done before breakfast. He is hoping that he can set out to return to Gothenburg tomorrow. Felix asks Greg when they can expect to set out to search for the sigil.

"Felix, there is one question I was meaning to ask you," Greg ignores Felix's question. "Do you remember what you and Gavinar came here for?"

"Do you mean the minerals I was to search for?" Felix watches Greg carefully.

"Yes, and by the way, what minerals were you looking for?"

"It was feldspar that the Alchemists needed, but I don't think it would be found here anyway." Felix tries to sound dismissive.

"Did you return to look?" Greg is bordering on interrogation now, and Felix is not happy with this turn of the conversation.

"What difference does that make? I decided not to return because I could not see the point."

"But why?" Greg is insistent with his questioning. "If your scientific group were relying on you to try, how did you explain to them the fact that you did not even return to try to find it?" Felix does not answer, so Greg does not push him further. Instead, he feigns tiredness by making sure to yawn hugely, he rises and bidding them goodnight, retires to the room in which he and Tim will sleep.

Shutting the door behind him, he can hear the others speaking, but he can't hear what they are saying. Quietly he removes his laptop and opening it, he connects to the satellite. As soon as he has power, he clicks on the university site and enters a search for 'riebeckite, feldspar'.

A page quickly opens giving the chemical formulae for what is termed 'gneiss-riebeckite-feldspar-quartz'. He reads avidly, and at last, finished with his reading, smiles grimly and closes the laptop, disconnecting from the satellite. It is just as he surmised. There is now no doubt in his mind that his assumptions about Felix's intention to construct another orb are indeed fact; his subconscious was working overtime to project to him this warning! He sits still thinking about how he can catch Felix out in this lie and what he is going to do about it if he can. It is now obvious to him that Felix is not what he seems. It appears likely that Felix has also somehow, and at some time, passed through the Curtain with the orb and managed to insert himself into the life here in Sweden. Whether or not Gavinar is also from another time, he cannot tell, but now he must make a plan to find out and well before they attempt to go through the Curtain again.

He quickly undresses and climbs into bed but without any intention of sleeping. He lays awake thinking, and a plan starts to form given the knowledge he now has about Felix. If Gavinar is not part of Felix's deception, then Greg knows he can find this out if he can get Gavinar on his own for a short time. How to arrange this? He will have to come up with a convincing idea to remove Felix from the lodge for at least an hour. Both Felix and Gavinar are expecting them all to search for the sigil tomorrow without delay, so what can he suggest that will absorb Felix's attention outside the lodge before they go to search? Or maybe searching is the best way; by again showing Felix and Gavinar the image of the sigil. This may be just what needs to be done. Yes, of course, since Felix knows what to look for, he can send him with Tim to start the search, but what can he use as an excuse to stay here and keep Gavinar here too? He needs to suggest something that requires Gavinar's presence, or that he knows one of them will want to take part in. Trust is still an issue between the two pairs of men, so what can he think of to do that one or other of them will insist on being present? Then it hits him, and he knows what he will do. Now, for the first time since they set out, he can relax and simply finetune the plan. It must be as foolproof as is possible, and then, when they know it all, he and Tim can make an informed decision about whether or not to take Felix and Gavinar with them. The last thing Greg thinks before succumbing to his tiredness is "Felix, you are about to be unmasked at last!"

Brandon

As Fellings waits for Brandon to wake, he lies in a kind of reverie, his mind casting back to a life as different from right now as can ever be imagined. How have they come to this pass, and what does it mean for humanity to be able to travel through the infinite plenum? What will the scientists do with this extraordinary knowledge? Perhaps it heralds the end of mankind and even the Universe as we know it. Unscrupulous men have already produced ruin with many discoveries that could have made the world a better place. How can the knowledge that has brought them here be protected from such men? He sighs deeply and is brought back to present reality by a spluttering cough coming from Brandon. His son is waking from an uneasy sleep. He moves closer.

"Where am I?" Brandon's voice is rough with dryness and fatigue, but at least he is able to speak this morning.

"You are with me, Brandon; we are on some primordial beachhead. Do you remember coming here?"

"I can't move, Dad, what is wrong with me?" Fellings smiles at the remark; Brandon knows who has spoken to him, so it bodes well for minimal damage to his mental faculties.

"You have broken an arm and a leg, and you have a large gash in your right cheek. I have stitched the gash and tried to set your broken bones as best as I can. Your right leg and your left arm. Don't try to move, I will get you what you want."

"Water," Brandon replies, so Fellings fetches the water bottle from the pack and gently raising his son's head he tips a small quantity into his mouth. This time, Brandon swallows the water greedily, but Fellings knows not to allow him to immediately slake his thirst. In small increments, he feeds Brandon the water until the bottle is empty. He fetches another from the pack, and placing it in Brandon's right hand, allows him to drink as much as he wants. This time when he speaks,

Brandon's voice is stronger, and he asks the questions that Fellings would expect after his ordeal.

"Dad, I don't remember what happened? Can you tell me please?"

"I will, but first I need to build up the fire and get you something to eat. Can you stomach a protein bar?"

"I think so, at least I will try, and can I please have more water? I don't seem to be able to quench this thirst."

Fellings hands him the second bottle again and moves to add more dry fronds to the fire. He decides to also try to make Brandon more comfortable by using the spare clothes from the pack to form a kind of pillow. This at least raises Brandon's head a few inches from the prone position.

"Let me know if you need to pee, I have an empty bottle here for that purpose." Fellings wants to see if Brandon can urinate as soon as possible; the sign that his kidneys and lower organs are not badly damaged.

"Sure, Dad," Brandon replies.

Fellings decides to make an inventory of sorts from the contents of the pack; he needs to work out how many meals he can give Brandon before he needs to revert to whatever he can catch. There are two packs of protein bars and some energy snacks of dried fruit and nuts. There are still six bottles of water, so this should last for at least two to three days. He will definitely need to hunt for more food today, and hopefully, if he can find another snake or two, or some seafood, he can cook it, and it will keep for at least another forty-eight hours in this cold climate. The fact that the air is tinged with sulphur should aid the preserving process too.

With two protein bars in hand, Fellings settles back down next to Brandon. Unwrapping one, he hands it to his son and watches as he takes a small bite. There is obvious pain with the stitched cheek but not so severe as to stop him chewing tentatively and swallowing. He breathes a sigh of relief. Brandon's throat and mouth are working. He is slowly checking every visible sign as his son eats. Could they be lucky enough that the broken bones are the worst of his injuries? Now he begins to relate what he knows of the events leading to Brandon's injured state.

"Do you remember we left Maui in the submersible and landed here, on this beachhead?" Fellings wants to find out how much Brandon can recall.

"Yes, Dad, I remember that. I also remember we went looking around here and found the waterfall in the fern forest. But I don't seem to be able to remember what happened after that."

"We decided that there was no point in staying here, so you recalled the submersible and gave me the packs and the transponder to hold, while you swam out to bring the submersible closer to shore. Do you remember that?"

"I sort of do, but it's all a bit fuzzy."

"Well, I was watching from the waterline, and I saw you grab hold of the submersible, but then suddenly from under the water, a giant form emerged. It was as tall as a ten-storey building and it come back down over you and the submersible, a giant maw opened, and it seemed to swallow you and the submersible. I was so shocked, I just stood there, open-mouthed until a giant wave of displaced water washed over me, and I was tumbled over the sand. I remember trying to get to the top of the water so I could breathe. When the wave subsided, I was left on the sand and the packs, the transponder, you and the submersible had all disappeared."

"Then how did I come to be here?" Brandon asks, "I don't understand."

"I'm not sure I do either, Brandon," Fellings replies, "but I will continue with the story. I spent the rest of that day trying to work out how I was going to survive here, and that night, I slept at the edge of the forest after burrowing down into the sand. I guess I was still in shock, but at least I had the sense to return to the waterfall and drink some water. I woke up from a nightmare, and I knew I had to prepare myself to stay here for the duration. I had absolutely no idea that you were still alive, and I had to decide whether to try to survive myself, or just lay down and die. I can tell you, both choices were equally forbidding!"

"When did you find me again, Dad?" Brandon is still confused.

"That next morning, I decided I would need to make a shelter if I was to stay here. I left the other side of the beachhead and wandered around the cove to a rocky outcrop that I could just see from the other side. By this time, I was very hungry, and I hoped that with the outcrop exposed, I might find something edible if there were any pools. I found a crab, and I smashed it to kill it, then I tore its body to bits and ate it raw. I had no way of making a fire at that stage, so anything edible, I would have to eat raw. I began to search along this side just in case I might find the packs, but I could not see anything. I was just about to turn back when something glinted in the sunlight. At first, I thought I must be seeing things in my agitated state, but then I saw it again about five hundred metres up the beach. I set off, then saw you lying in the shallows. You looked like a bundle of rags, but I knew that could not be possible, so I ran up to you and thinking you must be dead, I felt for a pulse in your neck. I was shocked to find one, even though it was fluttery and weak. The rest, my son, is history as we would say."

"How do you explain it, Dad? It doesn't seem possible from what you have said that I could have survived the monster's attack?"

"The only thing that I can think of that makes sense, is that somehow, you were washed out of the monster's maw by the massive displacement of water as it crashed back into the ocean." Fellings is even now thinking this through. "It could have been that you were small enough, in relation to the size of its maw, that it didn't manage to grab a hold of your body."

"I'm glad I can't remember any of it," Brandon says, "I don't think I could remain sane if I did."

"Then don't push yourself to remember," Fellings does not want Brandon to be subjected to further stress. "Just forget it now that you know. Let's concentrate on getting you through the next few weeks while your bones mend and then we can decide what to do. One thing I forgot to mention, I have already killed one snake; the pocketknife in the pack has already proven to be a great boon. I cooked it last night and ate some. It is quite good. I have also seen what looked like a cassowary, as we call them. It took fright when it saw me, but if I can catch or trap it, we will have some great meat for at least a couple of days."

"When did you find the backpack, Dad?" Brandon asks.

"When I found you, I raced back into the forest to try to find some fern fronds straight enough to do a makeshift job of setting your broken arm and leg. I found enough and I had shouldered them when I tripped and dropped them again. Once more, I picked them up, then tripped over something again. I looked to see what it was, and I spied a patch of blue, so I dug down and uncovered this pack. I have never before been as pleased to recover an object as I was when I saw it. Here was the means of providing what I needed to light a fire, stitch up your face, bind your bones and to feed you for several days. As soon as you are recovered enough for me to leave you, I will search again for the other pack. I will also try to catch more food. Perhaps we might survive all this yet."

"Thanks for not giving up, Dad; we would both have died here if you had!"

Henry

General Robbins and Dr Higgins stand outside in the semi-dark, watching as the RAF Hercules gathers speed along the lit runway and then lifts cleanly off the ground. Both men heave a great sigh of relief and look at each other for the first time. MI6 have now left, and at last they have the base back to themselves again. After giving orders to the ground crew to shut down the lights and return to their quarters, the General puts out his hand and Higgins grasps it in a full-blooded handshake. Both men step to the door and return to the warmth of the passageway.

"I think a drink is in order, what do you say, Higgins?"

"I think I need one all right, and a large one! Do you think we managed to convince Perkins and the others?"

"Oh yes, we did indeed," the General replies, "Perkins was so self-satisfied that he had at last won the day, that he didn't give it a second thought. He was too eager to make me feel hard-done by, and I did not disappoint him."

The two men enter the General's office, and while Higgins makes himself comfortable, the General takes out a bucket of ice and a bottle of Irish whisky. He takes a handful of ice, and after depositing it into each of two cut glass tumblers, pours two liberal amounts of the whisky. He looks at Higgins raising one eyebrow, but Higgins shakes his head. Both men need the full strength of the golden spirit.

"So, what do you think we should do now, Higgins?" The General asks, but the question is largely rhetorical; as Higgins is well aware the General is always at least one step ahead of the game.

"I am sure, sir, that you have already formulated a plan, and I can't wait to hear it." Higgins cuts short the preamble.

"I suggest the first thing to do is to get the sixteen men together and let them know they are staying here with us for the foreseeable future.

Once they realise that here they will at least have a certain freedom, compared to being kept in detention back in England, I imagine they will be cooperative. I then suggest that we interview each man to find out a bit about his personality and likes and dislikes so that we have a rudimentary profile. After that, it will be time to show them why we wanted them here; explaining why we made sure that MI6 was kept out of the picture." The General waits while Higgins thinks through the initial plan.

"So, you want me to take more blood before we reveal this?" Higgins asks, knowing the answer but wanting confirmation.

"Yes, Higgins, and before we speak to them, you can compare the latest results with the photos in my safe. When they see the problem, I am sure they will want to know what is going on as much as we do."

Higgins leaves the General's office and makes his way back to his lab. The rest of his staff are now off duty, and he does not bother to recall them; instead, he packs a trolley with everything he needs and heads for the rooms in which the sixteen men are being detained. As he enters Peter's room, Peter looks up and sits ready for the blood to be taken.

"What's happening?" Peter asks, "Are we to return to England with MI6?"

Higgins removes the rubber band and caps the test tube full of Peter's blood.

"The General will be calling you all to a meeting first thing in the morning," he replies, "so I think it best to wait and everything will be revealed to all of you then. At least I can tell you that you won't be kept in isolation any longer."

"Thanks, Doctor," Peter is relieved that at last, they will find out their future.

Higgins visits each of the men and gives each a similar answer to the same question. As soon as he has completed the blood collection, he quickly makes his way back to the lab and prepares the electron microscope to see what is now showing in this batch of samples. While he waits, he returns to the General's office to retrieve the photographs of the previous tests. The General has removed them from his safe, ready for Higgins and he reminds him to come back as soon as he has the results. Soon he will be able to compare the photos with the new blood tests, and perhaps there will be something that shows up that will make sense of the whole enigmatic problem. He can hope anyway!

As the first slide is inserted into the column, Higgins watches with bated breath. The microscope is already warmed up to the required frequency, and almost immediately the screen is filled with molecules. He is no longer shocked by what he sees, rather he looks closely at what is displayed; trying to make sense of the new molecules and trying to spot anything that may give a clue to what he sees. As he removes the first sample and loads the second, something jogs his memory, and he carefully peruses the new screen for what has come to mind. It takes him several seconds of careful scrutiny, but then he spots what he theorized he would see, and he turns the magnification to full. Satisfied, he takes a screen shot, then he sits back, his mind working overtime to try to work through what this could mean. Carefully, he checks each sample, and after returning them labelled to the cooler, he turns off the microscope, and again, sits still. Eventually, he decides to go back to General Robbins' office to make his report. He still has not decided how what he has seen — now in all the samples — can be explained and what it could mean. He hopes that sleeping on it may produce results that his conscious mind can't immediately bring to light.

The General is waiting for him, and as soon as he knocks, bids him enter. He sits down across from the General's desk and thinks about how to tell the General about what he has found.

"Have you looked at the new samples, Higgins?" the General asks, obviously very keen to hear what has been found.

"Oh yes, sir, but I am dumbfounded by something that came to mind while I was looking at the samples and which, after I checked for it, I was careful to ensure was in each." Higgins begins with this news first. "I have taken a screenshot of what is puzzling me."

He places an iPad with a large, coloured image from the microscope on the General's desk and moves around to the same side as the General is sitting to point out what he is referring to.

"Do you see this cell here?" he uses his finger to circle what he wants the General to look at, "It is what we call a carrier cell."

The General can see a small projection at the end of one particular kind of molecule displayed.

"Carriers are membrane proteins that complement the structural features of the molecules transported. They bind to the chemicals in order to move them across the cell membrane. Energy is consumed because the transport proceeds against the concentration gradient." Higgins knows that the General is unlikely to understand even this basic explanation and that he will have to think through the appearance of these carriers before he can give a cogent and simple reason for their appearance.

"What I wanted you to look at in particular is a tiny form called a cytochrome. It is the carrier protein in the electron transport chain.

"The only substance that fails to cross the cell membrane by carrier is DNA. It cannot do so, under any circumstances. And yet, this is what you are witnessing in this case. The cytochrome, which normally powers and transports electrons, in this image is acting as a carrier for the DNA molecule. This should be impossible, and yet here it is as plain as day. It goes against all the known biological constants, and I am flabbergasted by it. But that is not the greatest anomaly here. Human DNA molecules would normally appear as laddered strands in the helix form, but these have no such structure. What you are seeing here does not belong to the world as we know it, and my only reasonable guess as to what it could be, is something so archaic that it long ago died out of known existence. If I am right, and I could well be wrong, these men have been 'infected' by something when crossing through the Curtain. I use the word infected very loosely, because we are not talking about an incursion by a foreign body such as a bacterium or virus but something that has caused a change in the very DNA molecules of these men; in fact, another source of DNA seems to have been inserted into their normal DNA structure.

"From my own understanding, and the little I have been told about the top-secret experiment being carried out in Kettering, when the human body passes through the Curtain, it is first deconstructed to its constituent molecules which reform after the event. The process is apparently so fast as to be unable to be captured by any means, even nanotechnology. But if this is the case, and again I could well be wrong, then it is only at the deconstruction/ reconstruction phase that such changes could have been wrought. The fact that the changes are identical in each of the sixteen men points to the Curtain as the only constant."

"Have you any idea what this could mean, Higgins?" the General asks, knowing that there is probably nothing Higgins can add.

"Absolutely none, General," Higgins replies, "but I need to think on this quietly before I can even begin to tell you how it occurred, or what it means for the men involved as well as for all of us here at the base."

"Thank you, Higgins. It's time we got some rest. Tomorrow is another day, and maybe after sleeping on it, your mind may throw up something. Anyway, goodnight and I will see you in the morning. I intend to rise early to prepare for what we need to do with the sixteen men and to be ready for any further thoughts you may have on the matter."

"Goodnight, General, I will be up early too. Do you want me to come to your office first thing?"

"I think that would be best, then we can go over our plans for the sixteen before breakfast."

Higgins rises to take his leave, and both men vacate the office, each to go to his own quarters. For the next several hours, Higgins lays awake thinking, before succumbing to exhaustion and falling into a troubled sleep.

The Family

Canath returns to the tower room in a rush of frission; he has now to turn his attention to the two boys. Brian will return with them soon, and he hopes the boys have been able to complete their inner journeys successfully. He does not want to contemplate what will happen if that is not the case. He smooths his hair and beard, and takes the stairs down to the kitchen, where Florence, Antheia and Ladon sit eating.

"Is there any food left?" he asks cheerily, "I could eat a dragon!"

Ladon opens his mouth and laughs so joyously at this silly remark that the women start laughing too. How could this young baby understand Canath's joke?

"Oh, Canath, it is so good to see you," Florence rises to hug her husband to her.

"How did it go with Aletheia?" she asks this lightly, but her heart is beating with trepidation.

"It was as we surmised it would be," Canath begins as Florence serves him eggs and bacon and fresh bread. Although her heart is thudding, she pours coffee for him with a steady hand.

"She can physically see there, and she is comfortable with her task. The Power has enabled her with everything she needs; she has seen the threshold with her own eyes, and we explored the finite limits. I have also explained to her why we had to leave her and the children in Athens. She knows now that you are holding the universal stability, so that has galvanized her with serious resolve. She will be fine, Florence, and Kenneth and I will check in on her from time to time."

"Thank the gods," Florence's relief is clear in her voice, and the family remaining in the kitchen eat and chat. Ladon listens to everything as he chews more bacon. He may be a child, but he understands everything as he grows.

"The boys should be back soon," Canath says, "and I hope they will be hungry too. I will summon the kitchen staff to make sure there is plenty to eat." He stands and makes his way to the outer hall and speaks to the staff. Soon he returns and resumes his seat and his breakfast. Ladon reaches over and snags a piece of Canath's bacon. Canath looks on in surprise and says, "I will have to be careful not to be eaten by a dragon!"

Ladon collapses in laugher once more, and Canath reaches over and lifts him high into the air. Ladon clings on as Canath flies him around the room in his arms, then seats him on his lap. The child's eyes are filled with love, and his mouth is soon filled with food again. Canath and Florence exchange smiles as the family relaxes while they can.

Brian is aware of the room once more; shaking his head to clear away the visions, he gradually lifts himself to the sitting position. He still feels dizzy, but the memory of that overcoming spirit starts to lose its intensity. His body numb for several hours, now begins to tingle with pins and needles in all extremities as he resumes physical control. The painful effect helps to focus his mind again and he looks around him. He sees that both boys are still sleeping, but they do not appear to be in any way troubled. That is a very good sign. As soon as he feels that he can, he stands and stretches stiff muscles. He really is getting too old for these exhausting rituals!

As soon as he has his strength back, he begins to chant. This time the room stays stationary, and as the chanting increases in volume, the boys begin to stir. Soon they open their eyes and lay still listening. Brian stops chanting and claps his hands loudly three times and the boys sit up and look around. Phoenix looks at Kenny and speaks.

"Ken, are you all right?" he asks

"Sure, Phoenix, what about you?" he looks at Phoenix and then turns his attention to Brian.

"Brian, I had a really great dream," Kenneth begins, "and I know what I have to do now."

"Both of you have been on your inner journeys, and both of you have completed those journeys successfully," Brian intones, "well done, both of you."

"Are we to return to the tower now?" Phoenix asks, looking at Brian hopefully.

"Yes, Phoenix, we are finished here," Brian knows that Phoenix's journey has not been a pleasant one as Kenny's has been, and he feels sympathy for the brave boy/man.

"As soon as you feel like you can, I want you to stand up and stretch your muscles," Brian speaks. "Then we will leave here and make our way back to the boat. Are there any questions before we leave this place?"

"Will we need to come back here again?" Phoenix asks; he knows that if that is the case, he may have to go through a similar ordeal again.

"No, Phoenix, once we leave here, you will never return." Brian reassures the boys that this part of their training is now complete.

The boys stand, stretch and look around them. This truly is a magnificent and awe-inspiring room; the patterns begin to move as they look, and Brian leads them to the narrow crawlspace. Each boy enters the space and crawls back to the outside. The weather is cool and gloomy, mist rising in thin swirls from the lake, but the boys look around them thankfully and breathe deeply of the cold, crisp air. It is good to be back outside. With Brian in the lead, they head for the boat, and soon, Brian's swift rowing has them in sight of the tower. Suddenly they realise how hungry they are, and as soon as the boat is beached, the boys race up towards the kitchen door. As they enter, they can smell the delicious aromas of breakfast. The familiar scene in the kitchen brings such a joy to each boy that their spirits soar, and they greet their family with bright eyes and wide smiles.

Greg and Tim

Morning breaks with a cold and foggy dawn. Mist from the sea is blowing inland, obscuring everything except what lies within a few yards of Damon. He has already completed his chores and is now waiting for the others to wake and rise. He sits on the lodge steps and lights his long pipe. The talk from last night has him intrigued; the Curtain of the toast is puzzling him. What on earth can it be referring to? Never mind, he can do without any intrigue; he just wants to set off for home and get back to his routine world where nobody cares about Curtains or orbs. As he smokes, he hears the first sounds from inside. Knocking his pipe out, he stands and enters the lodge.

Felix is up and dressed and preparing to light the fire ready for making breakfast. He looks at Damon and nods to him, then returns his attention to the fireplace. Using a long poker, he rakes at the coals and adds kindling to get the flames going. It is not difficult; the fire has burnt down but has not gone out. As soon as the fire is roaring brightly once more, he takes a pot from the shelf and fills it with water, then spoons in coffee grounds. There will soon be coffee and that will ensure the morning is off to a bright start, regardless of the gloomy weather. Felix looks through the stores and takes out bacon and eggs, then takes a flat pan from a hook above the fireplace and places it to heat, along with the metal coffee pot, on the metal grid set into the stone hearth, and under which the flames leap. As soon as he considers it hot enough, he drops in the bacon and breaks in several eggs.

As he goes about this chore, he listens for sounds that indicate the others are rising; today he will most certainly get the chance to return home at last. He just has to make sure his subterfuge is not discovered before he can find the sigil and use it to pass through the Curtain. Then the orb can be taken back to where it belongs or remain here; he really is not fussed one way or the other, and he will, for the first time in many years, get to see his cousin again. Henry has much to answer for, and he is of a mind to make him pay. He has had plenty of time to concoct the appropriate punishment. The appearance of the two men from 2020 was fortuitous indeed! He is so, so close!

Dressed and ready for the day, Greg steps into the main room and nods to Damon.

"I hope we can send you on your way today," he says, and Damon answers this remark with a smile.

"Thank you, sir," Damon replies, "I certainly hope so too."

"Good morning, Felix," Greg greets the man fixing breakfast.

"Indeed, Greg," Felix answers, "how soon do you think we can start looking for the sigil today?"

"As soon as the others are ready and we have finished breakfast, Felix," Greg replies, "we need to find it post haste and get back home, although for you and Gavinar, this will be a journey into the unknown."

"Indeed," is Felix's reply. He has his back to Greg, so Greg cannot see the wry smile on Felix's face. Just then, Gavinar and Tim join the others and Gavinar squats by the fire rubbing his hands together. The smells of cooking bacon and brewing coffee meet them here, and they are all looking forward to a hearty breakfast.

"Well, today is the day, hey, Greg?" Gavinar asks the rhetorical question.

"Today is surely the day," Greg responds, making sure to sound positive and eager. He will drop the door of the trap after breakfast and hopefully, catch Felix. He has gone through the plan so many times that he is now sure he has covered anything that can go wrong. He must listen closely when Felix speaks.

"Will you show Felix and me the image of the sigil again before we set out?" Gavinar asks Greg, "just to make sure we have it in mind."

"Of course, I will," Greg replies, "just as soon as we have finished breakfast. We need to try to use it while it is still available to us."

"Do you mean that the sigils only have a certain lifespan?" Gavinar's surprise tells Greg that he genuinely does not know this fact, and Greg takes notice of this point. Now to try to trip Felix.

"Yes," Greg replies, "the sigils need to be sustained by human flesh apparently, or so our reading in Athens indicated. Isn't that right, Tim?"

"From what we read in Henry's files, which seems to be the case." Tim endorses Greg's statement.

"So, what happens if the sigil is no longer there?" Felix asks, unwittingly showing his hand to Greg. He has never mentioned the fact that the sigils disappear.

"I have decided to take out insurance against just that possibility," Greg replies, making sure to ignore the tell in Felix's question.

"What do you mean, Greg?" Gavinar asks curiously.

"I mean that when the three of you set out to look for the sigil, I will remain here and go through Henry's files once more to try to find out if there is any way, once the sigils have disappeared, that they can be reinstated again. That way, if we cannot find the one shown in the orb, so long as we can be sure of its original position, there may be some way to open it again for use."

The other three men remain silent for several seconds before Felix speaks.

"I think one of us should stay with you, Greg, to help with your research. Tim and I can start the search, and Gavinar could stay here and help. What do you think?"

Taking care not to show any sign that he is keen for just this situation, Greg appears to be thinking. He frowns at the suggestion as if he really does not want anyone else to stay with him. After a minute or so he replies.

"I suppose that would be OK, but it would be better for the three of you to search. The sooner you find it, the sooner we can leave. I am simply going to try to find an alternative if the sigil cannot be found."

"I know, Greg," Felix replies, "but it is better to be safe than sorry, and two heads are better than one. Tim and I will search, and you and Gavinar can go through the files."

Greg does not argue, but makes it appear that he is not at all happy with the plan. Felix announces that the breakfast is ready, so they all sit down to eat without further discussion.

"I will get my laptop and show you both the sigil again," finished eating, Greg stands up to do just that, but Tim says,

"Don't bother, Greg, Felix and I will search together, and I know what to look for, so instead of taking time to find the image again, you and Gavinar get on with looking through Henry's files."

"First we need the orb again," Greg says, "to pinpoint where the sigil is. That way, the image will be available to you at the same time."

"Yes, I forgot about pinpointing the exact spot," Tim replies, and Felix goes to get the orb box. Once he has it opened on the table, Greg closes his eyes and summons the orb. It rises, begins to spin and moves in front of Greg. He summons the image of the sigil to mind, and it is projected once more in the surface of the orb. Greg imagines backing away from the sigil; once more the cliffs appear and then Felix recognizes the spot because he knows the position of a dead tree trunk on the left-hand side of the view.

"Ah, I know where it is!" Felix exclaims excitedly, "come on, Tim, let's get going."

Greg returns the orb to the box and speaks once more.

"Wait just a minute, Felix, if you find the sigil, you need to come back here so that we can all shift to the position."

"Of course, Greg," Felix replies, "but now I know where it is, Tim and I should be back within the hour, so pack up everything before you get into those files."

With no further ado, he grabs Tim by the arm and leads him quickly to the door. "We will be back soon." He announces and the door shuts before Greg or Gavinar have a chance to answer.

"Well, he is excited!" Gavinar exclaims with a curious look on his face. "I have never seen him so animated, even when we found the orb in the first place."

"Why do you think that is, Gavinar?" Greg asks.

"I don't know." Gavinar responds looking thoughtful.

Intuitively, Greg knows that now is the time to spell out his plan to Gavinar and he knows also that he risks everything by doing so, but something in Gavinar's response to Felix eggs him on.

"Gavinar, what do you really know about Felix?" Greg asks, trying not to sound too curious.

"Well, I met him several years ago, when he moved to Gothenburg. We have been friends from the start, and he has included me in his work." Gavinar begins, "Why Greg?"

"It is just a thought, but something does not ring true about the man," Greg replies carefully, "where did he come from originally?"

Gavinar looks puzzled and strokes his beard. "Do you know, I don't know the answer to that question, or I can't remember," Gavinar looks perplexed, "I should know, but my mind is blank."

"I want you to listen to me now, Gavinar, and please don't interrupt me until I finish, OK?"

"All right, Greg, what's on your mind?"

"Do you remember how you tried to hypnotize that young lady we met before we left?"

"How can I forget?" Gavinar looks abashed.

"I want you to think about what you know of Felix; the fact that he was able to control us with his mind, and what about the clock just inside his house? Do you feel what it does when you enter?"

"Now that you mention it, I was curious about the way it made me feel, but Felix laughed when I told him; he convinced me that the feeling was me, not the clock and that I was feeling faint because I was hungry. Why do you ask?"

"Because, Gavinar, I know beyond a shadow of a doubt that Felix is not what he seems. I think he has hypnotized you to make you believe that you have known him for years. To do so, all he had to do is feed you with enough information about himself so that the suggestion would hold once you were taken out of the trance state. I think that is why you don't know where he really comes from."

"But that's absurd, Greg, how could I simply believe what I know to be the case?" Gavinar is shocked at the idea, but Greg persists.

"Then you should know how he came to be here and where from, don't you think?"

Gavinar frowns, trying to recall the details Greg has asked him to remember, but it is quite obvious that his mind is blank in this regard. Worry begins to beset him now; this has never happened to him before, and it is disconcerting to say the least. At last, he looks at Greg and speaks, "If what you are saying is true, how can I be sure?"

"Are you willing to trust me, Gavinar?"

"I don't think I have a choice," Gavinar replies, "but what do you suggest?"

"I would like to hypnotize you if you are willing. That way, I will know for sure and so will you."

"But how, Greg? If you put me in a trance, I will not know what is going on. You saw the reaction of the girl when you brought her out of the trance; she didn't remember anything."

"Yes, you will, Gavinar, because I can record what is said on my laptop. After I bring you out of the trance, I will play it back for you to hear, what do you say?"

Gavinar does not look at all happy about the idea, but after thinking about it for several minutes, he gives Greg his assent.

"Right, I am going to set everything up quickly, so we can do this before Felix returns. Just sit down and try to relax."

Brandon

As soon as Fellings has checked Brandon's broken bones and stitched face, he builds up the fire and sets off into the fern forest to collect more fuel; at least enough to last the day and night. He has taken the empty water bottles with him to refill at the river, leaving one in reach for Brandon to use to urinate. He has cut off the narrow neck to make it easier for Brandon to use.

As he piles dead fronds ready to take back, he thinks about what he can use to build a trap for the cassowary. Now that he has Brandon to feed, he needs to catch as much protein as he can. So far, he has eaten the rubbery seaweed as well, with no ill effects, so dietary fiber should be easy enough to find. As he works, he listens for any noises alien to those made by the task he is completing.

The piles are ready, so he heads to the river, following the marked trunks from yesterday. Was it only yesterday? It seems to him like weeks rather than hours since he lost Brandon and then found him again. Yet it has only been forty-eight hours. He squats at the water's edge and begins to fill the bottles. The water is flowing swiftly, so it does not take long. Soon the bottles are full, and he starts back to the spot where he left the piles of fronds. He secures the bottles in the front of his shirt and shouldering the fronds, sets off back towards the beach and Brandon. By the time he arrives back he is sweating regardless of the cold morning air. He drops the fronds in the place allocated earlier and returns to sit with his son. Brandon has been dozing, but by his side, the bottle is half filled with cloudy urine. Fellings picks it up, holds it towards the wan sun and then smells it. He can tell that there is a small amount of blood in the mix but nothing to indicate more than dehydration. Another great sign and about as far as he can go to check Brandon's physical state. So far, so good!

While Brandon sleeps, Fellings looks around trying to decide if he should construct a rudimentary hut for them, or whether he would be better using his energy to catch more food. The food wins out; until he can be assured of a regular supply of attainable food, the shelter will have to wait. Now, what can he do to make catching food more likely? Looking through the pack, his eyes alight on the packet of needles used yesterday. Searching through the rest, he takes out the cord he used to bind Brandon's broken limbs. There is not much left but enough to construct a rudimentary fishing line with a needle at the end to act as a hook. If he heats the largest needle, he may be able to bend it into a U shape. As he works, he thinks about how time consuming such a simple task is without the mod cons that he has, up to this point, taken so much for granted. It reminds him of childhood when he and his friends tried to construct such things. Now it is no longer a game for boys, but a deadly serious business, without which they may well starve here.

He has placed the needle on one of the flat rocks along the edge of the firepit, and when the needle begins to glow, he takes another piece of rock collected earlier and wrapping one hand in a t-shirt, lifts the needle and places it on a flat stone. Clumsily, with unpracticed wacks, he tries to bend the needle without snapping it. When he has done the best he can, there lies a slightly bent, thin piece of steel, the point somewhat battered but still sharp enough to snag at a fish's mouth. He still has some of the twine collected from the army fatigues to stitch Brandon's face, and he now takes this and threads the eye of the needle with it. He secures it to the end of the cord by stitching through the cord with the twine until it is as secure as he can manage. The fact that he has tried to shape the sharp end does not make this task an easy one. He carefully tests it for strength. It will do hopefully. One rudimentary fishing line! He is amazed by how much this simple task has taken out of him, until he remembers that he has not eaten yet today. He still has two pieces of the cooked snake, and he breaks both open and gingerly eats the white meat inside. He is about to throw the scraps into the fire but thinks better of it. Here is a kind of bait for the fishing line. Clumsily he threads a small morsel of the white flesh onto the end of the needle. Now, where can he test his latest invention?

Before he can decide, an image hits him; his imagination flashes the image of throwing the line in from the rocks at the end of the outcrop, only to have the megalodon take the hook and him with it. He breaks out into a sweat at the unwanted flashback. He hopes he will not catch more than he has bargained on! Perhaps he should try the river first. On this side it is wider and perhaps it harbors fish of eels. He soon rejects this idea; he knows he is much more likely to catch something from the ocean. Only the dire need to feed them both entices him towards the beach and the ocean edge of the rocky outcrop. He gazes out to the horizon, wondering, not for the first time, where in the world he is standing. In this primordial time, it is simply impossible to tell. He searches the water for what looks like the deepest part and sitting squarely down, he braces his sneaker clad feet to make sure nothing can pull him into the waves. Taking a deep, calming breath, he first winds one end of the cord twice around his hand, then he throws the rest of the cord with the needle out to drift on top of the water. He has nothing to use as a sinker, and he decides to find something before he returns to Brandon. Perhaps this rudimentary kind of fly fishing may work, if not, then he will have to attach something to act as a sinker.

For the first several minutes, he waits anxiously for the megalodon to rise up and engulf him, but the fear gradually abates, and he finds he is actually enjoying sitting here. He has done so little fishing in his life that he did not know how relaxing it could be.

His mind wanders as he watches the cord for any movement. Sometime later, and in a kind of trance, he feels a bobbing on the line, and he quickly brings his mind back to the task. It feels like something is gently nibbling at the line, and tiny ripples on the surface provide the proof. When he feels the bobbing start again, he jerks the line backwards. Suddenly, the cord dips below the surface and becomes rigid, and with all his strength, he pulls against the weight, transferring both hands to the cord for better purchase rather than just the one. He heaves the cord in and throws his weight backwards so that the whole cord is pulled out of the water, landing with a thud on the rocks behind him. There thrashing around on the end of the cord is a fish about forty centimetres long. He sits and watches until at last it stops moving. He can scarcely believe his eyes.

What to do now?

The first thing is to unwrap the cord from his right hand and look at what he has caught. It has fins and is dark on the upper side and silver underneath. Trying to remember what kind of fish were alive in the Cretaceous period, he thinks it might be an Apsopelix; it is the right size and colour, and they had fins, many fish of the period did not. He knows how lucky he is because as he now remembers, most of the fish from this time are different varieties of Coelacanths, savage creatures of much bigger size with wicked, razor-sharp teeth. Catching one of those could have been life-threatening. He picks up the cord, being careful not to get too close to what is hanging from the other end and begins to make his way back to Brandon. Perhaps the fishing idea was not really the wisest way to find food. To find food is one thing; to become food quite another!

As he comes into view, Brandon waves his good arm in greeting. Fellings holds up the line so Brandon can see what he has caught, and he gets a thumbs up from Brandon.

"Way to go, Dad," Brandon says, "do you know what it is?"

"I think I do," Fellings replies tentatively, "but I can't be sure. Anyway, I will cook it and we can try it." He uses the pocketknife to remove the needle from the fish's mouth and sticking it with the knife, puts it to bake on one of the stones around the back of the firepit. He does not bother to scale or gut it; he really has no idea how to do those things anyway. He figures that they must try to eat the whole thing and not be so delicate as to waste the innards. He surely has no intentions of going back to catch more; it is simply too dangerous. Fellings sits down next to Brandon.

"How are you feeling now?" he asks.

"Better, Dad, but still very weak and sore."

"I would expect you to be for some time yet." Fellings places his wrist against Brandon's forehead and is relieved to feel no excessive heat. At least for the moment, Brandon does not have any infection, and that is a bonus.

"Tell me what you think that fish is, Dad," Brandon asks.

"Well, from what I remember about the Cretaceous period," Fellings begins, "I think it is one of the few finned fish called Apsopelix. The shape, colour and size suggest that anyway."

"Does that give us any clues as to where in the world we might be, Dad?"

Fellings had not thought about that, but now he does. He casts his mind back to reading about this time, and he tries to remember.

"You know, I think these fish were found mainly in the Hudson seaways, and if that is so, then we are in Canada!"

"How good would that be, Dad," Brandon is smiling now.

"I won't be going back to catch more," Fellings says, "it's just too dangerous as we have already discovered."

"Then what are we going to eat?" Brandon is more worried that he lets on.

"I want to work out how we could catch one of the cassowary-looking birds," Fellings sits thinking. "Then we would have meat, for several days; especially if I cooked the thing straight away."

"What about snakes, Dad?" Brandon asks, he has shared one of the cooked pieces with Fellings, and it was quite tasty.

"That will be my very next task," Fellings replies, "to find snakes and anything that inhabits the river and the rock pools on the outcrop, especially straight after high tide. I will also collect some of the fleshy seaweed to eat. At a push I think we could survive on that if we have to."

"Do you think we will be here for the duration?" Brandon asks the question already knowing the answer, but suddenly, Fellings remembers the transponder in his pocket.

"There may be a very slim chance that we can get out of here," Fellings is careful not to build Brandon's hope, "but it is only a one in a million chance, so don't go putting all your hopes into it."

"What are you talking about, Dad?" the look on Brandon's face suggests that Fellings may have lost his mind.

Slowly, Fellings removes the transponder from his pocket and holds it up for Brandon to see. "I found this yesterday before I found you."

"Oh my God, Dad, why didn't you tell me sooner?" Brandon's face is alight with hope now, and this is exactly what Fellings did not want to happen.

"As I said, it is only a remote possibility. That is why I didn't tell you. I did not want you getting excited about something that may be impossible. Don't forget, the transponder was washed away from me and dumped further along the shore, so it will have been affected by the sand and salt water."

"No, Dad, you don't understand. It looks like plastic and metal, but it is constructed from newly developed materials that are impervious to damage in the normal way, especially sea water. Because the submersible operates underwater, all the components are constructed from materials that cannot be so easily damaged."

Fellings looks at the small box with renewed interest. If what Brandon says is true, then there may be more than a slight chance, depending on whether the submersible ended up in the belly of the megalodon, or like Brandon, somehow managed to evade that massive maw.

Henry

When Higgins knocks on the General's door first thing next morning, there is no reply. He carefully opens the door a crack and sees that the lights are on, but the General is not at his desk. He closes the door again and makes his way to the mess. The General is sitting alone, nursing a cup of fresh coffee. He signals for Higgins to get one for himself and then join him at the table. Both men still seem tired, and as they exchange greetings, each knows that the other has probably slept little.

"Well, this morning we must deal with several issues; the first is to tell the sixteen visitors that they will be staying here for the foreseeable future. I am hoping against hope that we don't have a mini riot on our hands."

"The best thing to do is explain why they need to be here and what the alternative would have been had they returned to England with MI6."

Higgins understands the General's concerns, but he is more hopeful that the men will see this as a chance to find out what is happening inside their bodies.

"We have enough staff here to deal with any problems in that regard, and a night in the cells would soon have a sobering effect." Higgins suggests.

"Is there a leader of the group?" the General asks.

"I have a fair idea of the pecking order, sir, and Peter is their spokesman. Another of them, Steven, seems to be the most reasonable of the lot."

"Let's get the two of them in first then," the General says, "perhaps they can then help with the others if it is necessary."

"Yes, I would say that's the best idea." Higgins replies.

Both men sit drinking their coffee in companionable silence.

Peter knows something is afoot but can't work out what. It seems like weeks that they have been confined to their rooms instead of days, and he is ready to take action if this continues. He has been exercising each day to the extent that he can, and he notices that there are changes in his body. He attributes those changes to the exercise. The door guards change at regular intervals, and he has been taking note of who comes and goes and when.

"Ah, Peter," Higgins greets him, and Peter startles out of his reverie.

"Will you please come with me? The General wants to see you and Steven in his office."

"About time," Peter replies tersely, "I want to know what the hell is going on, and I want to know now!"

"Great timing," Higgins says, "that's exactly why the General wants to see you."

Peter jumps up and follows Higgins out of his room. They stop just inside Steven's room to collect him too. The three men hurry towards the General's office, and Higgins knocks.

"Come!" the General stands up from behind his desk and offers his hand to the two men. They give him a cursory shake, and he invites them to sit down in the area near the window. A leather sofa and chairs surround a low coffee table, and he asks the men if they would like coffee. This informal approach seems to relax the two men, and they help themselves to coffee from a coffee maker on the low table. When they are all sitting down again, the General begins.

"I apologise for the room detention, but I had orders to follow. MI6 have now left here and will not be returning. Are there any questions?"

"How long have you got?" Peter asks the rhetorical question before launching into a tirade about their treatment here.

The General lets him work off some steam before repeating his question.

"I want to know what is happening and why we are still here," Peter replies, this time giving the General the chance to reply.

"Firstly, there is a very good reason why you are being kept here; if MI6 had taken you back to England, you all would have been kept in detention for the foreseeable future."

"But why?" Peter asks.

"Because what you have seen and had access to is top-secret and must remain that way," the General replies. "Here at least you will have a certain freedom, and we will give you plenty of work to keep you occupied. But that is not the main reason that we wanted you here."

"Then please be more specific," Peter is calming down now; his manners have at least surfaced again.

"As you are well aware, we have tested your blood several times while you have been here. Initially we sent a report back to Thames House which initiated the visit from MI6. Now, why do you think that happened?"

"I would like you to tell me without any further prevarication, please," Peter replies. Steven speaks up for the first time.

"You found anomalies in the blood tests, didn't you?" he asks

"We certainly did," Higgins now takes over answering the questions, "in fact not only that, but each subsequent test showed differences from the prior one. In the end we destroyed your blood and replaced it with blood taken from the staff here, so that it would appear to be normal and look as if something had been bungled to the extent that our report was mistaken. We set out to, and managed to hoodwink MI6, a feat not often accomplished." Higgins looks directly at Peter as he speaks.

"Why on earth would you do such a thing?" Peter is completely bamboozled now, but Steven smiles wryly at the news.

"I suspect that what you found is not something anyone would expect; that it was strange to the extent that you wanted to keep us here to investigate further, am I right?"

"Spot on!" Higgins replies, "now, not only will I explain, but I will show you what we have found so far."

He stands up to collect the photographs from the General's desk and opens the computer put there earlier.

"If you gentlemen will come over here and take a seat, I will begin from the beginning," Higgins says.

Peter and Steven look on, fascinated with the story as it is gradually unfolded by Higgins. The photographs act to reinforce what they are being told, and they both look carefully at the differences pointed out by Higgins. At last, he sits back and asks them if they have any questions.

Peter has paled visibly, and Steven sits frowning, obviously thinking deeply. At last, Peter says,

"Do you have any idea what this could mean, Doctor?"

"Not the slightest, except that I have figured out when this may have occurred. What do you understand about what happens to enable you to pass through the Curtain?"

"Nothing really," Peter says, "except that we lose consciousness and feel disoriented and nauseous afterwards."

"Well, from my understanding of the process, your body is broken down into its constituent molecules and then reassembled again. The time this takes is so minuscule as to be unable to be detected by the instruments of nanotechnology. This means, however, that something can occur after your body becomes molecules and before you are reassembled again. Something obviously can and has been introduced to change your DNA."

Peter reaches with a shaking hand for a glass of water. He is close to fainting.

The General takes over again and speaks gently.

"Now do you see the problem we had? We could not send you back without at least trying to discover what is happening to you. It could be that we need to treat you medically in some way. At least here, we can observe you as we observe the changes in your blood. Because we are a small base, Higgins and his team can make the time to work on this exclusively."

"I have no idea how to take this news," Peter says, "but I am damn sure the others are going to be as terrified as I am."

"That is why we wanted to speak to you and Steven before telling the others. We may need your help to keep them calm and quiescent."

"I think there may be two people who could be difficult," Peter replies; putting his mind to the task allows him to force his fear down, "Derek is not strong when it comes to anything frightening, and Max is somewhat the same. How do you intend to go about telling them?"

"What would you suggest, Peter?" the General asks.

"I think you should call a meeting in the mess, but make sure you have several soldiers to deal with any unforeseen outbursts. Steven and I will try to keep them calm by being reasonable ourselves, right, Steven?"

"Absolutely," Steven assents, "we need to try to find out what is happening to us as soon as we can. At least then we know what we are facing. I want to thank you, General, and you, Dr Higgins, for making sure we were kept here. I don't think MI6 would be treating us with the same concern for our wellbeing."

As the men file into the mess and take a seat, there is much mumbling and grumbling. The first thing they all notice is that Peter and Steven are already here, standing at the front with the General and the doctor who took their blood.

"What the hell?" Derek begins, but Peter walks swiftly up to him and says quietly.

"You need to shut up and listen if you want to know why we are still here."

That works and Peter returns to the front of the room. As soon as the fourteen are seated, Peter asks for silence and then introduces the order the meeting will take.

"I know you are all keen to know what is going on and why, so just shut up and listen, all of you. There are soldiers guarding the doors, so anyone who wants to cause a problem with be swiftly dealt with. Any questions?"

There is complete silence, and all the men give their attention to those standing at the front. The General begins.

"Thank you for your forbearance, men, I apologise for the room detention, but I had orders to obey. Now that MI6 have left, the detention will no longer be necessary. You are all to remain here for the foreseeable future, however. Had you returned to England, you would have been kept in detention by MI6 because what you have seen and taken part in, is top secret and must remain that way. Now I am going to hand over to the doctor, so he can explain to you why we also wanted you kept here."

Again, there is mumbling, but it quietens as soon as Higgins steps forwards. There is a smartboard set up at the front, and Higgins plugs his laptop into the board so that the screen lights up. He begins.

"Now what I am going to show you is very hard to believe, so I ask that you all let me finish before you ask questions. As you are well aware, we have taken blood samples from all of you, the last set yesterday. What I am about to show you is your blood under electron microscopic conditions."

Higgins taps his laptop keyboard and the latest blood test results are displayed in colour. Using a laser pointer, Higgins goes through the same story with illustrated proof that he already showed Peter and Steven. It is no less shocking to both of them the second time around; the others are shocked into speechlessness. When he has finished, Higgins looks over at Peter and then asks the others if there are any questions. The same question that Peter asked, is asked again, and Higgins gives the same reply. The only thing he can tell them is his assumptions of how and when the changes were initially wrought. What they mean are still an enigma. John is the first to recover his wits and asks,

"How do you intend to find out what all of this means? If you don't know what will happen to us physically, I don't see how you can help us?"

"The best way to go forward, as I see it," Higgins begins to answer, "is initially for the General and me to meet with each one of you to profile your personality and traits. Once we have worked up a profile on each of you, we can then begin intense observation while you get back to some semblance of normality, or as much as is possible here. We will need your full cooperation however, and it may become more intrusive that you are comfortable with. Rest assured; I will get the answers as soon as I can so that we know what these changes mean. Then at least you will know what you are dealing with. That is the best I can offer at this point."

Peter now steps forward and speaks to his colleagues. I think we are lucky to be here, the General and Dr Higgins will be working overtime to find out what is going on and how it is going to affect us long term. I for one want to know, so I am putting my trust and wellbeing in the hands of these two men. There is no other viable option, and I think we are lucky that we are not in England with MI6. I don't think our wellbeing would concern them at all. I suggest the rest of you do the same and pray that Dr Higgins' team can work this out."

The Family

The boys begin to eat, wolfing down their food with relish. Florence watches them kindly, but soon she orders both to eat more slowly so that the food does not give them stomach pains. The boys do as she has asked and then each of them tries to speak at the same time. Canath knows what they want to say, but he does not want them to speak of their inner journeys just yet.

"Now that we are all assembled here," he begins, "I want to tell you what the next step is in our preparations to deal with the universal damage rendered by Henry Bonnington and others of his ilk."

All at the table give him their attention, Ladon included.

"We are now at that time of the tipping point; the point at which healing the rifts or the damage becoming too widespread for us to heal is upon us. As you all know, Marcom and the Rift Spinner are working nonstop with the healing process, but it is no foregone conclusion that they will overtake the damage that is even now being wrought through different times and places. We must do all we can to aid their progress, and that means different things for each of us. I want you all to listen very carefully to what tasks you are allotted because although you may not see the point in what you are asked to do, you must trust that I do, and that what you are being set to do is integral to the whole enterprise. As you know, Aletheia is already carrying out her task, and I am going to tell each of you, what you must do next. Are there any questions before I begin?"

Canath waits, and as he waits, he looks at each face turned towards him. After several minutes he begins again.

"Florence, I need you to take Antheia with you and begin her education into the arcana necessary for her to help you hold the universal stability. At the moment, if anything happens to you, catastrophe will be upon us; you have the strength to go on, but without rest, eventually you will be unable to cope, so please, make sure she acquires all of your knowledge so that she can take over if needs be. That is the most important task, without that, everything is finished."

"I will do as you say, Canath," Florence answers.

"Father, what of Ladon?" Antheia asks, frantically worried that she won't be able to take him with her, wherever she may need to go.

"That is the next task, and it is up to you Phoenix to care for Ladon and guard him with your life," Canath looks at Phoenix, "he is eating solid food now, so it is time for you to entrust him to Phoenix, Antheia."

"But will I get to see him at all?" Antheia stares at her father with tears in her eyes.

"Not for the foreseeable future, Antheia. I am sorry, but our duty is grave, and I am sure your brother will care for him and keep him safe. He is born to this task."

"I certainly will do so, Father," Phoenix smiles at Ladon and then addresses his sister. "Antheia, I swear to you that I will care for, nurture and guard your son with my life."

"I know, dear Phoenie, but I will miss him dreadfully. I will do as you say, Father," Antheia adds sadly.

"What about me, Father?" Kenny asks, "don't I have a task too?"

"Of course, my son," Canath smiles at his youngest son, "you will stay with me and help me with overseeing everything and everyone. You know your task well already, for your inner journey set it out for you to see."

"Oh yes, I know, thank you, Father, I will do whatever you ask of me."

"There is so little time, and we must move quickly, so please say your goodbyes and get whatever you need to take with you. Phoenix, you and Ladon will remain here until I tell you otherwise, and if you need me, just think my name and I will come. Please make sure you let me know of any untoward events and only make contact with me if the situation is urgent."

"As you say, Father. Do you want me to begin teaching Ladon?"

"I think it will be Ladon that does the teaching," Canath replies, "but certainly keep him busy and feed his curiosity."

As each family member moves to do Canath's bidding, he sighs and wonders if they will ever come together again. There is only a hair's breadth of a chance that they will succeed, but if they do, he swears on all that is holy, that they will gather in this room once more. He goes to his and Florence's room to gather what he needs and to bid his wife goodbye once more. He holds her close for a long time before they separate, and with a smile, Florence leaves first to collect Antheia and then to take her away before the parting with Ladon becomes impossible.

Antheia hugs her baby to her and speaks softly into his silver hair.

"Remember me, little one, for I love you more than life itself. I will see you again as soon as it is possible. Be a good boy and heed your uncle, Phoenix." With one last kiss on his tiny nose, she hands him over to Phoenix, who understanding the pain of this separation, quickly takes Ladon downstairs into the garden. Kenny waits in the kitchen for Canath and smiles when he enters.

"Are you ready for the adventure of your life?" Canath asks, a twinkle in his eye.

"I have waited all my life for this adventure, Father, let's go!"

Canath sweeps the boy into his arms, and with a frisson of sparks, both disappear, leaving nothing but a few motes that hang in the air sparkling.

Florence wraps her arm around Antheia's shoulders and takes her daughter up to the tower room. Florence picks up a backpack of some shimmery cloth and together they enter a small, narrow passage and together they walk this narrow passage to the end. Just before they reach the end, they both begin to shimmer and then they disappear altogether. Thankfully, because at the end of this passage there is nothing but a dark void; stars twinkle, and colours move in and out of existence in the fullness of pure space time.

Deep within the plenum, Aletheia looks up and smiles. She has been informed by the Power that the others have set out on their tasks and soon enough the real work will begin. Already, she has stopped the spirit of

Henry from entering into the fullness of the Power: the infinite. It was as easy as swatting a fly but much more gratifying. To know that he has no way of interfering with the job that must now be done, fills her with a lightness of being. Soon enough Kenny will collect and hold him. She dreams of a time when everything is complete, and they can all meet again.

Greg and Tim

Greg places his laptop on the table next to the chair he has made ready for Gavinar. He sets up the recording app and checks to make sure it is working, and that the laptop has a secure connection to the satellite. Next, he asks Gavinar to sit down on the chair and try to relax his mind. He hums a lullaby very softly, and as soon as he can see that relaxation is underway, he speaks slowly and softly behind Gavinar's head. As he speaks, Gavinar begins to get sleepy and soon his conscious mind relaxes to the point that his subliminal mind rises to the surface. Greg tests this by gently lifting his eyelids; his eyes are fixed. He is now in a trance under Greg's direction, and Greg begins to talk to him.

"Gavinar, I want you to go back through time. I want you to go back to the first time you laid eyes on Felix." He waits several seconds and begins again. "Are you there now?"

"Yes," Gavinar answers Greg slowly and quietly.

"Where are you?" Greg asks.

"I am at home, and Felix has just arrived at my door. He looks at me, and I feel strange."

"Is he staring at you?" Greg asks quietly.

"Yes, and now he is telling me who he is and why I don't remember him. He is related to my cousin, he says. Now I remember."

"Does he tell you where he came from?" Greg asks.

"He says he is from Kettering and that we were friends and school chums there. Now I remember."

"What else does he say, Gavinar?"

"He says I have known him for many years, and do I remember? I have to think about this. Ah, I do remember now."

"Do you know how he came to be here?"

"He did not say, and I don't remember."

"Gavinar, I want you to come back to the present." Again, Greg waits for several seconds and then asks, "Are you back?"

"I am back."

"When you hear me clap my hands three times, you will wake."

Greg slowly claps his hands, once then twice and on the third clap, Gavinar looks up and sees that Greg is sitting just behind him.

"When are you going to start, Greg?" he says.

"I have just finished, Gavinar, and it is as I thought. Would you like to listen?"

"Oh yes, I need to know what you know now."

Greg plays back the brief conversation and all the while Gavinar looks on in astonishment. He has heard from his own mouth the facts that before were only Greg's assumptions. He sits brooding and stroking his beard before he speaks once more.

"What are we going to do about this, Greg? I can't for the life of me forgive what he has done to me. I have helped him financially as well as introduced him to the important men of my community. How are we going to deal with him?"

"I have to think about that carefully, Gavinar, and it is very important that you don't show him your hand. If he thinks we know about his subterfuge, he may be very dangerous, and we may all be in peril. Until we can find out who he really is, you will have to behave towards him as you always have. Can you do that?"

"I will try my best, Greg," Gavinar answers.

Tim and Felix have hurried across the fields towards the place where the dead tree trunk lies. As they get closer, Tim can see that Felix was right, so the sigil should be within the cliffs closest to the tree. As they come level with the dead tree trunk, both men look around on the righthand side until they notice a small opening in the cliff. The opening is so narrow that it is with difficulty that each man shifts and shoves his body to squirm through into a narrow passageway. Tim lights the candle he has brought with him, and they move sideways along the narrow slit in the rocks. Tim leads and he looks carefully at the walls from the floor to the rocks overhead, trying to glean anything that resembles the sigil. They have moved along the passage about two hundred metres, when the passageway gradually widens so that now the men can walk forwards instead of sidling like crabs. Their shoulders scuff against the sides as they go. The air inside becomes warmer, the further inside they go and soon both men begin to sweat. There must be some underground vent sending hot air into the passageway. Another hundred metres further, and Tim notices the rocks of the walls have taken on a glassy sheen. He stops and speaks to Felix.

"I have seen this before, in another place and time," he says quietly, "I don't think we should go any further."

"Don't be ridiculous!" Felix scoffs, "anyone would think you were afraid of your own shadow. You know how important it is to find the sigil, now move on, Tim."

Reluctantly, Tim moves forwards again and soon the passage widens so that Felix can walk abreast with Tim. Tim stops again, and this time he does not budge when Felix derides him.

"Felix, I am going back to get the others. We need to include them in deciding what we should do next, especially because I recognise the same signs as those Greg, and I found once before."

"Well, I am not coming with you, Tim. I am going on, so good luck."

With that Felix lights his candle and moves quickly ahead while Tim makes his way back along the passage towards the outside. It takes more effort to get back past the narrow opening going out from the inside of the cliff, and by the time Tim is outside again, he notices that the sky has clouded over, and the dark clouds look heavy with rain. He hurries back across the fields to the lodge and enters, breathless.

Greg and Gavinar are sitting by the fire, and they startle when he rushes inside.

"Where is Felix?" Greg asks surprised.

"He would not return with me, Greg. We found a narrow passage in the cliff and went in to search. I found the same glassed rocks in the walls as we found in Athens, so I wanted to come back here and get the two of you, but Felix refused to return. I am here alone."

"Just as well, Tim, because I want you to listen to this." Greg sits Tim next to the fire and turns on the recording from the laptop. Tim listens spellbound.

"So," Tim says at last, "he is definitely not what he seemed. You were right, Greg. If he comes from Kettering, then he must have come through the Curtain as we did. No wonder the orb showed the scene from Kettering! All Felix had to do was think of it and it was projected. But you know what that means, don't you, Greg?"

"Yes," Greg answers, "the scene displayed was the same one we know, so Felix, or whoever he really is, comes from our own time!"

As the three men sit thinking about the implications of their discovery, in another place and time, the family are setting out to begin their tasks; Brandon and Fellings sit considering their options, hoping against hope that when Brandon has recovered from his wounds, they may be able to move on again, and the men from Kettering try not to think about what the terrifying implications of their changes in DNA may mean.

In the tower garden, Phoenix looks on as Ladon plays. Ladon chants softly in the archaic tongue of his forebears as he watches fluffy, striped bees alight on the petals of newly born flowers. The Universe overflows itself into myriad living forms, and silently, Aletheia watches and waits. It seems to her that the Power of life is holding its breath for what is coming next. Whatsoever may come to pass, the guardians are on hand, and in the sunny tower garden, Ladon grows.

Bibliography

Ideas woven through this book can be found in the following texts:

Aristotle, (R. P. Hardie; W. D. Ross, Trans.) (1982), *The Works of Aristotle: Vol. 1,* The University of Chicago Press.

Bergson, H. (Arthur Mitchell Trans.) (1988), *Creative Evolution,* Dover Publications. Inc., New York.

Heidegger, M. (J Macquarrie and E. Robinson, Trans.) (2000), *Being and Time,* Blackwell, Oxford.

Heidegger, M. (Joan Stanbaugh, Trans.) (1969), *Identity and Difference,* Harper & Row, New York.

Heidegger, M. (Joan Stambaugh, Trans.) (1972), *On Time and Being,* the University of Chicago Press, Chicago.

Heidegger, M. (W. McNeill, Trans.) (1998), *Pathmarks,* Cambridge University Press.

Heidegger, M. (W. Lovitt, Trans.) (1977), *The Question Concerning Technology and Other Essays,* Harper Perennial, New York.

Heidegger, M. (T. Kisiel, Trans.) (1992), *History of the Concept of Time,* Indiana University Press, Bloomington.

Heisenberg, W. (2007), *Physics and Philosophy,* Harper Perennial, New York.

Hume, Lynn, (2002), *Ancestral Power,* Melbourne University Press.

James, W. (1985), *The Varieties of Religious Experience*, Penguin Books, New York.

Jung, C.G. (W. Dell and C. F. Barnes, Trans.) (1933), *Modern Man in Search of A Soul*, A Harvest/ HBJ Book, Brace Jovanovich, New York.

Jung, C. G. (2008), *Synchronicity: An Acausal Connecting Principle*, Routledge, London.

Jung, C. G. (1984), *Dream Analysis*, Routledge & Kegan Paul, London.

Jung, C. G. (R. F. C. Hull, Trans.) (1983), *Collected Works: Vol. 14: Mysterium Conjunctionis*, Routledge & Kegan Paul, London.

Jung, C. G. (R. F. C. Hull, Trans.) (1922), *Psychology of the Unconscious*, Moffat, Yard and Company, New York.

Jung, C. G. (R. F. C. Hull, Trans.) (1990), *The Undiscovered Self with* Princeton, New Jersey.

Jung, C. G. (R. F. C. Hull, Trans.) (1959), *The Collected Works: Vol. 9, Part 1: The Archetypes of The Collective Unconscious*, Routledge & Kegan Paul, London.

Kant, I. (J. M. D. Meiklejohn, Trans.) (1952), *The Critique of Pure Reason*, William Benton Publisher, New York.

Kirk, Raven and Schofield, (1999), *The Presocratic Philosophers*, 2nd Ed., Cambridge University Press.

Meier, C. A. (Ed.) (David Roscoe, Trans.) (2001), *Atom and Archetype: The Pauli/ Jung Letters 1932-1958*, Routledge, London.

Neitzsche, F. (Walter Kaufmann, Trans.) (1966), *Thus Spoke*

Zarathustra, Princeton University Press.

Ramsey, C.A. (2014), *Open-endedness: Towards and Encounter With Alterity,* Lambert Academic Publishing, Germany.

Spinoza, B. (Samuel Shirley, Trans.) (1992), *The Ethics, Treatise on the Emendation of the Intellect, Selected Letters,* Hackett Publishing Company, Indiana.

Suzuki, D.T. (1956), *Zen Buddhism,* Doubleday Anchor Books, New York.

Suzuki, D. T. (1957), *Studies in Zen,* Rider and Company, London.

Weil, S. (A. F. Wills, Trans.) (2002), *Letter to a Priest,* Routledge, London.

Weil, S. (Emma Craufurd, Trans.) (1951), *Waiting on God,* Routledge & Kegan Paul, London.

Unpublished Papers.
Ramsey, C.A. (2006), *The Soap Bubble and the Triangle: Mathematical Analogues of an Ethics of Difference.*

This book is dedicated to my three grandchildren, Phoenix, Kenneth and Florence.